Sphere's Divide: III
Tragedies of Emotion

J.C. Norman

Clink
Street

London | New York

Published by Clink Street Publishing 2017

Copyright © 2017

First edition.

ISBN:
978-1-911110-85-9 paperback
978-1-911110-86-6 ebook

This is one for Liz, Jo Jo, Julie and Deirdre.
The four who believed in this project as much as I

INTRO

Conner sat amongst his comrades with his hands pressed together between his thighs. They had been travelling in a helicopter for the last few hours ready for their important mission, given to them by Queen Angel herself. The night was bitterly cold, freezing in fact, he thought as he shivered and pressed his head against the side of the flying vehicle, trying to look down at the world below but only seeing plains covered in darkness; they were passing only farmlands, forests and fields, far away from any civilisation.

His team sitting around him all looked as cold as him. Feydon soldiers all trained to be the best in their field of expertise, he always admired how they were also a diverse team of different creatures. First there was the two humans, Richard and Vince. Richard was sitting upright with his arms crossed and his head back trying to find sleep through this cold night but wasn't finding much luck. Conner knew this because he was still wearing his helmet and mask and was breathing smoothly, and normally this guy snored far too much for Conner to bear.

Vince was sitting next to him with his rifle on his lap, inspecting it and checking for any dirt that could possibly jam it later. The whole team was equipped with these semi-automatic rifles but Vince was the sharpshooter, picked out for his talents that were needed for this team of specialists. Conner was concerned about using these weapons, forbidden for the last century after the Last Divide, and ever since being trained only a few days ago on how to use one had not really trusted them. But he knew his orders.

The strength of the group were two soldiers, Breneth and Jordan, an ursa and a tigian. The tigian, Jordan,

Conner had known for longer than anyone else. Tall with broad shoulders with dark black stripes down his coat of orange fur, he was a good friend and an old drinking buddy Conner had been lucky enough to be sharing a place in the special team with; but the ursa he barely knew at all. Ursas were at the moment divided from the rest of the world so seeing any around was rare. This creature truly was a bear, evolved from the beasts they used to be and now living alongside the other great creatures of Sphere. His fur was a complete coat of dark brown hair, thick like wire.

Jinpac was an ageing porcus, the only member Conner didn't understand. Not only was he, in his years, older than everybody else, but he also was a porcus, an evolved member of the pig family. Conner was not sure if he even liked the guy but he was the sergeant and Conner knew to respect him. Because of their snout nose the porcus helmet was shaped very differently from the others, but right now he didn't wear it and sat with his face exposed. He had wisps of white hair for his eyebrows, matching his head hair, and sharp blue eyes. His pig-like nose was at first strange to look at but Connor was a very tolerant being and never asked about it nor ridiculed.

Finally there was Suge, the human lieutenant of the group, and his faithful kingnine, Xer. Suge sat on the other side of the helicopter and also peered out of the window waiting just like the rest of the team, wanting to hurry up and finish this top secret mission the rest of the Feydon army didn't even know about. Xer only sat with her head resting on her paws, a metal plate helmet fitted over her head comfortably, covering her eyes and turning them red. This was something all Feydon soldiers, and especially kingnines, were equipped with and it gave them the ability to see in infrared. Apart from the ursas, kingnines had the best noses, which made Xer the best tracker of the group.

She was wide awake and staring out in Conner's direction when he met her red eyes.

"What are you staring at, little monkey?" she asked, finally breaking the silence. Everybody shifted slightly and looked at her, then looked over to Conner, the aeomon of the group.

"You know I don't like being called that, little doggy," he countered, smiling at her.

"Why don't you come a little closer and call me that to my face?" she asked again.

"And face your dog breath?" he sharply replied and watched her smile and even laugh a little. He noticed everybody around him snigger, all except the lieutenant and the sleeping Richard.

"Always got to have the last word, don't you, Conner? When a team of different creatures are put together, trust the monkey to be the jester."

He liked Xer, she may have been on four legs and answered only to her master, Suge, but he found a good connection with her – him as the cheeky, youngest of the group, known for being agile and quick, and her, who was quick to anger and feared by the rest, but to him more like an older sister.

When Suge finally saw what he was looking for he looked back at his crew. "Okay, we're here. Suit up, and someone wake up Richard."

Conner knew his mission but he was sceptical about it. In his briefing, they had mentioned that his target would be a leo. Naturally, Xer was the first to express her opinions on this matter and was excited that she could possibly be the chosen one of her kind to finally wipe the sphere of the last of the leos. Considering how the kingnines were originally created by the humans to rid the world of the evolved lions that had once owned the planet, she seemed the most eager to see this creature, more than the rest of the team. Conner, however, didn't know what to believe; he had seen many things while on his journeys with some of the soldiers here but never in all his life had he seen a leo and so thought maybe this was either a mistake or an exercise.

The helicopter flew down from the sky and soon the doors opened, blasting in the cold night air, and they looked down to see a train speeding through the night.

"You think you can handle this mission, bud?!" Jordan the tigian shouted to him over the sound of the propellers when the helicopter flew down to nearly touch the top of the moving train.

"Just watch me!" he shouted back.

"Okay guys! Masks on!" Suge called to his crew and put on his own helmet, which covered his whole face like a mask.

The helicopter pulled up as close to the train as it possibly could with the pilots calling in, "One minute!"

"Okay. Go!" Suge shouted and one by one the team climbed out of the side of the flying vehicle and dived on top of the train. Conner was first to jump and leapt, hoping not to over or under estimate his jump and miss the train, and when he hit the top he reached out with his hands and pressed down on the metal roof and with special, strong, magnetic gloves could support his weight until he found his balance. Suge was the last to jump out, followed by Xer, who needed the team to catch her since she had a different body type than her companions. Once the team were aboard, the helicopter took off and they checked their weapons and turned the infrared on on their visors. Conner turned his mask on and suddenly the world changed around him. He had done many exercises in infrared and never admitted it but always admired how the world looked when looking at only heat. Suddenly the cold sky above him was black, darker than before, and the heat from his teammates shone out in orange and yellow. This was the world the kingnines see every day.

"Remember, the target is the only important thing, all else is expendable," Suge said. The train was noisy but he only needed to speak in a whisper since they now were all linked by their helmets with little microphones and, in their ears, speakers.

"Let's go."

"Yes, sir," Conner said, cocked his rifle and followed his team to breach the train.

The front of the train was their first destination. They quickly breached the doors and silently killed the train driver, opened the door and threw him out of the side of the train to have him scrape against the stony floor, ripping the poor guy to pieces. They left Jinpac the porcus to keep the train at a steady pace and stop it if needed and together they headed for the passenger carts. Jordan kicked the door in and flew in first, instantly seeing screaming people and scared passengers who had no idea what was going on, and with his silenced rifle quickly shot the cowards trying to escape.

The ursa was the next to breach followed by Conner, who silently walked past with his rifle held high ignoring the coloured shapes of cowering people.

"*First cart clear.*" He heard the voice of Jordan come through the little speaker in his ear.

"Good, Richard and Vince, check the lower levels," Suge ordered his team. "Breneth, you're with me and Xer. Conner, you stay with Jordan and keep going forward."

"Yes sir."

With his back against the door and his hand on the handle Jordan waited for Conner and nodded when ready. Together they repeated the process of breaching the carts, shooting all who got in their way, and continued on their search for the leo.

"*Remember, once you see the target, keep him alive, he's mine,*" he heard Xer say somewhere, still on the train.

"Up yours," Conner said as he sharply turned to check a corner and had to fire as a hiding, wannabe hero passenger tried to jump him and instead got a metal cap in his chest.

They all felt the train tremble slightly and their ears all suddenly popped. "*Guys, the train has just entered the Great Tunnel of Angland. We've got approximately twenty-five minutes before it comes back out of it,*" Jinpac said, while still at the head of the train.

"*That's ample time, thanks, Sergeant,*" Suge said.

The train shot through the tunnel in complete darkness. The lights of the train had been turned off and now the only ones who could see anything were the soldiers, all still on their mission.

Five minutes passed and still no sign of their target but they still had much of the train to cover. Conner had to shoot a few passengers, something he wasn't happy about – he had no quarrel with these people and it wasn't anything personal. This was his mission and they got in his way so he had no choice. Still on the top floor Jordan and Conner searched the passenger carts one by one, silently, while they could. They came to another door but before they opened it Conner quickly knelt down, put his hand to his ear and pressed the button to switch on his microphone.

"We're coming up to the last of the carts now, so far nothing sighted. How are we doing on time, Sergeant?"

He waited for a few seconds but got no reply. He looked up to Jordan and saw that his head was tilted slightly down waiting too for an answer from the porcus at the head of the train.

"Sergeant? What is the ETA?" he asked again.

Still no answer and this time Jordan shot him a glance.

"His mic might be down," he heard Vince say.

"*Sergeant, this is Lieutenant Suge. Answer me.*"

When the lieutenant got no reply he said, "*Xer, go to him.*"

"*Yes, Master,*" she said.

"*Continue on as normal everyone, the mission carries on as planned.*"

Jordan nodded and opened the door, pointing his rifle up at a now almost empty cart. They had passed the first class seats and were now in the darker parts of the train. Even in the infrared Conner could see stains of water, or possibly urine, on the cotton seats. Small blobs of light from passengers poked out of the top of their seats and the lights from outside in the tunnel passed them quickly, lighting up the train like a strobe light.

"Move forward, buddy."

"*Master! The sergeant is down! Sergeant Jinpac is down!*" they both heard the voice of Xer shout through all of a sudden.

"*What!?*" Suge said.

"*An arrow, Master. Poor bastard never knew what hit him, got an arrow right in the back of his head, pinned him right up against the wall of the train.*"

"*Right, weapons free, people!*" he ordered his men. "*We got a vigilante on board!*"

Conner suddenly shot a worried glance at his tigian friend when another cry rang through his ear.

"*Ahhhh!*" called the familiar voice of Richard.

"*Nooo!*" called his partner, Vince, and gunfire rang through the whole of the train.

"*What's happening!?*" Suge called through.

"*Someone's attacking us!*"

"*Who, damn it?!*"

Vince made no reply but through his microphone the team heard a swift slicing sound and Vince gurgled on something then thumped as his body hit the floor and was silent.

"Vince! Vince! Everybody on me, now!"

Conner's heart suddenly skipped; no one had been expecting this to happen. They were supposed to be the silent killers on this train and now it looked like they were the hunted.

On top of the train, while it sped through the tunnel with lights quickly passing like a strobe, the hooded archer ran along the roof. Its two knife weapons dripped with blood as it had quickly sliced the human's throat and now targeted the rest of the squad.

Conner, Jordan behind him, burst through the door to see the other three still alive.

"What's going on, sir?" Jordan asked.

"I don't know but we're not quitting the mission now. You see anything moving, you fire at once!"

"Yes, sir!"

They all stood close by, staring around them, looking for anything, any type of body heat that would give their attacker away but saw nothing, everything was suddenly silent and no one made a sound.

A door clicked and everyone shot a glance over and saw nothing.

Suddenly Breneth's nose twitched. "There is something on board, sir, I can smell it."

"You're only smelling the passengers, Breneth," Jordan said, holding up his rifle and looking around.

"No, he's right, I can smell something too," Xer confirmed.

"Maybe it's cloaking its body heat," Conner suggested and quickly took off his mask to see the world with his own eyes. He dropped his helmet to the floor and peered out into the dark train carriage and still saw nothing. Only lights passing quickly above them lit up the empty carriage around them. The passengers had mostly fled now, leaving them exposed. Conner couldn't see anything but quickly heard the sound of something stretching, like the sound of plastic or wood bending, like the sound of a bow.

An arrow was cast into the air and straight into the throat of the ursa, who choked, gurgled and fell to the floor struggling to breathe.

"He's in here with us!" Jordan screamed and fired in any direction, seeing nothing.

"That's impossible, we would be able to see it!" Suge corrected, but clearly seeing the dying ursa at his feet.

Conner suddenly saw the figure at the end of the carriage – a hooded archer dressed in black with its hood covering its face.

"It's right there!" he called and lifted his rifle, but before he could fire, the shadowy archer leaped forward and twisted the lieutenant around, stabbed him in the back and held him as a shield that Conner fired up against, lighting up the train with every shot.

Jordan took off his helmet, realising the infrared was blinding him, grabbed Conner and shoved him back.

"Go to the target Conner! Leave me with him!"

"No!" Conner said, stepping forward as the hooded archer dropped the dead lieutenant and now faced the tigian.

"Come on!" Xer shouted and knocked him back with her head. She was suddenly frightened since she couldn't remove her helmet and was completely helpless against the attacker, who could mask its body heat from her. She was blind to it.

Conner could only watch as the tigian lifted his rifle to fire but the attacker was too fast and knocked his weapon aside, swiped its knife to one side and scratched Jordan's arms.

Jordan yelped in pain and looked down at this hooded stranger. Even in the brief moments of light he could not see into its hood and so knew nothing of what this was... too fast be a tigian, too strong to be a human.

Conner and Xer ran back through the train carts, just aiming to finish off their target. People still crying in desperation and cowering in fear were now also astonished and confused as to why there were only two of these soldiers left and what they were looking for. Since he didn't have his helmet on he had no idea of what was happening to Jordan, only hoping he was okay.

"Let's just kill the target and get off this train!" Xer suggested as they ran, her master dead but her mission still with a purpose.

"Agreed. Lead the way."

Jordan swiped for the archer, whose such low stance suggested that it must have had some sort of training in a martial art that Jordan hadn't ever seen in real life. He tried to swing but the archer was too fast and agile for him to hit. With the strobe effect above them it moved like lightning. Jordan saw the archer for only a fraction of a second before feeling pain across his body as he was cut and sliced, until he had no choice but to back up and draw out his knife. He held it up and peered out at the archer, who stood still now a few paces away. He knew its eyes saw from the dark void in its hood straight into his but all he could see were the shadows constantly shifting and changing around him as the lights above shot past them.

"Come on then, you bastard!" he taunted the archer and waited as it dived forward for him. The tigians were strong but also known for their speed, and even though this archer was faster than Jordan, he managed to finally catch it and swing it to the floor, pressing it down hard, and started ripping its two knives away from its hands. He picked it up and pressed it against the wall, now defenceless, its two knives, bow and arrows all at the other end of the carriage and a knife to its throat.

Jordan was finally about to rip its hood off and see what lay behind when it used the final trick it had up its sleeve. It grabbed Jordan's wrist, the hand holding the knife, flung its other hand out to the side and a small ice axe attached to its arm flung out, which it caught and stabbed into Jordan's shoulder.

He screamed, let go of the knife and fell back. The archer didn't waste any time but flung its other arm to its side, caught its second axe and jumped on top of the screaming tigian, then planted its axes in his chest, silencing the greater creature.

Conner was panting now; he had no idea he and Xer were the last two left and now felt as terrified as the passengers. Who or whatever this archer was, it clearly was trained highly enough to take out a whole team of specialist soldiers from the Feydon army in a very short amount of time.

They found their way almost to the back of the train now having no idea when they would reach the next stop, now just wanting to end the mission and leave while they still had their lives. The carriages were now cluttered with people all with their backs to the walls of the carriage knowing that Conner was the only one now still equipped with a forbidden weapon and wasn't afraid to use it.

Soon, though, Xer stopped and sniffed the air.

"What's up?" Conner asked from behind her.

"There is another kingnine on this train, in the next cart."

"It might be our target, let's go."

Conner opened the door into the last of the passenger carts and now found it had bloodstains along the floor. Xer sniffed the blood. "This is leo blood."

"Good, let's just kill the bastard and go."

They slowly took a couple steps forward, his rifle up to his cheek, wanting to find this thing as soon as possible. The blood around him was dry, maybe a few hours old now, but there was fresh blood soaked into one of the seats where his target had been only a few moments ago. A trail led them up to another door. He pointed to the door silently and crept forward, reaching out for the door handle, when the door snapped open.

His heart jumped and, hoping to see the archer but instead only seeing another kingnine, he fired his weapon over the top of it.

"Stay away from my master!" the kingnine shouted and pounced up at him. He dropped his weapon and screamed as the kingnine bit into him.

"Stop it!" Xer called and bit into the kingnine, pulling him away and snarling, "Why, brother? Why attack us?"

The second kingnine now stood back up and glared at both of them. Conner got back to his feet watching the second kingnine. It looked a little larger and younger than Xer, stronger and already had scratches and scars covering its body from previous fights. The strange thing, though, was that this kingnine was not fazed by the rifle now lying on the floor, like it had seen these weapons before and was not frightened of them.

"Whoever you are, kingnine, just know that we are here to kill a leo. If you are a real kingnine then you would step aside and let us fulfil our duty."

"I would die first!" it quickly countered.

"Stand aside, brother!" Xer said backing her comrade up and wanting to turn aside and leave it but feared turning her back on it.

The tense atmosphere in the room suddenly exploded into confusion as a window smashed in from the outside and the hooded archer appeared again, landing right on top of Xer and stabbing its knife into the bottom of her throat like a hunter killing its prey. She died humanely and silently.

Conner nearly screamed and fell back, crawling up to the door behind him, his rifle too far away now to reach for and he couldn't take his eyes off the hooded archer, who now had murdered his entire team of special forces.

The second kingnine stood there silent and sniffed the air, not fazed by the archer and instead, since he was also blind to it, just stood there, sniffed and listened, as if he knew this thing had been here all along but didn't know what it was either.

The archer stood up slowly and first looked over to the second kingnine. When it saw it wouldn't be a problem it turned for the desperate aeomon.

Conner yelped again in fright knowing his end was near and quickly turned and reached for the door, managing to close it in time before the archer caught him.

As he locked the door Conner stood looking out of its small window and trembled as the archer stood with its shadowy face on the other side. Conner waited, staring at the cloaked figure before it turned and disappeared, passing the second kingnine without a second thought.

Conner, his heart drumming, his hands shaking, sighed and tried to catch his breath back. He went to turn around, when he walked into a huge, armoured chest. The chest of a leo, an evolved lion, that towered over him and panted in pain, holding a wounded side. Before Conner could think of anything the leo grabbed him by his neck and lifted him off the floor. Conner struggled all he could but even though his target was weakened, this leo would always be stronger than an aeomon.

"Please…"

Conner tried all he could to beg for mercy but the leo finally snarled and slammed his head to the ground and cracked his skull. Conner's breathing slowed and he could only lie there dying and watching the leo open the door and step through.

"Are you okay, Master?" the second kingnine asked the leo as it sat back down in agony.

"Yeah, I'm fine Zou'," the leo replied, but that was the last thing Conner ever heard as his heart stopped and he died on the floor.

The archer ran to the very end of the train and jumped down into a cargo carriage it was using to hide in. With its mission complete it opened the door into the silent room and looked over its shoulder. The leo was safe but it still had some unfinished business to attend to. It reached out with a cream coloured, furry, clawed paw and closed the door.

1

Nightfall at the Bastard Camp was always quiet. The walls were so thick it was sound proof to the torture and screams of the tormented souls. The guards outside were no different; either because of boredom or because the truth of the place that they were paid handsomely to protect scared them into a silence every night. Most of the guards took their pay from the Bastards down in the Entertainment Corridors in the sub level of the complex but a few were decent enough to just get paid and leave during the day to be with their families and never speak of the horrors of what every night witnessed in that hellish place.

Down in the darkest dungeons of the place lived the Bastards, kept in a giant dark hole with cellar doors above them leading into rooms where they would be molested, raped or even killed in gruesome ways and it all depended on how rich and crazy the paying customer was. This was all they ever knew though; they were not people. They accepted their life if they needed to survive. Outside the complex were long wooden huts. More Bastards were kept here but these were the prettier, even slightly educated Bastards. Some could even be nice enough to call themselves whores; these were the most expensive Bastards but the price comes with the quality. But these damned, poor souls were not prisoners here since a prisoner would have to know freedom to begin with. They had lived here all their lives and knew nothing else in the world. The real prisoner in this complex was contained in the first floor, away from the Bastards, in a dark room. The prisoner was tied in a crucified shape to a wall to keep him vertical, his hands bound either side of him and his feet only just touching the floor.

The owner of this complex was a large tigian named Dimitiry Taylor, a rich, powerful and intellectual monster who made his riches originally as a common pimp but moved on to bigger things when had he gained his millions. He paid for this land in Angland out of his own pocket and now ruled this place like an emperor. People would come from all over the world to take advantage of the Bastards. Some were just like the usual punters he used to deal with as a pimp and would pay just to have sex with the pretty ones that lived outside in the huts. There were also the rich men who wanted to know what it felt like to kill a man and so would torture and kill the Bastards in the Entertainment Corridors. The more controversial and crazy men would come a little more rarely and kill the Bastards with tools, cut them open and have sex with their organs. These sorts of people never made it long outside because of their sick and perverted nature, but to him, so long as they paid, they were not judged. He even thought of himself as a saint and thought that giving these psychopaths the killing they wanted would prevent them from killing innocent people outside the camp. Killing the Bastards is something he would only stop when the numbers grew thin, then he would only cut his prices down and give a few months while the Bastards gave birth to more Bastards and in only a few years would rebuild his numbers again. Tigians lived longer than humans and so this time was nothing to him and the price drop always meant more business and so would actually make more money in this time.

But he was also a collector of rare and valuable items. He once had a very special item that was stolen from him in his home mansion in Walshraw. One of the thieves was the very prisoner he had contained, which is why he wanted him away from the other Bastards. He needed this one alive.

He stood staring out of a large window in his office. He always admired the view of his land and loved knowing he was successful in life. His vanity was one of his favourite things about himself.

His door opened and a toned, armoured Feydon soldier walked in. He usually didn't do business with any sort of army and kept himself away from the politics of war but this matter was different. He had been trading with this soldier recently to have his complex equipped with cannons and forbidden weapons recently remade. They were an excellent defence weapon to ensure the safety of his company from the law outside.

"So, Baron, are you gonna let me kill this pest of mine yet?" the soldier asked him, referring to the prisoner.

The baron didn't like the man and despised the fact that even though he was a powerful tigian this man could kill him easily, but he also knew the soldier needed him too. He wanted the prisoner dead and he wanted to do it himself, and had been pestering him to kill the prisoner since he arrived.

"No, Miles. I have told you countless times now. The prisoner shall not be harmed. He is *my* prisoner and I am waiting for him to break and tell me where my artefact is."

Miles sneered. He had been through this argument with the baron for two weeks now. He could kill the prisoner and still find this 'artefact' for the baron if he wanted it so much, but the baron was stubborn like all tigians and would not give in.

"You know, you keep denying me this luxury; I'm just going to kill him anyway, then kill you after for standing in my way."

"And if you kill him my men will outnumber yours. You only have a small squad here, Miles. Not your whole army. My men will outnumber you and I have already given the orders to take all of your squad and throw you down with the Bastards. You will live like them and be treated like them if you so much as curse at us, then we will lobotomise you all and before you know it you will be fucked in the arse more times than you've had hot dinners."

Miles stood silent. As much as he didn't like to admit it, the baron was right. Miles was good, very good, but he couldn't take this whole complex on his own or with the small squad with him. He could kill the tigian but at a price that was frightening even for him.

"To be honest, Miles, I don't even know why you are still here. We have done good business, with myself buying some of the cannons from your army and you have brought a fine young woman to me in exchange for the office equipment you needed. You have used these and she has escaped and now you just linger here. Don't you have other orders to attend to?"

"Only my master will give me orders and he has said no word as of yet. Since my orders haven't been updated yet I am here on my own free will to make sure your prisoner is dead. It's personal."

"Well, you will be waiting for a long time, Miles, I assure you."

"We'll see."

The door opened again and one of the Baron's guards stood there, "Sir, there is someone coming to the gates."

"Another customer?" Dimitiry asked.

"We're not sure. We ask if you could check this one out for us."

The baron nodded with a pleased smile and thought to himself, *excellent, another crazy, rich psychopath, probably wanting to murder a couple of Bastards. Business is good when the nights are cold and dark.*

The baron was led outside with Miles following out of interest to see how this process worked. Many of the people that came to the Bastard Camp were harmless but some were vicious and ruthless murderers and so the baron ensured that every time a real violent man came to the doors, a special welcome would be brought forward for the protection of his men.

The sentry lights on either side of a fifteen foot metal gate shone down on a cloaked figure standing outside, his head down and the shadow of his hood covering his face.

"Positions, men!" the baron called and waited for his men all to stand in a large semicircle around him and the gate. He never wanted anyone loose in his complex and so this was normal protocol. Some men also grabbed their bows, arrows and crossbows and went to certain spots from where they could fire immediately if needed.

"Open the gates!" the baron called when everyone was ready.

The gates opened electronically. The stranger waited in the dark and cold until the gates were fully opened. There was absolute silence.

More Feydon soldiers ran out of the complex seeing the commotion and went to Miles.

"What's happening, Commander?"

"I don't know yet. Get your weapons ready though, guys, and bring out the cannons that were delivered here last week. I want one man on each and aimed at whoever this guy is."

"Yes, Commander!" they yelled and ran back to their own posts, waiting for further orders.

The baron stood in the silence of the night staring at the stranger as he finally stepped forward slowly. His every step brought confusion and fear into the guards. Never had someone entered this place like this before, so slowly. He walked like death itself, not looking up at the armed guards above him like most of the crazies that came before. Normally *they* are the ones to strike fear into the crazies but there was something about this one that was different.

"That's far enough!" the baron called out and waited as the stranger stopped. The two lights of the sentry towers shone down on this stranger as a spotlight in the dark. He still stood there, menacingly, waiting for the baron to continue.

"State your business here!" he called again, strongly wanting to show his dominance in the situation.

The stranger waited. "You have a prisoner with you!" The voice was female. "I want him!"

The baron glared, trying to see through the stranger's cloak but still only seeing into the black void of the shadow under the hood.

"The prisoner is not for sale! He is my prisoner and he will be released when and where I see fit!"

Miles had already seen enough. He knew exactly who this was and wondered how she was so bold all of a sudden. He raised his hand to the soldiers behind him and signalled them.

"What are you doing, Miles!?" the baron shouted in shock.

"You should have let me kill him when we had the chance. Boys, on my command…"

The stranger finally looked up, seeing and hearing the voice of Miles.

"Fire!"

Instantly the cannons behind them lit up and their thunderous sound killed the silence of the night.

The stranger lifted her hood revealing her face in the light. Her hair was as black as the night around them and her eyes were a perfect white, with no pupil nor iris but both eyes as white as the sclera, perfect white, absolute white. Even with the projectiles fired at her, the white eyed Acarlie showed no signs of fear to the small army that stood before her and only lifted her hand sharply with her fingers stretched out. The cannon balls and shrapnel speeding through the air all slammed into the large, blue, circular shields she summoned using her mastery of magnetism. Just like at the Battle of Hiro, she stopped these large, metal balls simply by ordering them to stop with a simple gesture of her hand. When they struck, the noise hit like lightning and the blue circles instantly appeared, lighting up the sky and disappearing as quickly as they came, leaving the projectiles to float harmlessly in front of her.

The baron stared dumbfounded at what he was witnessing, as was every guard and soldier, who could only stand and watch, waiting for the next move.

Acarlie breathed steadily; she was so calm and composed, almost like she wasn't in her body at all. Her shoulders hunched forward, her head lowered and her breathing deepened as if she were controlling the energy inside her. Miles noticed the baron's eyes widen watching this elementalist now acting differently from anything else he had ever seen. She slowly pulled back her still stretched out hand slightly and they all noticed the floating projectiles also moved slightly toward her. With a loud, animal-like scream she thrust her hand forward, then all the shrapnel and cannon fire she controlled now flew back in the direction from which they had come. At thrice the speed the cannons had fired them, they now shot like bullets back at the complex and crashed into the building causing instant damage to the complex.

The baron shielded his eyes and turned in recoil as his precious building now only stood as a target for the powerful elementalist now enraged with so much anger it was like she was possessed by a demon of unspeakable power.

"Keep firing!" the baron screamed to his men and together as a unit the soldiers and guards from the complex all lifted their weapons and fired towards the elementalist.

She shielded herself from more cannon fire and bullets from their rifles again by creating a large magnetic field around her so strong that nothing metallic could pass through but, instead, deflected off it to fly in every direction.

When the soldiers all needed to reload, after carelessly all firing at once, she quickly threw her hands to the floor and used her Element of Ground to cause a spherequake to tremble and quake the ground beneath their feet. A wave of energy shot from under the ground itself and aimed at the complex again, hitting its target and causing part of the building to shake violently and start to collapse down into thick sheets of poisonous dust.

"She's going to kill the prisoner!" Dimitiry cried out over the sound of the destruction. "We must not let this happen!" He quickly pointed to her this time and ordered his men to charge.

While drawing their weapons this time the men charged toward her.

She stood strong and waited for the first to arrive, swinging his sword to kill her, and instead of using her shield, this time she held her arm out to block the attack. Her arm instantly turned to diamond when the attack struck and countered with a diamond fist; she heard the bone and cartilage break in the guard's face and turned to the next guard instantly.

As the battle waged on, more tried firing at their target but without the necessary training they were poor marksmen and either missed or hit their friends, who were now so close and personal with the white eyed Acarlie they risked being shot among the stray bullets.

The ground kept shaking and parts of the complex still broke from their foundations and fell; in all this commotion nobody noticed another figure leap over the gate from a quiet corner and sprint toward the complex.

Cannon balls still fell from the sky as more attempts on Acarlie's life failed and crashed down into the ground around the figure's feet, causing him to move continuously and duck and dive his way to the doors that were protected by a few guards still concentrating their attention on the elementalist. He ran wearing tight black leggings with a short brown cotton shirt and his scabbard tied to his back. When one guard finally saw the figure he tried to sound the alarm but instead found the figure's sword inside his chest. The figure ripped out the sword causing blood to spray out and cover his comrades, who screamed when covered in their friend's warm, oily blood. They again turned to attack their new foe but were blinded as the figure's blade now burst out in a blaze of fire.

Since Val had been captured in an attempt to rescue Acarlie from this complex two weeks previously, Dude had been in a constant programme of training and exercising formulated by the pirates. This obviously was nowhere near as long as what they wanted but since he was to carry out this part of the rescue mission on his own it was up to him to ensure he was fit and able if he were to succeed.

He hated it, the last two weeks had been unbearable for him. He was given eight hours a night to sleep, but after that, it was a strict regime of exercising in the morning that would last through until the afternoon. He was given five small meals in his intervals of rest which would mostly only contain protein; he hated fish.

Even on his days of rest he was made to perfect his katas, given to him by some of the pirates and Rezosa. These were the most painful lessons of all and the only time in his life he was thankful for the fact that he was mute and could not talk to her but instead just listened and did as instructed. The first couple of days were hell for him but he knew he had to do this if this plan was to succeed. Acarlie was far too distressed to train with him but the only piece of comfort he got was when Mitis, the blonde nurse from Toshiro, decided she would train alongside him. This was a relief for him. He had been there for her when she last needed somebody and now she was returning the favour. She was a slow learner at first but with a few lessons with Rezosa, the beautiful ex-sergeant of the Feydon army, she started learning more.

After the two weeks, Dude's body ached and needed a whole day to rest as much as he could but even in that short amount of time he could feel his body was stronger. He felt tense but strong and the time he spent practising weapons training with the pirates was now finally paying off as the guards before him all fell at his feet and he stood amongst blood and tissue, catching his breath and looking at his bloodstained hands. From the once frail, weak and bullied, self-hating aeomon, he was now turning into a deadly weapon. However, he was still unstable from his episode back in Donolan, and the two weeks of Rezosa, the person he lusted over, either barking orders at him or ignoring him completely didn't help. He thanked Sphere, though, that Mitis was there.

He held his chin to the sky and breathed in some of the dirty, dusty night air and slowed his heart down from the excitement, opened his eyes as another cannon ball smashed into the building and remembered who he was here for.

He took his scabbard from his back and tied it to his waist for a quick and easy access to his sword and entered the building while the battle still raged on outside. He knew he had to be quick in getting Acarlie's guide back.

The staff from the building had all escaped and fled leaving the corridors empty for him, with only a couple of Feydon soldiers spotting him and, thankfully, believing themselves to be enough to stop him, rather than calling for support. As another two soldiers fell at his feet he reached the large metal door that led down to the Entertainment Corridors and he opened it to instantly smell the pungent reek of death, sweat and body waste. He gagged at first but knew Val must be down there and went to step down, when he heard a whimpering in a nearby room. He quickly kicked the door and when he couldn't open it the macho way he preferred he turned the handle and found a receptionist cowering from him in a corner. He may have not have been able to kick the door open but this had managed to scare her a little more so he used this, drew his sword and held it to her chin. He knew he wouldn't hurt this woman but she didn't know this.

"Purihoah!" he shouted to her.

"What!?" she cried.

"Purihoah! Ware ih purihoah!" he ordered again trying to pronounce his words as best as he could without a tongue.

"I don't know what you're saying!" she suddenly wailed, crying.

He knelt down this time to face her and opened his mouth to show her his severed tongue. Once she'd seen his tongue was missing he tried again.

"Puurihh-oh-aa," he tried one last time using his hand to try and force the correct words out.

"What?" she sobbed. "P...prisoner?"

"Hei!"

"Upstairs! Please don't hurt me!" she cried, but he didn't answer and darted out of the room and left her there unharmed.

"Their attacks are doing nothing to her!" cried Dimitiry as more of his men were ordered to their deaths in trying to overpower the white eyed Acarlie.

Miles was already drawing his blade Razor and quickly tilting it to the floor causing the oily gel to trickle down the edge and instantly dry and sharpen the blade, "That's because all your men are incompetent fools! They're guards, not soldiers."

"Then what do you suggest?"

"I already gave you my suggestion, Baron! To lobotomise her when you had the chance, now she's pissed off with what we have done to her. Just leave her to me!"

He charged into Acarlie, knowing his Razor would be no use so instead used it as a distraction and threw it towards her. The blade cut through the dusty night as it spun in the air at her. Her head jerked as she saw it in the corner of her eye and instantly the sword stopped as it hit her magnetic shield. Miles knew this would happen and still ran in and dived toward her, spearing her into the ground, and went to punch her but was quickly thrown off. By swiftly swinging her hands to her left, she turned to her side and lifted from the floor, lowering the gravity, then strongly thrust her hands to her right and caused every guard within ten feet of her to fly backwards in a strong gust of thrown wind energy, giving her space to concentrate on the one she wanted.

He quickly rolled back, sprang back up on his feet and waited for her to attack; and sure enough, when she went to kick him he turned, grabbed her leg and twisted, throwing her back to the floor, and lifted his knee to stamp on her throat but missed as she rolled to her side again and back onto her feet like a cat.

He tried attacking her again but felt himself stopped immediately. She knew she was too slow to attack him physically and so turned to another option: she held out her hand and used her magnetism to grab his armour and lift him from the floor.

He cursed as he remembered what had happened last time and had forgotten to take his armour off but luck was on his side. Acarlie didn't have enough time to finish him like before since the other guards were now back on her and she only had enough time to push her hand forward. Miles catapulted backwards and tumbled to the floor in a heap.

Dude finally found the room he was looking for but a guard were standing on either side of it and they drew their weapons. He drew his sword Fireshaver from his side and blocked the first attack, kicked the second guard, turned and sliced down into the first's chest, nimbly stepped aside and waited for the second to regain his stance and try again. With only two short and quick manoeuvres the second was also on the floor in agony but Dude didn't have the time to finish them off and opened the door to find their prisoner.

His knife was on a table stained with his own blood next to his staff, weapons Miles wanted to torture Val with, loving the irony that he would be tortured with his own weapons.

His violet/purple cloak was at his side and the same bandages still covered his head, only leaving his mouth and right eye exposed.

The bed he was on was tilted almost upright. His hands were stretched to either side and tied down, the rope tightly tied to his wrists burning and scratching them, leaving sore, red marks. His head hung down with his chin touching his chest. He was clearly unconscious and Dude tilted his head to see the bandages had recently dried, saw the water stains and hoped this didn't cause any infection in his already broken face.

Dude took Val's knife and cut the ropes, threw his purple cloak over his shoulders and left his staff, only concentrating on trying to carry the wounded man out with his feet dragging across the floor.

He managed to get back outside and saw the carnage

and destruction the monster that was Acarlie was still doing to this complex and tried jogging away from them. He was halfway across the field when he heard a loud, snarling cry and turned to see Dimitiry Taylor, the baron himself, charging for him.

Way back at the start of his journey Val and Dude had been made to steal the blade Fireshaver from this tigian, this highly evolved tiger, and had successfully managed to, and now he wanted his precious artefact back and dived into the aeomon. Dude had no choice but to drop Val and try to defend himself against the baron. An aeomon against a tigian? This kind of encounter only ever had one outcome in history.

"Ah! Bitch!" Miles cursed as he got himself back to his feet. His back was sore and he needed to stretch after the fall he had just taken but it was nothing that could slow him down. He glared angrily at Acarlie as she still took on small waves of soldiers and guards one at a time without breaking a sweat. She moved like the whole thing was a game to her, with perfect technique and precise aim. With her eyes white, the person inside her body was gone and this meant that her emotionless body had brought her to a state of perfect concentration. He marvelled at her. This is the power his master had recently told him about. Right now the once sweet Acarlie was an effective weapon against even the strongest army. As this was just one elementalist, he wondered what could an army of them could do.

But as much as he marvelled at her he still had his orders. She had to die and so he this time took off his armour and anything else metallic and charged for her again.

She turned her concentration after punching one of the soldiers and saw Miles running. He looked up and saw deep into the perfect white eyes. There may have been no pupils in her eyes but he knew she, or it, saw him. Whatever it was, it wasn't Acarlie.

She held out her hand to attempt to copy her previous move but instead found it ineffective since Miles wore no metal and she now stepped back as Miles brought the fight to her with everything he had. They exchanged blows, fists and blocks, trying to outperform one another. Miles knew if this was the real Acarlie then he could easily defeat her. She wasn't a fighter outside her precious Elemental Battles.

He swung his arms and waited for her to block, parried her counters and punched her in the chest. As she recoiled in pain he thrust his leg to kick her again but flew up as she caught his leg and lifted it too high for his balance to cope with.

More guards and soldiers tried again to jump on her but when she only lowered the gravity they rose off the ground and flew backwards as she commanded the elements around her to disperse her enemy.

The baron Dimitiry Taylor didn't wait for any monologues when he saw the aeomon and tried to kill him as quickly as possible. Unfortunately for Dude, the very blade he had strapped to his waist was the very reason that the baron wanted him dead. It also was the very reason why Val had not been executed immediately after being captured. After being bundled to the floor, Dude had to think fast before he found his head in the jaws of this superior creature and jabbed a fist at the baron's throat. A cowardly move, but one that saved his life. As the baron choked, Dude scrambled away and drew Fireshaver. Immediately the red steel burst into flames, something that only enraged the baron even more since he was never able to succeed in doing this when he had owned this blade previously.

Dude screamed over the sound of the excitement of the night and tried swinging his blade of fire toward the baron, who jumped back and tried parrying the katana away enough to grab the small aeomon and finish him off.

The size difference of these two creatures was amazing; like a real David and Goliath they fought, Dude with speed, grace and agility and Dimitiry with enough strength to pull the aeomon's joints out of their sockets.

Dimitiry tried swinging for the aeomon, who ducked and rolled out of the way of his claws and, more importantly, his teeth. But Dude had a weapon of his own, a legendary blade that burned like fire and blinded its opponents before slicing them open. The baron swiped again while Dude ducked and swung a punch of his own. A punch that turned the baron's cheek but nothing to do any real damage and the baron retaliated by backhanding Dude and swung a punch with his opposite hand which nearly knocked Dude's head clean off. Dude fell to the floor and tumbled over. His neck hurt from the whiplash and his cheek felt swollen and fragile. The baron picked up the aeomon, who tightly gripped onto this blade still but was weak and still in shock from the heavy attack. The baron lifted him up by his neck and tilted it to an angle, smiling as he saw the white flesh of Dude's neck, and bit into it.

Dude screamed as his neck all the way down to his shoulder was now in this tigian's mouth, his teeth puncturing his skin and drawing blood to trickle down his chest. Without a second thought Dude gathered all the strength he could muster and lifted Fireshaver, burning even more than usual, and thrust it into the tigian's chest.

With a blood-curdling scream the baron dropped the aeomon before having the chance to rip out his throat and instead left him with large tooth marks on his already scarred body and fell to his knees. Dude, once back on the floor, yanked Fireshaver out of the tigian's chest and aimed it back down to pierce his sternum below his throat and forced the fiery blade down into the tigian's chest.

The baron's eyes widened as he felt the hot steel burning his organs and his last thought was that of irony. Once he spoke of killing this aeomon and all for the very weapon now piercing his heart. His body convulsed and began to spasm before dying instantly before the aeomon, who drew Fireshaver back out of the baron's body and wiped the blood on his cloak.

Dude couldn't believe it. What had he become? He was hated by his fellow people and aeomon since he had his tail removed but now he had succeeded in something that only a very few aeomon in all of history had done, win in a one on one fight against a tigian. Even though he *did* have a very special weapon on his side, the chance of this happening was still remarkable. He had no time to congratulate himself though as Val still lay on the floor. Dude took Fireshaver and its scabbard from his waist and strapped them to his back and turned, when something made him stop in his tracks. A strange feeling came over him he didn't understand. Time seemed to stop. The night became silent and the destruction of Acarlie and the army now seemed many miles away. The night crept around him and smothered him in a void of silence. He felt an urge to turn around and when he did, the deceased body of the tigian lay before him with blood seeping out of his chest and soaking into the dusty ground. Something inside him wanted to cry. Tears begged to roll down his cheeks but his confusion denied him. A great, warm feeling of accomplishment swelled inside his chest and he felt like stabbing the dead tigian more and more. He knelt down to see into the dead eyes of the baron but still didn't understand. He felt happy, like he had succeeded in something; maybe it was the fact that the baron was a tigian? No, he thought, it wasn't that. It felt more like the satisfying feeling of vengeance, like long ago the baron took something from him. But if this was so, then what? Dude had first met the baron when he and Val stole Fireshaver. The baron captured him and nearly killed him; maybe it was this, he thought, but something still felt different. He was angry with the baron, a lifelong anger he never knew he carried until now, now he was dead by his hands. He felt accomplishment but also profound confusion as he never knew why. A cannon ball struck the floor and woke him from his thoughts and back to his responsibility. With one more look down at the puzzle before him he turned away. He would have to think about this later.

Miles was thrown again by the white eyed Acarlie and got back to his feet with his team now staring at him for direction. None of them could attack the elementalist successfully and now even the guards had no idea where their boss had gone and were about to flee themselves.

Miles spat blood onto the floor and looked up to see still the fighting soldiers and screamed for them to pull back.

"Fire everything he have at her!" he ordered his men.

"Everything?" they asked.

"You heard me! Everything! All at once, let's see how her elements can save her here!"

They all ran back to their cannons and filled them with everything possible from cannon balls to chained balls, metal shrapnel and even rocks and rubble, piling in everything they had while the rest all reloaded their rifles and aimed at her.

Acarlie, however, used this time to catch her breath back and hung her shoulders forward again and breathed deeply, like a beast.

As soon as she saw them all readying their weapons she held her hands to the sky and in the blackness of this once peaceful night a bright white sphere of energy appeared above her head and grew as she held her hands to the sky.

"Fire!" Miles screamed and pointed to her and they all fired everything they had and suddenly every rifle and cannon started belting out lethal rounds towards her.

She screamed even louder now. Her voice echoed over the sound of the gunfire as all the flying ammunition now changed its course and flew straight into the white sphere above her head with a loud crack as they compacted closer and closer together. The ball of energy now even fizzed like electricity as she compacted all the elements around her closer and hummed louder and louder until the whirling sound was the only thing in existence. Finally, using a combination of all the energies she could gather within her body she released this ball toward the complex. The black sky now lit up into a blinding white light. The ground shook like a wave of water and rushed in front of the white sphere and when it reached the complex it exploded with a force no one had ever seen before. The whole complex didn't know what hit it and suddenly was forced back into rubble. People caught up in this wave of energy were blown back like ants by a torturous child's breath.

Miles could only cover his eyes and hide under anything he could, realising this was the power his master spoke of, and still on a small scale.

She stood there, her outstretched hands now tense and she screamed whilst still destroying the whole complex and massacring whoever was close enough.

The building exploded into fires like a bomb had hit it and the underground Entertainment Corridors now also burst into flame as wild and flaming Bastards sprang out of their cells to scream and run wildly, falling to the ground burning.

Finally, one last light lit up as the Scarlet Arise now arrived, firing more cannons back at the already missing complex that now stood like a sandcastle ruined by a child's older sibling.

There was nothing left but smoke and fire to remind the survivors of what once stood here – and all this destruction caused by one elementalist who had broken her conditioning and awoken the true power that lived inside *every* elementalist. Acarlie still stood panting, her hands still stretched out and her eyes still white, until she felt a hand touch her shoulder.

"Acarlie!" said Zahied as he appeared from behind her. "We got him, Val's safe!"

As soon as she heard his name Acarlie's eyes rolled back into her head and she collapsed into Zahied's arms completely unconscious. Zahied caught her and ran back to the Scarlet Arise as the soldiers now crept out from their hiding places. Miles was one of these and he got to his feet, picking up Razor from the floor, while Zahied ran Acarlie back on board the ship as it started to lift from the ground.

Miles was too late and was left standing defeated, staring up at Dude and Zahied as they looked down with the two unconscious companions in their arms.

Fireshaver was still strapped to Dude's back and a dead tigian lay at Miles's feet. He looked down at the deceased evil baron and back to the wounded but still able aeomon, smiled and nodded as the ship took off.

2

The Great Forest of Angland gleamed in the morning sun. The morning dew soaked into the moss that covered the trees and decorated every leaf hanging from the trees and shone like tiny diamonds, reflecting the colours of the spectrum in the early hours of the morning.

Two tigians trekked through this great and deep forest, one female with orange and black stripes over her fur, the other male with white and black stripes. He wore dark grey tigian-made leggings and over his chest wore only his standard, police issued, dark blue stab-proof vest, attached with black Velcro straps. He thought it useful since it had big, deep pockets down the chest and because the tightly woven materials within made it difficult for attackers using knives. His department called it the stab-proof vest and it made good armour. It wasn't completely impenetrable but gave some security so he decided to keep it on on his journey. This land was foreign and alien for Keppal. His white and black fur suggested that he originated from a distant and cold environment called Glacias Terras. Not that he minded; he had left his home when he was still young and set out to make something of himself, becoming a police officer for the city of Toshiro, rising up the ranks until he was made a detective. Unfortunately, though, what had brought him this far away from his home and job was the disaster of Toshiro a few weeks previously, but still fresh on his mind. His team of officers had been killed alongside thousands of other people when what will be known now as *The Great Storm of Toshiro* destroyed his home and lifestyle. He believed that a young man named Val and his companions were responsible and he had now been given, by the Elemental Lord Zane himself, a special and top secret mission. He was to find this human, Val, who was a sacred guide and guardian for an elementalist named Acarlie. Once he found Acarlie and her team he was to stick close to them until he was near enough to Acarlie herself, then kill her. He believed her to be a menace and terrorist of the people of Sphere. A mission he was reluctant to achieve, but after murdering Dusty, the ursa of the team, with his bare hands, he realised now he was far too deep into this mission to back out. He despised murderers since his last job had been to catch and arrest them, but now he was one. He hated himself for this. There was nothing personal with Dusty, only that the large, evolved bear had found out about Keppal's mission and needed to be silenced. Now Keppal marched with one of Acarlie's closest companions, Sheeria, planning to stick close to her whilst she arranged travel back to Acarlie, then he would kill her. Then, once he was face to face with Acarlie he would wait until it was just him and her and then he would strike. He would kill this elementalist, relieve the world of this menace and become a hero, and maybe have his old life back. This, of course Sheeria was completely unaware of.

She walked ahead of him through the thick forests, her feet crunching the dead leaves as she strode. She was bare footed and wore common tigian gowns tied tightly to her so they didn't drag and tear on the forest; around and over them she wore her traveller's cloak made of tigian velvets, soft, but hard to tear and the colour of warm, fresh blood; she wore her hood down to rest across her shoulders.

After Donolan was attacked she lost her elementalist and her friends when they all split up to look for the nameless mute aeomon. Feydon attacked the city led by Zane and Queen Angel and once again lives were lost and another great city known for its elemental stadium was left in ruins. She needed to get back to her elementalist before she carried on with her pilgrimage, leaving Sheeria lost and without purpose in this world. Sheeria had already lost a previous life thanks to the humans who wiped out the leo species to near extinction and now risked losing another. She was reluctant about travelling through this forest for it meant facing her old tribe again, but this was the only way she could think of crossing the waters back over to Anavrin to get to the city of Chippenham, where Acarlie would surely go next.

Together they marched through this thick forest. The soft mud on the hidden paths was gentle on their feet and the morning air was welcoming to their lungs. They had just slept, with Sheeria helping Keppal to build a temporary shelter by tying a large rectangular sheet at a sixty degree acute angle to four trees and sleeping under them.

Keppal was wasn't used to this sort of adventuring and found it hard to sleep, but eventually found a few hours. But he was still pleased to be back on the road.

"Are you sure you still know the way?" he couldn't help but ask whilst trekking closely behind her.

"Yes of course I still do, it may have been a long time ago when I was last here..."

"Remind me how long again now," he cut in.

"Well, let's see, it was at the start of the Leo Divide, which dates back to something around a hundred years ago now."

"One hundred years? So how old are you?"

Sheeria laughed. "Keppal, you have more manners than to ask a lady her age, don't you?"

Keppal smiled. "Forgive me, Sheeria, you just don't look over a century that's all."

"Well, thank you, Keppal. To tell the truth, I was very

young when I lived here. I was a young mother who society would have frowned upon, but no matter how long ago it was, it was still my childhood here so my memory of this place will stay with me until I'm well over two hundred."

"You plan to live that long?" he asked.

She laughed again and looked over her shoulder to him and smiled. "Of course I do, Keppal, doesn't every tigian?"

"I guess." He nodded and smiled but when she turned around his smile turned to a frown and he thought again, how would he kill her, in her sleep? Did he really have it in him to kill her as she slept? He had to if he wanted to save the world from Acarlie.

They eventually came to a crossroads with a wooden sign posted. A human skull decorated it, with red paint spelling "Go Back" on it.

"How barbaric. What kind of place is this, Sheeria?" Keppal asked, astounded by this sign.

Sheeria frowned and stepped closer.

"Bloody kids," she said to herself.

"Sheeria?"

She stepped up to the sign and took the skull from it and handed it to Keppal, "It's plastic. A kid's prank trying to empower the tigians and scare humans away. It's signs like this that give our species a bad name."

Keppal looked at the harmless plastic skull in his hands and couldn't help but smile again, admiring the way Sheeria handled this. She showed strength and wisdom beyond her years. He threw the skull aside and watched as Sheeria took to the road ahead, completely ignoring the plastic threat that would scare most people off.

They walked in conversation for another hour until they finally came to another post. This one was only a small yellow flag pinned to a tree but when Sheeria examined it she frowned and turned to Keppal in concern.

"This means we are entering archer space. This is now a hunting ground for my people so don't make too much noise or you will scare off prey and piss my people off."

"Won't this mean that they won't know we're coming?"

She turned back around with her eyes to the trees. "Oh, they already know, Keppal."

"Really?"

"Of course. This is their home. You don't think they don't know everything that happens in this forest?"

"So what's going to happen?"

"No doubt they think we are both travellers trying to find this place and are planning to either lead us astray or kill us and call it an accident. Or they *can just come down and speak to me in person!*" She shouted the last part to the forest knowing her voice was heard by more than just Keppal.

An arrow shot out from the trees and pierced the tree beside Sheeria. Keppal jumped suddenly but Sheeria looked more offended than scared.

"Was that supposed to frighten me?! That was very immature and foolish! Show yourself immediately!"

Keppal almost gasped at the way once again she completely ignored this obvious threat and instead lectured their stalker.

Their stalker finally revealed himself as a tigian not much older than Keppal himself.

"How did you know, tigian? I kept my movements to a minimum."

"Don't give me that! Come here!" she demanded.

The archer raised an eyebrow still with the bow and arrow in his hands. "And who do think you are, telling me what to do?" he countered.

Sheeria ripped the arrow from the tree, stormed over to him and threw the arrow at his feet. "What kind of archer pulls stunts like this? Someone could have got seriously hurt!"

"That might have been the intention," he wittily replied.

Sheeria wasted no time and raised her hand to strike the cheeky tigian but stopped when she realised he wouldn't be alone.

"Where are the rest of them?" she asked.

The archer laughed and applauded her. "Wow, no one has ever seen through this trap. I applaud you, tigian." He turned and shouted to the trees, "It's okay guys, come down!"

Suddenly another four archers appeared from their hiding places and sheathed their weapons.

The tallest and broadest walked up to her.

"No one outside this village has managed to see through our traps and warnings. I take it you must be from here."

"You thought right. My name is Sheeria Katsan and I used to be a member of this tribe long ago and have returned to speak to the council here."

Once she said her name they all fell silent; the leader even stuttered, "Katsan?"

"Yes." She glared at him, but more at the weapon he was equipped with. It looked almost electronic, a crossbow that worked on cogs that the tigians never used.

"What's that?" she asked, but the tigian ignored her question and ordered his men. "Okay, we'll escort them to the village. Come Sheeria and your white companion. It's this way."

"One thing first," she quickly put in and turning to the first archer, who had fired the warning shot, backhanded him across his cheek.

"That's for firing at us! Sphere's divide, you should have known better than to fire at unarmed travellers! What did you think you would achieve by firing at us?"

The archer held his cheek. With the smile wiped from his face he looked now like a disciplined child and said nothing, completely gob-smacked she had struck him then lectured him too.

Keppal still stood stunned and watched as Sheeria started walking away after not getting an answer out of him. He had greatly misjudged this tigian. She had just marched in after all these years, seen through all their defences and disciplined their best hunters in a matter of minutes, and now led the way back to her old village. He wondered why they had acted so strangely when she said her name and why they didn't just kill her on the spot. He followed now out of curiosity to see what made this tigian so special.

The 'village' of Rowsena finally revealed itself to be a magnificent town of wooden huts that stacked high into the trees. Keppal stared in disbelief at first. This looked more like a wooden city than a village or a town. The tree houses climbed high into the sky next to giant trees that acted more like buildings, skyscrapers. Great glass mirrors sat on the walls of each tree-house and masked their upper heights, with only the base visible to people below.

"What the–," Keppal began, dazzled by the size of the trees.

"They're just trees, Keppal," Sheeria began. "A member of the Redwood family, largest trees in the world. We use them as support for our homes."

"How high do they go?" he asked, having to crank his neck to see the top of one.

"I don't know, I never thought to ask," she shrugged, but noticed something else about this place that troubled her.

She witnessed at the bottom of one of these great trees a kind of elevator, powered by a generator at the bottom that ran on cogs and steam. It screamed and whistled as a lever was pulled when a tigian stepped onto the elevator and a number of cogs and wheels began frantically turning. A pulley system that looped all the way up the tree and back down to the elevator next to it started turning, slowly pulling the elevator up past the small huts that acted as flats for the tigians.

It was then that Sheeria noticed the change in the village she grew up in. It was so much more advanced from what she remembered. The tigians wore different clothing from the usual robes and garments. Some were even in suits with hats, reflecting the human and aeomon fashion sense, with pocket watches hanging from chains. Some were getting onto lizzier-pulled wagons and even a primitive form of M.V. (motorised vehicle) they had to wind up from a lever at the front, chugging like a steam train as they drove away.

"What's happened to this place?" she asked, bewildered, when her answer walked straight past her in the form of an aeomon wearing a fitted black suit and tie.

"Aeomon?" She looked to the leader of the archers. "Since when did aeomon live here?"

The archer gave her a warm smile. "For the last seventy years now. We have shared our home with them and they have returned the favour by helping us with their technology to help with our lives."

Sheeria looked back at her changed home. "When I was here it was so much more peaceful, primitive yes, but peaceful. How do the aeomon make your lives better here?"

"With their know-how of machines similar to the humans' but without the stress and pollution. Their machines all run either on steam or cogs and use very little electricity like the humans use. They are not as efficient as the human technology but we will gladly live side by side with these peaceful creatures rather than the ignorant and pompous humans any day."

"You'll find life here is much better with small contraptions to help with some jobs," the first archer said, breaking his silence to Sheeria since she struck him. "And everything they use here is recyclable and friendly to our forest. Everything we use, we give back to the forest to ensure its prosperity."

She wanted to criticise it. Her old home had now gone from the vision she remembered, but the experiences gained from leaving and living in a human world made her admit she was impressed. They had a perfect society here of tolerance between two species who lived in harmony with each other. Tigians walked past peacefully beside the smaller human-like aeomon, all dressed similarly and even waving and greeting each other like neighbours. The aeomon, all walking a little hunched with their monkey tails following behind them, waved back, tipped their hats and continued on happily.

"So who is in charge, then?" she asked as they were led through the town of busy tigians and aeomon.

"That would be Audie Katsan."

Sheeria's ears pricked up. "Audie? Audie Katsan?"

"Yes. We noticed you share the same name as him. Which is why we brought you here. Do you know him?"

Even Keppal looked at her now to wait for her reply.

"Yes, I know him. He is my brother."

Audie Katsan was a proud tigian in the prime ages of his life. He lived happily with his family and was the chief executive of the Rowsena people. He represented his tigian people and it was he who had decided to allow the aeomon to live with them. There was a small government that was elected and as a nation they still answered to the human President Sahota of Angland, but to this forest and the tigians living there he was the chief and had remained in power since he was elected at the beginning of his reign.

He sat at his desk in his office at the top of one of the great trees with a view of the whole forest to his right. His office, like the rest of the village, was made mostly of wood but since the aeomon lived there his office reflected the aeomon technology. It was the aeomon who had found the idea of putting large mirrors on the outside walls of each tree-house to mask them from the outside. Each tree's mirrors would reflect the other trees around it, effectively making it disappear. Inside every hut the tree would reach up through the centre. The huts were connected and clamped down tightly to the tree's trunk in the centre with adjustable bolts to loosen when they became too tight and therefore allowed the tree to grow.

Solar panels sat on top of the office and ran a small amount of electricity to a generator, which powered some of the small appliances in his office. One was a small wooden box by his side with a speaker, a small bell and a button on it.

He was working on a folded out, large suitcase that opened to be a primitive form of laptop. The keyboard on the bottom had buttons like an old typewriter which he tapped constantly while working.

A little red light appeared and a small bell chimed on top of the box diverting his attention away from his work. He pressed the button and spoke into it. "What is it, Synthia?" he asked.

"*Mister Katsan, sir, there is someone here to see you,*" the voice of his receptionist replied.

He pressed the button again. "I'm sorry, Synthia, but I have no appointments today and am very busy. Please take their name and arrange a suitable day for them, thank you."

"*Actually, Mister Katsan, I think you may want to speak to this person now. She says she knows you personally.*"

He thought for a moment. This wasn't his wife since Synthia would say and his mother had passed away years ago.

"Okay then Synthia, send her in."

His two sliding doors began jerking outwards run by a number of cogs, and there standing before him was a face he had thought he would never see again.

He gasped, his heart jumped and his throat suddenly gagged. Her face showed signs of ageing but her eyes still had the same youthful glint that he remembered from all those years ago.

She smiled when their eyes met for the first time in ninety-eight years.

"Hello, brother."

Even her voice was the same; all this time and she hadn't even picked up an accent.

"Sheeria?" he said as he rose from his chair, walked over to her and welcomed her into his arms.

"It's been so long. I thought you were–"

"Dead? No, I'm sorry little brother. I'm sorry it has taken me so long to contact you. I'm sorry I left without saying a word. I'm sorry for so many things I did to you."

Audie said nothing but kept his sister in his arms. Finally he let go. "A long time ago I would have sent you out of my office. Cast you away and left you to die for breaking my heart and leaving like you did but it has been so long now that it doesn't matter. I may still be young for a tigian but old enough to know that life is too short for grudges. I'm just glad you are safe. Come, sit down with me."

"Thank you, Audie."

She remembered her little brother as only a cub when she left. The divide that killed her husband and child left her torn and needing to escape but knowing she left her family behind had hurt her. But now she saw her baby brother as a chief of the people she was filled with pride for him and shame for herself.

He had so many questions for her but sat down and asked the question that had been burning on his mind for years now.

"Why, Sheeria?"

"You know why, brother," she answered bluntly.

He stopped and remembered what few memories he had of his nephew and brother in law all those years ago. "I mean why did you not say anything? Not a word, a letter, nothing. You left me to pick up the pieces of a torn society on my own. The forest burned after the humans came before the divide was announced, the leaders and chiefs gone and my only family run away."

"And for that I'm sorry, brother. It hurt me more I assure you, but at the time I couldn't stay."

"Where did you go? What happened to you?"

"That is something I wanted to speak to you about. After travelling for a long time I found refuge and a home in Eloma. I became friends with an elder and became a trainer of elementalists. After years of sending more and more elementalists I had nurtured like a mother to their deaths I finally decided to become a guide for one them."

"You're a guide? For who?" he asked amazed.

"For a young human elementalist named Acarlie. Currently we are on a very important mission and need your help."

This time he frowned and leaned back in his chair, making a pyramid of his furry fingers.

"Help? You are gone for all this time, saying not a word and now you arrive unannounced at my office and ask for help? You offend me, sister."

"I apologise, Audie, once I am done then I promise I will return as soon as I can and make up for the time I lost with you. I want to sit down, meet your family and speak to my little brother, proud of the great tigian he has become and what he has done for our home."

He paused again and avoided her stare, "This is not your home any more, Sheeria. You made that clear with your actions over the years. What makes you think I will just help you only for you to leave all over again?"

She paused knowing he was right, this was what she was expecting from her only remaining family. "I don't know, brother. If you will not treat me as family then I beg you to treat me as an old member of your tribe. I desperately need passage across the waters to Chippenham."

"So it is your intention to leave again?" he asked coldly. She could tell she offended him, and who could blame him? She hadn't said a word for years and now asked for help from a brother she had left to fend for himself.

"I..." she hung her head. "I don't know what to say, brother."

He sat silently staring at her. She still hung her head and waited for him to speak. As much as it pained him to stare at his sister looking defeated in her chair of guilt and dishonour he couldn't help but feel merciful.

"If I treat you as an old member of the tribe then you will receive all the old customs. You know what this means, don't you?"

She looked up slightly. "Yes."

"And you are still willing?"

"Yes, brother. I know I may seem selfish right now but you have no idea how important it is for me to be reunited with my elementalist."

"In that case you are dismissed. I will have everything arranged for the day."

"While I wait, brother, could I spend some time with my brother and his family? I would love to finally meet them."

This was what he had been waiting for all the while. He smiled and stood up from his chair, walked over to her and put his hands on her shoulders. "It would honour me, sister. This doesn't change anything about–"

"I know, brother. This is just important to me."

"Then please speak to Synthia and speak to me when I finish today's work."

Keppal was waiting outside when Sheeria finally emerged from the building.

"How did it go?"

She carried on walking and spoke over her shoulder. "I have to fight to the death to prove myself to the tribe."

3

Edwin Townsend was finishing his shift. The hour was late but the lack of sunlight down in True Hiro made the day always night anyway. Only his body clock confirmed to him what time it was. The factory he worked in was almost empty. His fellow workers waved to him as they passed and allowed him to mop the last piece of the floor before he wheeled the mop bucket away, waved to his superiors, signed out and left the factory.

He stepped out into the damp darkness he was so used to now and breathed the cold air and sighed, feeling he was finally free from the responsibilities of work. The dank streets were alive with people; Edwin recognised them all. Distant voices were heard from all around, passing traffic and street lamps caused the long shadows made by the people to scatter into the darkness. But as alive as the streets were to Edwin it still felt like a dead part of town. The tall, stone buildings surrounding him were all old and all too familiar, so much so that he knew exactly which window was broken in the abandoned building beside him and where the glass had shattered but had never been cleared and still lay scattered on the path. He knew when the deathly, oily smell from the take-away's waste bin outside would hit him and exactly when it would leave him; it hadn't been changed all month. He walked like a tired zombie, following the crowd of people in front of him, pulling his raincoat close to him against the bitter wind that was unforgiving and sharp. He stared at the ground while he marched and questioned his life, following the same crowd he did every day. He felt like an ant falling in line with the others, all perfectly identical to one another and all thinking in sync rather than with the individuality of the other species on the planet.

The same old, dirty, stained tram arrived exactly when it always did and he sat down amongst the same faces and against a window. He pressed his head against the glass and in the darkness he could see his reflection staring right back at him. He was a tall and skinny young man. His skin was pale white, as everyone else's, the total lack of sunlight saw to that. His face was gaunt and the only colour present was the dark blue bags under his tired eyes. His nose had been broken once years ago and it hooked slightly to one side. A small childhood fight with his best friend, Jacob, had caused him to fall straight into a lamp post; a small fight easily forgotten and a lesson learned about friendship. His hair was usually short but now looked a little overgrown. He had dark brown wisps starting to curl behind his ears and his fringe now reached down to his eyebrows in a messy fashion.

The tram ascended a hill, a small ten seconds he always enjoyed on this journey since it always gave him the view of the underground city. Considering it was in perpetual darkness, True Hiro was a city that never slept. The city always brimmed with energy, both positive and negative. Crime was a certainty here but the people were accustomed to it by now, and screams of either anguish or happiness were always heard echoing from the walls of the tall, closed in, stone buildings bringing a sense of security to the public, but always with a pinch of caution. The hundred giant stone pillars stretched down as far as he could see until there was only a black void in the distance. The streets were decorated with lights, smoke and small fires; pollution was extracted through giant vents reaching way above them and clean, recycled air was always circulating around the city, but still the air was constantly stagnant and moist. The sky, taken from them by the rich folk that live in a magnificent city above them, he had only ever seen on the TV. This place was the gutter of Sphere, but it was his home.

He finally reached the door of his rundown apartment and entered with another sigh of relief and hung his coat up. Now his work life was over his home responsibilities came into action and he walked upstairs to a room in which an elderly woman lay in her bed, staring into the television in the dark, the blue light from the TV flickering in her dark room. The woman was sickly pale and had taken a fever Edwin knew wouldn't end well. But he found a tired smile when he greeted her.

"I'm back, Gran."

The old, weak, bedridden woman smiled. "Ah, there you are, Edwin. I have been waiting for you to return. I got your friend Jacob to run to the bakery for me, look." She smiled and pointed a skinny, bony finger at a fresh loaf of bread to the side of him.

"It's your favourite."

Edwin glanced and found the bread. "Oh, Gran, this stuff is expensive. You shouldn't worry about buying this. It's only bread."

He still cut himself a slice though, buttered it and bit into it. It was crunchy. He really did love this bread.

She smiled, the colours of the flashing lights from the television reflecting off her white, stringy hair.

"Don't you worry about that, darling. A life like ours, you should learn to love the little things."

Her voice was beginning to become shaky, her condition was deteriorating. He sat down at the end of the bed.

"How have you been today?" he asked her.

"Oh, don't worry about me, darling." She took his hand; her touch was cold as ice to him. "I have lived long down here in the dark. The True Hiro Sickness has finally caught me. Remember when you last had it?"

The True Hiro Sickness was a common illness that the public got. It was the lack of sunlight that caused everyone to eventually grow weak and pale. Everyone suffered from it but some worse than others. It caused many deaths, especially in the young and the elderly.

"That was a bit different, Gran. I was seventeen, they took me up to the hospital above us where I finally saw the sun and I was back in a month. They had me locked in the big hospital with hundreds of other Sickness patients, where I would sit in the sun for hours. They should send you there. All you need is some sunlight."

"Oh, I'm far too old for them to waste money and resources on me. You should know that by now."

As much as he wanted to prove her wrong he sighed, knowing she was all too right. She was too wise for her own good sometimes. She glanced out of the window and began telling him what she always said.

"We live in a hard place, Edwin. The world forgets about us and gives us only what we need to survive, and that's only if we work hard for it. People born here never leave, they only do what they can each day, and so you should make the best of it."

Edwin, however, was too tired now for her repeated counsel. "I know, Gran." He covered a yawn with his wrist and took another bite of bread.

"Then you would understand why I buy the bread you like so much." She reached out with her cold hand and pressed his cheeks tightly together, lifting his smile up.

"You should smile more, Edwin," she said lightly and let go.

His face dropped back to where it always did. "I don't think I can, Gran, I don't have your strength." He finished his bread and stood up.

All his life his gran had been like this. His mother had

died birthing him and his father caught the Sickness when Edwin was only five. After that, when it looked like he would have to be moved down to the streets with the other orphans of the city, his father's mother took him in; she was like a mother to him.

"Then you should practise," she suggested.

"Practise?"

"Yes, practise. Go look in the mirror and smile. Hold it there and keep doing it. People respond better to a smiling gentleman like yourself."

This time Edwin sighed and raised an eyebrow. Her counsel was strange sometimes.

"I think you'll find it's the actions of a man that people respond to, Gran."

"True, but a man who helps with a smile will always be more appreciated than a man who helps but has the face of a smacked arse."

This made Edwin finally lighten up and laugh; he loved his gran, she always had some way or another to teach him things schools and the streets just couldn't teach. Her counsel was strange, yes, but effective and always accurate.

"I remember once telling a young aeomon the same thing. He always wore the same expression as you so I made him practise smiling. Every time I saw him I made him smile. He used to tell me it was the only time he ever did, so I took comfort in that. Even if it hurt his cheeks he smiled for me," she explained, still with her shaky voice almost stuttering.

"And what happened to him?" Edwin asked.

Her head jogged slightly like it was balancing on her shoulders while she searched her memory and looked back at the television. "He caught the Sickness, went up top and I never saw him again."

The door downstairs was knocked four times lightly.

Edwin knew this knock well. It was Jacob's knock.

"That will be Jacob, Gran. I'll put this bread away for you and tell him I'm going have a quiet one in tonight."

"What did I just tell you about enjoying what you have, Edwin? Go out, go to the bar with your friends, and smile."

He was still tired but again took her advice. Jacob was waiting outside the door. He was Edwin's age and like a brother to him; the two were inseparable but where Edwin lacked confidence sometimes Jacob made up for it. He stood slightly shorter than him but with spiky, gelled, black hair. He was also as pale as Edwin but with a more muscular build and more of a youthful energy to him.

"Sup bro, are you coming out to play?" he asked sarcastically. Edwin had lived in that apartment all his life and that used to be like a catchphrase when they were younger.

"Shut up, Jacob," Edwin ordered while locking the door.

"What's up your arse?"

Edwin rubbed the tiredness out of his blue eyes and sniffed, clearing his airways. "Nothing, just tired. Where are we going?"

"Where do you think we're going, dick? The bar."

Edwin took one more look at the window of his gran's room, the blue, flickering light from her television lit up like a strobe.

"Okay, lead the way."

Police tape surrounded the train stop in Tirendal, a small city in North Angland, miles north of Donolan. Crowds of people huddled around to witness the deceased being carried away on stretchers. It had quickly become the talk of the city, that a train had been hi-jacked by special soldiers and both they and many passengers had been slaughtered in a single night. News reporters and journalists reported a count of thirty deceased and many injured. One of which was a leo that was taken instantly to the Tirendal hospital after it was reported that it was injured.

The soldiers that had been carried away were all taken away privately by Anglish soldiers under direct orders of President Sahota as soon as the words of the train disaster reached him.

The ambulance that carried the leo raced back to the hospital with the now unconscious leo lying still with an oxygen mask over his face and a kingnine by his side.

Raiden's body reached the hospital's doors, the rushing paramedics nearly breaking them down, then, quickly, the stretcher holding him was handed to the doctors, who needed the help of two tigians to push the stretcher along the long corridors of the hospital.

Zoudiva now felt useless as he could do nothing that would help except to leave the doctors alone and not get in their way.

The day seemed to go all too fast for Zoudiva until he was given time to wait, then suddenly it was like time stopped. Since he was a quadruped half wolf, half leo he had always been treated differently from all the other intelligent creatures of Sphere. He was used to the majority of it by now. Humans were his natural masters since it was they who genetically engineered the whole of his race in an attempt to wipe out the leo species in the Leo (Last) Divide that took place somewhere around a century ago. This meant that servitude of the humans was always a part of his life, he had been born into it; but unlike the leos and the elders, whose relationship was between both species as a whole, the kingnines answered to one human at a time. This was down to the fact that the humans always craved power and owning a kingnine was something only great men of wealth or power had the privilege of. Zoudiva was not very old even for his kind and so never saw the Leo Divide, as Raiden and Sheeria had, but knew from birth that the only reason he was brought into this world was to extinguish the leos and to serve the human master he was appointed to.

He never looked at the world as a place of repression for his kind, but it was on days like today that he did notice that there may be some things wrong with their lifestyle. While in the hospital corridors he waited on the cold, hard floor since he could not simply sit in a chair like the rest of the world, and had to wait for hours while people rushed past either ignoring him or even looking down at him like he was a dirty mongrel and didn't belong in the clean hospital in case he spread diseases.

He sighed as yet another doctor walked past him and he continued to wait for any kind of news until a young boy walked over to him.

Zoudiva looked up at the boy through his metal-plated helmet and red eyes that were given to every kingnine; it was part of the Feydon armour that helped them see in infrared. Around a colourful hallway of heats the boy stood before him in blue with orange cheeks and dark eyes.

"May I help you, child?" he finally said after he knew the child wouldn't simply walk away.

The boy just looked like he had too many questions that burned in his mind. "What's wrong with your voice?"

Zoudiva couldn't help but smile, this boy had obviously never heard a kingnine talk before or maybe this was the first time he had ever seen one in person.

"This is how I always talk, child. This is how all kingnines talk, our voices are naturally deeper than yours."

"But you sound sick. My friend is a tigian and he does not have a voice like yours. You sound sick or like an old man," the boy said, talking in quick, eager sentences, like many human children do.

56

"Yes, our voice is different from ursas' and tigians', child. I have heard many people say my voice even sounds like a whisper. It is because our mouths are shaped slightly differently from humans' and tigians'."

"And what about your eyes? Are they really red?"

Zoudiva chuckled a little at this naive child. "No, my eyes are brown, at least I hear they are. I have never seen them without my helmet. It is only my helmet that makes my eyes appear red. They don't frighten you, do they?"

"A little," the boy shyly replied.

"Then I shall close them for you."

Zoudiva closed his eyes and smiled. "How is that, child?"

He heard the boy laugh. "Why are you here, sir?"

"My master is hurt, child. I am here waiting for him and hoping he gets better."

Before he got a reply he felt the boy patting him on the head. He opened his eyes and saw the boy smiling.

"You have ears like my dog," the boy stated and lifted his hand from his head.

"Yes, that is because we are of a similar family," Zoudiva said, raising an eyebrow. He knew this kid was naive but clearly didn't see kingnines in the same light as other beings otherwise he wouldn't have petted him like a dog.

"James! Come away from that thing!" He suddenly heard the voice of the boy's mother, who appeared and grabbed his hand.

"I'm sorry," she quickly said and hurried him away.

For what? The fact that your son was asking questions about something he didn't know or for you referring to me as "that thing"? Some humans are so ignorant, Zoudiva thought as he placed his head back on his creamy brown paws. *I hope my master is okay, and Master Raiden too. I wonder where my master and my elementalist have gone to.*

Night eventually came and even though the hospital was

still active, the halls were quieter than some other parts of the hospital.

A door slowly opened and the hooded figure walked in, its weapons and backpack not on its person now and only its silky black robes covering it. It still wore its hood tightly over its head and crept up the hallways of the hospital searching for the leo. Luckily some of the hallways were darkened since patients were sleeping and so it could use the cover of darkness to slip silently from room to room. Doctors, nurses and patients still walked the hospital every now and again but the emptiness of the hallways made their footsteps echo from a distance, giving the stranger time to hide whenever it needed to.

It wore no shoes and only cream coloured paw-like feet touched the floor, making its walk as silent as a shadow. Even its breath was silent, as if it had mastered a way of becoming so silent it was like a part of the night itself.

It heard distant voices coming from farther up the hallway and stopped to see two young nurses walking in each other's company.

The hooded figure stopped and waited, poised on the spot, and waited to see if these two nurses would change their paths, but when it saw they wouldn't it had to resort to pressing itself against a wall.

They walked closer until it could even smell their perfume but it didn't move. There was nothing to hide under and no time to escape but the figure didn't need those. The nurses were still chatting quietly and walked straight past the figure. There was little light in these corridors so darkness was not the issue, but they simply didn't notice this tall, lean figure standing so obviously right next to them. They continued past the figure and disappeared around the corner.

The figure stood away from the wall and lifted its nose

slightly into the air, sniffed and caught the scent of its target not far away.

It now knew also that its target was alone as it entered the ward primarily used for injured tigians. It knew the leo was alone in here. All except for a kingnine asleep at the foot of a door leading to the ward. The figure slowly crept up to the door and stopped as it approached the kingnine, who winced in its sleep, winced again and slowly opened its eyes. The kingnine sniffed twice sensing a presence near him but could not see the figure who was less than a metre away from it and staring straight into its red eyes. The kingnine saw nothing and the figure noticed its eyes glaze over and look straight through it, scanning the room and sniffing again.

The figure held out its hands and waved them slowly and elegantly over the kingnine's head and, as if a spell had been cast, the kingnine started to close its eyes and fell back to sleep.

The figure stepped straight over the kingnine and approached the leo, who was now sleeping in a stable condition in the hospital bed. Finally it was face to face with the leo and reached down with its cream coloured paw and touched the leo's cheek, inspecting its face and tilting it from side to side.

It noticed a document at the end of the leo's bed, reached for it and read what actions the doctors had taken. When it found what it was looking for it grunted in disappointment and looked back down at the leo, threw the file down at its feet and silently walked away.

Zoudiva woke from a deep sleep with a strange dream about waking up in the middle of the night and dismissed it as just that. He stretched out his paws and looked back to see Raiden still sleeping soundly, but with a number of doctors around him.

"What's wrong?" Zoudiva asked as he entered the room and saw the concern in the doctors' eyes.

The doctor frowned and looked to his superior for a nod to explain and when he got the all clear he invited Zoudiva into another room.

"I'll repeat my question, doctor. What's wrong?"

The doctor was young and had to bite his lip in answering, "I'm afraid I have some slightly upsetting news."

Zoudiva said nothing and waited for him to continue.

"I'm afraid we here at this hospital had made a great mistake which nearly cost the leo his life."

"Why? What happened?" he asked suddenly concerned.

"We had been treating this leo as if he had been a tigian and had been giving him the wrong kind of medication, medication usually prescribed for tigians, and even giving him a wrong blood type. We have corrected what we have done wrong–"

"I should think so too. How could you get something like that wrong? Also, if you were wrong then how was it pointed out to you?"

"That, sir, is a mystery no one in this hospital can answer. We have come in this morning and found that his medical file had been tampered with."

"What do you mean 'tampered with'?" Zoudiva asked.

"I mean someone came in and changed the file we had for the leo, broke into our medicine cabinets and changed his medication. To the *correct* medication. The file also pointed out something important which concerns you. Now previously we had been treating the leo like a tigian but now this file is telling us to actually treat him more like a kingnine. It seems that because you were created as a by-product of the leos then your blood is actually the closest to theirs, not tigians'. This is why our head doctor has come down here and has seen the file and regards it as correct."

"So you're saying my blood could possibly match my master's?"

"That is what I'm saying, yes. We could possibly order some kingnine blood to be delivered from Septura."

"That won't be necessary. My fellow brothers and sisters would not understand and would most likely refuse to help a leo. If my blood matches I want you to use mine."

The doctor smiled. "I was hoping you would say that. Please follow me."

He never knew how long he was asleep for but eventually Raiden opened his eyes. Groaned and breathed in and saw Zoudiva sitting at to his bed side.

"Welcome back, Master."

Raiden felt terrible. He had a splitting headache and had to massage his eyebrows and focus.

"Update me."

"We are in a hospital in Tirendal. It's been a week and a half now. The doctors managed to stitch you up but there was a slight problem with the blood they gave you. They messed up and gave you the wrong blood type."

Raiden groaned again. "Typical."

"They gave you tigian blood until it was revealed to them that the nearest thing they had to leo blood was kingnine blood."

Raiden still had his head in his hand and felt slightly dazed but opened his eyes when Zoudiva said this and looked over to him, shocked.

"I have kingnines' blood now?"

"It was the only way I could save you, Master. I know the history of our species has been terrible at best but I could not stand by and let you be taken from this world."

Raiden fell back down to the bed with his hands covering his furry nose. *Kingnine blood? Why of all the creatures did it have to be the blood of the beings that wiped out my entire race?*

Zoudiva saw how this news was upsetting for him and looked down at the floor. "I'm sorry, Master."

"No," Raiden finally said and opened his eyes again and glanced over to him. "No, it's okay. I'm just a little shocked, that's all." He sat up again and took a breath still not believing what he was hearing. He smiled lightly, "So now the last leo not only has a kingnine by his side but also the blood of them inside his body. My brother would kill me."

"Master, I–"

"It's okay, Zoudiva, I'm not angry. Thank you for saving me." He reached out and patted him on his head. "This does mean that you cannot call me Master any more."

"What?" Zoudiva suddenly asked fearing Raiden would disown him now and leave him far away from Val and Acarlie.

"We share the same blood now, Zoudiva, now you will call me brother."

"It is improper for a kingnine to refer to their master as anything else."

"Hey, if I have to make sacrifices then so do you. Val is your true master anyway. We have been through much, Zoudiva, and now we have proved to the world that the rivalry between our species was futile. Once your kind would have gladly let me die and now it was actually a kingnine who saved me. I shall not forget this, brother."

Zoudiva almost choked hearing the word 'brother' from a leo. Raiden was right, though, the day before Zoudiva met Val he would have rather died than call a leo his brother and here he was.

"Yes...brother."

"Okay then. So what else have I missed?"

4

The hour was turning late, the day was tired and the air was stagnant but still the young blonde girl stood there, sweat dripping from her brow, punching the air in front of her. She had been practising for hours now and had to concentrate every breath in time with her punches like she had been taught. This was the only time she had to herself since she was the only qualified nurse amongst the ship of pirates but felt that she could do nothing to help the team unless she was stronger. She never usually liked any type of violence and pitied and despised all the fighters who would come into her hospital in Toshiro with broken wrists, injured backs and legs, missing teeth all in the name of sport. But her life was so different now. Even after this short amount of time since she first met Val, everything about her was different, now she felt violence was necessary in order to survive. She was beginning to get out of breath but punched the air again; with every strike she tried harder than the last and thought of what she had witnessed in these last few months. Her home in Toshiro had been destroyed and her life would have been taken too if it hadn't been for Val and Keppal. Ever since then she had been through an emotional journey trying to get over the death of her previous love and get revenge on Zane, the Elemental Lord who was the cause of all this. She may not have been there at the start of the journey like the rest of them but this didn't matter, especially to her. After she and Ursa Dusty helped the lost Val be reunited with Acarlie, the team made their way to Angland, where she witnessed Dude, the mute aeomon, go mad and began desperately trying to help him. She chased him down with the help of Raiden through the streets of Donolan while Acarlie fought her Elemental Battle with an aeomon called Electra. Only a day after those events she again witnessed the destruction of a great city of Sphere as the Feydon army attacked and the team was split up looking for Dude again. Mitis went with Raiden and Zoudiva but was split from them and still did not know what had happened in their fight against the soldiers who attacked them. She was forced to run and was eventually saved by Dude, who helped her to the ship, the Scarlet Arise, where she had been ever since. After her scare with the soldiers she had been in constant training but with every fist she threw forward she couldn't help but notice her small hands: not ever being like the weapons Rezosa or even Acarlie had, they were too fragile. She had healing hands, not hands for damage.

She threw one more fist forward and yelped out the last of her energy, fell forward and leaned her hands down to rest and catch her breath back.

"You know, you should be practising in a lower stance."

She panted and looked to see Rezosa behind her. The tall, dark haired beauty was her personal instructor through most of the week when Dude needed to train and Mitis took it upon herself to train with him. But in the last couple of days she had been training on her own. Rezosa walked up to her wanting to start a friendly chat and corrected her.

"When practising, you should stand in a horse riding stance, bend your legs and keep your back straight. That way your body is level with each punch."

She showed her, quickly standing in the uncomfortable stance, but standing perfectly for Mitis to copy.

Mitis wiped the sweat from her brow. "But that one really hurts my legs. I can't stay in that one for more than a minute."

"Then that means you're doing something right. The pain will get better trust me, plus the guys love a woman with strong legs," she joked and made Mitis stand in this stance then started tutoring her again in her exercises.

While punching with Rezosa standing behind her in a secluded part of the cargo room of the ship Mitis couldn't help but notice she was now being watched. Her head flinched and she thought she heard a scuffling from somewhere above her in the ship. Rezosa heard this too but said in a lower tone, "Concentrate Mitis, eyes forward and keep punching."

She did as instructed for another three minutes until she had to straighten her legs again and panted, feeling done with tonight. Rezosa, however, sighed and stood in front of her.

"May I ask you something?" she asked.

"Yes, of course."

"Why are you doing this? I mean you know you're not a fighter. You're a nurse, Mitis, and if you ask me then that's what you should stay as. Don't get me wrong, there is nothing wrong with exercising and taking part in training with the rest of the crew but do you really feel it's necessary? You're a lot more useful to us as a trained healer."

Mitis was still panting when she answered. "I'm training because I have to, Rezosa. Yes, you're right, I know I'm only a nurse and I'll never be as good as you but after what I've seen I can't just sit back and watch everybody put their lives at risk. I want to contribute and to do so I need to be stronger." She paused briefly thinking of how she could say the next part. "When I was being chased in Donolan I was so scared. They cornered me and had me on the floor ready to rape and kill me. I had never felt so scared and defenceless in all my life. I wished I could be strong like you and fight them off but I couldn't. All I could do was lie there alone and if it wasn't for–"

"It doesn't matter how strong you are in a situation like that," Rezosa stated. Her eyes glazed over as she remembered herself being raped by this army. Mitis knew about this but chose not to answer and let her continue. "The fact is that if you had fought in a situation like that it wouldn't have made a difference. There were just too many of them. You were lucky that Monkey was there at the time to save you. He was there for me too but unfortunately he was a little too late for me."

"Is that why you're ignoring him?" Mitis asked.

Rezosa now shot a glance at Mitis. "What's that?"

"It's my turn to ask a question now. Dude, Monkey, whatever his name is. Is this why you're ignoring him? Are you mad at him for not being there when you needed him? It's just that we both know he can't take his eyes off you. Even now he's probably watching us. He really likes you, Rezosa, and it's hurting him that you are treating him this way."

Rezosa sighed and looked down at the floor in annoyance of this question but answered, "No, not that this is any of your business but–"

"I only care for the welfare of–"

"–*But*, I'm only doing this for Monkey. I know it hurts him but, trust me, this is the best way for him to deal with it. We both know he's had a hard life, growing up in the darkest part of True Hiro, resorting to theft just to feed himself, but this isn't my problem. Right now he's hurting but he'll get over it. He only needs a little tough love. I've seen this many times before."

"You mean this isn't the first heart you've broken?"

"Careful now, Mitis," Rezosa warned and stepped closer. "You're getting a little out of your depth now."

"I'm sorry but it's just I can't help but think you're handling this the wrong way. He's not a college sweetheart you can play with. He's so much more…"

"More what?"

"More...mentally unstable. You weren't there when myself and Raiden chased him through the streets. You didn't see the desperation in his eyes. He's not used to this type of torment."

"Then he'll get used to it. I've seen him fight, he's a lot stronger than he looks. He will get stronger. Trust me, Mitis, this is the best thing for him."

"At the cost of what?" she countered, but this time Rezosa was finished with the conversation. There was just no convincing this woman. She turned her back and walked to pick up her weapon, Hevana, the short metal pole-type of weapon with two spikes concealed inside it. She pressed the button in the middle and the two spikes shot out like a spring and handed the weapon to Mitis.

"Okay then, Mitis, you really want to fight like me? Then take this. I'll teach you."

Mitis said nothing at first, feeling she had more to say, but eventually took Hevana and silenced herself and listened to her instructor again.

It was now late and Mitis felt exhausted again when she finally finished, showered, changed and readied herself for bed with the rest of the crew in their quarters. There were both male and female quarters and so she only had to share with Rezosa, Midia the quartermaster and second in command of the ship and Acarlie, but before she turned in she wanted to check up on the elementalist who had been in the infirmary in the sub-level of the ship.

She walked into the infirmary to see Val still asleep in his hospital bed, his head still covered in bandages but in a stable condition.

Acarlie was now sitting at his bedside and still holding onto his hand gently. She was wearing her traveller's cloak, the very same one Mitis had found and given to Val, and wore it with her hood up with her eyes closed, falling asleep herself.

All Mitis could hear was the droning of the ship's engines and the steady bleep from Val's heart rate monitor and she walked up to Acarlie and gently put her hands on her shoulders.

"Acarlie, it's getting late. You should get some rest. Val will be waiting for you here tomorrow. Please get some rest."

Acarlie's head jogged slightly when she felt Mitis's touch but then stayed still.

"Acarlie?"

"He came back for me," she finally said in a low tone. Mitis could feel her emotion as if it were her own. Acarlie was depressed. After she and Dude went to rescue Val Acarlie had fallen unconscious and since she had woken up rarely left Val's side. Mitis didn't *see* what happened to Acarlie when she was imprisoned in the Bastard Camp, nor did she see what happened when Acarlie went to save Val, but she knew what had happened. Acarlie was raped while in that hellish place and since Val saved her that night had changed into the shadow of the person Mitis remembered, and she had retaliated by smiting the whole camp off the face of the sphere. She had broken more sacred rules and killed maybe dozens of people, maybe more. Elementalists don't kill normal people, 'Innocents' as they're known by the elementalists. They only kill each other in arenas in front of thousands of people and if they do kill Innocents they immediately terminate themselves for bringing shame onto their home and their way of life. Acarlie now had broken so many rules and now it looked like it was really starting to take effect.

"He knew what was happening there. He knew what would have happened to him there and he came anyway.

He gave his life for me."

"Of course he did, Acarlie. He's your guardian and wanted to make you safe, which he has done. Now please come and rest. I know I'm not a guide but I am a nurse so as a member of this crew you're partly my responsibility. When Val wakes up you're going to need your strength."

After another pause Mitis noticed a slight nod.

"Okay," she whispered.

Acarlie let go Val's hand and Mitis helped her to her feet and walked her to the door.

"Do you need help getting back?" she asked.

"No," Acarlie whispered again and slowly began walking back.

Mitis noticed how she was carrying herself. She walked so slow with her head low, she was worried. She only saw this kind of behaviour from people who had just lost their partners and were close to suicide. She knew she needed to keep an eye on her but Val also needed attention since he was back in another light coma. She turned her attention back to him.

Val seemed to sleep so peacefully. This wasn't the first time he had been in this condition. Mitis had seen it before, just after the now infamous Toshiro storm and also when she first met him. She checked his head by tilting it slightly and noticed his wounds were very nearly healed up. It was amazing. She marvelled at how they managed to heal and remembered the doctors in Toshiro saying it was a miracle he survived being attacked that night when Miles jumped him and beat him to near death with a brick. It was only then that she noticed that every time Val was unconscious he would heal quicker. After the attack, the storm, Acarlie's E.B. with Zane and now this and every time would wake up stronger than before. Maybe this was a new elder healing trick, she thought. She had been a nurse for a few years now and had never seen anybody react to injury like Val did. She just didn't understand it. This was another mystery of Val. None of them knew his real identity, not even himself since he had woken without any memories, and he also possessed a strange power not even the sacred elementalists could equal. He somehow was linked to a metal staff, a six foot bo staff, and could summon this staff from wherever it was straight to his hand; also he could alter the shape of it, making it a very useful tool on his journey. There was no such thing as magic in Sphere, only tricks of the elder, who never in all the years of history have explained to the humans how they perform these, and the elementalists are the only living people who possess such a power. But it would be hard for people seeing a trick like Val's and not think it was magic since there was no way of explaining it yet. She sighed as she looked down at Val and after she was satisfied with his condition left him to his sleep.

The next day was bright and sunny. The Scarlet Arise elegantly soared through the sky, its destination Chippenham, the capital of Magna and the elder capital of the world. The ship's captain was standing in the middle of the cockpit glaring out at the view of a constant horizon of international waters. His name was Kaza Caines, a tall and strong man with a golden brown complexion, short, black hair and almond eyes he usually kept covered with his pair of sunglasses. He wore the clothes of a pirate: thickly woven, dark green trousers with cuts and holes in the knees and a matching shirt with a black waistcoat over it and a black webbing he filled with clips for the pistol he tucked into the back of his trousers. He wore some jewellery, none of it of any real value. Over his wrists were thin bangles of different coloured metals ranging from copper, tin and titanium to bronze, silver and gold. His neck was decorated with a string necklace of coloured wooden beads and his ears were stretched with big, black spikes of plastic. In front of him was his pilot Dillon and co-pilot Smythy operating the ship between the two of them, and by his side was his quartermaster Midia, the beautiful pirate, and Zahied the caster.

"What's the order, Capt'n?" Midia asked him, regarding the current situation of fuel.

Kaza stood proud with his hands at his waist. "There really is no alternative, is there? We need to stop briefly. As soon as we see land we're going to have to re-fuel then make our way to the city before Feydon catches sight of us. Inform the crew."

"Yes, Capt'n."

Dude was by himself again. As much as he liked being here with these people where he had a purpose he couldn't stand the idea of being locked into a small space without the freedom of going away somewhere on his own. He spent most days away from the crew and was the only crew member apart from the captain who chose not to sleep in the crew's quarters but made his own space near the engine room. He had been in this one room nearly all day now and was at this minute exercising again by doing sit-ups. Overhearing what Rezosa was saying about him last night to Mitis upset him as he only wanted to impress the woman he admired. Lust hurt him, more than any wound he received; even having his tail cut off and his tongue removed didn't have this mental effect on him. Mitis was right last night, he wasn't used to this kind of pain.

But he thought if he could strengthen his body and prove to Rezosa he was worth it maybe she would change her mind; if not then at least his toned body could now benefit him in other ways, like escaping from this place.

He heard a door open behind him and immediately his mind raced and thought about whom he wanted to see but instead of seeing her he saw the blonde nurse standing behind him.

"Hi," she smiled. "The Captain said we're landing soon. The ship needs to refuel."

He looked from where he sat, his hands still behind his head, with a confused look on him as if to say, "*And that's what you came here to say?*"

Mitis shifted uncomfortably with his natural silence. "I brought you a sandwich. I thought you might be hungry."

She walked up to him, sat down beside him and handed him the food she had brought.

He was a little confused at first but knew he was hungry and took the sandwich, turning to sit up straight against a wall to eat it. She just turned and sat next to him, bent her legs up to her chest and wrapped her arms around them and watched as he bit into his food.

"So how are you?" she asked being the only one concerned for him. Everyone else on the ship now just saw him as an anti-social weirdo, Rezosa had voiced her opinion last night and Acarlie had her own problems to deal with. Also, Mitis was the only person who understood what was now going on with Dude.

Dude looked down at the floor not liking the question, half because they both knew he couldn't answer because he had no tongue and half because they both knew the answer anyway. He only shook his head and carried on chewing.

"Look, Dude, I know what's happening here and this really isn't the way this should be resolved. Rezosa is being stubborn right now, I know that, but you need to pull yourself together. Like it or not, Dude, you can't always have the person you want." She tried explaining to him and his silence only looked like the reaction of a stubborn teenager. He finished his mouthful of food and looked to her shaking his head. She naturally didn't know what this really meant but only took it for a negative answer that mimicked his silence.

"Life is hard, and love is even harder but you should…"

She was cut off as he almost slammed his head back against the wall now and shook his head again, this time putting his hand on it.

She doesn't understand, he thought.

"Oh," he finally said.

She gasped, this was the first time she had heard him speak. This was progress, but she didn't understand what he meant.

"Oh?"

"Oh, ihh eyor ha."

She tried mimicking his mouth but still didn't understand, "Ihh eyor ha?"

He sighed, realising it was no use. There was no getting through to anyone. No one understood him, no one would understand what he ever said. That's why he gave up all those years ago.

"Yhou whown urherha," he said, standing up now and passing her the other half of the sandwich. She sat there bewildered by what he was saying at first and still surprised that he was finally opening up to her, even if it was only a little. She noticed he was starting to walk away though.

"You're not going to leave me here are you? It's cold here."

He reached the door and stopped when she said this as if he were considering coming back, but walked out. Mitis sighed when he left and was looking down at the sandwich when he walked back in. She was going to say something when he appeared with a coat in his hand and passed it to her.

"Here," he whispered and exited, leaving her to sit by herself.

"Kill me, Val! Please kill me! Kill me! Please!"

"Nooo!" Val cried, the body of the dying Acarlie resting in his arms, his knife lodged deep in her chest, her dark blood leaking from her wound and staining his hand as he held the knife that killed her. More blood leaked from her mouth as she started choking and convulsing on her own body fluids as they started filling her lungs. He held her tightly, crying desperately for her to stop but she wouldn't. Her eyes rolled back in her head and closed as she died struggling to breathe.

Val woke with a jump from this nightmare. His memories flashed up, Miles was standing over him, torturing him with water and the last time he saw Acarlie she was unconscious and was picked up by the Scarlet Arise. This recurring dream had been haunting him ever since, this vision of a bleak future which showed him slaying the one he had vowed to protect.

He expected to find himself still in the dark room of the Bastard Camp with Miles standing over him but instead the first thing Val noticed was the young blonde nurse who saved him before. She seemed startled at first by how he woke but then smiled in relief and touched his shoulder.

"It's okay, Val, you're safe. You're back on the Scarlet Arise."

He breathed heavily. "Where are we?"

"Back in Angland. We're stationed at the moment, the ship needed to refuel."

He sat up and rubbed his head and remembered his

face was still covered in bandages. He only needed a second to get to grips with reality again when he realised that.

"Where's–?"

"She's safe. She's currently outside. She has been by your side ever since you were rescued by the mute. I had to order her to go get some air. She's not looking good, though, Val. We've all been hoping you would wake just so you could give her some confidence again."

His head hurt from guilt when he remembered what had happened to her, what he had saved her from and now she must have been traumatised. He still had so many questions, like how he got here, but this wasn't the time.

He tested his feet and slowly stood up. He felt so relieved to be back on his feet since he had been tied up all the time he was imprisoned, but felt a little weak and needed to summon his staff to balance himself.

"Take me to her," he ordered.

They found her sitting outside, a few hundred yards away from the ship, which was stationed at the top of a hill on the outskirts of a small town. It was hard for Kaza to find skyship fuel there but he eventually found enough to get them to the city.

She was sitting hugging her knees under the late afternoon sun with Zahied watching over her from a distance.

Val waved Mitis away and then Zahied and approached her.

"Acarlie."

As soon as she saw it was him her head tilted to the sky, "Oh, thank goodness," she sighed. "Are you okay?"

"Yeah," he said sitting next to her and realising why she'd picked this spot looking across acres of farm space. The sky was open and warm with shades of red and orange stretching out into the horizon and burning the sky for miles.

"It's you I'm worried about. I hear you've been–"

"Trust you to be more worried about someone else, Val. You've just been locked up for too long, being tortured and…" she couldn't even finish her sentence but instead avoided his look and brushed her hair behind her ears.

"But it's you who had the harder experience in that place, Acarlie. What I went through was nothing compared to what…he did."

He winced in guilt again and she looked down and remembered; she may have been drugged at the time but she remembered every detail. A memory she would happily erase forever if she could but instead like a nail in her mind it stuck and stung every time she thought of it.

"I'm so sorry. I should have just done as you said and walked you back to Donolan," he confessed.

"No, Val. If you had stayed then Miles would have killed you and I would still be there. That argument saved both our lives."

As right as she was Val still couldn't help but look at her and know she was raped because of him. She, however, also felt the painful sting of guilt when she looked over to him and saw the bandages still covering his face, a constant reminder of how she nearly got him killed.

She bit her lip and looked him in the eye. "I missed you."

"I know." He smiled this time, "we've done this before."

She looked away hiding a smile, this was no time for jokes, she thought, and looked at the horizon. "Miles took the item by the way, it's gone. And we still don't know where the others are."

"Then we'll get it back, also, Raiden said to all meet up again in Chippenham, so once we're there we will wait for them."

He started scratching his face and started pulling at his bandages, beginning to unravel them.

"Stop," she said and turned to him. "Let me do it."

She reached out and took his hands away from his head and reached up for the bandages. Her fingers tingled when she touched his face and reached around to find the end of the bandage. Once she found it she slowly started unwinding it from the back of his cheek and round his face. The first one was just under his nose and above his lip.

Val closed his eyes and leaned forward as she gently unwrapped his head, his heart racing when he realised this would be the first time he could use his left eye in what felt like a lifetime, and she would be the first thing he saw.

The bandage passed his cheek and already Acarlie's heart sank when she noticed the hideous scar reaching up across his whole face and circling his left eye.

She slowed down as her heart skipped when she got past his left eye; she finally saw what her stupidity had cost Val back in Toshiro, this was the punishment he had, to pay for her mistake. There was no healing completely from this wound. This scar was permanent.

She took off the last of the bandage and dropped it to the floor. She lifted his chin up so she could see in the light what she had done to him.

Her hands dropped as her heart thumped against her chest.

"Oh, Val," she whispered in grief.

He opened his eyes, blinking at first, feeling sensitive to the sunlight and when he focused he knew how bad it was from the look on her face. He could almost see his scar from the reflection in her moist eyes as she stared at him, trembling.

He wanted to say something, he knew how bad he must look but when he looked up again at Acarlie he only saw what Miles had done to her. His failure as a guardian shone through everything about her. This scar will be his memento.

She reached up again to gently touch his cheek where the majority of the scar was and as soon as her finger touched his skin he stopped her, taking her hand.

"I'm so sorry," she nearly cried.

He could feel her heartbeat from the pulse in her hand; it matched the pace of his own. He lowered it but when he did he saw she leaned closer to him, so close he could feel her breath against his lips.

He felt emotion driving him to lean forward and hesitated at first and noticed she felt the same but still they leaned forward and he finally tasted the soft skin of her lips. Everything became dark as he closed his eyes but all the colours he knew lit up in his mind, bright and vibrant. An energy only the sun could match burned in his chest and filled his whole being with warmth. His heart felt like it doubled in size as he could still feel her lips against his. He lifted his hand to touch her neck and slowly slid up to the back of her ears and leading to her silky black hair. She lifted her own hand and pressed it against his chest. She felt his heartbeat and wrapped her arms around the back of his neck, fell into him and together they shared the warm, tingling feeling within them, trying to control their breathing as their hearts elevated, together in each other's arms. The warm and bright sky mirrored the sensation within them. They took their time and enjoyed their moment while the bandage by their side picked up as the wind blew it slowly away from them, to disappear into the great world around them.

5

At Sheeria's apartment, given to her by her brother, Audie, two knocks sounded on the door. The room was very basic and could easily have been mistaken for a cell had there been a lock on the door.

Audie ordered a local tavern to provide them hospitality, with rooms reaching up into one of the highest trees, which gave an excellent view once the morning sun brightened up the blue sky.

"Come in!" she called, as she was only sitting down at a table with a large cup of coffee in front of her.

Keppal walked in and she smiled as she looked up at him. They had spent a while now in each other's company and she was beginning to open up to him a little more and could see a very familiar look in his eye.

"You want something, Keppal?" she asked.

"Only to ask you something."

She nodded and gestured to a chair beside her.

Keppal sat down and first looked into Sheeria's eyes before he started speaking, as if he were calculating her answer before he even asked.

"Do you know what I'm going to ask you?"

She smiled into her drink and glanced back over to him. "You want to know if you can take my place in the fight tomorrow."

Damn, she is smart, he thought.

"How did you know?" he asked, folding his arms and leaning back in his chair.

She now smiled again, feeling triumphant, as though she could read this tigian's mind like a book. "Because you're a good tigian, Keppal. Someone who protects people and takes responsibility. Right now you're faced with your friend having to fight and you feel you want to protect her."

Keppal's eyes shifted when she said that. He knew well that wasn't the case since he had murdered Dusty only a few weeks ago. She, however, saw his eye movement as something else and continued.

"Also that you don't know how to take compliments. You're modest and probably don't know your true potential. Maybe another reason for you asking this is to find out something about yourself? Am I right?"

She's not that smart though.

"No, Sheeria. I'm asking because I know I am stronger and faster than you. Look, I know you want to do this to both win the approval of your family and re-insert yourself back into a community you left so long ago, as well as finding your elementalist, but there is nothing wrong with assigning a champion to your fight. I can do this, Sheeria. Being bred as a tigian from Glacias Terras my fur is naturally thicker due to the cold conditions and my body is stronger. With my training from the Toshiro Police Force I make an excellent opponent, worthy of any battle ritual, be that tigian, human or even leo."

"This is my family though, Keppal. My fight. A tigian doesn't show their strength by letting others do it for them. I can do this, Keppal. You underestimate me."

"No, Sheeria I do not. I know you're more than capable but we need this done quickly. If I'm right then we have no idea how much time we are dealing with to meet up with the others. Also once we do find them, I don't know this Acarlie but what will she think if I let you go by yourself and put you in danger?"

This time Sheeria nodded when she thought about not just Acarlie but another member of the team and what he would do if he found out Keppal put her in danger like this. Her mind drifted briefly as a horrifying scenario appeared in her mind and she quickly blinked and looked back over to Keppal sitting there waiting for her answer.

"Yes, you're right, Keppal. We need to make our way to Chippenham as soon as possible. I will go and ask my brother now."

"Thank you, Sheeria."

"There is only one condition to you doing this."

"What's that, then?"

"You end it quickly. This isn't like an Elemental Battle where the audience is waiting for their money's worth. You end it quickly and we'll be back on our way the day after."

Keppal nodded. "I understand."

The royal chamber of Queen Angel, the Queen of Feydon and the ruler of the Septurian continent, was dark and warm, how she liked it. Her skyship was still making its way over the international waters and she had just received her newest present from her beloved tigian husband, Zane, the Elemental Lord.

She was the vision of beauty, her face looked as if made by gods, with small cheekbones, small pink lips and large dark eyebrows. Her eyes were large with piercing deep sapphire blue irises, a black ring outlining them and matching her pupils and long eyelashes reaching out. Her hair was brown, but as dark as it was, still reflected the light, and reached down her back and over her shoulders to her bare breasts.

She lay beside her newest lover and snuggled up against him, waking him.

"Good morning," she whispered as she watched him blink and saw his eyes adjust, discombobulated from sleep.

Her lover groaned and sniffed, clearing his airways, and

looked over to his perfect woman beside him. Angel, the most desirable woman on the planet, cuddling up against him and gently biting his ear in a playful fashion.

Angel had many lovers, presents, concubines from her husband, but this one in particular had stunned her over the last few days. Handsome and strong, with much battle experience and with very few scars, the only ones he did have she thought cute. He was built like a soldier but he didn't act like one; she liked that; her husband had picked out a good man for her here.

He grinned in his arousal as she rolled on top of him, her skinny belly pressing into his and he slid his hands up her long legs and up her side to her soft breasts and kissed her.

"So where are your other lovers, then?" he asked.

"I had them executed, darling," she said and sat up and began to grind against him slowly, guiding his hands to hold her hips as she did.

"Ever since I found you I feel I don't need them any more. You are perfect for me," she said and leaned down to him again until her brown hair rested on his shoulders.

He smiled again knowing he had her full attention now, this beautiful dark haired angel now belonged to him, had already killed for him.

"Now are you going to fuck me?" she asked with a demanding tone.

He groaned again while she still pressed her pelvis against him, waiting for an answer she knew was coming.

"Yes. But not now," he said and took her and threw her aside on the bed. She hadn't been expecting this.

"But Miles, I–"

"I need a shower," he said and stood up and stretched. "My master still has a mission for me so I need to do it."

"Your master is my husband, Miles, and he asked you to do *me*."

"And I have. Several times. Now get off my back."

She was gob-smacked, never had she been denied. She was not some lonely virgin incapable of finding a mate, she was the Queen, the most beautiful woman around, and here he was denying her. This was what she loved about him. All her life she had got what she wanted, every wish fulfilled, every desire met. Until she met her husband. He had something she couldn't have, for he was a different species and so sexual congress was out of the question, and when she knew she couldn't have something, she wanted it even more. Now Miles gave back to her this desire, there was something about Miles, something feral she couldn't have, couldn't control, and now she knew she couldn't have it, she wanted it.

Miles walked into the shower and stood under the warm, falling water, when she walked in after him, pushing him against the wall and kissing him, wrapping her legs around him so he had to hold her up by her firm buttocks and turned her around and up against the wall.

"You don't understand, Miles. I always get what I want."

"Tough shit. I have to go soon."

She kissed him again now as her soaking wet, warm body now started to slip from his grip.

"I'll have you executed," she said with a raised eyebrow.

"What? By who? Alberto? Your shiny, most valued and skilled guard? I'll strip down that glorified girl's doll and embarrass him in front of all his men. I'll have him dancing for his life then chop him in pieces so small the kingnines won't have to chew."

"But you forget I have an ace up my sleeve, darling. I have Proto-Weapon. Any time I want you and anywhere you are in the world I can send Proto-Weapon after you. You may be the best human fighter in the world but you are nothing but vulnerable prey to the likes of Proto-Weapon."

She held onto him tightly; she could sense his arousal as well as the obvious sign pressing into her hip.

"You kill me then who's going to fuck you?"

"I'll find someone."

"Like me?"

This time she had no answer.

"Exactly, you won't kill me, woman. You want me too much."

"And you want me." She smiled now.

"I don't need to want you, I already have you. Now shut up. After I'm done I have to go. No bitching, we both still have the same person to serve and the same goal to accomplish."

He started to rub her soaking wet breasts and kiss her neck, when she pushed him back a little.

"That's something I seriously wanted to talk to you about, darling."

"Okay, but it can wait now."

She nodded and pulled him closer into her.

"Thank you all for gathering here today, people of Rowsena. We have with us today an old member of my family who is also an old member of this community, ready to fight for her place back in this community!" Audie called out to the crowd of tigians all whistling and clapping, making a large circle in the middle of the village.

"Now, we all know the rule of this village. One that my dear sister once forgot all those years ago and now she stands beside me asking for my forgiveness. Now I am a fair tigian, a tigian who knows the value of family as well as mercy, and so I have accepted her offer of this ancient ritual if it means she can once again have a say in our matters and we can once again call her sister. But today, not only has she brought up this ancient tradition, but she also wishes to change it. This is what I said I would ask you to consider."

Sheeria was standing beside her brother in the centre of this circle of tigians while he explained what she had asked him the night before. The crowd now stood silent and waited for Audie to ask.

"She asks you all if she can choose a champion to fight for her. Since this has never been done before I promised I would ask you all so you can decide."

The crowd started murmuring to one another and Sheeria quickly glanced aside to Keppal. His different colour fur made him stick out of the crowd. He stood there with folded arms waiting for the crowd's answer.

There was a moment of whispering and passing of opinions then an elderly tigian called out. "When this used to happen I remember the rules stating that these fights should only be between two tigians. Some time ago before the Divide a tigian tried to cheat and brought a leo in with him. If she wishes to choose someone to fight for her then her choice would have to be of our blood."

Keppal looked up and took this as his cue. "Then this matter is for you to now decide: if I qualify for this."

Everyone stood silent and watched the white tigian walk and stand beside Sheeria. Keppal had had lots of awkward stares from these tigians the whole time he had been there, gawking at him as if they thought he had a skin deficiency, something he now felt he had the chance to clear up. "I am Keppal from a distant land known as Glacias Terras. There the snow falls thick and the cold is constant. My ancestors are the same as yours but mine chose to live and survive in the cold and dark and so my fur has adapted to a different kind from yours. I may look different but if you say that only a *tigian* may fight then I qualify for that. I am a tigian and have asked Sheeria if I could take her place."

The crowd again started murmuring and rustling against one another before finally accepting Keppal's proposal, accepting him into the arena.

The tigians now all took another step back, making the circle in the middle of their village even larger, and a single young tigian stepped up and faced him. Keppal stared at his opponent and waited for Audie and Sheeria to take a step back.

Audie nodded when he faced them again. "Let's get this over with. Franco, make this quick."

Keppal's opponent nodded and immediately stepped forward to Keppal with his guard raised waiting for the first attack.

Keppal wasted no time and immediately sprang forward and grabbed the young tigian and started wrestling him to the ground in one of the textbook manoeuvres he learned during his police training, but to his surprise, instead of taking to the ground, Franco nimbly stepped aside and kicked Keppal in the jaw. The kick knocked him straight onto his back and he heard the crowd call and "Ooohh" at the sound of his head thumping the ground.

Immediately dazed, Keppal was now on the floor and Franco jumped on him, digging his knees into Keppal's shoulders and started repeatedly throwing punches at his nose. After the fifth punch he felt his nose pop and Keppal caught the sixth attack and grunted as he threw all his weight over to one side to throw the tigian off him, giving himself a second to catch his breath.

He panted heavily while his vision blurred back into focus and wiped the blood from his nose and looked up to see Franco throw another kick. Keppal held up his arms to block the attack and caught Franco's leg and lifted it, knowing this would soon throw him off balance. But again to his surprise, Franco used this support to jump up and swing his other leg all the way up and smashed it into the side of Keppal's head, landing back on his feet.

The crowd clapped and applauded Franco as Keppal was back on the floor now in agony.

Having seen many Elemental Battles in her time Sheeria knew what she was looking at here and glanced over to her brother. "So when did you start allowing martial arts to be taught to tigians, brother? Was that not something our ancestors and predecessors thought weak and unnecessary?"

Audie grinned and kept his eyes on the fight, while Keppal was back up again and trying to fight a losing battle against the nimble and quick tigian. "Since the aeomon started living with us, sister. It was something they contributed to our society. Our ancestors were wrong, tigians are strong and teaching them to fight like a human or an aeomon is the best way forward. It teaches them discipline, speed, agility and to even learn the opponent's technique. Observation is one of Franco's strengths, he's not only fighting the white tigian but he's also watching him, learning what his strengths and weaknesses are."

"And there you were worrying about me breaking the rules of these sacred fights," she smiled.

"There is nothing to say *how* the tigian fights, Sheeria," he quickly countered.

Keppal had now changed his tactic since Franco had managed to jump up again and swing a roundhouse kick straight into his temple, caught him before he fell, twisted his wrist and yanked it in an unnatural direction, forcing him to the ground. Once Keppal was back up he lifted up his guard and now tried fighting defensively, jabbing his opponent when he could, and managed to find one successful strike through Franco's defence and punched his jaw.

"It's just a shame that your Franco isn't fighting with any proper technique," Sheeria stated again.

"Oh, and how would you know that, then, sister?"

"I've already explained, Audie. I have been raising elementalists for decades now, brother. My current elementalist, Acarlie, has mastered the arts and I have watched her since infancy and helped tutor her as well as many other students. So I am telling you the truth right now when I say that Franco has speed, power and strength but his technique is sloppy, his stances are too short, the ones that need to be long are too long. Keppal doesn't know it yet but all he has to do is swipe Franco's ankle and he could have him on the floor."

Audie frowned when he looked down and saw she was right. Franco was good and was getting the better of Keppal but it didn't mean he was the better fighter and soon Keppal had managed to finally catch the nimble tigian, throw him on the floor and sink his teeth into his shoulder.

"Maybe you're right, sister. You do seem to have knowledge of the art of fighting. Maybe once all this is done you can return here and teach the students. It will bring strength as well as wisdom to our community."

"So you will accept me back in? Because it sounds like you need me now."

He frowned again. "Let's see what happens to your champion first."

Sheeria nodded and looked back down at Keppal, who was being very unforgiving to Franco and now had his arm wrapped tightly in a lock and was pulling trying to break his arm while his opponent screamed and refused to tap or call submission.

"What is the meaning of this!" called a voice.

Everyone stopped as a small, smartly dressed aeomon

stormed into the circle followed by a small crowd of aeomon.

The aeomon was middle aged with a grey suit, a top hat and pocket watch hanging from his pocket, small round glasses sitting at the end of his nose and a long moustache. He had no trouble in walking straight past the fighting tigians and up to Audie.

"Stop this fight immediately, Audie," he demanded.

"Sanders, please step aside. This is a tradition of our culture that you are witnessing right now," Audie tried explaining.

"This is nothing but a pathetic excuse for violence. This is barbaric! Stop this immediately!"

Audie only tilted his head slightly to one side and continued, "Sanders, I hope you know that I do not enjoy watching this right now but this is a tigian family problem that is being settled in a tigian way."

"No, Audie. When we moved into this community with you we agreed that this would be a shared society. An aeomon would have the same rights as a tigian. Now I am the head of the aeomon community here and sit beside you in our councils and I demand we sort this problem another way without violence. We are not animals any more, Audie. I understand why you want to carry on with the traditions of your ancestors, I have no problem with that, but killing in order to settle a debate is far beyond the line. You are better than this, Audie."

Audie looked down at his friend and partner and back over to the fighters. Keppal, still with Franco's arm in his grip ready to break it, was waiting for him to speak.

Everybody was looking over to Audie now. The crowd was silent, some wanted to carry on while the others nodded and agreed with Sanders and the aeomon standing behind him.

Finally Audie nodded. "Yes, you are right. None of us are the tigians our ancestors used to be. I guess that in order for us to evolve as a society we have to walk away from certain traditions and become something better than our predecessors. Stop the fight! Sheeria, Sanders, we should vacate to my office. I think we have much to talk about."

She was led back to Audie's office with Sanders. Back up the wooden elevator that lifted them up the giant tree and to the secured office high above the ground. Audie walked in causally and gave her a seat while Sanders had a small chair in the office he had used many times before. Before he sat down Audie went to a cupboard and opened it to reveal some small glasses, which he lifted down.

"Okay then. I believe we have some business to attend to now." He reached up to the corner of the cupboard and pressed a hidden button that clicked and slowly, using cogs and wheels, the back of the cupboard slid down to reveal three bottles of different coloured spirits held onto the walls with spirit bottle dispensers similar to what is used in bars. He poured himself a drink and another for Sanders and offered one to Sheeria, but she politely refused. Once he was sitting down behind his desk he sipped at his glass and began.

"So tell me again about your predicament, sister."

Sheeria nodded. "I am a sacred guide for Elementalist Acarlie of Eloma. Myself and Keppal were separated from my elementalist back in Donolan."

"What happened there?" Sanders asked, still unaware of the current events.

"Feydon invaded the city. The city was fired upon with forbidden weapons. After her battle Acarlie had some business to attend to, something I wish I accompanied her to but it was too late. We are separated and now I need to find a passage across the ocean back to Anavrin and to Chippenham."

"Forbidden weapons you say? Why is this? I thought the forbidden weapons were a thing of the past?" Audie asked once she mentioned them and caught his attention.

Sheeria noticed his immediate concern about these weapons and wanted to be open with him. "Yes, they were, brother, but on our journey we discovered that a human businessman named Campbell was manufacturing them in Toshiro."

"I heard Toshiro was destroyed by a great storm. Is this true?" Sanders asked again.

"Yes, Feydon stepped in but it was led not by Queen Angel but by a large fleet led by the Elemental Lord Zane. It was he who stepped in and took control of the city and seized the forbidden weapons, equipping his army with them."

"The E.L. Zane you say? Are you sure? Maybe there was some mistake?" Sanders asked in amazement.

"This is true. I saw it with my own eyes, sir."

"But maybe this was –"

"Sanders. This is my sister we are speaking to. My older sister, the eldest of the Katsan name. There is no lie in her words. What bothers me though is why he would do this."

Here it is, the hardest part of the story to tell anyone. I don't know what to say, usually Raiden keeps the information about this mission a secret as to not scare the people of Sphere. But I really need to win the confidence of these two.

Audie noticed her eyes were unsettled, as though he could hear her inner monologue. He knew there was more she had to tell.

"I know that face, Sheeria. You pulled the same face when you tried to protect me from our mother when I broke her jewellery when we were cubs. Tell us what is going on."

"I'm hesitant to say," she admitted.

"Why?"

"Because I fear my words will be dismissed as lies."

Now they both sat silent. Audie lowered his head and glanced over to the aeomon in disapproval and bit his tongue but it was Sanders who nodded and said, "We do not think you a liar, Sheeria. As Audie mentioned earlier, you are a Katsan, the older sister of the leader of this community."

Sheeria sighed again uncomfortably and rubbed her forehead. "I...I do not wish to lie to you, brother. I need your support and want to tell you everything but you must promise to listen to me. These facts are hard to hear..."

She told them everything: Zane's immortality, the black hole, the items under the elemental schools, the rocket, everything. When she finished there was a silence. Audie said not a word but finished his drink and had to go back to the cupboard to pour himself another and Sanders just sat in deep thought, swirling his drink under his nose.

"I'm sorry you had to hear that, but I promise you this is nothing but the truth."

Audie finished his drink in one this time, poured himself another and sat back down. "I really don't know how to take this, sister. I don't know whether to laugh you out of my office or shout at you for telling me such a story."

Sheeria hung her head.

But it was Sanders who spoke up, ending his silence. "But what if it is true, Audie? This would explain why Feydon has invaded all these cities before. Mecroyles, Toshiro and Hiro are facts, the news has spread across the globe now. Mecroyles and Hiro *were both* invaded, Toshiro *was* destroyed. Not just the countries, not just Racoves, Calmeron and Anavrin, but the three cities. All three have elemental schools. And if Sheeria's story is true about Isolies then this would also explain why Lachine was not invaded."

"Oh, come on, Sanders. Think for a minute, Feydon has always invaded whatever it seems to want. Remember Decrenia a year ago? Remember the Battle of Osiris? Hiro, Mecroyles and Toshiro were coincidences. Lachine was not invaded because it has nothing Feydon wants. Their elemental schools have nothing to do with it."

"The Battle of Osiris was only a short war to reclaim Feydon's land that the old Ultra Soldier Osiris and his army claimed for themselves after they were deemed obsolete once the kingnines were created before the Leo Divide," Sanders countered in one long sentence.

"So what does that mean?"

"It means, my friend, that the Battle of Osiris was about land. Meaning Queen Angel would have ordered and Lord Zane would have had no part in it. I am troubled by this story but I know my history, Audie, and so should you. I bet a story like this would have been told to many people and treated the same way back when the sun was dying. Before the First Divide."

"Brother, if you do not believe me then that's okay. But if I can have a passage across the waters I can at least pay you for your troubles," Sheeria cut in now, feeling she was never going to win her brother's support.

"There is nothing you can possibly have that I want, sister. Save your bargains for when you have something of value." He silenced her and thought about what Sanders was saying again.

"But I do have something," she said, remembering his reaction at a previous point of this discussion and realising what was really on his mind then. "I can give you one of the forbidden weapons we have attached to our ship. A cannon. You can bring this back here and study it, and with the help of the aeomon you can remake more."

This seemed to anger him slightly more now. "And now, sister, you tell me this? More promises and stories. You forget how long you have been away, sister. Since the Last Divide you have been absent in my life and now you come here unannounced and feed me stories and promises for a favour for you. You test my patience and my trust, sister."

Sheeria was silenced again, her heart thumped in her chest. She didn't know what to say and the look of such disappointment in her own brother's eye felt unbearable to her.

"I believe her," Sanders said, cutting the tension.

Audie looked back over to him and let him continue.

"The details in her story seem too precise to be fictional."

"Only the best lies have details, Sanders. Unsupported and un-researchable."

"But they're not unsupported. If this was false then why would Feydon leave Toshiro in the state it was in when they arrived? I bet if you ask and research about Donolan tomorrow the fact will be presented then. All of these facts could possibly have been woven into a high tale, yes. But with Donolan the fact is unsupported. Out here we receive news of the outside world late but Donolan being destroyed by Feydon is a fact that won't go unheard. This is the fact that will fully win my confidence if proven tomorrow. Also it calls the question: why would she provide us with this unbelievable story when she could have easily used the fact of Mecroyles's invasion to promise us the cannon? Sheeria, I have a zeppelin that is waiting to make its maiden voyage once some final preparations and modifications have been made. If your brother shall not assist you, then, providing the fact of Donolan's invasion is proven true, you will have the support of the aeomon of this community. If it's

Chippenham you need to visit then I think it will be a good time for me to present myself to the Senate there and try to make a connection of trade between our two settlements."

Sheeria nodded. "Thank you. The news is true, you have my word."

Sanders looked back to Audie, who sat stubbornly in his chair but nodded. "I will trust you sister, and you, Sanders. My decision will be made on the arrival of this news of Donolan."

Keppal sat down on his bed, his wounds still healing, with a knife in his hands.

His room was identical to Sheeria's, a room on top of one of the high trees with a scenic view of the Great Forest. The light from the two moons shone down on his knife and reflected back up at him, making the weapon gleam in the night. He sat and thought, locked deep in his mind about what he would have to do eventually and wondering how he would accomplish it successfully. Sheeria had now been in talks with her brother and the aeomon leader of this town and it was likely that she had managed to arrange a lift so they could make their way to Chippenham at long last. But the matter still lingered in his mind; she had to die. The Elemental Lord Zane had given him this secret task of eliminating this team of crazy psychos. The elementalist Acarlie was his prime target, she was apparently the leader of this team and after he had assassinated her he would then take that Val out. He still blamed Val for the deaths of his team back in Toshiro. He closed his eyes and remembered his team, Roy and Dean, Sonia and Mitchell the aeomon, all dead and, apart from Dean who had died beforehand in an M.V. crash, Val was the cause of it all. He sighed as the phantoms disappeared and the face of the tigian he travelled with now entered his mind. Like the leos, tigians responded to strength and confidence and she glowed with it with a natural talent. There was also a wisdom about her too that Keppal found comforting. He didn't know Acarlie and so couldn't judge her but he found it difficult to believe Sheeria was capable of being a terrorist but trusted Zane and believed him.

At a knock on the door he quickly hid the knife behind his back; Sheeria walked in holding a bottle of wine with two glasses, one of which already had an orange liquid in it.

"I just wanted to thank you in person for what you did for me earlier on, Keppal. May I come in?"

"I…Yes, of course. Please, sit down." he smiled up at her and gripped onto the handle of the knife he hid. *Maybe this is my chance?*

She sat down and poured him a glass. "The lead councillor of the aeomon people here, Sanders, gave me this. It is fine aeomon rose wine, known for its flavour. Here," she said and handed him the glass.

He took the glass reluctantly at first with thoughts flying through his mind of what he should do. If he killed her now then it could jeopardise his mission, but then again with her dead he could still possibly get a lift to Chippenham. Who would suspect her closest friend here to be her murderer? She could have many enemies here, even her brother would be a suspect. He winced when he thought about springing up and planting the knife in her chest. *No, I am not a murderer! I'm a police officer, I…damn!* he cursed in his mind when he remembered the blood stains on his hands when he murdered Dusty.

"Thank you. Will you be joining me?" he asked but she held up her glass in front of him.

"No, I have my own drink here," she smiled.

"Not really much of a drinker then?"

"No, I tend to stay away from it."

Keppal smiled back and sipped his wine whilst still thinking about how he would kill her.

Completely oblivious to the demons in his mind Sheeria carried on. "The aeomon here say they have a zeppelin that can take us to Chippenham, we will have to wait a day first though. It's quite amazing what technology they are capable of really. All their power is reusable and friendly to the environment. The humans could learn a thing or two from their way of life."

She carried on her idle chat while Keppal gripped on tightly to the knife and sipped from the glass, fighting temptation in his mind.

No, wait, we're not on the zeppelin yet. I should wait until we are face to face with Acarlie then strike, killing Sheeria now will only delay our flight.

"So...Keppal?" she said realising her conversation was boring him. She stood up and walked to the window and sipped at her glass of orange. "Tell me a bit more about yourself."

He finally released tension on his knife and stood up, concealing it behind his back, and faced her. "What do you want to know?"

I have to do this! If I don't do it now I might not get another chance! He took a step closer.

"Well, I've seen a frown like yours many times before. You are haunted by a murder."

What! How can she know!? He took a step back.

"What do you mean?" he asked.

"Maybe your first ever kill. Tell me, Keppal. Who was your first kill?"

His heart raced, but he breathed in relief; she still didn't know. He remembered his first kill like it was yesterday.

"A year ago now, in Toshiro. A serial killer was stalking the streets. I got the report that this thing was killing and even eating its victims. Dressed all in black with a bow and arrow this thing was a silent killer, stalking and murdering its prey. We called it The Archer."

He loosened his grip on his knife again and this time concealed it behind his clothes. He drank again as he reminisced.

"It moved like a shadow, using all sorts of cunning hunting techniques from fast poisons to trapping and ambushing its prey, taking them away leaving almost no trail behind. Sometimes it would even vanish before people's eyes. It was my job to track it [a story you will all know one day, Readers] and I found one of its old hideouts one day and discovered the skeletal remains of its victims. It liked porci, or even children, human babies and their mothers. We had to kill this monster."

"That sounds terrifying, Keppal, what happened?"

"We trapped it in a warehouse once. I had to fight it."

"And what happened?"

This time he paused and closed his eyes as if to not see what was appearing in his mind. "I killed it."

"What was it?" she asked now.

This question burned a hole in Keppal then and Sheeria noticed this, it was like he cared more about what it had been rather than the details of its death.

"It doesn't matter," he said, turning from the conversation.

Sheeria paused for a brief moment then reached out and touched his shoulder. The second she did his heart raced again; here she was, being sympathetic to him, and here he was contemplating her death, and why? Because Zane, a tigian he didn't know, told him too?

No, Zane is the Elemental Lord and greatest tigian that ever lived. She must die!

"Well, I'm sorry, Keppal. But at least this evil monster is dead now, right? Sphere doesn't have to worry about The

Archer any more. Come on, let's go visit my brother one last time before we depart."

The Archer was crouched high above an empty hallway staring down at the leo. Raiden had found some space to practise and sharpen his skills since he was now out of the hospital and waiting for some response from the President of Angland for passage to Chippenham. He was unaware of the hidden archer above him, which now stood up and slowly pulled out its bow. Its recent visit to the hospital meant it could use the drugs there to make a worthy poison, and it dipped the end of its arrow in it, pulled back on the bow and aimed down at the leo, still punching the air in its low stance, training.

"Brother, there you are," called the voice of the kingnine.

Zoudiva walked up and Raiden used the moment to rest.

Damn that kingnine! The Archer thought. *Looks like I can't take the leo on its own. No matter, I will kill the kingnine.*

"A representative of President Sahota of Angland is here to speak to you, Raiden. He is just outside."

What? Damn them!

"Okay, thanks, brother."

"There is something that is troubling me though, brother. Ever since we were on that train I feel a presence around us. I see and smell nothing but it is a feeling I cannot shake."

"You're probably just paranoid, Zou'."

"But this would explain what happened to the soldiers on the train. It would also explain who changed the file at your bedside. I think we are being followed, brother," Zoudiva croaked in his deep, seemingly old voice.

The Archer kept the bow and arrow straight, wanting

to release its poison arrow when the doors in the distance opened and a crowd of humans walked in.

"I think this is something we will have to ignore now, Zou'. We will see what they want first."

"Hello, Leo Raiden. I hope you are well now. As you know after the attack, President Sahota has more pressing matters to attend to but wants to assure your safety and passage back to your elementalist. I am here to ensure this happens. Please follow me."

The Archer grunted after its only moment was ruined by this and had to quickly and quietly escape without anybody noticing.

It sped across the rooftops of this small town using the ice-axes to climb difficult areas and found its current lair. A broken and secluded farmhouse, away from any human, that stank bad enough to repel them. The air was quiet but as The Archer returned to its current hiding place a young infant's voice was heard crying. The Archer ignored this at first and took off its bow and arrow and stashed them away, as well as its ice-axes. The baby still cried as it now approached it and took out its two knives. Its dinner was now ready.

6

The days passed quickly as the Scarlet Arise took the final few hundred miles to Chippenham. The ship was now silently passing over the plains of Anavrin in the mid afternoon sun. Val had since used the time to rest and get used to the terrible scar that now sat on his face like a burn victim's. He was as upset as anybody would be that his youthful looks now elicited a glance of pain and pity from the people who now saw him. He tried all he could to take his mind off it but every now and again found himself feeling the scar with his fingers like a child would a wound. So instead he started his training to take his mind away from it.

He was currently in an old room of the ship, the very same room in fact that he was first thrown into bound with the mute aeomon back when the pimp Gendrick owned this ship, but right now was down on the floor doing push ups.

"Twenty-four...twenty-five...twenty-six...," he counted to himself. He heard the sound of footsteps close by.

"Twenty-seven...twenty...eight...."

He panted as his arms started to tire but saw Acarlie walk into the room and look down at him.

"Oh, hi Acarlie. Seventy-seven...seventy-eight...seventy-nine. I didn't see you there...Eighty!"

Acarlie had not been herself since he woke, but was better and couldn't help but smile a little at his poor attempt to impress her with his bogus push up count. She thought of a quick way to help him exercise as well as teach him a lesson and stood over him.

"Eighty-two...eighty...threeeeeee."

She smiled again and put her hand over Val's body

and ever so slightly increased the gravity around him and watched him suddenly slam into the floor and howl in pain then begin a mixture of laughing and crying.

"Come on, Val, you can do one," she said cheering him on. "Come on, give me one."

"No, please!" he pleaded in pain but still couldn't stop smiling. "I'm being crushed under the weight of my bones!"

"Push, Val!"

"Ahhh!" he called and slammed his hands into the floor, to push himself up, now feeling twice as heavy.

She knelt down still with her hand hovering over his body and smiled as she tortured him.

"I hope you're enjoying yourself!" Val said as he strained his arms and tried with all his might to push up; but he was now feeling like he was pushing the ground away from him so as not to slam face first into it.

"I'm having a great time, Val. Come on, Val, you can do it!"

Val screamed again, slowly pushing himself away from the floor, but now his arms started to shake violently.

"Okay, okay, okay. I give in! Please stop!" he pleaded and she did as asked and put the gravity back to normal. She even made it a little lighter for him but not enough to stop him now face planting the floor in exhaustion.

He lay there panting while she even started to laugh a little. "What did you learn?" she asked sarcastically.

Val smiled again and looked up at her. "That I can always make you smile," he replied, noticing the first real smile she'd pulled since he woke up.

While looking down she tried to see the funny side and appreciate what he was trying to do but all she could see was the hideous scar on his face and her guilt sank in again, wiping away her smile.

Val saw this, stood up and started stretching his arms thinking of how to save the moment. "Did you see how many I did, though?"

"Val, I could hear you counting from outside in the hallway."

"Yeah, I…always count like that. Counting in twenties makes it feel…easier."

"You're such a liar!" she joked and jabbed him in the ribs.

Still feeling weak Val started caving in like a child and held her back.

"I'm kidding! Stop hurting me!"

His plan had worked and she gave him a final push and grabbed his hand to pull him.

"Come on, I came down here to show you something."

He followed her to the deck of the ship, where they saw other pirates, either mopping the deck or taking a break, and even Mitis standing at the edge and peering over.

"What is it?" he asked.

"Come here, look."

She took him to where Mitis was and pointed down at the Great Plains of Anavrin. The afternoon sun glazed the plains with a warm, orange glow and Val could see thousands of wild animals below them. Some he knew; a herd of elephants marched across a riverbed with the young ones playing in it. A great herd of lizziers and antelope grazed side by side in the fields and giant flocks of birds flew down near the riverbed.

Val was amazed by the sight of it. The Scarlet Arise was too high in the air to disturb any of the wildlife there but low enough for them all to see.

"What's that?" Val had to ask, pointing to a particularly large furry beast he saw hiding in the long grass, watching its prey.

Acarlie squinted, "Wow, that's a Magnan Tiger Wolf."

Mitis now glanced over at Val and saw this look of amazement. "Tiger Wolves are the biggest wolves in the world. So big that they have taken over the role of apex predator in its natural habitat. It's called a Tiger Wolf because of its stripy fur, very similar to what the tigians once had millions of years ago. Since the tigers and lions evolved the wolves stepped up and became the big predators of the world. I take it you know what that is, Val?" she said and pointed to the river bank where a familiar looking large reptile surfaced from out of the water.

"Sure I do, that's a crocodile," Val smiled.

Mitis squinted. "Interesting. You seem to have knowledge of all the ancient creatures that have been around for millions of years. What about that?" She pointed now to another large, armoured creature walking and grazing the plains. It was a large, grey quadruped with four horns growing out of its nose and even its tail was like a battering ram, spiked with small bones.

"It looks like a rhino," Val guessed, squinting down at it.

Acarlie was impressed. "Wow, Val. The rhinoceros has been extinct for the last few thousand years now. How did you know?"

Val looked blank. "I don't know. I just see a picture of it in my head, just like how I know what a lion is."

"This has to have something to do with why you don't know your identity, Val. Maybe you were an archaeologist before you woke?" Mitis suggested.

Val just smiled reluctantly now; he knew very well that wasn't the case, but she was right – it was strange how he could tell a catalogue of ancient creatures apart from another but knew nothing of the modern ones. One day he knew he would find out who he used to be and why he knew all this information.

Soon after, the night fell, followed by a bright and promising morning, when they finally reached the magnificent city they had travelled so far to see. The capital city of Magna and the elder capital of the world. The city of Chippenham.

The city's buildings stretched out as far as they could see. The Scarlet Arise entered the city for the air station. The morning sun gleamed down and reflected off the glass windows of the tall human built buildings, lighting up the rest of the city in a magnificent portrait of wonder to the eyes of the beholder. Even the first sight of the sparkling clean Hiro with its defence system of the giant electric shield dome was underwhelmed by this city and, of course, it was not the human skyscrapers and buildings that gave this place such a renowned view but in fact the elder-made buildings. Built so differently from the conventional tall rectangular shapes of the human-made buildings the architecture of the elders had been made into works of art. Coming in all different shapes and sizes, using all different tools and ideas. Some were stabilised into an egg shape and coated in glass letting in light from all directions, while others even took ideas from animals. Val noticed a particularly prominent building that had the shape and style of a snail's shell, and another resembling a tortoise shell with great pentagons of glass on the top and spikes reaching out and curling back around with spotlights at the end to light up at night. There were the countless cathedrals, monasteries and temples that were made to look like they had been built from wood but actually the large beams were of marble and concrete, and it was Acarlie who pointed out to Val the stadium.

The Universal Elemental Stadium of Sphere was its name and it hosted the C.E.L.: the Chippenham Elemental League. A league of its own, separate from the League of Elementalists, in which all elementalists took part at the cost of their lives. Since the C.E.L. was a separate league the rules were different. In the League of Elementalists, the elementalist would travel the world and gamble their lives in the Elemental Battles in order to learn each element from the schools. In the C.E.L. however there was no death since there was never an element to learn. A travelling elementalist would often stop here and leave their pilgrimage behind, instead becoming a legend of a different kind. One could never hope to become the Elemental Lord here but instead could become a champion of the C.E.L. This, however, often meant that the C.E.L. was shunned by the traditionalists, who were loyal to the strict rules of the League of Elementalists, but the contenders always had the choice of gambling their lives for greatness or settling down in the C.E.L. and becoming champions; an easy choice for most.

The Scarlet Arise landed at the city's station; the captain of the ship was the first to step off and inhale the fresh air in the morning sun and behold the sight of this city before him. Kaza was closely followed by his quartermaster Midia and Acarlie, when they were greeted by station Security. It was Acarlie's job to speak to them all and arrange a quick audience with their bosses to get permission for them to stay while she visited the stadium. They were quick to react when she spoke to them. By now Acarlie had realised her face had now been seen by many people around the world. Out of her seven battles, five had been broadcast around the world and now she was really beginning to make a name for herself as a possible contender to one day challenge the Elemental Lord Zane for the title.

Their stay was permitted and the Scarlet Arise was granted a safe port to stay in while the crew were given the rest they deserved. As in the other cities they had stayed in they were given accommodation while Acarlie and her close guides were given a more secluded and private accommodation.

At the entrance to their hotel, which all the elementalists stayed at, Acarlie and her guide, Val, walked up to the counter to register.

"Could I take your full titles and names, please?" the receptionist asked.

Val had never gone through these procedures before, he normally left that to Sheeria, and so stood back and watched Acarlie handle this.

"I am Elementalist Acarlie of Eloma."

"And your title and name, sir?" the receptionist asked, while writing down Acarlie's details.

"Val," he said bluntly and leaned closer to the desk.

The male receptionist now just stared back plainly. "Your *full* title and name, please, sir?"

Acarlie now nudged him a little. "Val, you have to say your title."

He whispered back, "I don't know what that is." He then leaned back to the receptionist. "Mister Val," he tried to correct, but still the man look impatient with his ignorance.

Acarlie had to quickly remember Val's condition and pulled him back slightly to give him a quick lesson.

"No, Val. Here, our title goes: species, name, family name. Haven't you noticed that yet? That's why people would always say 'Leo Raiden' or 'Tigian Sheeria'."

"Oh right. Then why wasn't your title Human Acarlie?"

"Because I'm not really human, Val. Elementalists are technically a separate species. We have no family name either since we are all brought up by the elders."

Val nodded and understood and leaned back to the reception. "Okay, I'm Human Val."

"And your family name sir?"

Val stared blankly. "I don't know."

"Well, what's Raiden's family name? Surely you would share the same name as him, right?" Acarlie asked.

Val tried to think, searching his memory for an instance of Raiden mentioning his name.

"I don't know. Just leave it blank," he suggested and pointed to the paper.

The receptionist now sighed, being fed up with this conversation, and filled in the form.

"Okay then, Miss Elementalist Acarlie and Mister Human Val Blank–"

Acarlie glanced at Val, who smiled and shrugged.

"Please follow me this way."

"Before we do, sir, I want to also put the titles of my other guardians who are just not present yet. Please also include Misses Tigian Sheeria Katsan, Kingnine Zoudiva and Mister Leo Raiden."

"The leo's family name?" he said, writing all this down.

"He's the only leo left, sir. I don't think his family name will be relevant. When you see a leo, that's him."

The man sighed again. *How can they not know each other's names!?* "Very good then. Please follow me to your quarters."

Zahied looked at himself in the mirror after freshly cutting his hair and trimming his beard down to a goatee and inspected his face. He knew this place very well and had been dreaming of visiting it ever since he started his Casters' Pilgrimage. As a caster Zahied had always wanted to see the elder capital of the world. He knew that if there was any place that could teach him a thing or two it would be this city or the monasteries in Aragorth, but he had missed the chance to visit that. His appearance here would be vital and he was happy with his new look.

His room was in a hotel that he shared with the rest of the crew and currently he shared the room with both of the ex-soldiers Rezosa and Major. He, Kaza, Midia, Mitis and the mute were all invited to visit Acarlie and Val in their hotel and he intended to quickly visit a few places before he went. He walked out from the bathroom to find Major and Rezosa standing on the balcony chatting while staring at the view.

"I see you have cut your hair, Zahied," Major said while rubbing his own bald head. "Maybe one day you'll cut it as short as mine, yeah?"

Zahied chuckled while picking up his blue and silver cloak and throwing it over his shoulders. "Maybe not that short, Ragnor. Not just yet anyway. My hair may be turning a little grey but there's no need to cut it all off just yet. I've still got a few years on me yet, young man."

He smiled at the two younger soldiers and stood at the mirror and fastened up loose ties and buttons on his clothes, still inspecting his appearance.

Rezosa took a step forward and leaned against the door. "You look fine, Zahied. You look ten years younger."

"Do I look young enough for you yet?" he joked and glanced over to the dark, brunette beauty to see her smile back with a small pleased look in her eye as if she took that as a compliment. He knew there wouldn't be an answer and laughed. "Not yet then, no? Never mind. I will be back in a while then, you two. Be good."

He quickly checked he had everything he needed and made his way out of the door giving Rezosa one more quick glance as he walked out and saw she was still standing there, watching him leave, wearing the same smile for him.

When he finally arrived at the other hotel to find the others the afternoon sun was blazing down, bringing joy to the city. Mitis opened the door and Zahied entered the room in Acarlie's apartment to find he was the last person to arrive. Both Kaza and Midia were already seated next to the mute and Val was in the kitchen speaking to Acarlie.

"Sorry I'm late everyone. I just needed to find a few files from the elders here."

"That's okay, Zahied. Did you find anything useful?" Mitis asked as both Val and Acarlie now noticed him and walked into the lounge with the others.

"Oh, just some more of the more offensive elder tricks. I doubt very much I'll ever use them."

"Well, now we're here maybe we can discuss the next plan of action," Midia stated and sat upright. Zahied nodded and found a chair to sit in.

"Yes. So remind us what we're doing here again. I mean, there is no element for Acarlie here, right?" Mitis started.

"That's true. Even though there are more Elemental Battles here than anywhere else on Sphere I can't learn anything from anybody so myself taking part in this is only going to prolong our stay," Acarlie explained.

Kaza sat forward now. "But it's not like we're in a rush at the moment. Back in Donolan Raiden told us to all meet up here. We can't go anywhere until we all regroup again. You could use this time to take part in these battles, Acarlie."

Acarlie looked a little unsettled now. "I really don't think this will help us, Kaza."

"Of course it will. You may not learn an element here but you can gain experience here from other elementalists. Competing in this league will not only demonstrate your skills without the worry of death but will also let Zane see how you are still here and still the biggest threat to him."

"But let's not forget why we're here," Val added, leaning against a table at the back. "There is still a black hole out there. Information about this rocket to the space station is hidden somewhere in this city. We have to speak to the High Elders of this city. They must know of you, Acarlie, and are probably expecting to speak to you."

"An audience with the High Council of Elders in Chippenham will be harder than in most other places, Val. To most of the rest of the world I can still find and speak to the leaders of countries but to the elders I'm still just a human with the elemental gift. The only elementalist who could see them this easily would be Zane," she tried to explain.

"This isn't entirely true," Zahied said again. "There is also the Senate here in Chippenham."

"What's that?" Val asked.

"It's the council where a few selected beings of each different race on Sphere stand in and represent their own race. This is the council that decides on divides. Right now there are representations of humans, elders, tigians, porci, elementalists and aeomon in the Senate. The only ones who are not in this council at the moment are kingnines since they only serve individual human masters, ursas since they are currently divided from the rest of the world, and extinct creatures such as leos, pardi, vulpi and the goalaria, for understandable reasons."

"What about Raiden, then? Would he not be a part of this council since he is a leo?"

"Well, I guess there is nothing to stop him but then again he would only be able to represent himself since he's the last one left."

"You said there is also an elementalist there. Who represents them?" Val asked again.

"Take one wild guess who represents them, dumbass!" Kaza broke in, now feeling Val's questions were boring him.

Val thought for only a second and wanted to turn and look at Acarlie but as soon as he realised who would be the highest member of the elementalist line the answer soon came to his mind. "Oh right, sorry, carry on."

"What I'm trying to say is that, Acarlie, you can find the Human Prime Minister Sarah Celadore since she will be the closest link to your species and ask for her to speak to the High Elders."

"Actually I am to speak to her later on today. Since we have just landed here there is no king nor president here apart from the elder council so she is the one I have to address to admit myself into the C.E.L. I guess I can ask her then."

"In that case would it offend anyone if I were also there? I may not be the best political speaker but I think if anyone here from our group apart from yourself can persuade them then it's me."

Acarlie thought for a minute before nodding and accepting his proposal. "Well, I don't think it will hurt to try, Zahied. My appointment with them won't be for another hour yet but maybe we can get down there sooner rather than later, with you, myself and Val."

Val looked a little stunned then. "Am I coming too?"

"Of course you are, Val. You're my only guide present," she nearly snapped at him, also beginning to tire of his ignorance.

Val looked a little stunned at first but quickly got over it and stood up. "Right, I better get changed then."

The Senate was gathered in a small group outside the parliament buildings of the city, enjoying the heat and sun of the afternoon sky. A giant stone courtyard with a large marble table set with their refreshments rested in the middle of them, and bright plants and flowers hung decorating the walls around them. They all welcomed Acarlie when she arrived with her two guests, Val and Zahied.

The human of the group, the Human Prime Minister, stood up and was the first to greet them.

"Good afternoon, Elementalist Acarlie and her guides. My name is Human Sarah Celadore. Thank you for joining us today."

"Thank you for welcoming me here today." Acarlie bowed. "This is my guide Val and the gentleman behind him is Zahied. He is a caster and has asked if he could join us today."

"But of course he may." The tall, dark skinned, female prime minister held out a hand and shook Zahied's. "I see you are from the more tropical parts of the world," she smiled.

"That is right, madam. I am originally from one of the islands neighbouring Myrrh."

"Then we have something in common. Please sit and join us."

Val was a little nervous here and didn't want to embarrass himself or Acarlie so he just kept his mouth shut, smiled and thanked the ministers and stood a little back. He was only her guide, a guardian and a manager; any political conversation was beyond him.

Acarlie sat in between a porcus and a tigian. Both were dressed smartly with the dress sense of their people. The porcus had a very similar dress sense to the humans, as did the aeomon, but the tigians dressed in more of robes or tunic garments such as the chiton and the himation, a heavy cloak that tied at the shoulder. Their thick fur naturally warmed them in the sun and their big build made them seem strange wearing tailor-made suits designed for humans and aeomon and gave them more of an elder look. Cecil Vurbute, the tigian of them, sat to Acarlie's left in white, tunic garments in a wheelchair. He, like the others, was the highest political tigian leader and took his role deadly seriously, sitting upright with his fingers under his chin.

"Now that you are here, Miss Acarlie, maybe you would like to tell us your business here."

"This city is not required in your sacred pilgrimage and it is a tradition now that a journeying elementalist should speak to this council and state their business when entering the city," the short porcus started, leaning on the table, taking a sip from a chalice-shaped glass.

"Can we be expecting to see you in our own league?" Sarah asked.

"Yes, I do aim to participate in the Chippenham Elemental League but I do not expect to stay. My real business here is to speak to the High Elders of this city. I have some important business with them and ask you if an audience with them could be arranged."

"An audience with the High Elders?" the tigian from the group, sitting next to her, started. "What business could you possibly have with them? These elders are not part of your pilgrimage and do not stand anywhere within either Elemental League."

"My business with them is not regarding my pilgrimage, my lords."

"Would this by chance have anything to do with the Elemental Lord Zane's business with them last week?" the aeomon asked.

Acarlie looked stunned, "Lord Zane was here?"

"Yes, he was. He joined us in a meeting last week representing all the elementalists around the world. It's not very often we get blessed with his presence, especially nowadays with all the hard work he is doing in helping the other countries. I believe you were even there when he helped in the restoration of Toshiro."

"Yes, this is something we wanted to talk to you about, Miss Acarlie," Sarah stated. "It is clear to the world now that your pilgrimage seems…tainted."

"Tainted?"

"Yes. Everybody knows about how you destroyed the stadium in Hiro. The secret match you had with Elementalist Eliza that led to her death and then the match with Lord Zane himself which you fled from. Your reputation precedes you, Acarlie, you have had a memorable journey so far but it comes with a sense of controversy to the people of Sphere."

"Yes, I agree," started Cecil, the tigian. "If we allow you to join the city's league then what kind of reassurance do we have that you will not destroy our stadium?"

Acarlie looked stumped now and turned pale as the ministers all looked at her for her answer. She knew she hadn't killed Eliza but it was part of her promise to the elders of Selodia to take the blame for her death and keep the real story secret.

"I…" She tried to think of what to say and glanced quickly over to Zahied, who got the message immediately and leaned forward.

"If I may, Council, the actions of Acarlie's pilgrimage are not subject to the political decisions made by this council. Everything was done to ensure Elementalist Eliza's death was avoided and the stadium of Hiro was a beautifully designed stadium but was faulty by being made of glass. This could have happened to any elementalist."

"This still doesn't explain why she had to flee from the battle with Lord Zane," the tigian countered.

Zahied thought quickly. "I think we can all agree that the battle with Lord Zane was biased. Acarlie was not ready to fight him and nearly died in that battle. Yes, a rule was bent to ensure her safety but–"

"A sacred rule was broken, you mean? An elementalist should never run nor flee from an E.B. If the elementalist is not strong enough then they should pay the same price that every other weak elementalist has to pay. Her act of cowardice has embarrassed both of the Elemental Leagues. It is only by Lord Zane's mercy that this rule has been overlooked and she is still accepted on her pilgrimage."

"Lord Zane wishes me to continue?" Acarlie asked now, stunned.

"Yes, Acarlie," Sarah said. "We discussed the matter last week when Lord Zane was with us and he told us that this rule will be overlooked this time as an exception."

"May we ask what Lord Zane's business was here?" Zahied asked politely.

"His real intentions of his visit here he did not share, Zahied," Sarah answered.

"I believe that our business here may be for the same reason, which is why I ask again, can an audience be made with the High Elders?" Acarlie asked, wanting the discussion to move away from her pilgrimage.

The tigian next to her spoke up again. "I'm not sure this can be arranged, Miss Acarlie, and if you ask me, I also think that your contribution to our league will also only end badly."

"Yes, I agree," the aeomon of the group added.

"Hold on a second," Val said and stepped forward. He couldn't hold his tongue for another moment. "Pardon me, but isn't this a council that represents the different species of Sphere? How does Acarlie's pilgrimage have anything to do with–?"

"VAL!" Acarlie snapped, silencing him immediately.

After seeing the look of thunder in her eyes Val bit his tongue and stepped back.

"Please excuse the interruptions of our friend Val," Zahied recovered quickly. "He is new to these parts and has not yet learned such mannerisms required for this discussion. I assure you he will not contribute again."

"Yes, well, the decision still stands. An audience with the High Council of Chippenham is out of the question. What will the world think if we allow her to contribute after the offences she has committed? Even to the Elemental Lord himself?" the tigian said.

"I'm afraid Lord Zane is guilty of offences of his own," Acarlie now added, feeling the conversation was digging into her reputation. She felt she couldn't hold back this information any more.

"What do you mean by this?" the porcus asked.

Acarlie sighed, feeling she had already started, and went on, "The attacks on the four cities around the world, Mecroyles, Hiro, Toshiro and finally Donolan, have all been by the Feydon army. An army led by the Elemental Lord."

"Such an allegation would need some serious explanation," the tigian prime minister now said, turning to her.

Acarlie looked petrified now. She tried looking over to Zahied again, who only stared back and silently shook his head, trying to tell her not to continue, but she carried on. "There...there is a black hole outside the sphere's atmosphere. A sight that was foreseen by the Elder Amber–"

"A what!?"

"A black hole. We have discovered that there is a way of neutralizing this threat but Lord Zane has–"

"What Elementalist Acarlie means to say is that both ourselves and Lord Zane are currently working together in finding a solution to this problem. This is why we ask about his latest attendance at this council. This is also why it is very important that we speak to the High Elders," Zahied quickly butted in. Acarlie had already said too much but he thought he could at least stop the council turning against them by telling them the truth of Zane.

"What would the High Elders have to do with this?" the tigian asked.

"This is something that we cannot share with this council. My apologies, but these matters have been given to the kings and presidents of the world. We don't wish to alarm anyone here. This a minor predicament that will soon be resolved, but we need a small piece of information from the High Council first."

"But what of this black hole? If this is outside the planet's atmosphere then surely this means planetary devastation?" the aeomon now asked.

"I'm sorry, but this matter is beyond this council and may only be discussed by the leaders of the countries of Sphere. I assure you this is nothing to be alarmed about and this matter will be resolved very soon, ladies and gentlemen. As for the army, it is a known fact now that the Feydon troops have invaded the cities of Hiro and Toshiro and the small town of Mecroyles. This is a matter that the presidents of Calmeron and Magna and the King of Racoves have already discussed and have already made their decisions on how to deal with the actions of Queen Angel. Please forgive Miss Acarlie for bringing up these foreign affairs but you have scared her into a panic."

The speech seemed to work, everyone's concern now died down and the attention now turned back to Acarlie, who now felt as if she had shrunk in her seat. She quickly bowed. "Yes, forgive me. I am only an elementalist and my contributions to this table should concern nothing more than my pilgrimage."

Prime Minister Sarah Celadore now sighed. "Well, I'm glad that is now settled. If this matter you speak of is true then I sincerely hope you and Lord Zane find a quick solution for this. I hope that everyone at this table understands the measure of concealment this table must now keep. Something like this must never be revealed to the public. But I'm afraid Prime Minister Tigian Cecil Vurbute is right, an audience for yourselves and the High Elders may be beyond our abilities, but we shall certainly try though. As for the matter of Elementalist Acarlie and the C.E.L., after talks with Lord Zane I see no problem with allowing Acarlie into the C.E.L. Even if it is just a few exhibition matches. There will be no deaths involved and that means Acarlie be able to represent Eloma safely. We haven't had a representative from Eloma in over a decade now, this will enlighten the spirits of Chippenham and all of Sphere. Will you accept our proposal Acarlie?" Sarah asked.

Acarlie bowed. "Of course. Thank you Prime Ministers and thank you having me here today."

"You're very welcome and I look forward to seeing you in battle. I hear there is about to be a very special event that will be taking place soon at the stadium. It would benefit you to compete in this event and show the world your abilities."

"I will, Prime Minister Celadore. Thank you."

Kaza was waiting for them outside when the three of them left.

"So how did it go?" he asked.

"I don't think we can speak to them just yet," Val said.

"No thanks to you," Acarlie snapped again.

Val turned.

"You can't just blurt out what's on your mind like that, Val! Those people are the very council that decides on divides. Having a human there who speaks to them in that way makes it look bad for the rest of them. You have to understand that even your presence there is something that is recorded by the other creatures. If one person does something it reflects the whole species to the rest of them."

"Okay, I'm sorry, Acarlie. I just felt like it had to be said."

"Well, it didn't. Zahied was handling that fine. By the way, thank you, Zahied. I'm glad you were with me then."

"That's okay, Acarlie. Although I have to say that probably wasn't a good idea mentioning the real intentions of our stay to the council."

"I know, I really wish I'd kept my mouth shut, but they kept digging into my pilgrimage and reputation."

"Well, they would do that, especially Cecil. Zane is a tigian and so the Prime Minister of Tigians would always take his side."

"I guess so."

"So what can we do now?" Val asked as they started to walk back.

"I don't know about you but I cannot take no for an answer. If we cannot make an appointment with the High Elders then I'll have to make my own appearance." Kaza said. "We know how important this is and whatever is so important that we cannot see them can wait. If this is for the planet then we're going to have to intrude a little on elder affairs."

"What do you mean by that?" Acarlie asked now.

"While you are in your battles, Acarlie, I'm going to the Elder Temple where the High Council will be and I'm going to find them myself."

"There's no way you will be able to walk straight in there."

"That's why the mute aeomon is coming with me. We're going to break in there if we have to."

"You can't do that!" Acarlie protested.

"Yes I can, Missy. Your appearance in the C.E.L. will be all the distraction needed to pull this off. Zahied, you should come too since you're a caster, Midia will also accompany us."

"What about me?" Val asked. "I should come to."

"No, Val, you're staying with me," Acarlie ordered.

"But what if they need me? This sounds like a mission where they need that extra person."

"That is true, maybe your help would be needed," Kaza said.

"Val!" Acarlie held tightly on his elbow and pulled him away from earshot. "I don't want you doing this. They can do whatever they like but you're my guide. You should be with me while I battle."

"But–" Val started.

"No, Val. I won't let you. Not this time. This time you're staying with me. If they need the help then they have a ship of pirates. Please, Val."

Val looked down at her, her eyes reflected the hideous scar across his face and reminded him of their last argument. His memory flashed and he remembered what she went through last time he disobeyed her and now her eyes screamed for him to cooperate. He knew there was only one answer this time.

"Okay, I'll stay. I'm sorry."

"So what are you doing then, Val?" Kaza called back.

"You guys can go ahead. I'm going to stay with Acarlie. I'm her guide after all so I should start acting like one."

"Thank you," she whispered to him while they caught up.

"It still concerns me though that Zane was here before us," Zahied mentioned.

Kaza looked over and thought for a second, "This would explain his absence in the Donolan invasion. After it all happened Rezosa reported to me that she intercepted a fallen ship of the Feydon fleet. She squeezed information out of the officer on board and reported to me afterwards that Zane was nowhere on that field."

"So what does that mean? Did he know we would be coming here?" Acarlie asked.

"I think that is a possibility. If what Kaza says is true then we can't afford to believe that this is a coincidence. He must know our next move too. He is already a step ahead of us. We should hurry to the council, who knows what he has already told them. This could explain why we cannot see them so easily. He could have told them we were coming and made sure we could never seek the information we need to catch up with him," Zahied added.

"Then he could already be here, right?" Val asked. "They said he was here last week, didn't they? So where is he now?"

Zane stepped down from his personal one-man skyship, a mini version of the large people-carriers that easily transported him around the world. Still large enough to carry enough fuel to cross the oceans and with a fancy auto-pilot function to keep the ship flying if he needed to rest but small enough for the thrusters on the bottom to shoot him across the ocean faster than any ship could. Many rich ambassadors, and especially elemental lords, used this means of transport but it was far too expensive and rare for normal people of Sphere to get hold of.

The gloomy sky of his surroundings suggested autumn was now on its way and an impending rain was only an hour away when he arrived at his destination. A little buzz went off on a device on his wrist and when he saw what it was he pulled a small earpiece out of a pocket of his cloak and fitted it in his ear. He then turned his attention to a long, fitted device that covered his forearm. He found a tiny catch, unclipped it and fingered the edge to locate a concealed, paper thin plastic film, which he pulled out, unwinding it from the wrist device until it could go no more. Once at the end it clipped out and held its position while he held his arm out. This plastic film was a new amazing invention of the humans and posed as a touch screen monitor that folded and rolled up like paper. The screen lit up and he pressed a button with his other hand and a face appeared on the screen. He finally pressed a button on his earpiece and opened the link so he could hear the voice of the person.

"Good afternoon, Master," the face on the screen said.

"Miles," he answered coldly.

"I'm reporting that I am ready and in position like you ordered."

"What of the elementalist?"

"I tried selling her to the Bastard Camp Master but she escaped. I'm sending you the information you asked for though."

A small beep sounded and a tiny icon appeared on his screen. Zane's face lit up.

"Excellent. You have done well, Miles. I was right in choosing you."

"Thank you, Master. I must ask though if it is necessary to leave me here. I'll be waiting here for days, even weeks. Why don't I–"

"You will do as I order you to, Miles. Where is my queen? I trust you have been obeying me and keeping her entertained as I ordered."

"I have, Master. I believe she is falling in love with me though. Is this a problem?"

"No, this is exactly what I want. Now she won't be following my movements so much and will probably start chasing her own selfish desires. Just wait where I have commanded you to, Miles, and keep me informed on your progress."

Miles sulked a little here but nodded. "Yes, Master."

"Good," Zane said and turned the monitor off and rolled it back into the device fitted to his arm.

"Ah, if it isn't the Elemental Lord Zane!" called a familiar voice and he turned and smiled when he saw the face he was hoping to see.

"Ah, Elder Argo. It has been so long, how are you, my old friend?"

He hugged the old elder in their greetings and Argo started walking him into the town he hadn't seen since his first pilgrimage before he was Elemental Lord.

"It pleases me to finally see your face again, Zane. What brings you here?"

"I actually just wanted to visit all the places I did in my pilgrimage again, Argo, and maybe see what talent you are training nowadays."

"In that case, Lord Zane, I have an excellent pupil here who is training in the stadium at the moment. He would be thrilled to spar with you."

"It would honour me, Argo. Please take me to him."

Elder Argo walked him across the town and into the small elemental stadium where a young man was under the grey sky training by himself.

"Barry!" called Elder Argo.

The young ginger man looked over to his master and, to his surprise, the Elemental Lord standing beside him.

"I have here Elemental Lord Zane, who wishes to spar with you."

Barry knelt down. "I…it would honour me, my lord."

An evil grin appeared at the side of Zane's mouth as he admired his plan. His hands started to glow with fire as he concentrated on his elements and glared down with a look of devastation and destruction in his eye at the young man bowing before him.

7

The Archer moved with speed and grace regardless of the weight it carried. Clutching onto its backpack tightly and was equipped with its bow, still with its two knives tightly attached to its chest and its ice-axes tied and attached to its forearms. Its tight robes masked it from any eyes and its route to the skyship led it above ground level where eyes could not see. It was now late, the moonlight shone down and cast long shadows that it expertly made use of as it ran across the rooftops of the industrial part of town.

It hopped over pipes, climbed down fences and dashed from one shadow to another and soon the leo was back in its sights.

Raiden was stepping onto the skyship beside Zoudiva. The ship had been hastily provided by the President of Angland as soon as he heard the leo was in hospital and was the target of Feydon forces. Also, since Raiden was a member of the Scarlet Arise and a guide to Elementalist Acarlie, whose team had helped in the protection of his capital city, the president felt it necessary to help the wounded leo back on his journey.

"How long will this journey take?" Raiden asked the representative of the president.

The human looked up at the large cat. "This is a fast ship, leo. Maybe even the fastest there is and can ensure you get to the city in three days. You will find this ship to your liking. After the prototype ship your crew now possesses was originally stolen the ideas used for the Scarlet Arise have been recycled and used again. This ship uses the same aerodynamic build and is a slightly smaller ship so the weight would make it faster. Unfortunately it does not have all the same capabilities as its predecessor. For instance, this ship may only travel over the water and cannot sail on top or even swim underneath like the Scarlet can. This does mean, though, that more effort has been used in creating a faster, more effective ship. You could call this ship the Scarlet Arise Mark Two. Or since the first was only a prototype this could even be the true Scarlet Arise."

"Yes, I still don't understand why the president didn't take back the ship when we arrived in the city," Raiden said.

The man nodded. "Yes, I asked myself that too. I even questioned my own commander and leader on that topic and he assured me of a few reasons as to why he let the Scarlet go. Firstly, that you and your crew on board the Scarlet were with our brave soldiers led by the great Commander Chez in the Battle of Hiro. When the men finally returned home they told the story of your journey with them and helped each other as brothers in arms against Feydon. Secondly, when your crew arrived, and just before the attack of our city, the captain of your crew had a private word with the president about keeping the ship in payment for using it and its forbidden weapons against the attack. He also gave the president the knowledge of the forbidden weapons so we ourselves could manufacture them if ever they were used against us."

This shocked Raiden. "So Angland now has the knowledge of using cannons? These have all been forbidden since the extermination of my race."

"Yes. This is true. The president expresses that they will be made in secret and used only as a means of defence if ever they are used against us. Thirdly, after your captain bought the ship off the president, he let it go because he believed it was now obsolete anyway, inferior to the ship you stand on now."

"So what is the name of this ship?" Raiden asked.

"This ship is named the Soaring Grace, the heir to the sky."

Raiden nodded in approval as he stepped inside. "It's a nice title. But is it truly the answer to the Scarlet Arise?"

"Well, my friend. Would like to see for yourself?"

The ship was beginning to fly away. The ship's doors began to close as the last of the crew boarded so nobody saw a quick, dark figure chase the ship as it began its descent and dive for the cargo doors as they lifted, hauling itself up and entering the ship.

The Archer wasted no time and immediately found a dark corner of the cargo hold and started lifting up the floor tiles and sliding underneath the ship's walking space using shafts and crawl spaces to hide away. It finally found the engine room. There were members of staff all checking the engine and ensuring the ship's safety and it used its expert skill to slip past them until it found itself under the ship's engine and in a small room, secluded and dusty. It knew no one would ever come down this far. No one ever did.

It laid down its backpack and bow and sat thinking. The sound of the engine was a terrible droning noise but it was something it would have to deal with. The leo was still unreachable and it knew it now needed to wait for at least three days. It needed food and water.

Raiden was below deck with Zoudiva by the time the ship was fully in the air and they were on their way to meet up with Acarlie.

"I hope my master and Acarlie are safe," Zoudiva croaked and sat down with his head in his paws.

"Don't worry, brother. I'm sure they are fine. There is a monitor here on the ship which will broadcast the

Chippenham League tomorrow. We have been given permission to watch it. That way we can know for sure."

"Can I get you anything, sir?" a porcus employee approached and asked them.

"No. We're fine, porcus. Thank you though," Raiden gestured.

"Very well then. You will be sleeping with the rest of the crew in the cabins below. You may relieve yourself whenever you see fit."

The porcus bowed to them and left them to their peace; it was late for him too and the last of his duties were now fulfilled and he too could relieve himself and climbed down some stairs towards the crew's cabin when he heard a rustling from underneath the stairs. No one could enter these and so he believed rats or vermin had maybe nested there. He walked down the corridor and to a cupboard and pulled back the wall to poke his head in to see what was there. In a flash his life was over: a clawed hand reached out and grabbed him, silencing him immediately and yanking him behind this wall before it was put back in place.

The shadowy archer slit the porcus's throat and began dragging him back to its den under the engine where its bow and backpack were. The Archer now stripped the porcus down, talking a large plastic sheet it had in its backpack it often used as a cover from the rain and laid it down underneath the porcus, and began cutting the deceased pig open and feeding on its meat. This would last it the journey.

The day of the big event finally came. They only had to wait until the end of the week and suddenly the city was buzzing with excitement. News of not only a new elementalist but an elementalist that hasn't journeyed this far away from their home in over a decade had the city full of enthusiasm and anticipation. People flooded in from all over the country and the heart of the city was now brimming with a mixture of great creatures, all congregating in harmony to watch the sacred elementalists' battle. Within hours the stadium was full and even some smaller side stadiums were also packed and still the people of Sphere flooded in and filled up the national park outside. Just like all the other stadiums, large monitors were set up outside for the non paying customers and the unlucky souls who couldn't get a ticket in time would watch from the outside and cheer on their favourite elementalist. It wasn't just the arrival of Acarlie either that had the city excited, but for the first time in years they had two different journeying elementalists arrive at the same time from different cities.

Acarlie was concentrating in meditation in a secluded room in the stadium. She could almost feel the walls vibrating from the crowd and tried to block out all thoughts and stresses of her pilgrimage. Somewhere out there still was Sheeria, her closest friend and guide, and her other two guides, Raiden and Zoudiva. She wished and prayed they were okay and were on their way to find her. Her thoughts sat on her mind like a weight and all she could do was try to relax and lift this burden from herself and thank Sphere Val was still here for her. *At least this is the C.E.L.,* she thought, *at least there will be no death here.*

These matches will only be exhibitions for her pilgrimage and so she was in no real danger, which was a relief. She didn't think she could handle fighting for her life again. She still did not know what was going on in her mind, she was still unaware of how she had killed Elder Khan back in Selodia. She was also still scared of what was happening to her. No one had spoken to her about the rescue of Val either; she remembered walking up to the gates, she remembered telling Kaza and the crew she would go in alone to save him but then her mind went blank and she woke up on the Scarlet Arise, Val was safe and the Bastard Camp was gone, and nobody said anything. Were they scared? Did they even know? Something was inside her and she was starting to fear the worst but as much as it scared her, she knew this wasn't the time to worry. Her battles would start soon and she needed to clear her mind. She sighed as she realised this negative thinking ruined what effect the meditation had had and she started again.

The door was knocked and she opened her eyes. "Yes?" she said.

Val opened the door and poked his head in. "There are two people who would like to speak to you, Acarlie. They say they are elementalists."

She stood up. "Okay, Val, send them in."

Val nodded and opened the door. A red-haired human female walked in and shook Acarlie's hand.

"Hello, Miss Acarlie. My name is Vix, I am one of the elementalists of the C.E.L. It's great to finally meet you."

Vix was a little shorter than Acarlie and wore traditional elementalist garments. Before Acarlie's time the female elementalists would wear kimonos; she herself used to train in them when she was young but her own master, Argo, decided the garments weren't practical when fighting any more. She did still wear some when not in battle as she always did like the comfort of wearing them and respected the elementalist who still wore them in battle. Vix looked to still hold up the ancient traditions with honour and respect, Acarlie admired that. Her kimono was cotton and silk with sleeves that hung down like capes from her arms; green as summer grass with dashes of red to match her long auburn hair. The kimono reminded her of her own white dress that she would wear whenever she presented herself to important people on her pilgrimage and she wondered if Vix's was green also to represent her element.

Acarlie blushed a little. "You must forgive me, Elementalist Vix, but the records of the C.E.L. are not really shown much to the other elementalists and so I do not have any knowledge of your pilgrimage."

Vix just smiled. "Well, I am an elementalist from Delta."

Acarlie gasped. "Delta? The second element of Feydon? The Natural Element!"

Vix chuckled and held out her hand and Acarlie watched as her hands turned to a grass green and a rose appeared to emerge from her skin and rest in her hand. "Yes, Acarlie, the correct term is the Element of Nature. Delta is the second school of Feydon. I have been waiting a very long time to speak to someone like you."

She handed the flower to Acarlie for her to examine the sharp thorns in the stem. "Why me?"

"Eloma is the second school in Racoves to Hiro, yes? The Element of Wind has always been undermined by the Element of Water just like Delta has undermined the Element of Fire. We are like two younger sisters of two great countries. Each of us is always in the shadow of our two opposing older siblings, Water and Fire. It pleases me that an elementalist from Eloma has come out from the shadow and is showing the world what the Element of Wind is capable of. Just like I did all those years ago now."

"Thank you, and yes, we do have some things in common. When were you on your pilgrimage?"

"Twelve years ago now. My journey took me from Delta to Mecroyles, Hiro, Toshiro and finally here, where I decided to stay."

"So you already have four elements?" Acarlie smiled.

"That's right, I specialise in Natural but I also train in Ground, Water and Diamond. I hear they are the ones you have under your belt too, and Electricity if I'm not mistaken?"

"Yes." Acarlie blushed again.

"Then I can't wait to see you battle, it will be a pleasure to test your skills against mine. Hopefully we can have a battle the C.E.L. will never forget."

"Are you trying to make friends again, Vix?" said a voice from behind and Vix suddenly sighed and turned around to introduce Acarlie to a male elementalist. He was a tall and handsome man with broad shoulders, long arms with large hands. His eyes were a misty grey and his hair ink black, similar to Acarlie's hair but thicker and much shorter, shaved from behind his ears and cropped on the top. He stood wearing a shirt which was purposely tight to show off his chiselled chest, abs and biceps. It also displayed his sponsor's logo. The man looked like he could fight a leo; towering over the short Acarlie he was over six feet tall and had looks to make even Rezosa blush.

"Please ignore Sharcole. This is his way of being friendly. Unfortunately they don't teach such manners in Alpha."

"Alpha? So you specialise in the Element of Fire!?" Acarlie gasped.

Sharcole grinned, loving the attention, and Vix continued, "Yes, this is the current champion of the C.E.L."

"Well, I *do* come from Alpha, Vix. That seems to be a winning city these days." He grinned egotistically.

"Wait a second," Val now said from behind them, leaning up against the door, overhearing the conversation. "I thought Zane was the elementalist from Alpha."

"Well, of course he is. This is why I went on my pilgrimage. I had no chance of beating Zane ever, the tigian even trained me. So my best chance was to become the best in the C.E.L. I went around Sphere knowing full well that I could never hope to become the E.L. so I went to Mecroyles, Hiro, Donolan and even Eloma." He winked at Acarlie. "I didn't bother with Delta and Lachine since I think they are weak elements."

"Arrogant bastard," Vix stated bluntly. Acarlie saw now another reason why Vix wanted to see an elementalist in her shoes compete like she did. This Sharcole clearly always gave her a bad time, calling her home element weak.

"I would have liked to visit Toshiro though," he said, ignoring her.

"If you didn't like the weaker elements why did you go to Eloma?" Acarlie asked now. She knew very well that her element was strong, but for the rest of the world, and in the history of its origin, Eloma was always considered the weakest of elements.

"It was just close. Who did I fight there again? Tristan? Yeah, that was it, Tristan. Whatever happened to him?" Sharcole asked.

"He was murdered and eaten by demons in Plainess," she said bluntly.

His face suddenly dropped. "Oh, I'm sorry. What happened?"

"It's a long story. Lachine's elementalist was a fake. The President of Isolies stole the magnetism trait of my school and infested a linking city between our two schools with lobotomised aeomon. This is why an elementalist from Eloma hasn't been seen in ten years."

Both Vix and Sharcole looked pale in the face now. "Oh my gosh, that's terrible. So what happened?"

This time Acarlie stepped forward and looked Sharcole in the eye intimidatingly on the behalf of Vix. "I cleared the city of the demon aeomon and destroyed the Elementalist of Lachine. That school and its whole element are now no more."

But Sharcole smiled when she said this. He grinned. "Great! It looks like I will finally be facing some real competition then. I can't wait. Remember though, Acarlie, I already have the Wind Element and so know all your tricks already. And I already know that you are not as strong as your story says you are. I have here another elementalist who has also just started her pilgrimage. I believe you two know each other."

Acarlie looked puzzled but someone with a familiar face stepped through the door. She was slightly taller than Acarlie and wearing a chocolate brown, long sleeved shirt and black leggings with small, subtle yellow lines of electricity. Her hair was black like Acarlie's but tied back into a long ponytail that hung over her shoulder. Her eyes were as blue as the sky and she sported the long, light brown tail of an aeomon.

"Electra!"

"Hello again, Acarlie," said the aeomon elementalist she had previously fought in Donolan.

"Electra has been telling me about your battle, a battle in which you both died, I believe. Two equally faced elementalists. I can't wait."

He ushered Electra in to catch up with Acarlie and pulled Vix away from them.

"We'll leave you to it. Just be ready for the arena in an hour, the crowd is waiting."

The door closed and the two journeying elementalists stood facing each other once again. Each one looked as scared as the other as the thumping of the crowd within the stadium now sounded louder.

This was new for Electra, Acarlie could tell. Just like her she had been almost imprisoned in her home and schooled until she was ready to leave on her pilgrimage.

"Please sit down, Electra." Acarlie smiled seeing the discomfort in her face. "Are you okay?"

"I'm fine," she said. "Just nervous. This is my first time away from home."

"I know that feeling," Acarlie smiled. "You'll be fine. So why are you here if you don't mind me asking? You came straight to Chippenham. Why not learn some different elements before coming here?"

Electra looked over to her, "Because I died in our last battle, Acarlie. I killed you and you killed me. When it was over I realised I never wanted to go through that again. I couldn't stay home any more, especially since Donolan was invaded, and I don't want to go through that pain again. I don't want my guide to go through the pain of being an alanode. So I decided I would come here to the C.E.L. It will be safer here and I can represent my element in peace without dying again."

She then looked puzzled as she worked something out and looked back to Acarlie.

"Wait, isn't this why you're here? Don't tell me you're only stopping for just a while?"

Acarlie sighed and nodded. "I'm sorry, Electra."

"Don't you remember our fight?"

"Only too well."

"Then you remember the pain, the fear, the thought that your loved ones will live on without you?"

Acarlie remained silent.

"Why?" Electra asked.

Acarlie bit her lip; Electra wasn't allowed to know. "To become the Elemental Lord."

Electra frowned, as though she saw Acarlie's lie, and put her head to the wall behind her and together they listened again to the crowd.

"Females and males of all species of Sphere! Humans, elders, tigians, porci, aeomon and ursas! Welcome to the greatest show of elementalists on the planet!" the ceremony announcer's voice called from the speakers to the audience.

"Once a week we show you battles of great elementalists within the C.E.L. but today, to celebrate the arrival of not one but two new elementalists, we want to give you something special. Thank you all for your attendance on this short notice. Today we have a very special knock out tournament with different stages for the elementalists!"

Val was seated in the arena looking down at the empty, dusty floor of the large arena. He was seated next to a male aeomon who was Electra's guide. His name was Felix and he was not only Electra's guide but her partner too. Not being able to handle the fact that the aeomon he loved would be sent out into the world to her eventual death he committed himself to being her guardian to see her safe and was even the one responsible for nudging her into her decision to remain in the C.E.L. Now that she was safe in the C.E.L. he was relieved and now only concentrated on supporting her from a distance like every other guide there.

Having not spoken to anyone the aeomon was quiet at first but found Val was an easy person to talk to since they shared something in common, and they soon were talking like friends.

"So how far have you travelled?" Val asked as he paid for two cups of coffee from a seller making her way through the stands.

"Actually this is the farthest I've ever been. I once went to North Angland when I was young. Went on a holiday with my parents near the Anglish desert, but other than that I've stayed near the elementalists to help in their training. Have you ever been there?"

136

Val laughed as he reminisced. "Me? Oh yeah. I've been there."

"Sounds like you have a story to back it up," Felix said.

Val chuckled again. "Yeah, I kind of got lost out there in the desert this one time. I had to carry my friend with me, he was like you, an aeomon I mean, well, an aeo-*man* to be exact."

Felix crossed his arms and raised an eyebrow, "You know an *aeoman*? I hate those guys, cutting off their tails like that. It's disrespectful to the whole of our race. Every aeomon should be proud of their tails, and not cutting them off to be more like humans."

"I don't think he meant to do it. He's lost his tongue too, the poor bastard. I think someone cut it off."

"His tongue or his tail?"

"Probably both, mate. He's not a bad guy, just had a pretty dark childhood, growing up in True Hiro. I went to his flat once, it wasn't something to write home about."

This suddenly made Felix change his tone and sip his coffee. "Someone cut his tail and tongue off, turning him into an aeoman? That must be pretty bad for him. So not only will his people resent him but he can't ever tell them differently. I take it back you know, I'm sorry for him."

"Now everyone please put your hands together for the elementalists that will be entertaining you for the next few hours!" called the announcer again and suddenly, down on the arena floor lots of bright rectangular lights split through reality like a door and through the light doors the elementalists appeared.

The crowd erupted in applause that echoed throughout the entire city. Acarlie and Electra stepped through side by side as well as what looked like another thirty elementalists, including both Vix and Sharcole.

Acarlie stood and looked at the crowd surrounding her above and felt blinded by the afternoon sun now beaming down into the centre of the arena.

"I never knew there were so many elementalists here!" called Electra over the noise.

"This is a special event, Electra. One that every elementalist in the C.E.L. is taking part in. There are elementalists from all over the world here, all having different elements fighting at once," the redhead Vix explained.

"Does this happen often?" Acarlie asked.

"Not very, last time we had something like this was last year after the Battle of Osiris. The people were depressed and we had to give them something special to lift their spirits."

"So what's going to happen?" Electra asked.

This time Sharcole answered and stepped forward. "You will find out soon enough, young one."

He stepped out and found his own space, held out his hands to the crowd and flexed his power by firing jets of fire from his palms.

Every other elementalist did the same after that, flexing their abilities in their own special way. Acarlie watched as they either held their hands out, summoning water from the air and holding it up for the crowd to see or turned their body to diamond. From these displays she could tell where each and every one of these elementalists came from. Some were from Donolan like Electra and were fizzing and cracking while they concentrated on the electric element they specialised in and some held their hands to the floor and commanded parts of the floor itself to rise up and form objects like shields as though the sphere beneath them was just putty to shape and mould to their desire.

"Now, introducing the two new elementalists! From

Donolan, Elementalist Electra, and for the first time in over a decade we finally welcome an elementalist from the small town of Eloma, Elementalist Acarlie!"

The two just stood there still side by side and watched as the crowd cheered their welcome, even the elementalists around them were now clapping, centring them into the middle.

"Nervous?" Acarlie asked her.

"Yeah...You?"

Acarlie smiled. "Yeah."

"Okay then. Now we are all ready! Release the Kingnines!" the voice bellowed, followed swiftly by the screams of the crowd.

"Wait, what?! Kingnines?!" Acarlie gasped as doors from around the arena now opened and a large pack of kingnines now stepped out. Tiger Wolves followed and marched beside them towards the group of elementalists.

"Everyone bunch up!" Sharcole cried in command.

"What's going on?!" Acarlie called in fear. "Kingnines are not allowed in E.B.s!"

"This isn't your league, Acarlie! This is the C.E.L.!" Vix called back as the elementalists now bunched up tightly together as the oncoming kingnines and the large stripy wolves closed in on them.

As the crowd screamed the elementalists shook their nerves and remembered their training. Some were new to this event, some were veterans and had experienced this different kind of E.B. Acarlie and Electra stood close to one another and watched what it was they had to do. Two male humans stepped out to take on the first of the kingnines. Standing in a low stance, ready for the attack the two readied their elements. The first kingnine pounced up. The first elementalist threw his hands to the ground and, like the floor was made of water, the ground morphed and rose up instantly into a rock that the kingnine fell straight into. Another tried to pounce around the new rock as it descended back into the ground as quickly as it appeared, but again the elementalist jumped aside and thrust his hand to one side and what was left of the rock broke away from the floor and struck the kingnine away. A Tiger Wolf now sprinted forward and jumped up, its clawed paws reaching up for the elementalist's head. He had to duck aside but was saved as his companion fired a projectile of water into the wolf, causing it to hit the floor and roll aside. His companion turned quickly as another kingnine tried swiping his feet and he punched the kingnine in its metal helmet but was tripped as the first kingnine took its opportunity and pounced on top of him, pinning him to the floor.

"I yield! I yield!" he quickly called out, expecting the kingnine to release him, but the kingnine did not listen but instead scratched his face with its claws then bit down into his neck.

"I yield! I–AHHH!" he cried, but now the other kingnine jumped on him too and bit into his arm and together the two kingnines started ripping the elementalist limb from limb.

"Noo! He yielded!" his partner cried, turning his attention from the kingnine and Tiger Wolf he had previously fought off and he too was subjected to the claws and teeth of the ravenous beasts who now sprang up and tumbled on him and started pulling the flesh away from his body with their teeth.

The whole crowd suddenly screamed in a new tone as they watched two elementalists being slaughtered and ripped apart, staining the beasts with fresh blood that excited the other beasts around them.

"As mentioned before, people of Chippenham, today is a very special event for the C.E.L., for today we bring in a new and exceptional rule for this one occasion! The rule of death!"

"What is this?" the elementalists started crying, watching their friends now far from being mauled by the beasts and now just pieces of fresh meat flying around them.

"This isn't supposed to be like this! This isn't why I joined this league!" they began to cry as now the fear of death was all too real for them and suddenly a fresh danger was upon them.

"Everybody calm down!" Sharcole tried to call to them and fired a ball of fire towards an approaching kingnine. "We can do this! Just stick together and fight them as one unit!"

Electra now started to shake. Acarlie looked down at her hand next to hers and noticed it was nearly vibrating and she became white from fear. Acarlie too was now frightened of what was happening but kept herself a little more composed and took Electra's hand.

"It's going to be okay, Electra."

She saw Electra wasn't even paying attention now, instead her eyes were shifting around the stadium and she started to weep. "Felix," she said as she started to tremble.

"What's going on!?" Val now screamed and stood up from his seat after seeing what everyone else was still watching. Another elementalist was now pulled away from the group and left screaming, being dragged away and torn into pieces.

"Electra!" called Felix, who stood by Val's side. All the other guides were now just as much tormented as Val but knew there was nothing they could do.

"We have to go down there!" Val cried, but was held back by Felix.

"This is the way it is, Val, remember your training. Remember your sacred vowels as a guide. We cannot intervene!"

Val knew he was not a guide like the rest were. His story of how he became one was unique and he knew what was really going on here. The guides were just as brainwashed as their elementalists, brought up with sacred promises and vows that were only made by the elders to stop them from saving the elementalists when they needed them. But since he was the only one who knew this he couldn't convince them of it.

A female tigian guide began to cry as another elementalist was killed by the beasts. Val couldn't tolerate this for another second and turned to them.

"Are you just going to stay here and watch your elementalists die!?"

An old, bearded man with a tear in his eye answered, "We *all* knew this day would come, son. This was the promise we made as guides. We would protect them outside the arena but inside the arena they belong to fate."

"Screw fate!" Val cried, catching their attention. "Screw all of you!"

"You're not going down there, son! We're not going to let you dishonour your elementalist by jumping in there. We'll bundle you down if we have to!"

More screams from the arena cried out and now the group was starting to break up as the elementalists started to fight back.

"You can't change anything, son! You just have to sit here and hope."

"Hope!? That's your plan? Hope!?" Val was completely stunned and turned to Felix.

"That's your aeomon out there, Felix! Your Electra!"

"I know, Val!" he cried back. The young aeomon was not used to seeing his beloved in danger like this and it was distressing him severely. "But what can I do!?"

"You can't change the rules!" the old man called again and made Val think.

"Yes we can. You can stop me from jumping in there but

you can't stop me from going up to the office of this place and beating the announcer until he changes the death rule. Sphere's divide, people, these are your elementalists! You're supposed to protect them! Right now they are in danger and you're going to sit here and watch!"

"You're not going anywhere, son!" the man called again and stood up to approach him. Val held his hand out and summoned his staff, which appeared in his hand and shocked the guides. "Just try it, pal! I'll break your face!"

The man looked shocked, more so by Val's trick, and hesitated. Val looked around again and saw these scared guides.

"I'm going to save my elementalist. Who's coming with me?"

At first no one answered but Felix was the one to step up. "You're right, Val. I can't go in there but I can stop this event. We were lied to. They promised us the C.E.L. would not have death involved. This is the whole reason why myself and Electra came here. I'm coming with you."

They both turned to go, when they were stopped again. "Wait!"

Val turned to see the guides now standing up from their seats; even the old man now changed his tune.

"The kid is right! We were all lied to. We have to stop this!" one called.

"Our elementalists need us!" another called.

Val looked to the old man to see him now change his mind, realising there was nothing in the rules and vows that stopped him from sabotaging this event. The man nodded to him. "Lead the way, son."

8

So how do you expect to pull this off?" Zahied asked Kaza as they peered around the corner of one of the buildings adjacent to the Elders' Temple.

Kaza was staring over to the temple standing tall and broad with a white domed roof, high concrete walls which were all too high for anyone to climb and only a large metal gate opening to a tunnel leading to the front door was the only way in or out. The High Council of Elders was in there somewhere and it was essential that they spoke to them. But this was no ordinary building they had to get into. This building was where the highest of all elders congregated. Entry would be no easy feat here.

"First tell me the security they have here. Is there any surveillance?"

"Elders do not use such human inventions. They have their own way around these things."

"That's good then. So can you do your old trick like you did before at the army camp?"

Zahied frowned. "Not with the elders. My tricks are based on simple elder techniques, techniques they teach infants. It would be pointless and embarrassing to try it here. The best I can offer here is knowledge since I study elders."

Kaza sighed and looked over to the mute aeomon, who was scanning the temple. Still having to wear the dark goggles in the sunlight to protect his eyes Dude was in deep thought. His skin was now starting to tan and look more like a normal person's and his new regime of exercise was now starting to show.

"What do you think?" Kaza asked and Dude shook his

head and bit his lip after seeing nothing he could use. He had broken into many places before but the building here looked very well secured, every wall was too high with smooth surfaces and with nothing to climb on. Opening the large gate and going through the tunnel looked the only way to gain any kind of access.

Kaza turned back to Zahied. "So what can we expect in there then?"

"Lots of guards and doors that lead to nowhere. It's possible that most of the rooms in that place will only be accessible by light doors. Those things the elders conjure to teleport them from one place to another. Otherwise they might be using certain tricks in there to confuse and disorientate us, maybe even kill us. Since we don't know where we are going I really don't think we should creep in there."

"Well, we have no choice here. What about you, Midia?" Kaza asked, turning to the second in command of his ship.

The dark haired pirate grinned and just pointed to the gated front door. "Remember when we had to steal the safe from the Ultra Soldiers in Decrenia just before the Battle of Osiris?"

"Yeah?" Kaza said. Suddenly a grin appeared as he remembered that day the pirates successfully managed to rob the most highly trained humans before they were slaughtered by Feydon. "It's not a very good idea out here though, Midia. These elders will be smarter than that."

"I'm sorry, Captain. I didn't know you had a better idea. Do you want to share it with us?"

"Watch your mouth, smart arse, I'm still your captain."

He then scanned the building one last time before turning to Dude and Zahied. "Okay then. The front door it is. Come on, guys." He stood up and walked across the empty street confidently with Midia beside him. Zahied raised an eyebrow wondering what Kaza was up to but Dude only jumped forward and caught up not wanting to be left behind.

"Look out!" one of Acarlie's neighbouring elementalists cried as the kingnines now took their chance and attacked, separating out the elementalists. The elementalists all tried to stand their ground as now the battle had begun, many were immediately turning to their abilities and elements. The diamond elementalists from Toshiro seemed to have the best defence against the kingnines by turning their limbs to diamond. But it meant they could not move so much and soon were completely surrounded by kingnines and Tiger Wolves. They resorted to crouching into a ball and concentrating all the could before they lost their concentration and turned back to skin and were immediately pulled in different directions by teeth and claws. Acarlie crouched down and shielded Electra while the other elementalists fought for their lives. Electra had now succumbed to her fear and was terrified of fighting these beasts.

"It's okay, I'm going to get you away from here!" Acarlie called and tried to take her hand and pull her to her feet, when a loud growl caught her attention. A large kingnine stood low, ready to pounce and presenting to her a full bed of sharp teeth and a look of murder in its eyes. She hesitated at first and could only shield her eyes, when it pounced and she fell back to the floor screaming. Only when she hit the floor the kingnine yelped, and she looked up to see it had been caught as it pounced by a sudden conjuring of vines and thorns now entangling it. The vines rose out of the ground and wrapped around the kingnine tightly, and in a flash, the thorns and vines whipped apart and the kingnine seemed to instantly rip apart with them, the sharp teeth of the thorns bit deep into its fur and the force of the sudden separation ripped the kingnine into pieces. It yelped instantly but soon only showered Acarlie and Electra with its blood. The vines disappeared back into the ground and Vix stood behind them.

"Fight them, Acarlie!" Vix cried turning her attention away from a wolf behind her, who pounced up for her hand. Vix quickly held her hand out and, like the elementalists from Toshiro, turned her arm to diamond, shielding them from the teeth, and struck the wolf away.

Everything around her looked hectic. Kingnines were mauling elementalists, elementalists were striking them back and battling them with any element they could use. Sharcole was the only elementalist here who had mastered fire and he was helping the weaker, younger contenders.

Acarlie's heart raced but she took a breath and tried to control herself and turned back to Electra. "Stand up, Electra. Fight with me."

She got up and concentrated, the atmosphere was electric but she remembered her previous battles with Zane and Khan and remembered feeling she had had more to worry about with them. These were only kingnines she tried to convince herself.

Two kingnines approached her and snapped at her. When the first jumped she raised her hand and with her ability to control magnetism she caught the kingnine by its armour. At first it yelped like a struck dog and she threw it straight into the second one, who only dodged and pounced on her. The heavy beast landed on top of her and she could only grab its head and try to push it back as it started snapping its mouth, trying to bite into her pretty face.

She screamed, the creature pressed its weight down on her but now Electra was up and she touched the back of the beast, jolting it with electricity. The shock, however, also zapped poor Acarlie on the floor but the beast now rolled aside, its metal armour, especially the metal helmet it wore, now seemed to smoke like it fried its brain. The beast was stunned and could not move.

"Are you okay?" Electra said and went to Acarlie, who felt just as limp as the beast.

Acarlie remembered this pain, this was the wrath of Electra, and remembered their last battle as soon as she experienced the familiar pain.

"I'm sorry, Acarlie," Electra told her whilst lifting her up.

Acarlie groaned and tried to stop her head from spinning.

Kaza was the first at the large, metal, black gates and at the sign marked 'Closed for tourists today due to C.E.L.'.

"I think it's closed today," Zahied said, stating the obvious.

Kaza only grinned and started ringing a small bell, pressing it every three seconds in a way annoying to the person on the other side.

"If they're really closed then they won't mind me doing this."

He kept ring for another half a minute then the two gates finally reacted and opened by command.

Kaza quickly turned back and nudged Zahied's shoulder. "When there's a will, ay?"

Zahied shook his head as they entered the tunnel. "They have probably already called the authorities on us, Kaza; we've just announced our arrival to the whole building. I take it you have more to your plan than ringing the doorbell?"

"I might," he countered.

The tunnel darkened the further they went in until

sunlight became distant and instead the tunnel was illuminated blue by multiple torches of blue flames on either side of the wall. The wall glistened with tiny blue crystals. Zahied explained to them that these were made of ground up plants. Acarlie and Val had witnessed a very similar thing when they were at the monastery in Aragorth. The flames, however, he needed to examine. The air felt denser the further they went, with an odour that felt a little discomforting, even worrying – like smelling gas when walking into a room.

"What is that?" Midia finally asked, which answered a quick question for everyone else, all wondering if it was just them that felt it.

They were now shrouded in blue, the tunnel had now taken all sunlight away from them and left them in only the stunning but cautious blue tint of the fire and illuminated walls.

Zahied inspected the torches and noticed they were all fuel powered. The answer came to him immediately.

"Suggestive Oil. I thought this stuff was forbidden."

"What's that?" Midia asked, but it was Kaza who answered.

"Damn it, woman, read your history some time. Suggestive Oil was what the elders used in the old wars and divides. It's like a harmless poison once in the air. We're breathing it in now and will be absolutely fine until we piss off the elders. Then, all the while we're breathing in this gas they can command us to do anything. This stuff was forbidden just like gun powder. I guess they saw it as still useful to protect their sacred temple. What I don't know is why they're using so much here. I can almost taste it in the air. Why so much and so obviously?"

"It's a warning and a promise," Zahied explained. "Remember some tourists come here. They're making sure everyone understands that once inside we play by their rules. We will be cured once we breathe in fresh air again and will be fine so long as we act accordingly."

Kaza sniggered. He still walked very confidently with a cheeky grin on his face.

"I hope you're enjoying yourself, Captain. We've just been given our first warning," Zahied said.

"Oh yes," he countered, with a childlike smile on his face, giddy with excitement. "Breaking into the most sacred of all places, breathing in a poison that has been abolished for a century. There's so much scandal about today, don't you think?"

"You really are enjoying this, aren't you?" Zahied asked again.

Kaza let out a single loud laugh. "Piracy can be exciting sometimes."

"And the other times?" Zahied asked finally, but Kaza now remained silent and led the way down the tunnel leading to the front door.

They all walked through the door into the giant temple to find a security guard there. A tigian stood before them with a halberd axe at his side.

The temple was massive, with artwork engraved on the concrete decorating the room with pictures of old elders and telling stories of previous elder victories. Concrete pillars and wooden beams supported them and a stained glass mural domed the ceiling with lights behind it drawing the attention of any visitor straight away.

"The temple is closed to the public today, sirs. Can I help you?" the tigian said blocking their path. He already looked irritated. Kaza guessed that it was he who had answered his call when he rang the bell.

"Yes, you can," Kaza said, looking around at the empty hall and the doors around them. Kaza thought it a little strange that he was the only guard here but continued on. "I was having an argument with my friend here," he said, referring to Dude. "And he tells me that," he pointed to the first door to his right, "that room over there is actually a secret elder brothel."

The tigian looked over and raised an eyebrow. "Is this some kind of joke?"

"No, not at all. I just wanted to prove him wrong."

The tigian clutched onto his halberd tightly in frustration and was about to threaten the captain when he continued.

"Look, we'll go. It's not a problem. Just please, tell my friend this is not where they keep secret elder gang bang sessions, in the last place people would ever suspect."

The tigian sighed, pan faced. "No. It's just a storage cupboard."

"What? There's just stuff like utensils and cleaning stuff in there?"

"Yes. Just normal items."

Kaza turned to Dude. "You see! I told you."

Dude blushed and shrugged.

"Come on, guys, let's go...Oh, and one more thing, sir," Kaza said, turning back and quickly whipping out a pistol he had concealed behind his back and putting it to the tigian's head. The tigian knew exactly what this was and knew what it was capable of.

"Drop your axe and get in the cupboard."

Val was leading the charge of upset guides through the higher levels of the stadium. The hallways were high up on the top of the stadium and lined with glass windows that overlooked the gory battle still happening down below. To the elementalists and guides it was a horrendous display of lies and distrust by the promoters, and even the elders who arrange these battles, but to the audience it was just a more exciting battle and they loved the real intensity of the death rule and cheered even more for their favourite elementalists.

"Where do they keep them?" Val asked the other guides and was shown the way to the offices of the announcers but was stopped by Security.

"I'm sorry, sirs, but you cannot come up here. This is no place for the sacred guides, who are only permitted to use the designated stands where they can watch their elementalists."

Val stepped in front of the first few guards; the guides still outnumbered them though.

"We have to see the announcer and change the death rule," Val ordered.

"I'm sorry, but we cannot let you pass. Sacred vowels you all took mean you cannot ever pass these lines without breaking the oaths you made as guides and therefore eliminating yourselves and the elementalist you represent from these games."

This statement reminded all the guides of what it was they were actually doing, but it was Val who reminded them of why they were here. "Good. Take my elementalist out of these games if it means she will live."

This shocked the security guard – never had a guide done this before, going against his oath.

"But, sir, your elementalist–"

"Hold them down," Val ordered the angry guides behind them, who jumped forward and did as instructed, took down the guards and bundled them to the floor. Many other people who saw this suddenly stood back and watched the guides march through.

They finally found the office door in front of them. Val tried opening the door only to find it locked. He banged on the door at first and when no one answered he tried throwing his weight into the door and kicking it violently to open it.

"Stand aside," one of the tigian guides said and also started throwing his weight into the door. Eventually the door smashed open and there in the room was a cast of scared humans, all with their backs against the wall, white from fear as the angry mob stormed in.

"What is the meaning of this?" one of the announcers cried as Val grabbed him, kneed him in the stomach, knelt him down next to the table and smashed his head against the side of it, startling him.

"You! Change the death rule!" he demanded and again smashed his head against the table.

"Now!"

The others tried pulling him off but were held back by the other guides. Even Felix now stood forward and swung a punch for the announcer.

"You lied to us all! You promised us our elementalists would remain safe in the C.E.L.! Why have you lied to us!?"

The scared, now bruised man hesitated. "I'm only the announcer. I only call out the rules. I don't make them."

"Well, it's your voice that the audience takes notice of. Change the rules!"

"I can't, it's too late!" he cried.

"Why were they changed!?" Val screamed.

"The…the Elemental Lord was here last week. He said a new rule would be announced for this day if a certain elementalist should arrive. He said should this new elementalist arrive then this special event should welcome her. He ordered the new rule and even paid off the elders who manage the event to finalise it. Please don't hurt me!"

"Lord Zane ordered this?" the guides started questioning.

Val grunted. *Zane! I should have known he would be behind*

this. That bastard is always one step ahead of us. I guess this is just another idea to try and have Acarlie executed. I know she won't approve of me intervening, but screw it. I have to do this.

"I don't think this is right!" one called out. "Who are we to question the Elemental Lord? If he wishes this event then I think we are directly disobeying the E.L. by doing this, and that goes against everything we have ever sworn not to do."

Val ignored the sudden change of mind of his mob. "Where are the elders who manage the event?" he asked the announcer.

"In the next room, they are concentrating on taking the remaining elementalists to the next stage."

"Next stage?" he asked. "What next stage?"

The elementalists were now fighting more fluently, the kingnines' and wolves' numbers were now decreasing and the elementalists started to finally finish off the last of them. Vix had just finished striking a kingnine. Her arm had turned into a plant-like form and lots of buds and spores from the little bulbs on her hand flew into the face of the kingnine, blinding it, and with a diamond hand she struck the kingnine on top of the head to have it run away blinded and concussed.

"I think it's over!" called Sharcole, circling a whip of fire and whipping a wolf with it, setting it ablaze only to be extinguished by a nearby water elementalist who blasted it away with a jet of conjured water.

The beasts now realised they were outnumbered and started hesitating. Then as in all unsuccessful hunts regrouped away from the elementalists and took what meat they had made and took off with it, carrying arms and legs of the fallen back to their cells.

Electra had now also found her fighting spirit and

shocked the last one and sent it running, with Acarlie using the last move she had to blow a gale force wind in its direction and blow it away from them.

They all stood silent when they realised it was over, the crowd cheered and they started congratulating each other, when light doors started appearing.

"What's this now?" Acarlie asked.

Vix panted and straightened her back. "We made it to the next round. We just have to wait for the announcer now."

They stood silent and waited for the announcer to call their success but found themselves and the rest of the crowd waiting in eager silence.

"What's going on?" they started to ask.

Acarlie looked up at the top of the stadium where the elders and the offices of the event would be and wondered. She glanced down and into the stands and noticed Val missing and, more importantly, that the whole of the guide stands were empty. Her heart jumped into her throat.

"Oh, you idiot!" she cursed.

Again the door was crashed into and Val stormed into the elders' office to find them standing in meditation, giving the elementalists down on the arena floor the light doors to the next stage of the event. Val looked down and saw a tiny figure he recognised as Acarlie looking up at the window and searching for him in the stands where he should have been before walking into the light door with the rest of the elementalists and disappearing completely. Once the last one had walked through, the doors disappeared and from the ground many large monitors that had been hidden away rose up on metal arcs to show the rest of the tournament to the crowd in the arena.

The elders now opened their eyes and saw the angry

guide mob.

"Is there a reason why you have barged in here unannounced?" one asked calmly.

"Forgive us, elders, but–" one guide began to say but was cut off by Val.

"No. I'll handle this. What do you think you're doing!? Bringing in the death rule and killing off our elementalists? This is the C.E.L., right? I thought this wasn't allowed here?"

"The death penalty is not something unheard of here. I admit it has been a few decades since we last had this rule but never have we had sacred guides rudely intervening. You have to trust your elementalists."

"I do trust Acarlie. It's you I don't trust!"

This brash statement stunned the room. The elder was just as shocked as the rest of them. "You must be Acarlie's guide Val. We have heard of you before. It was you who intervened in her first battle in Lachine."

"An intervention that saved her life and I'm only doing the same now for the same reason."

"You do know we can punish Acarlie with this act and abolish her from her pilgrimage, and you know what that will lead to, don't you?"

Now Val was the one to hold his tongue. The elders, guides and humans present were all silent as the tension in the room could now be cut with a knife. Val, however, was the only one there who truly understood what this meant. Once an elementalist has gone against the rules they always terminate themselves; this was not a warning from the elder, this was a threat. Val also knew this was also a bluff. "No, you can't. This is only the C.E.L. and is a different league from her pilgrimage. You banish her from this league then she loses nothing but instead gets to keep her life. You can't threaten me with anything here."

"Val, maybe you should–"

"Shut up, Felix," Val snapped, silencing the interrupting aeomon while keeping eye contact with the elder.

"The death penalty has been introduced in this event by the E.L. himself. It is meant to provoke a real emotional response from both the contenders and the audience. This already has become a very famous event and it is already an exceptionally successful one since it has provoked the guides in a fashion like this. Think of what the audience is thinking right now. Now guides, because of this rule I will overlook completely the acts you all have committed today. You all love your elementalists and are protecting them in an excellent fashion by even challenging the elders themselves, but only if you return to your seats and remain there until the end of the event."

They all stood silent. The elder's words were seeping into them. Val was losing his mob.

"No, change the rule now!"

"The rule cannot be changed," the elder now said, raising his voice. "This whole event will mean nothing if the rule is called off."

"I don't care, call it off!"

The elder stood strong now. "I will not."

Val stared into the eyes of this stubborn creature. He knew he couldn't punish him, as he had the announcer. The guides would turn against him but he also couldn't back down, he had to intervene.

"You have no idea what you are doing today!" he warned, stepping closer to the elder. He remembered what Raiden had taught him about striking fear into his enemies and stood toe to toe with the elder until his scarred face was right in the elder's.

"If you won't change the rule then you will send me in there."

"You cannot save your elementalist, Val."

Val stood firm and still, dominating with his presence, and repeated, "Send me in there."

"Val, let it go, it's over! There's nothing we can do!" the elderly guide called to him.

"You may be willing to give up so easily on your elementalist but I'm not, so let me do my own thing here!"

The elder thought about Val's command.

"You have to send me in there, and I'm not leaving until you do."

The elder finally considered his proposal before looking to the other elders and nodding. "Very well. Just know that this goes on Acarlie's record. She will never again be allowed in the C.E.L., where she could live out her days in peace," he told him and opened a light door for him.

Val stepped closer and before he walked in he turned back. "Who else cares for the welfare of their elementalist? To forget the rules and protect them, like you vowed?"

No one answered.

"Screw you all then, don't say I didn't warn you."

Felix then stood up. "I care for my Electra! I don't care about the rules. I just want her safe."

"Then follow me. We're going to get our elementalists away from this lying death trap."

"You realise what this will do though?" the elder finally asked.

"Actually, I think I'm the only one here who really *does* know what is happening here. Come on Felix, let's go."

Val didn't wait a second longer and in his impatience he stepped through the light door with Felix running behind him and instantly passed through to what looked like an abandoned warehouse. The ceiling was dirty and looked to have started to erode, the whole complex was dry and dusty. Brick walls were stained with old paint that now chipped away and covered the floor with the dirt.

As soon as Felix stepped through the light door it closed behind him and he stood beside Val and looked around this suddenly strange new destination.

"Umm, Val? Where are we?" Felix asked, now standing in disbelief, as was Val.

Val cursed when he suddenly realised what had happened. "We're not in the stadium any more."

"So where are we?"

"Probably somewhere out of the way where we can't interfere with the event. Damn!" Val smacked his head and cursed his impatience and his stupidity. "We should have brought an elder in with us. That way we could at least have forced him to create another door to the event."

"So. Where are we?" Felix asked again.

"I don't know," Val answered. "Let's just find a way out and get back to the stadium."

Felix looked around and suddenly panicked when he noticed the four high, brick walls surrounding them and how dark this big empty room was. The only light let in came via some small, dirty windows high above them that only just lit the room.

"Umm, Val. There are no doors."

Val jerked his head around and realised Felix was right.

Four walls surrounded them. They were trapped inside. Val walked up to the wall and leaned into it. "How could I be so dumb!" he cursed and cursed again before falling to his knees and sitting up against the wall in defeat.

Felix sighed. "I never thought the elders were capable of lying." But Val didn't answer but sat with his head in his hands.

"Fuck!" he cursed again.

9

Keppal was standing at the edge of the zeppelin, a wine glass in his hand and tourists and aeomon around him. The day after Sheeria spoke to her brother she was suddenly the centre of attention. News of Donolan's destruction reached tigian and aeomon ears and suddenly Sheeria was treated with more respect and the zeppelin was readied for their trip. Now a couple days into the air and she really had the chance to spend time with her younger brother with some joy and promises of how she would return once Acarlie had become the Elemental Lord. This of course upset Keppal as he knew she never would become the E.L., he would make sure of that. It broke his heart to stand there on a sideline and listen to Sheeria talk to her brother, a sibling she hadn't seen in somewhere around a century. He knew she had to die but the more he watched and listened the more this hatred burned in his chest. He felt like he was at war with himself. Lord Zane had specifically ordered him to kill these people and he trusted his lord, but the way she smiled seemed too innocent for her to be a threat to Sphere and he felt he couldn't sink to the level of the criminals he used to protect people from. He was after all a police officer and he tried to convince himself, but every time he tried to force his sense of justice into his mind he only remembered Dusty and his own bloodstained hands after murdering him. The thoughts became too much so he left to stand near the window with his glass and just stare out, the relaxing view of the calm ocean was all he had to soothe the battle in his mind.

This is all Val's fault. If he had never fought Lord Zane's servant then my team would have never been killed in the attack.

But maybe he was telling the truth? What if he was attacked? What if this Acarlie, Val and Sheeria are standing on the right side of justice and Lord Zane really is this menace? No, it can't be true! Zane is the Elemental Lord and is racing these terrorists to these cities to save them from this team of psychopaths. Why would Lord Zane want to destroy everything? It doesn't make sense! But from what I've seen...

"Damn!" he cursed and pressed his head against the window. He hated this.

"Thank you," said a voice behind him. He turned to see the smiling face of Sheeria standing behind him. He drank the contents of his glass and looked back out of the window.

"What for?"

"For accompanying me on this journey. Without your help I don't think I would have had the chance to speak to my brother after so long. I am still worried for Acarlie but right now I feel I haven't been happier."

This only angered Keppal even more. *How dare she say that! How dare she put all this guilt onto me like this? She has to die but...*

"That's okay," he said in a low tone and looked into his empty glass, wanting more.

"Sheeria! Sheeria!" called her brother. "Come quick! You too, Keppal!"

She turned to see the sudden dire look in his eye. "What is it, brother?" she said as he reached her.

"We have a communal monitor set up in the lobby. There is something on screen that you must see."

"What is it?" Keppal asked, now feeling tense. Not knowing what was going on.

"There is a big event being broadcast from Chippenham. A massive Elemental Battle, several deaths have already been reported, but come see."

He led them to the lobby the crew and people on

board were all bunched into staring up at the big monitor. He made his way to the front and showed them. On the screen were two elementalists walking along a dark, narrow hallway. A box was at the top of the screen displaying their names and elements with a presenter's voice in the foreground.

"Isn't that your Acarlie?"

Sheeria looked up. "Yes, it is." She sighed, relieved, knowing she had made it.

Oh thank goodness. She made it to Chippenham, and with a guardian too. Maybe this means Raiden and Zoudiva found them? Maybe I'm the last one to arrive.

But the presenter's voice made her heart sink when he revealed the words on everybody's lips in the city at the moment: "Death penalty."

"Death penalty? Chippenham does not have a death rule! Why is Acarlie in this event? She knows there is nothing to gain from this. If the death rule has suddenly been introduced then why did she do this?"

Keppal just looked up at the girl walking, finally putting a face to the name. *So this human is Acarlie? Such a small and delicate thing. How can Lord Zane be afraid of this little thing? This makes things even worse. But at least I can hope that my job will be easier if she does die in this tournament. But what am I thinking? Wishing a small human's death like this? Why is this happening to me?*

He kept his thoughts to himself and stood still, staring up and watching this young, delicate terrorist walking down with her aeomon companion.

"Where are we going?" Electra asked. They had been lost for an hour now. Walking around aimlessly, alone and lost in what looked like a giant complex of metal walls and corridors stretching down for as far as they could see. They guessed they were below ground level because there were pipes all around them. Stretching all along the ceilings and sweating from heat. Steam clouded some parts of the hallway and the heat was starting to feel uncomfortable.

"We're going to find a way out of here, Electra. I don't know where we are but I don't want to stay here any more. The other elementalists are somewhere in this complex too and I don't want to run into any of them. This is still an E.B. after all and so we would have to fight them to the death and I don't think I can handle that at the moment."

Electra glanced up to Acarlie. Since they had teleported to this next part of the E.B. she seemed to take charge of the situation. She walked with a confidence about her but it came with a sense of confusion, fear and worry.

"There has been so much death on my pilgrimage, Electra. More than any other elementalist has ever seen. In the months that I've been journeying so much has happened already, and now this."

After this sentence Electra noticed how bad Acarlie was really looking; all this confidence was really a mask for the audience.

"Are you okay?" she whispered, walking past the cameras fixed to the walls and shifting over, watching them.

Acarlie put her hand to her head and tried to rub out a headache. "I don't belong here."

"What do you mean? Here in the C.E.L.?"

"No, I mean…Never mind, forget it."

She carried on walking with Electra tailing behind before she finally found a door and opened it. The room they were in was pitch dark.

"What's in here?" Electra asked.

"I don't know but this is the only room we have found since we got here. I'm taking it."

Electra stepped in before the door shut behind them

and for a brief second they were cast into darkness. The lights came on and they saw there was nothing in this sealed room but two doors either side and four, floating, sphere shaped cameras all pointing at them. The ceiling itself was a large monitor that flicked on and suddenly the roar of the crowd back in the arena was back with them, sending a chill down their spines in fear of what was coming next.

Back in the arena the largest of all the monitors present turned on its axis and sat horizontally above the arena ground and faced up so the whole of the stadium could now look down at the screen to see the two elementalists walk into this room side by side.

The C.E.L. had now become a whole day event and they had witnessed E.B. after E.B. of elementalists now battling each other. Many more were killed only for the amusement and cheering of their own fans. And now it was Acarlie and Electra's turn.

"*Oh, and now it looks like Acarlie and Electra have found their arena!*" the announcer called.

This monitor had cameras on the corners and presented the two elementalists a view of the crowd now looking down upon them.

"Oh, and now it looks like Acarlie and Electra have found their arena!" they heard the announcer call.

"*Acarlie, Electra! Can you hear me!?*"

Acarlie walked forward to the centre of the room looking up at the crowd; their noise was deafening.

She said nothing but the announcer continued, "*You have reached the second part of the event. In this stage there is only one exit. The door will only be opened once one elementalist has fallen. This is a specially-made room in which the elders have ensured you cannot use your elemental gift. You two will now face each other, the old fashioned way.*"

"Acarlie?" Electra asked, feeling fear creep back into her.

Acarlie felt it too and glanced back at her friend, but now her next opponent. "I'm only just noticing how barbaric these Elemental Battles are."

"Now remember, ladies. The death penalty is still present. The door will mechanically open once we see there is a winner. So, ladies, take your positions and begin!"

The crowd roared and left Acarlie and Electra to stand and stare into each other's eyes. They could both feel the tension in the room and see the look of desperation on the other's face.

"No, this is wrong!" Acarlie called and looked back up to the ceiling, "Myself and Electra have already battled! In Donolan we fought and I was announced winner after a sudden death call! It is against the rules for the same two elementalists to do battle for a second time after one has been declared the winner!"

"Acarlie, this is the C.E.L.! It is a different league to yours and therefore has different rules. Here two elementalists can battle as many times as they like!" the announcer called back. *"But don't worry, this does not affect your pilgrimage should you wish to leave, the events of the C.E.L. are separate from the progress of your pilgrimage."*

"What are we going to do?" Electra asked.

Acarlie sighed. "There's nothing we can do. I have no doubt they will keep us in here until we do as they say. We're locked in."

"But we don't have to. We can do nothing, and bore the crowd until they want to watch another battle."

The announcer heard this. *"I'm sorry, Electra, but should you not wish to cooperate then that goes against one of the first rules set upon your training by the elders. You will not only be excluded from the C.E.L. but will be expelled from the entire Elemental Order and you and your alanode shall walk the sphere shamed as a failed elementalist."*

"So much for 'events of the C.E.L. being separate from the progress of the pilgrimage'," Acarlie stated sarcastically.

"I guess that's the only law they abide by strictly."

"I don't want to become a failed elementalist!" Electra shouted. The instant fear was still conditioned in Electra and so the shame of her name was still a fate worse than death and would lead her to instant self-termination, leaving Felix to wander alone as an alanode, much like Ceaser, the alanode they had met earlier on their journey.

"Electra, it's okay," Acarlie said calmly and put her guard up. "Let's just get this over with."

Electra had to breathe to calm herself down but eventually put her guard up and faced her friend.

They stood there for half a minute staring at each other, the crowd chanted their names and screamed for them to fight but they just ignored this and tried to calm themselves.

"You know, one of us is going to have to throw the first punch," Electra said.

"Then be my guest," Acarlie said and welcomed her with a gesture to strike first.

"Okay...I'm sorry, Acarlie."

She struck Acarlie, and a good strike too, connecting with her cheekbone just above a pressure point to the side of her left eye. Acarlie staggered back and Electra didn't want to start again and so struck her again, kneed her in the stomach and struck her to the floor.

Acarlie's face instantly bruised and she held onto her cheek and tried to get up but Electra swung a kick and kicked the bottom of her jaw and sent her back to the ground.

"I'm sorry, Acarlie," she said as she turned Acarlie

around on the floor and threw more punches into the side of Acarlie's head.

The pain overwhelmed her, she cried as more strikes kept coming. The world became blurry and she had to act fast and wait for Electra's fist to raise before she rolled to one side and let Electra punch the floor. Electra yelped and Acarlie quickly got to her feet and slammed her elbow into Electra's nose, planting her on her back.

With the few seconds spared Acarlie staggered back. She was dazed from pain and needed a second before her vision came back and the pain in her temple subsided. She stepped back, still blinded and swollen, and reached back until she could feel the wall but by now Electra was back up and charging into Acarlie, spearing her into the wall and head-butting her. After the strike from Electra's head, Acarlie's thumped the wall and she couldn't do anything as Electra swung her own elbow into the side of her head again and sent her back to the floor. Acarlie rolled and tried to get some distance from her but she staggered like a dizzy child. So much pain in her head concussed and confused her. She tried to swing her arm to one side and use the wind element to force Electra back but when she failed to control the wind she heard the muffled sound of Electra ringing in her ears.

"Um orry Cary," and another strike was swung. This time she forced her arm up to block Electra's attack and grabbed her arm and pulled her towards her, stepped aside and threw Electra to slam into the wall and thrust kicked her in her back.

Electra screamed and turned again for Acarlie who now fought more offensively and began desperately trying to get Electra to the floor. In this fight Acarlie should have had the advantage since she was better trained, had more battle experience and as a human would always have a slight physical advantage over the aeomon. But since Acarlie had taken all this pain to her head she felt dazed and couldn't concentrate on her attacks as she wanted to. But she soon managed to fight back enough for Electra to slow down too and tend to her own pain.

The crowd still cheered them on while they took a couple steps back to each catch their breath. Acarlie wiped sweat and blood from her brow and gasped for breath, looking up to Electra, who was now holding onto her side and struggling to breathe.

Acarlie already felt defeated. Electra would kill her just like she did before. But she couldn't let her do this. Acarlie had to survive but killing Electra seemed too harsh. Electra was a fine elementalist, a strong fighter who held up the laws of the pilgrimage proudly. Sphere would do well to have an aeomon such as this as the E.L. but Acarlie couldn't allow her to live. If Acarlie wanted to continue on with her pilgrimage, if she wanted to save Sphere from this black hole and from Zane, Electra had to fall. She sighed and stepped closer.

With her guard raised Acarlie tensed and punched Electra, who retaliated and threw another punch and the fight became a moving symmetrical picture with each fighter swinging their fists and trying to knock the sense out of the other.

Acarlie finally predicted Electra's next attack and used it to her advantage, stepping aside and throwing Electra to the floor and she tried to slam into her but the nimble aeomon rolled aside and when Acarlie hit the floor, she dived on top of her and began punishing her with punches and elbows until Acarlie could take no more. The floor was stained with her blood and her eye was so bruised she couldn't see. She felt like Val must have felt when Miles assaulted him. She choked and tried to catch her breath back.

Electra was now crying, her tears falling down onto the mess that was Acarlie, and she threw one more punch that now weakened Acarlie to the point where she was defeated. Acarlie had lost and now could only lie there waiting to die.

Electra hesitated though. Looking down at what she had done to Acarlie destroyed her. She wept and cried, "I'm so sorry, Acarlie."

Acarlie could not answer, only try to breathe and endure this pain that defeated her.

"*You must finish her, Electra! To help with this the elders have now released the seal upon the room enabling you to use your elements again!*"

Electra began to cry and held onto Acarlie. "No!"

She lifted Acarlie up and buried her head in her shoulder. Acarlie had already beaten Electra, learned her element and now shouldn't even be in this situation. It was already announced that Acarlie was the better elementalist and here she was near death from Electra. She stood up and looked up at the crowd, who looked more upset about a lost bet than the death of Acarlie, but sure enough, like the announcer said, she could suddenly feel the electric element inside her once more. She wiped her eyes and turned back to Acarlie lying helpless on the floor. She held out her hand and saw a tiny arc of electricity flow around her hand and knelt down and put her hand over Acarlie's head, covering her eyes so she wouldn't have to see.

"Acarlie...," she whispered in her grief and felt the current of the element inside her.

"*Kill her*!" the crowd cheered as she screamed, quickly took her hand away from Acarlie's head and pointed it to the ceiling and suddenly the monitor exploded and its electricity reached down like lightning and into Electra, charging her. She stood up and instead of finishing off Acarlie and before the elders and announcer could do anything she dived across the room to the electronically locked door and slammed her hands into it and pulsed all the energy she could into it. She overcharged the door and the lock system and finally the door flew from its hinges backwards into a small room with towels and a sink there. Another door at the end was only wooden and could be opened easily. This was where the winner was supposed to clean up.

Electra turned back to the defenceless and defeated Acarlie now lying amid broken glass, scratches and cuts covering her, and picked her up.

"Come on, Acarlie, if they want to ignore the rule of re-facing two elementalists and lying to us then I'm going to ignore the death rule. There was nothing in our upbringing about going against the made up laws of the C.E.L. anyway."

She carried Acarlie over her shoulder and sat her up against the sink and began treating her wounds, giving Acarlie time to recover.

"Electra…," Acarlie whispered.

Electra shushed her. "It's okay, Acarlie. It's over now. We both made it alive so let's call it a draw again, yeah?"

"No, you won…you beat me."

Electra stopped. She had beaten Acarlie. Acarlie had made a great name for herself, killing Eliza, destroying Hiro's stadium, surviving an encounter with Zane, and she had defeated her.

This meant a lot to Electra but she just dabbed Acarlie's head with a wet cloth. "Let's just get you back on your feet, okay?"
Val was pacing up and down in the large hall they were trapped in. It was so silent there that his footsteps echoed. Felix was sitting up against a wall now and brushing the dirt from his tail.

"We have to find a way out of here. There probably isn't much oxygen in here and if there is it might be poisonous,"

Felix said.

Val was in a terrible mood now and still paced. "Don't be stupid, Felix. The air is fine, it's not the air we have to worry about, it's Acarlie and Electra."

He paced some more and still looked around at the room and shouted out, "I mean, what is the point of this building?! A warehouse with no doors? What possible purpose would this building be used for?"

"It's just a room, Val. I don't think it serves a purpose other than containing people like us," Felix suggested, but Val dismissed the idea instantly.

"Nonsense, if the elder wanted to contain us he would just have teleported us to prison or somewhere. Instead he sends us to what is basically a modern tomb. A big, dusty, dirty warehouse with nothing in it but dirty old storage shelves with nothing on them and a bunch of old junk and debris cluttering up the room! No one could possibly make use of this place if they are unable to enter it!"

"But some can enter this building, Val. Elders can with their doors they conjure."

"Yes. That's right. Tell me, how do these doors work?" Val asked now.

Felix looked confused at first. "Are you not a guide, Val? Everyone knows this. The elders can create doors that teleport them from one place to another; they have to visit the place themselves first to do so though."

This caught Val's attention. "So wait. If that's true then this building must have been created by the elders, right? Because no man or any other creature would be able to enter it without an elder."

"I guess so. What does that mean though?"

"Well, if that's true then it raises a question. Why would the elders need a building that only they have access to? And if the individual elder has to have once been on the other side then the elder who organises and manages the C.E.L. has been here once before."

"So?" Felix asked again.

"So...This warehouse has to have something to do with the C.E.L. Think about it. Only elders can come here, but not every elder. I bet that only the elders who manage the C.E.L. have access to this place. They must have needed it for some reason. There are no doors and only windows up so high that no one could enter, but if they did they would only find the place empty apart from the useless junk scattered around. Maybe this place was made for security reasons, or maybe this is where the elders would come to enter the arenas if they needed to."

"You're talking rubbish, Val. Elders won't need this empty building to enter the C.E.L. since they have light doors."

Val thought for a minute. "Maybe so, unless this place isn't for the elders to enter but for elementalists to leave. Maybe this place is where the elementalists come once they are knocked out of the tournament, or even a place where, if something should happen, humans and other species could enter and exit, say if there was an accident?"

Felix just put his chin against his knees and sighed. "If anything like either of those scenarios happened, Val, then the elders would use light doors. That way the secret arenas would be kept like that."

"Secret arenas?" Val asked.

"Yes. The light doors that our elementalists walked through would have sent them to the next part of the event, yes? That would be a separate complex, only elders know where it is."

"But what if there was a fire in this arena? Surely then the elders would need to have made a way of allowing emergency services into this secret complex, right?"

Felix now groaned. "They would use the light doors,

Val!" he shouted in frustration.

"No they wouldn't, Felix. Yes, at first they would but once inside the services wouldn't be able to get back out unless the elders knew exactly where they were. I think this room was made for this reason. So if any elementalists needed to evacuate for any reason then they would come to this containment space. Also, look!" Val walked over to the empty shelves and started rummaging through the scrap pieces of junk before he found several boxes with a familiar sign on them.

"These shelves used to be filled with first aid boxes!"

Felix now stood up. "Will you listen to yourself, Val?! Every building has first aid boxes! You're trying to find things that just aren't there. This isn't like a fire exit or a place where humans would enter the complex if they needed to, Val! It's just a room that the elders made probably to keep tampering guides like us from ever intervening in the E.B.s!"

"No. Trust me on this one, Felix. The elders don't have to worry about interfering guides. We're the only two." He turned back to look at the surroundings again and whispered to himself, "There is far too much conditioning in the guides' minds to rise up and intervene."

He turned back and pointed at Felix. "I'm going to start searching for a door or something. If I find anything, you owe me a steak."

Felix tutted and let Val begin. He started with throwing all the shelves aside and sweeping all the junk and debris away desperately and moving it all around the floor. He continued this search until on the stone floor he noticed a tiny piece of dirt fall between two laid stones. As he inspected it closer he noticed there was a small gap where concrete wasn't laid and the stones were separate. This gap stretched down in a perfect line. With his fingers he followed this line until it reached a corner and sharply turned. Val's heart jumped with excitement. He suddenly started sweeping the dust and dirt away until he found a large dent in the floor with a metal ring attached to it and yanked it up, opening a trap door.

Felix watched the whole time and stood dumbfounded when he lifted the trap door up, stood forward and beside Val and peered down some stairs and into the metal hallways of the elementalists' complex and sighed. "How do you like your steak?"

10

Kaza checked the last knot of the ropes they had found in the cupboard and tied up the tigian with. "You just stay there and look after this cupboard for me, pal," Kaza told the bound tigian and closed the door, sealing him inside.

"So where do we go now?" Midia asked.

Kaza grinned and looked around from wall to wall.

"Well, we start looking."

"For what?" she asked again but her question was in vain, Kaza had already gone to check around. At first they found nothing more than the reception and large rooms with fine woven rugs and carpets and many pictures hanging on the walls, each room leading to nowhere around them, and finally a small kitchen area for the sentry. The place was empty and quiet, the silence began to bother Kaza and made him wonder where the elders actually were.

"Why doesn't this place lead anywhere? There are no hallways, no room leading to another. It's like there is so much more to this great temple but we can access no more than six rooms. So where's the rest of the building?"

They soon realised that they were completely alone in this small place; since the C.E.L. had been opened no one but the single guard remained. They walked in each room around the fancy decorations of oil paint portraits of famous figures, mostly humans and elders. Each was framed in gold and vases of bright, colourful flowers sat around them. The rooms looked more like a museum than a temple.

"Like I mentioned before, Kaza, this is only a part for the elders' security. They have other ways of keeping their secrets safe. The rooms we have here were most likely only for formal meetings with the other species, tourists or the guards," Zahied explained while they examined the rooms and portraits.

Many figures they recognised except for Dude who was never taught such history in his youth. Old war generals of the elders stood proud in their old canvases, dressed in the same uniforms they wear now: straw conical hats, woven masks and light armour made of thick leather. Others were much older and brought mystery to them. A young and pretty human woman dressed in tight black robes stood in a leaning posture with a hood down showing her face, piercing blue eyes and long, brown hair hanging over her right shoulder. She wore a pair of sai at her sides that both glowed tinted blue like rushing water. '*Alixia Laguna, we will remember,*' was inscribed in fine golden ink at the bottom. Another was a tall and powerful leo, with a long brown mane plaited down its back dressed in shiny blue armour of 'leoium alloy', the old leo metal. He appeared crouching over a battlefield of deceased leos but reaching down and touching the subtle and weakened hand of an injured human dying on the floor. '3041 LW' was titled on the brows of the portrait. Zahied noticed this date and told them that this was the final year of the three thousand year divide when the leos took over Sphere. A story that was only a legend now. It was Dude, however, who pointed to another finely written name inked in gold at the bottom, signifying the name of the strong leo liberating the humans.

"Zane!" Midia read out loud.

"He must have been the legendary leo that ended that terrible divide all those years ago," Zahied explained but closed his eyes and shook his head in disappointment. *Why Zane? You have been our saviour for so long and been there for every world event. Why have you decided now, when Sphere needs you so much, that you don't care?*

He opened his eyes and another portrait caught his eye. He knew this wasn't the time for history lessons now but he couldn't help it.

"Hey, look at this one," he called back to the others and pointed to the largest painting at the back of the wall. There standing on a great hill with a heavenly light behind him was a dark skinned human. He wore a long brown overcoat with a high collar and a tightened belt around his waist. His hair was short and cut in a way that people wore no more. With hands outstretched, his eyes closed and chin raised the man looked like he was falling backwards into the great light behind him. Many humans and elders stood at the foot of the portrait; one caught Zahied's attention. A strong looking, middle aged man with tanned skin and a short and neat beard crossed his arms, shoulder to shoulder with the others around him and looked up to the great figure in the light.

"What is it? Found anything that we could use?" Kaza asked as he looked up.

Zahied only chuckled now and pointed to the figure. "No, but he kind of looks like you."

Midia looked up and sniggered seeing the aged bearded man before them but Kaza only laughed in sarcasm.

"Sphere's divide, that guy looks fifty, what are you trying to say? Stop wasting time and look for something here."

"I told you before Kaza, I don't think we're going to find anything more than these rooms. The elders would use light doors when accessing the rest of the building."

"Well, it's going to be a long night then isn't it, Caster?" Kaza answered sarcastically.

The two human males continued their arguing banter with Midia searching with the mute aeomon at the end of the hall. More portraits hung around them now portraying old and wizened elders, one of whom they recognised as

Elder Amber, the previous High Elder of Chippenham and highest in command of all the elders worldwide before she moved to Walton for her retirement. Her portrait showed her sitting in a great red velvet chair wearing a warm and comforting smile. The portrait sat high above them with a brick wall below that stretched from one corner to another. At first glance and from a distance it looked to be nothing of interest but it was Dude who stepped forward to touch the bricks underneath her portrait, something about them seemed different from the rest of the room, but instead of touching the wall he stumbled forward. Midia caught him and pulled him back. Dude was astounded when he felt his hand slip past where he thought the wall was; in actual fact the wall was a metre behind a small doorway. The brickwork was painted on the floor and sides perfectly, creating an optical illusion and concealing a small doorway. Midia called the others over to show them the wonder they had just found. Dude stepped into the doorway and felt around the walls until he found another sharp turn; when he followed it, it looked to the others like he had stepped out of reality altogether, but he returned, pointing downwards to show them a hidden staircase.

Zahied chucked in marvel and turned to Kaza. "This is exactly what I was talking about. No doubt this was an ancient elder trick to confuse intruders."

Kaza grinned as he followed Dude and whispered now, "Is it all they can muster though?"

"I expect not, remember this is only the first room, who knows what else they have down here for intruders such as us?"

"Intruders? I like the term 'pirate' better," Kaza countered. "You wait here then if you don't want to 'intrude'. We'll go and then tell you about it when we return."

Zahied smiled and followed. "It's a little late now for that, Captain. Lead the way."

They all followed Dude further down the tight, narrow, spiral staircase with many stairs that wound down a tight, vertical cylinder like a lighthouse. The paintings and wall decorations now were gone and only dark cream plaster and concrete surrounded them, the dusty stairs moulded from the ground beneath them and it became very dark as soon as they left the light.

The bottom, however, came suddenly and led them to another brick wall. When the staircase came to a halt Dude nearly walked straight into it. He reached out again but found this wall was real, solid and unmovable. He pushed at it to no avail. The others both turned to Zahied.

"Another elder trick?" Kaza asked.

Zahied frowned and stepped past them until he was at the wall with Dude and touched it.

"Maybe this was where the entrance used to be." He looked back up the staircase. "The first door wasn't nearly secure enough, even an inquisitive aeomon saw past it. No offence." He nodded to Dude, who just waved his hand as if to say, "*None taken.*"

"Maybe we should try looking elsewhere?" he suggested.

"But isn't this what the elders would want us to think?" Midia pointed out.

"Midia, it's a brick wall!" Kaza explained, stepped down, pushed it and thumped it with the side of his fist proving a point of how solid it was.

This time Midia waved the boys out of the way and stepped down herself. "Stand aside. You men find it all too easy to give up sometimes."

She brushed her long, black hair behind her with her fingers and started looking around. They all stood waiting for her at the bottom of the spiral staircase in the closed in cylinder-shaped space with nothing but the hard steps above them.

Kaza shuddered after a minute of Midia pressing and kicking bricks thinking they would be buttons. "Hurry up, woman. I'm starting to feel claustrophobic down here."

When she found it was no use Midia sighed and sat down. As she looked up she saw a part of the cylinder room was different from the rest. A circular line haloed the last few remaining steps and brought her hope and understanding.

"This part of the wall is separate from the rest above us. Look!" she pointed to the line in the brickwork. At once she understood what this meant.

"We're pushing the wall the wrong way. It's not supposed to be pushed forward but..." She pressed her hands to the wall and slid them sideways. The wall shuddered and groaned but began to turn counter-clockwise. Slowly and in protest like a woken child it moved, slowly and creakingly. They all leant their strength on it and soon a doorway hidden behind the staircase appeared on their right. An opening to a tunnel appeared before them with black walls, dark as the deepest of blacks but with a bright light illuminating the passage like a portrait of optimism before them. They all marvelled at the clever secret door and stepped down and entered the tunnel.

"I told you, men all give up too easily," Midia stated.

Zahied noticed. "That's a good point, it must have been an elder trick to put doubt in our minds as soon as we saw an obstacle..."

"Yeah, yeah. You just can't admit that you were wrong."

"Shut up, you two," Kaza snapped now and stepped forward in front of them. He began to sneak up to the end of the tunnel. The further they ventured the more it seemed to glow at the end. Kaza was the first to reach the opening at the end and gasped as he took in the view. The tunnel now opened up to a gigantic deep cave that glowed blue and violet. The cave floor ventured and tunnelled in different directions like an ant farm, with bridges of oak leading over the huge deep hole of glowing energy in the centre of the cave. Each bridge had decorated railings with green vines and leaves spiralling them. Deeper and deeper this giant cave seemed to go until they could see distant bridges so far down the purple, mystifying energy shrouded them like fog. The walls were still the cream plaster colour of the staircase but now decorations only portrayed the elders. Statues of silver and gold of great legendary elders stood upon pillars that overlooked them all from above. Paintings now were painted on the walls themselves in glistening oils and other paints, sparkling in the light, portraying landscape views of distant lands and ancient elders. Only Dude noticed a very particular portrait that was so old the paint was cracking but portrayed an elder under a dark sky with a red sun casting a blood red sunset. The ground was black and grey, like grass was a stranger there, and smoke from distant fires of war polluted the sky. Finally, small fireballs rained down like red and yellow snakes in the background of the portrait, exploding on impact over the horizon. The elder looked haggard and wounded and had his hands raised and looked to be giving a human a sword. The human wore armour Dude had never seen before (at least he thought it was armour), large and black with padded shoulders, and the human seemed to wear some kind of helmet with a glass visor, thick gloves and boots and something over his mouth. He looked as if he needed this to breathe the air around him. The sword, however, is what Dude noticed for it was the very same blade he was equipped with, on his back. There was Fireshaver, in a portrait that looked like the oldest here, in this most ancient place of Sphere, and it looked as if since then it hadn't aged a day. He blinked in wonder and reached up. What was this blade? How old was it truly and how had it managed to stand the test of time? All these thoughts swam through his mind when he realised the elders must know about Fireshaver. He thought maybe they could explain it to him. When he finally escaped the thoughts in his mind he saw Kaza and the others had left without him. He suddenly felt a little frightened and ran to catch up.

The cave still appeared empty but the air seemed thicker further in and they looked down where they stood to what looked like a bottomless pit of bright and colourful air, thick with what looked like fog or dust.

Zahied was the first to speak, understanding what he was seeing but not believing his eyes. "I didn't think this was possible!"

"What is it?" Midia asked, peering down and trying to sniff but finding the purple dust had no scent.

"From what I have gathered on my pilgrimage as a caster, what we are looking at now is what the elders call 'Spirit'. Supposedly this is what the elders see everywhere they go. I think we can only see it now because it is so compacted together. It is an energy that the elders use, they can tap into their gifts by using this energy wherever they go. This is the very reason why humans and other creatures don't have the same power and understanding of Sphere as the elders do. Acarlie also mentioned something about this."

"Yes, I remember, but she said she couldn't control it yet," Midia added.

"True. This is the energy of Sphere itself, its life force, and here we are in the centre of a mine full of it. This must be why the temple was built on top of it. No wonder the elders want this place so secure. We must be careful not to be discovered. I don't think they will just arrest us or let us leave if they catch us." They continued on still unaware they had left the aeomon behind. Kaza took the lead and stepped down a couple of steps and onto a stone floor that spiralled around the giant cave with a red carpet with golden vines sewn on. Zahied noticed the pistol still hanging out of the back of his trousers. "So when did you start using forbidden weapons?" Zahied asked him as they made their way further into the elders' temple.

"Since I was handed one. You forget what I am Zahied. I don't care for the laws of the people here. I've been living by my own rules for years now and they haven't seen me go too far astray."

"Apart from that time we had to save you from prison when you got drunk and slept with the daughter of the Mayor of Kennington. Then knocked him out when he found out," Midia quickly stated.

Kaza smirked. "Yes, please stop reminding him of our previous ventures, Midia. You're giving me a bad reputation."

"Yes, Captain."

"So where do you think we're going now, if you don't mind me asking?" Zahied asked again.

"We're going to find one of the elders here but first...," he stopped when he realised. "Where is the mute?"

Midia being the last one in their single file looked back to see Dude was missing.

"Oh, he's gone. He's so quiet sometimes I can hardly tell if he's there or not." She stood upright and put her hand to her mouth to call his name, when Zahied stopped her.

"We're still trying to be discreet, Midia. We can't call him. The elders will hear us."

Kaza noticed what he said. "Yes, speaking of the elders, I am finding it very hard to grasp that there is no one here.

Where are they all?" Kaza asked now.

They followed the winding path further down until the glowing purple mist seemed like fog to them. They held onto the wooden banisters that crossed the bridges over the glowing and mysterious deep hole, when Zahied stopped.

"Yes, you're right…" He stood and looked over the side of the wooden bridge and down into the abyss below. His mind was racing with thoughts and ideas, then he finally realised. He slapped his head, a slap that echoed down into the beautiful but deadly, glowing pit.

"Sphere's divide!"

"What is it?" Midia asked.

Zahied sighed in defeat. "The elders know we're here. We are not seeing anyone because they don't want us to see them. There is an old caster trick that masks people from the eyes of others. Makes them unnoticeable and undetectable unless caught on surveillance. We have ventured all the way down here and believe we see it empty. In actual fact that is far from the truth. They probably are watching us right now."

Kaza and Midia remained silent and began to look all around them, seeing nothing but the same walls they passed, pillars holding up the ceiling, the statues, paintings and decorations and purple mist around them before the silence was finally ended.

"The human caster is correct. Stop where you are. You are all under arrest."

Many elders appeared from either side of the wooden bridge, dressed in sentry uniforms with straw conical hats and woven masks revealing only their eyes. They each glowed a subtle colour of violet like the mist around them and wore its aura like armour. Each one held a halberd long axe horizontally, blocking off their escape.

"It goes against the very first rule the humans and elders made thousands, even millions of years ago to sneak around in the most sacred of elder temples. This sort of act leads to divides. Tell me, are you spies of humans? Sent here to infiltrate our temple after so many years of peace? Speak, human," an elder demanded of Kaza and stepped onto the bridge toward him. In a move of desperate defence Kaza whipped out the pistol from behind his back and fired. The shot rang out and echoed down the hole and all around the deep and open cave. The straw hat of the elder was no defence against a speeding bullet and it pierced his skull leaving brain and bone to scatter behind him as the exit wound seemed to explode the back of his head. The elder fell over the bridge and disappeared into the purple fog below. The elders behind him, now all soaked in their friend's blood, shrieked and cried.

"Shut up!" Kaza ordered and pointed the gun to the next elder's head. "You know what this is?"

The elder suddenly turned pale. "You bring a forbidden weapon here to this place of peace. This is an act of–"

"I said shut up!" he ordered again but this time found he couldn't fire. He felt paralysed to the spot and couldn't even speak. Zahied and Midia also felt this strange imprisoning feeling. The elders from behind them on the other side of the bridge all stood with their hands held out, controlling their motor skills and freezing them to the spot.

"Halt!" one demanded and turned his hand. As if their bodies were controlled they began to turn against their will towards the opposite elder.

"I am the head of security in this sacred temple. We have watched and followed silently ever since you tied poor Rupurto up and locked him in that cupboard and ventured down here. We hoped you would have turned back by now or at least when we mentally suggested to you to leave at the spiral staircase, but now you have gone too far and have even murdered one of our friends. Tell me now, before we kill you, what is happening here? Why are you here?"

The elder released his grip on Zahied just so much that he could speak. Zahied's mouth opened. He knew this imprisoning feeling must have come from the Suggestive Oils they inhaled. "We are not spies, elders. We are here only trying to force a short audience with the High Elders here. We mean no one harm and will leave freely as soon as we speak to the elders in charge here."

The elder frowned and looked back at his colleagues who were holding the others behind them. "You cannot speak to who is in charge! The High Elders here have too much very important business to waste their time on the criminal antics of pirates. You are all under arrest under the treaty of the human and elder laws. Your case will be met by the highest courts of both species and you will be hanged!"

"No please! We mean no harm. I apologise for the death of your friend. It was not our intention to hurt anyone here. We are only here to speak to the High Elders regarding the–"

"Silence! Before I command you to jump from the bridge. Be thankful I don't want to taint the Spirit with the bodies of humans and that I haven't already done that."

"Elder, please listen!" Zahied protested. "We here have been assigned a mission by the old Elder Amber of this temple, who now lives in Walton, to find out information about a black hole that rests in space and is slowly heading towards Sphere. If you elders are as powerful as you make out I'm sure you are already aware of this, correct?"

Now the elder looked shocked. "How...? That's classified elder information!" he warned.

"Elder Amber foresaw this, elder. She is not as ready for retirement as you all made her out to be. She has sent a small group to help in this secret mission so as to not alarm the rest of the world but now our journey has led us and Elementalist Acarlie here so we could speak to the High Elders. Please cooperate with us so we can achieve what an old leader of this temple, your old master, has ordered us to do."

When Zahied mentioned her name another elder stepped out from behind the security. This elder was dressed in fine white gowns and silks, had long white hair that hung down and even a small beard, which was rare for an elder.

"You speak of Amber? Who are you? Guards, release your control of them."

"But Master...," the first tried to protest.

"Do as I say, son," the elderly one commanded. Once the three were released Zahied quickly turned and commanded Kaza to withdraw his weapon. When Kaza did as instructed the guards around them seemed a little less tense.

The elderly one stepped slowly onto the bridge to have a look at the three intruders. He had never seen Zahied nor Midia before but stopped when he reached Kaza.

"What is your name, son?"

Kaza felt frozen again at first but took a breath and answered, "I am Captain Kaza Caines of the Scarlet Arise."

The elder peered and squinted, looking deep into his eyes. "Yes, of course you are." He finally turned back to the others. "These men will harm us no more. They are my guests."

Everybody looked at one another. Midia especially looked over to Kaza, who only shrugged, confused as to what was happening.

"What about this one, sir?" called another, and the missing aeomon was dragged up to the bridge.

"He's one of us!" Zahied quickly pointed out. "We just lost him."

"Off stealing was he?" the head of security asked.

"No, no, no. Stop insulting my guests," the elderly one said and walked over to Dude. "He too has not come here to harm any of us."

"How can you be so sure?"

"Because of this." The elder reached back to Dude and pulled the red katana from its scabbard on his back and showed the elders, who all looked amazed and dazzled by it.

"Behold Fireshaver! No person wielding a legendary elder blade such as this could possibly be here to harm or destroy us."

With this excuse, to the surprise of the prisoners, the elders all now backed off a step and looked to be releasing them instantly.

Zahied had to ask, "Who are you, elder? And how is it all of a sudden you believe us? What has Fireshaver to do with this?"

The elder now smiled and gave back Fireshaver to Dude then turned back to Zahied.

"But my friend, it is you who intrudes into our home. It will be me who asks the questions first. Come, let me take you to whom you seek. Right now we have lost a dear friend, an expense that could have easily been avoided." He turned to Kaza. "I'm sorry, Captain Kaza Caines, you shall pay for the crime you have committed, but I regret to say there are bigger issues to deal with right now. I will take you where you wish to go. Please follow me."

11

Acarlie was back on her feet with the help of Electra. She was still sore and weakened but soon managed to pull herself together. She drank as much water as she could at the sink provided and had her cuts and bruises cleaned up.

Electra remained silent when Acarlie was finishing the last of her first aid, feeling extremely guilty. Acarlie noticed this and asked, while dabbing a wet cloth to her bruised eye, "Was this your first win, Electra? You never defeated an elementalist before?"

"No," she answered quietly. "I mean yeah, I defeated the elementalist at the end of my training when I was back at home but those battles are never to the death. You were supposed to be my first when you arrived in Donolan. I remember facing you and feeling so confident and proud that I was representing Angland."

"That was your first real E.B.?" Acarlie asked.

Electra smiled. "Yeah."

"But…you were amazing, Electra. That was one of the hardest fights I've ever had. We fought for nearly half an hour. You even killed me in the end. And that was your first?"

Electra shrugged, "I guess our fight wouldn't have been as bad as your fight with Eliza…the one where you killed her…"

Acarlie fell silent. Electra, as well as the rest of the world, still believed that Acarlie had killed Eliza in a secret E.B. organised by the elders, when the truth was far more brutal.

"Electra…I didn't kill Eliza," Acarlie admitted.

"Then who did?" she asked.

Acarlie felt a painful sting inside her knowing Electra wasn't supposed to know but couldn't help herself. "The elders did. I was just supposed to take the fall for it."

She expected an ocean of questions from her then and so was surprised when Electra just said, "I guess that I'm not supposed to know then? I won't ask, Acarlie. I guess I've already seen today what the elders are capable of."

"I wish I could tell you, Electra. I wish you could know the truth of what is happening here. Why I'm really here... But I can't."

"I don't care why you're here, Acarlie. I'm just glad you are. I can't think of a better elementalist I would rather have at my side right now. I just wish you can forgive me for..." she gestured to Acarlie's swollen face, "...this."

Acarlie laughed. "Last time we spoke you tried to kill me, Electra, and now you're guilty of some bruises on my face. What if you had killed me in Donolan?"Electra thought for a minute. "Then I wouldn't have you here with me now and would probably be dead too. Come on, Acarlie, let's find the last round and finish this and go back to our guides. I can't help but worry where my Felix is right now."

"Do you know where you're going?" Felix called to Val as they both ran through the underground complex looking for the elementalists.

"Of course I don't!" Val called back, running down the hallways and searching every room he could find.

"But this place is massive, Val! It could take us forever to find them."

"That's why we're running, Felix!"

Val saw a door in the distance of one of the hallways and ran to it, opened it and peeked inside.

The room had recently seen a fist fight; there was blood smeared all over the floor and the wall was dented in several places. Val scanned the room until he saw a dead male lying on the floor in a dark corner. His head had been battered and his body just left there to rot.

"Anything there?" Felix asked, catching up.

Val closed the door. "No, nothing. We're getting close though."

Val took a breath after what he'd seen and walked away. Felix peeked inside and he too saw the dead elementalist lying defeated, and closed the door, struck silent.

"You don't think Electra and Acarlie–?"

"They're fine, Felix. We just need to hurry up and catch them up."

A bang echoed in the distance, like the sound of something heavy falling or thrown to the ground. Their ears pricked up.

"Let's see what that is," Val suggested.

A light door opened and Kaza and the others stepped out beside the elder to a large, underground elevator. A large squared metal floor held them and looked as if it would travel diagonally downwards when activated. It had enough room on it for a large amount of people and seemed even to have carried heavy machinery.

Whilst stepping onto it, Kaza noticed how advanced this piece of machinery looked, far too advanced for the elders to normally use and clearly had had some help from human hands. He had to ask, "I thought the elders weren't ones for using such human-made contraptions?"

The elder present didn't say anything but walked over to a control panel and began pressing some holographic buttons that had lit up when he'd approached. The elevator slowly began to slide downward diagonally.

"The High Council below us set up a room that no light door can cut into. It is impossible for any other elder apart from the council themselves to enter unless they use the front door. This is always strictly prohibited except in urgent situations. This is just a security measure. Right now you are some of the few humans ever to have come down here and the quiet one behind us is the only aeomon in history."

Midia glanced over to Dude, who stepped closer to the edge of the elevator and tried looking down, but found his view was restricted by the angle that the elevator was going in.

"This still doesn't explain why you have human-made technology here," Zahied said.

"This elevator was made with the help of humans thousands of years ago as a means of escorting the council out if anything should happen. It is a safety measure and also a safe way of entering without the use of light doors."

"I thought the light doors are the best way of travelling for the elders?" he asked.

"No, human. Light doors are useful but have always been faulted. The elder casting the door could be mistaken and trap himself or elders somewhere or accidentally think of a different destination and end up somewhere dangerous. Also, the light doors only stretch so far and mean only a few people may pass before the door closes. If anyone should be half way through the door when it closes it will leave half of the person in the desired destination and the other half in the previous. Many limbs and even lives have been lost by using light doors. Also, they have never been used to transport heavy machinery or even medical equipment. If a home was to catch fire then an elder could send a fireman in to save the people but would not know where they were to be brought back to, and the fireman could not send his hose in so they all would die. This is why we elders often end up using human technology as a last resort."

"Can't beat a good old human-made machine, right?" Kaza smirked.

"On the contrary, elevators such as this need maintenance; cleaning, re-oiling and servicing. They could break down or the power could give in and we could be stuck. No species' way is superior, but if you ask me, one species that has a good idea is the aeomon."

Dude looked up on hearing this. No one ever compliments the aeomon.

"The aeomon technology is quite like the humans' but is easy to make and understand, safer and better for the environment using less efficient but more recyclable resources, being friendlier to the environment."

"True, but it doesn't get the job done as well as ours does," Kaza said, backing up his race.

"But it does get the job done, no?" the elder asked with a warm smile aimed at Dude.

"Elder, may I ask now how you came to trust us so easily?" Zahied put in. "Why is it that once you saw us, and more importantly Dude's sword, you concluded that we are not a threat?"

The elder smiled and nodded. "Ah, yes." He looked back fondly at the katana at Dude's back. "I could spend my whole life time left telling you the history of that blade and still would only be telling you small tales of its true story and heritage. This was one of the great legendary elder weapons forged at the beginning of the counting days and has remained with this planet ever since. Yes, we elders all know the legends, and I expect that you know some yourselves."

Zahied blinked and looked back at Dude, who stood intensely listening, trying to gather every piece of information he could about his only item of value in the world. "Yes, I admit I know the legends…"

"And I assure you the legends date back further than you think. A touch of elder influence on an item makes it impossible to erode; when it lights like fire it regenerates in a way, sharpening the blade and restoring it to the condition it was created in. I was told in my youth that the blade was created to respond to the wielder's personality. It is very particular about what kind of person it gives its power to. Since it has found its way here to the temple, we know that its reason is honourable. This is why I believe you to be no threat."

"Are there more?" Midia asked, now getting into the conversation. "You say '*one of the legendary weapons*'. I take it there are other blades similar to this."

The elder shook his head. "Not any more, many were destroyed, more were lost in time. We have since tried to copy the idea but back then, without the right materials, we could only make smaller inferior models. There was a time not long ago when elders attempted to copy the technique of creating a blade that would not erode and sold them off to humans. These blades were sharp as razors and made to contain a gel that when tilted onto the blade would dry on it and sharpen it. However, these copies, as great as they were, could not stand against a weapon such as the one bound to the quiet one behind us, which has remained like a prince of steel among us mortals."

"Yes, we know of a blade such as this. 'Razor' he calls it," Zahied told them, remembering the damage that blade had caused at the Battle of Hiro and the life it took from the valiant, broad shouldered archer of Plainess, Zack, on a day that seemed years ago now.

"What about me? You already decided we were not a threat once you looked into my eyes," Kaza asked now.

The elder, however, avoided the question. "Ah, look. We have arrived."

The elevator reached the bottom and before them was a large, metal door that resembled a safe. The elder stepped off the elevator and opened the door by inputting a code in an adjacent panel. They all stood and waited as the door slowly opened. A large wheel turned, unscrewing a giant bolt that fell downwards and into a hole in the floor and the door itself began to rise up finally revealing to the pirates the inside of the sacred elder council.

But to the elder's surprise the place had already been disturbed. The beautiful decorations of the elders had been torn off the walls. The carpets looked to have been burned away. Book shelves had been tossed and thrown aside. The whole place had been turned upside down and set ablaze.

"What has happened here!?" the elder cried and began rushing around this once peaceful room that now looked to be the result of a terrorist attack.

"Masters! Masters!" he called and began searching.

"Who could have done this?" Midia asked and Zahied knelt down to inspect the burned carpet.

"I can think of only one person who could have done this. The members of the Senate did say he was here a week ago," Zahied suggested.

"Sphere's divide! So are there any left on the council?" Kaza asked.

The elder seemed to be in shock now and paced around before he found the burned, deceased remains of the High Elder Council and moaned in grief. The others followed, he fell to the floor and wept, reaching down for the burned carcasses of the dead.

"Why?" he cried.

"Midia, help him to his feet," Kaza ordered and took Zahied by his elbow, stepping aside while Midia and Dude tended to the weeping old elder.

197

"He was here, wasn't he?" he asked.

"I have no doubt. These bodies look to have been dead for days now. The place was set ablaze, no doubt as a broom to his tracks. He knew someone would follow him and he wanted nothing to be found."

"Damn him!" he cursed. The weeping old elder still cried and moaned.

"Who shall guide us now? Who can we elders follow for instruction?"

Kaza paced up and down trying to think when he realised that the crying elder was damaging his concentration. He needed him out of the room.

"Dude, escort the elder back to the rest of the temple. Have them bring down the security. Elder…," he now said and knelt down to comfort the elder and bring him back to his feet.

"Let me handle this," Zahied broke in, knowing Kaza was never subtle with words, and addressed the elder. "Elder, with your permission we would like to just have a look around here. We are here because we know that some vital information we are looking for was down here. I know these elders have been murdered because of this knowledge."

"I…I don't have the authority to grant you the clearance here. I was only supposed to show you the door but now my responsibilities have changed. My masters must be found and buried. The safety of all elders worldwide now may be compromised," the old, white elder cried.

"I assure you the safety of your people is still assured. It is the safety of the planet itself that is now compromised. All I ask for is a few minutes to find out what it was these elders have died protecting."

The elder was lost for words still, not knowing whether to trust these people, but when he again saw Dude's blade on his back he closed his eyes and nodded. "I will likely be hung for this but I know of the danger outside the atmosphere…I believe this is the reason why you are here. I will give you a few minutes while I go back and gather the guards. I will use the elevator to buy you more time. Please be ready by the time I return. They will not understand if you are caught going through the contents of this most sacred of places."

"Dude, go with him," Kaza ordered him again and placed a hand on the elder's shoulder. "Thank you."

They waited for the elder and the mute aeomon to disappear again in the slow elevator.

"Right, we probably don't have much time left then. Let's not forget we're still intruders who killed an elder to get in here," Kaza said.

"You! *You* killed an elder to get in here," Zahied corrected.

"Whatever! Just find whatever it is we're supposed to find!"

Acarlie and Electra finally found a door that didn't lead to more deceased elementalists in rooms that mirrored their own and found they were the last to enter into a giant hall that all of the other elementalists were now battling in. The last round which was a last-man-standing stand-off, was in progress. The whole arena was a large circular room held up by beams, with a metal grated floor and a long fall beneath.

Sharcole was fighting off two attackers by channelling the fire element he had conjured into two whips. He was swinging them around in an artistic fashion and scolding his two attackers.

Vix was leading an assault of her own against a water elementalist and using her natural element to cast a shield of plants and bark around her whilst pressing her hands into the metal floor and causing vines to rise up under the feet of her opponent, tangling him to the spot. Many other elementalists were now battling, again with the crowd watching from above, but now instead of a giant monitor above them the ceiling domed up and the dome lit up a giant holographic image of the crowd in a three dimensional live feed back in the original arena. All these elementalists were now the winners of their individual fights, which they had won by killing their opponents with their bare hands and now they were all as crazed and shell-shocked as one another. Water elementalists were casting jets of pressured water into the pit and drowning their opponents as well as trying to defend themselves from the elementalists who had mastered electricity, like Electra, who could easily shock the water around them.

"We're here, Acarlie. Are you ready?" Electra asked.

Acarlie frowned, looking at all the competition that now faced them. "I think so. I think it's best that we fight as a team here. The only advantage we could have against so many is that we stick together."

"Agreed."

They marched in, terrified and wounded but keeping their composure as they entered the pit. The crowd screamed and chanted and the announcer called their names as they entered.

"And here is our final finalist and it looks like she has spared her last opponent and brought her to the final with her! A clear violation of the rules but since we are just and fair we shall overlook this offence and instead congratulate Electra on her mercy and grace. Welcome, Electra, and a very special welcome to you, Acarlie! You have been given an extra chance and have been accepted in the final by a wild card. We all hope you can use this chance and defeat all the elementalists here. I shall remind you though that even if you two shall both see the end, you will again be faced to one another!"

"He talks too much!" Acarlie now shouted to her partner over the confusion and screams of the battle. An elementalist beside her, fighting in a blind rage, twisting and breaking the neck of his opponent, turned straight to Acarlie and tried to pounce on her but she instantly held up her hand and stopped him in mid-air. He froze where he was and she threw him back into another two fighters, now revealing herself to the final of this event.

"I can hear something happening from down here, Val!" Felix called as Val checked another room. They now began to feel a little out of breath and slowed down their search but they were still both determined to find their lost elementalists.

"Where?" he asked, returning to him.

Felix pointed. "There. Listen."

The hallway was silent but a very faint scream was heard, a scream that Felix knew immediately. "That's my Electra!"

"Okay, let's hope we make it there in time!" Val took a quick breath and began dashing down the hallways towards the distant echo of Felix's partner.

Electra screamed as she was thrown down by a tigian elementalist from Mecroyles. Being from a school that specialised in the sphere and ground below them his disadvantage meant he could only rely on his weaker elements and his tigian strength to win and he dived on top of Electra, who quickly jolted his head with electricity and fried him immediately but was then stuck under the weight of him.

"Help!" she called to Acarlie.

Acarlie had just finished blocking an attack from a human male and quickly snapped a diamond fisted punch into his ribs and knocked him away, when she heard her friend call and saw the heavy weight on top of her. Another elementalist had just seen Electra's trouble and went to make an easy kill but Acarlie quickly pointed to the deceased tigian and lowered the gravity off him, letting Electra easily push him aside and get back up. Doing so though caused Acarlie to take a jet of water suddenly, casting her across the floor and pressing her up against the wall of the arena struggling to breathe. She tried to deflect the water but her power of the element was weaker than her opponent's.

Electra managed to fight off the elementalist approaching her and looked over to Acarlie, tightly pinned against the wall by a vicious jet of water. It crossed her mind to touch the water and fry Acarlie as well as the elementalist casting the water, but didn't. Instead she threw herself into him and freed Acarlie, trying to give her enough time to get back to her feet.

Chants, cheers, claps and roars filled the air from the audience watching above them. With the death rule announced the audience had the greatest battle viewed in centuries. Not caring for the lives of their champions they only cared for the bets they'd made and their entertainment. This event truly was something special. The elementalists all fought with so much vigour and drive now they were all fighting for their lives.

I hate the C.E.L.! Acarlie cursed as she took a moment to catch her breath. She was still sore from Electra's beating and was now beginning to tire again from exhaustion. *Why bring in this forsaken rule? It makes no sense killing off all the elementalists in the C.E.L. They must know that there will be no league left if there is only one elementalist left. But they don't care, they only care about what suits them. They can always take young talented elementalists from their schools and start a new league. I hate it! I hate it!*

Her arms began to shake as her emotions began to build again while she lifted herself up; her eyes began to burn and fill with tears. She felt rage and anger now driving her and looked back to the pit to see so much violence; so much unnecessary violence all in the name of entertainment. Her heart raced and pulsed adrenaline around her body and she ran forward, not caring now for anyone but Electra, her friend, and forced her hands forward. A vicious gale was forced in the direction of the pit and suddenly everyone was blown back against the other wall. The closest to the wall were pelted with debris and bodies and crushed under the weight of the other contenders. Everything suddenly fell silent. Acarlie's power stunned the audience and the pit alike. They all got up stunned and speechless.

She stood there, shaking, her eyes closed and her heart racing, still trying to control her rage.

"What on Sphere was that?" Sharcole asked, getting to his feet and seeing that the only elementalist on the other side of the arena now was Acarlie.

Electra was also thrown to the wall but jumped back to her feet and ran to her friend.

"Acarlie!"

Acarlie's eyes opened when she heard her voice. "Electra?"

"Are you okay?"

Acarlie looked down at her hands; they were still shaking. "I don't know."

The elementalists all got back up. One took a breath and looked to a previous opponent; he used this moment of silence to get the first punch in and smashed him in the nose, starting off the fight again.

"Found anything yet?" Kaza called over to Zahied, who was now sat down and reading as fast as he could through historical books to find anything useful.

"Nothing! What about you?" he called back.

Kaza was himself searching all the walls and desks, moving anything he could. He removed all the paintings he could remove but some were fixed to the wall or were engraved in large metal slabs that were irremovable. Midia was walking around aimlessly at first trying to ignore the smell of the week-deceased elder whom they had dragged into a corner. They checked the pockets of the dead for anything significant but found nothing.

"Maybe whatever it was Zane already found it and has gone away with it?" Zahied suggested.

Kaza grunted, dismissing the idea, and found a particularly large desk standing beneath a large metal world map attached to the wall. This clearly was the desk of the highest of the elders and the picture was used to create strategies for old wars and divides. This desk had to be important and Kaza began ripping open the desk draws and searching for any kind of hidden buttons.

Midia walked up to help him when a particular metal globe caught her attention. It lay on its side in a dusty heap of lots of burned books, under wooden shelving and various debris. When she stood it up she found it was a very large, metal globe of Sphere. As it measured five feet, she struggled to get it to its feet and spun it when she finally did.

"Captain? How old is this place?"

Kaza looked up. "What? I don't know, thousands, millions of years? Elders have been around before the humans remember? So this place was probably used way before the First Divide."

"If that's so then why is this here?" she asked, spinning the globe again.

"Every military or leadership building would have a world map, woman! Quit asking stupid questions and get to work."

"What I mean, Captain, is, why is it like this?"

"Like what?"

"You know, like this? Old, ancient even. If this council is so old and undisturbed then why would they have a globe like this? Especially when they have a world map above your head too."

This now caught Zahied's attention and turned him away from the books. "She's got a point, Kaza. Over millions of years planets change. Continents shift and drift apart and merge into others and the planet changes. Back in the First Divide the Sphere would have looked nothing like that."

"So they upgraded their map, so what?" Kaza said, but stopped on his last word.

Midia again spun the ancient relic of a globe of the modern world and now inspected the small metal engravings. There was ash and chalk on the floor. The globe itself looked ancient but held its structure perfectly, even the tiny numbers on the side and bottom were still there.

"You don't think...?" Kaza began to say as he stepped forward and Zahied stepped closer to inspect the ash and chalk on the floor.

"Someone copied this map and then failed to burn it away."

"Quick, where are the items we have from under the schools!" Midia demanded and Kaza shrugged.

"Back on the ship, I didn't want to risk losing them. What were the coordinates though?"

"Latitude thirty-four," Zahied said and began searching the map for the number. Sure enough, there it was.

"I think this may be the world map we are looking for. It would explain why Zane copied it and tried to destroy it after. Quick, find some paper! The only problem is that there are two."

"Two?" Midia asked now.

Zahied sighed and pointed them out. "Yes, on a globe the central line of latitude is zero, so there would be a northern and southern hemisphere. I think this is the map we are looking for but now we don't know if it means latitude thirty-four north or south. I guess we will have to go with both for now."

"This still doesn't prove anything! Any world map could have a latitude thirty-four," Kaza said, but did as instructed and started finding pieces of paper and some black chalk.

"What makes this map so special? Any globe or map could give us the same coordinates. Why come all the way down here for this one?"

"Maybe this map is different. Maybe it is a little inaccurate compared with all the other maps but its sole purpose was to guide us. Whatever the reason was, Zane seemed to believe it too or else he would have also tried to copy the map above the desk. The age of this map also has to be something useful. And where better to hide such an important piece than a place where humans haven't been in millennia?"

They all took the paper to the engraving and started rubbing away it with the chalk and copying the globe onto paper. It took them a few minutes since Zahied wanted it as perfect as they could make it.

"This is good. I can copy this once we're back on the ship and make a better map. Once we have the next coordinate we can at least find where this island is, and once there we can find this supposed labyrinth we have a map for. All we need to do now is wait for the elder to return and deliver us back. Hopefully we will not be arrested when they discover us down here."

"I've got a better idea," Kaza said and rolled up his sleeve, revealing a hi-tech communicator attached to his arm. He pulled up the paper-thin screen and turned it on to see the face of Rezosa.

"Umm, Captain?" she said, a little confused at first by how to work this contraption at her end.

"We think we've got what we want, Rezosa. Go and assemble the crew back on ship, send your friend Major out if you need to but make sure I have every member from the city back on the ship and accounted for. We will be escorted out of the Elders' Temple soon and might need a quick exit. Probably nothing to worry about because we think we have someone to speak for us but this is just a precaution."

"Yes, Captain."

Zahied started putting together all the pieces of this map and stared at Kaza's new toy.

"Where did you get that? They're state of the art and cost thousands. Did you steal it?"

Kaza scoffed. "Steal? Now what gave you the impression that I'm a thief, Zahied? I don't steal."

"Yes you do. Are we going to have to deal with the police here now?"

"Of course not. I paid for this and the other four with *legitimate money.*"

"And how did you get this legitimate money?"

"I sold some blueprints to this city on how to make the cannons on our ship."

"You what!? How could you? You've been selling cannons – forbidden weapons to the city!"

"Not selling cannons, Zahied. Just the knowledge on how to make them."

"But–"

"Relax, Zahied. If it wasn't for my selling abilities we wouldn't have even been able to keep the Scarlet Arise from leaving Angland."

"Angland has them too!? What have you done, Kaza? You may have ended the universal treaty that ended the manufacture of these weapons that killed off the leos!"

Kaza raised his eyebrow. "Zahied, I was going to give you one but now I'm starting to reconsider. Stop worrying, my friend, everything is going to work out. These things are necessary for our journey. Also, with the money I managed to re-stock the ship completely with both food and fuel and I also found a blacksmith to make ammunition as well as do any maintenance needed."

"I suppose you also sold them the knowledge of how to make the pistol you have on you now?"

"Don't be stupid, Zahied. I'm a pirate. I always keep the best for myself."

Acarlie was thrown across the floor and quickly rolled back onto her feet. Her attacker was an elementalist from Hiro and trying to conjure water and shoot her with it but now she was full of adrenaline and dived aside and approached him, her guard raised, and grabbed his hand, twisting it around. He tried to swing his other hand but she quickly retaliated and terminated his attack by bending her finger and pressing down hard with her knuckle into the pressure point in the back of his hand. He knelt down in pain and she made use of this to twist has hand further until he was on the floor and then chopped hard into his neck, slamming his head against the floor and knocking him unconscious.

There were now only a few elementalists left. All of the more talented and experienced elementalists, like Acarlie, had successfully managed to just knock their opponents out, while the less talented still needed to resort to killing them.

Sharcole, the fire elementalist, was now battling both Vix and Electra and a third elementalist, who tried to overpower him.

"Acarlie! Come over here and help us!" Vix called over to Acarlie, who now dragged the elementalist she had just knocked out to the side of the arena and out of harm's way.

Sharcole blocked Electra's attack and parried another and kicked her away, turned to the other elementalist, conjured fire in his hand and with a small explosion he blinded the elementalist briefly. He held the attacker by his throat, picked him up, slammed him into the ground and threw him aside once he was unconscious.

He turned now to have Vix attack him. With her arms turned to diamond he had to resort to using the advantage of his physical strength to defend himself against her. Acarlie dashed forward realising the truth here. Sharcole here was the strongest and so getting him out of the way first would make it easier for the rest of them. He, however, knew this and clutched onto his life just like the rest of them and used his advantaged element of fire to immediately burn whoever tried. His strength was also an advantage against the female elementalists or the aeomon, but Acarlie, however, was trained in a way to see past this.

She thrust kicked him in his ribs and waited for his turn and counter, which was inevitable, and assumed a low stance, caught his wrist as it swung and pulled it forward into her, lifted her knee to strike his ribs again then smashed her elbow into his cheek, sending him away.

Another tried to take advantage of the direction of her attention and lunged from behind but she now swivelled around and caught the elementalist, blocked his attack and kicked into the knee he was stupid enough to lock and caused his knee to break backwards.

He cried out and fell to the floor and she cast him away by ordering the wind to force him back against the wall.

Sharcole was back on his feet and defending himself against Electra again. Acarlie tried to help her friend out but the fight suddenly turned for her. Sharcole kicked Electra and flicked his hands to one side. Two fire whips appeared, under his control, which he aimed for Acarlie. She screamed when she heard the crack of the whips and fell to the floor avoiding the first attack but could only turn around and try to escape when he whipped them again.

She screamed in agony. The burning sensation shot through her body as quickly as the whip itself. Both whips simultaneously and in parallel slapped her back. Two vertical lines of fire began immediately to burn on her back. She rolled on the floor, shrieking and wailing, trying to put the fire out by cutting off the oxygen but couldn't. The fire burned and would have reached her hair if Vix hadn't then got to her, turned her around and pressed her hands down on the fire, extinguishing it with the water element. She couldn't stay long enough to help Acarlie to her feet, however, as Sharcole still needed dealing with.

It still felt like the fire was burning but her now soaking wet back convinced Acarlie that the fire *was* extinguished. She groaned in agony and slowly pressed her knees into the ground to push herself up. She could smell the steam evaporating from her and the smell of her smouldering back. The pain almost paralysed her but eventually turned to just a painful sting she could deal with. She looked up to see both Vix and Electra trying in vain to battle Sharcole. He was still the stronger fighter and the stronger elementalist. Electra was fighting gallantly and to the best of her abilities and Acarlie wanted to help. Her friend was now in need and she had to help her. Acarlie forced her hands to the floor and began to pick herself up; her adrenaline from the pain now overshadowed her fear and hesitation. She found her feet and glanced up to see Sharcole form another whip, crack it in the air and whip it toward Electra. The whip found a perfect route in the air and wrapped around her neck, and in an instant Sharcole whipped again and Electra's head left her shoulders.

Acarlie's heart stopped; she couldn't move. Suddenly nothing mattered. Electra's head now fell and bounced close to where Acarlie stood and she fell back to her knees. Electra's body now slumped and fell to the floor in a heap. Acarlie wanted to scream but couldn't find her voice. The sudden shock constricted her and wrapped her tight in vines of disbelief. In only a second Electra's life was extinguished and now she lay as a decapitated body.

She finally opened her mouth when she snapped back to reality but it wasn't her voice she heard screaming, but a male voice, that of Electra's guardian, behind them.

"Electra!" Felix cried and went to charge in.

Acarlie glanced back to see a male aeomon being held back by her own Val, trying to stop him.

Felix was a picture of distress and instant heartbreak and he ignored Val's attempt to hold him back and instead reached for Val's knife that he had received from the Battle of Hiro and pushed him away, screaming like a wild animal for Sharcole.

Sharcole, however, only used his control of wind to force Felix back with ease and concentrated on still fighting Vix, who now was trying to avenge Electra and take him down.

Everything was happening all at once now. Acarlie still was kneeling down not knowing whether to run to Val or run to Sharcole. Felix was thrown to the floor near Electra's body, where he clutched onto her in a fit of tears, crying her name over the sound of the cheering audience.

Acarlie had seen a familiar face on Felix then. She had even felt that heartbreak he was witnessing. Unfortunately though, she could not see a second into the future to stop his next action and instead was forced to witness him in his despair clutch onto Val's knife and drive it into his chest.

The knife pierced his broken heart and his body fell on top of Electra's. His blood soaked through the metal tiled floor and dropped down to the darkness below, agglomerating with the rest of the spilt blood of the elementalists. She couldn't even blink. In the space of a minute two innocent lives had been taken in front of her. Electra and her guide had only come here to escape death from the Elemental League and now they lay together as two victimised lovers of the C.E.L. She suddenly felt her heart throb painfully and she was subjected to the very familiar pain she had felt back when her own heart broke on the empty field in Selodia forest. Her blood raced and she still couldn't take her eyes off the two lovers, now only corpses. Empathy overwhelmed her and she finally closed her eyes and tried to breathe.

Val noticed Acarlie now kneeling on the floor and trembling next to the two bodies of Felix and Electra and dashed forward for Sharcole, his own heart racing.

Sharcole looked away from knocking Vix down to see the charging Val, who dashed straight passed Acarlie and stopped when he got to him.

"Quick! We have to get out of here!" Val called over to him, to all the elementalists.

"What?" Sharcole asked. "Why are you here? To save Acarlie? You can't save her from this tournament unless–"

"I'm not here to save *her* from *you*! I'm here to save *you* from *her*!" Val cried back. Sharcole looked into Val's eyes and saw the sudden fear and worry in him then.

Val pushed him back and turned to face Acarlie. Her body was shaking from her heartbreak and she suddenly screamed out, stretching out her burned back and tensing her forearms out to her side. Her eyes snapped open revealing the white eyes of the monster within.

12

The whole underground stadium began to shake as Acarlie screamed and lifted off the floor to levitate before them. Her head arched upwards with her white eyes looking straight through the domed ceiling and an aura seemed to glow from her. As her body tensed and her voice echoed, the glow stretched further. Val had witnessed this energy from Acarlie before; this was the very thing he had come down here to try to prevent. The aura around her seemed to wind back and compact closer to her. She was building up all the energy within the room.

"Get out of here!" he cried to the other elementalists, but his attempt was too late. The energy surrounding her exploded in a shock wave and sent everyone back in every direction. The dome above them fizzed and cut out, leaving the audience completely cut off from the action now and all of the little cameras surrounding them dropped to the floor and short circuited. Her blast of energy acted as an electro-magnetic pulse and cut out all electronics in the complex. The people screamed suddenly seeing this monster appear before them in the body of the sweet and beautiful contender Acarlie.

Acarlie finally stopped screaming, took a deep breath and looked down from where she floated. Her body felt charged and her bodily control had now been completely passed over to the beast inside her.

She looked down. Her all-white eyes scanned the room without blinking and the first one she saw was Sharcole crouching down and looking up at her in fear. She could feel the energy in every elementalist around her and by the way he was covering his eyes from the blinding light she emitted convinced her that he was scared. He tried to turn but at a gesture from her hand he froze and lifted from the floor. Everyone else now began dispersing and rushing for the door with Val there trying to hold it open, when he noticed Sharcole being lifted up and towards Acarlie.

She still floated metres from the floor, her breathing pattern now found a fluid rhythm of deep breaths, while he began to now tremble at the sight of her.

"What on Sphere are you!?" he cried but she never answered.

She remained silent and only lowered her head and narrowed her white eyes to look straight at him, as if she was looking through his eyes and deep into his soul.

He tried to say something else but she silenced him with a feral bark. Her voice echoed like nothing ever heard from a human before. Val saw Vix was still on the floor, knocked there by Acarlie's shockwave, and began dashing over but again was too late in his attempt. She screamed, "Electra!" as though it was the real Acarlie deep inside her own body trying to escape and Sharcole slammed into the floor.

Acarlie screamed and pressed her hands downwards, controlling the gravity, and Sharcole was now subjected to the wrath and power of the most threatening elementalist on the planet. His body now became a weight he couldn't lift and he yelped feebly. His lungs pressed hard against the metal floor and stopped him from breathing. His spine now pressed down heavier into his organs until they punctured. His skull cracked and the crack quickly spread as the weight still increased and finally Acarlie pulled her hands back briefly and forced them down even harder and the ground itself opened up. Sharcole's body was forced through the metal floor. Squares of metal tile flew down and the beams holding up the arena caved in and they all fell. When the floor suddenly tilted Val also slid down next to Vix, slammed into one of the beams and tumbled down beside her until they hit the ground below them with a thump.

When Val's head struck, a very familiar high pitched whistling came from behind his ears. He remembered this unbearable pain from the storm at Toshiro. It subdued and he had time to glance around to see the scenery surrounding him now. The dome was way above and only small pieces of the floor now still stood up there. All the rest, metal beams and tiles, were now all around him and he quickly checked his body to see if he was injured from this fall.

He blinked and felt relieved all his organs were still intact and sighed again in relief when he noticed his knife that Felix had killed himself with had also fallen down with him and landed close to his left ear, pierced into the floor and was still wobbling where it had only just struck. He couldn't believe his luck and quickly pulled out the bloody knife from floor and stowed it where it would be safe.

Val rubbed his head, held out his hand, called his staff to it and used it to pick himself up. Sharcole was gone; nothing but a mess of bone and muscle on the floor; surrounding him were other bodies of the elementalists. All dead, except for the body of Vix, who lay there still but breathing and slowly coming to her senses.

Acarlie floated down smoothly, her eyes fixated now on Vix as her next victim. Vix was slowly getting to her feet when she saw the wild and powerful Acarlie float down to her and hover above her.

"Please!" she began to plead but Acarlie was gone and so could not hear her beg, and the white eyed, beautiful monster had no remorse whatsoever and lifted her hands again and all the metal shrapnel began to lift from the floor.

"No!" Vix cried and tried to turn to run away.

Acarlie lifted the metal shrapnel from the ground and aimed it towards Vix, but Val dived in front of her to protect her.

"Acarlie!" he called up to her. "Don't do this!"

As soon as Acarlie saw his face she screamed again. Her head flinched and she suddenly grabbed onto her skull in agony. She began battling inside her mind screaming, "Val!"

The shrapnel was thrown. Val quickly activated his electric shield, the means of which he always had on his left arm, – a long fingerless black glove he had received in Hiro that reached all the way up to his elbow. A button in the centre of the palm would activate a translucent, blue, oval field of energy the people used as shields. The large shrapnel was scattered and the smaller was diverted away from them as he lifted his arm and took the impact to save their lives. The walls and ceiling were now pelted with the shrapnel from the previous floor and some parts of the walls fell down, revealing heavy machinery previously used to power the room above. Everything fell down again and the room rumbled and shook with the impact. Val could only turn around and lift his shield again to protect Vix from falling debris. Again Val was fortunate to not feel the weight of the heavier objects but still screamed in agony just from the force of the distance that these metal squares of flooring fell from and slammed into his shield.

One part of the machinery that had recently been unaffected by Acarlie's previous EMP blast fell from its foundations and crumbled against a wall high above them. It looked like a spinning metal wheel attached to a vertical conveyor belt which spun on an axis and turned cogs which powered lights as a backup generator behind the wall, but now the still spinning wheel fell against a metal beam that held up the ceiling. It shrieked of metal against metal, grinding away and causing millions of sparks to jump out into existence and rain down.

Once everything had fallen down again and settled on the floor he turned off the blue shield and helped Vix to her feet as Acarlie now got up from the floor herself. He struggled at first; his arm was aching, his legs bleeding, his heart racing.

"Go! Get out of here! Get help!" he ordered her and looked back.

The sparks now filled the room and lit up like raining fire. Acarlie was back on her feet and breathing deeply.

Having dropped his staff he called it again and stood strong and assertive, disobeying the painful commands of his body to rest and sit down.

"Acarlie! It's me! Calm down!" he tried to call, but now her head snapped up only seeing him as an enemy.

"Please!" he cried again but she only screamed and dived for him.

He caught her by her arms and tried to push her back. She didn't even stumble, her feet were in perfect harmony with the rest of her body and even when forced back she turned and forced her feet to the floor. Instantly balanced, with agility and grace she turned, jumped up and dived back into him and, together, Acarlie and Val began their desperate fight under the sparks, which were the only light they had to see each other by.

Val tried all he could to avoid her attacks while screaming to calm her down. "Stop!" he cried, "it's me!" but she could not hear. She continued on with her assault on him like he was an enemy she wanted to destroy. She fought differently when she was in this state of perfect concentration. Her fighting skills elevated, her speed increased, as did her drive and anger. Val could only block, parry and avoid her punches and soon she recognised his honourable defensive tactic and used it against him. She deliberately held out her hand knowing he would react to it and used it as a feint and quickly snapped a punch for his skull, precisely aiming for his cheekbone, and stumbled him back.

He tried to swing an arm up just to grab hold of her and hold down her arms but she caught his arm and twisted it around and kicked him away again.

Fire fell around them as the sparks still fell and decorated their noisy arena. Val found himself on the floor looking up at his Acarlie and breathing in the dusty air around him. His blood felt like it was on fire, his muscles crying in desperate agony for him to lie still and recover. Her skin was still the soft white skin he remembered, her hair was still the silky black but her eyes were hollow. With no pupil nor iris it was as though she saw completely through him and didn't see him at all. She whipped her hands out to one side and by the millions of sparks that fell around her Val could see the air around her following her orders and circling her. The sparks circled around her in the brief moment of existence they had before she threw them all towards him. He shielded his eyes from the flash of light and before he could lift his arm down she was there again. He dived aside while she kicked and swung. He stepped aside of her as she swung another and for the briefest of seconds forgot who he was fighting and raised his own hand. As soon as he did he saw the sweet face of the girl he vowed never to hurt looking back at him and hesitated. She thrust an open hand forward and hit him with an instant force of wind that struck him like a giant fist and sent him flying back to slam against a wall. The howling, screeching noise behind his ears rang out again and deafened him while he tried to come back to his senses. She stood over him again with her hands raised to one side and tensed her arms until the veins almost popped out of her skin. Val recognised this stance and remembered his dream.

Is this it? Is this when it happens? Am I supposed to kill her? he thought while trying to get back up.

The room started to tremble; everything metallic lifted from the floor as she raised her hands to the ceiling.

No, this is different. This can't be it!

She now held her head up and screeched like a wild animal as more shrapnel began to lift from the floor and above her head. What was left of the metal ceiling above them now started to shake violently and break away. Val noticed the whole thing was going to fall on them both.

"No!"

Val felt as if he couldn't move at first but leaned forward, tensing the muscles in his thighs and all the way down to his toes, and forced himself through the wall of pain to spring forward for Acarlie. He grabbed her tight with both arms and fell with her to the floor.

The ceiling gave way and everything fell. Val knew he was dead, but he couldn't let go of Acarlie and instead shielded her from what was now falling on top of them.

He cried and waited for the eternal silence, clutching onto her, protecting her. He pressed his eyes tight shut and squeezed out his tears, his heart shuddered but he felt no pain except a deafening slam, enough to pop his ear drums, around him. It sounded like a giant bell falling and he was in the centre of the impact. The whole plane of existence that he knew shook, like the world itself and everything in it vibrated as in a spherequake. He screamed but could hear nothing but the ringing of his ears. For a brief moment Val thought he was dead and this new pitch black ringing sensation would be his eternity. The ringing faded, however, and he opened his eyes to see a flash of blue. An electric domed shield covered them and kept the falling debris from them. He panted and waited another second and the metal that deflected off the shield slammed into the ground around them. Everything became suddenly silent. They were now in a perfect circle surrounded by debris. Val looked back over his shoulder to see Acarlie's hand was raised under his arm. He quickly looked back to see with relief the pretty brown eyes of Acarlie looking back at him before they rolled into her head and she fell unconscious and he was left alone, holding her, surrounded by the destruction she had caused.

Her head swam in a sea of discomfort and discombobulating blurry images. She felt warm and unharmed, lying on a soft bed. She was somewhere safe. There was a blurry image of a figure sitting beside her. When Acarlie's eyes finally focused the saw the smiling face of the very person she had been waiting so long to see.

"Hello Acarlie," that person said, her face lit up with the glow of a mother, a sister and a best friend all wrapped up in one.

"Sheeria," Acarlie replied and reached up from her bed and embraced her closest guide and friend.

With her arms wrapped tightly around the orange and black stripy tigian Acarlie didn't notice she was back in a hospital bed, but wouldn't have cared anyway. Sheeria laid her head back down.

"It's okay, I'm here now."

Acarlie lay back down and this time felt a painful sting on her back, as if the bed she lay on had two hot rods underneath the sheets burning her back. She jumped back up in agony, yelping in pain and was caught by Sheeria.

"It is okay, child, it's just a wound from the fight."

"What is it?" she asked, frightened, still feeling the hot

burning pain up her back. She slowly reached behind to her back and felt that it was bandaged up. As soon as her fingers felt the wounds on her back she flinched again. She remembered Sharcole's attack then, the two fire whips that scorched her back leaving two large vertical lines of burned tissue to scar all the way up her back in parallel.

"Are you okay, Acarlie?"

She breathed in and endured the pain and waited several seconds for the stinging sensation to settle and she slowly lay herself back down.

"Yes, apart from the mark it will leave on me, I will be fine. What happened to you though, Sheeria? Where have you been? I've been so worried."

"Not as worried as I have been, child. I assure you of that. I had a bit of trouble getting here. I had to go back to my village to ensure I got passage here in time."

"You went to Rowsena?" Acarlie asked, stunned. "Oh, I'm sorry I wasn't there. I know how difficult that must have been."

"That's okay, darling. I'm glad I went for I found my brother after so long. It was he who helped me get here. I'll tell you all about it later but right now I have to introduce you to someone. He has been with me since your E.B. in Donolan. If it wasn't for him I wouldn't be here."

Sheeria looked back and signalled for a figure to come in and Acarlie glanced over to see a white and black tigian. She smiled, knowing his name. "You must be Keppal."

Finally, here I am. Face to face with her. Keppal took a step forward and stared down at the young human female lying on the hospital bed. This was his target, this was the person Lord Zane had ordered him to assassinate, this small, skinny human. He began calculating in his mind what she was capable of.

Since the aired E.B. she had recently fought in was cut

short after her outburst he and Sheeria never witnessed the aftermath, only seeing it until poor Electra lost her head, when the power cut out. This meant her power was still a mystery to him. She looked weak, especially at this moment, lying there on a white bed smiling up at him. He could kill her now, Sheeria would not be able to stop him.

"Thank you for helping my Sheeria. And Val and Mitis for that matter. Without your help, none of us would be here." The young terrorist smiled up at him.

She was so oblivious to his intention, smiling at him like a dog at the barrel of a gun. Flashes of her murder filled his mind as he stepped forward. The white sheets stained in fresh blood. The crying of the tigian next to her and her wincing corpse afterwards. He would be arrested, he was not afraid of that, Zane would see him released, he was sure of it. His eyes widened as he approached, his fists opened and he extended his claws. He breathed in and focused but withdrew suddenly for some reason he couldn't understand.

"Yes," he said. He didn't know why or what he was doing but continued, "I'm glad to finally meet you, Acarlie. Sheeria spoke very highly of you earlier."

There was still hesitation in him, this was his chance but the way Acarlie smiled up to him made him pause and think.

There must be some mistake.

Acarlie's innocence glowed like an aura that made him question even his lord, Zane. It was like his detective instincts he had trusted all through his career were screaming for him to stop but the loyalty to his lord were urging him further.

Acarlie, being oblivious to the battle in Keppal's mind, turn her attention back to Sheeria. She still had so many questions.

"So where is your brother? I have always wanted to meet Audie."

"He is on his way, child. He is currently with the presence of Captain Kaza. The only way I could get passage here was by striking a deal with my brother so the pirates can teach them how to make cannons."

This, however, now won the battle in Keppal's mind. *Giving others the knowledge of creating great weapons of destruction? Maybe they are terrorists.*

Acarlie, however, looked shocked, "But Sheeria, those are forbidden. We cannot go against the universal treaties like that."

What's going on?

"I know, Acarlie, but there was no other way to get back on this pilgrimage with you and to stop the black hole."

Yes, Val mentioned a black hole, it still doesn't explain why Zane would want to use this to destroy Sphere though. Maybe they are using this as a way of defeating Zane. Maybe they are trying to convince this Acarlie that he is evil so she can defeat him in battle. This all sounds insane. What are they not telling me!

This time Sheeria had a question. She reached down and stroked Acarlie's head with the back of her furry hand. "What happened to you in the C.E.L., Acarlie? The event was cut short, something happened there, didn't it?"

Acarlie looked up and saw the worry and concern in Sheeria's apple green eyes. It felt like so much had happened since they last spoke in Donolan after her battle with Electra, in a hospital bed just like this one. She wanted to tell her everything but couldn't. She couldn't bring herself to tell her that Miles raped her and that she somehow destroyed Donolan, the Bastard Camp and the C.E.L. Her memories were all completely blank but luckily for her she didn't need to.

"I destroyed the C.E.L.," Val said from behind them.

They all turned to see Val leaning up against the door. He too had been treated for some minor injuries after their encounter but Val always did seem to heal quickly. Seeing him here produced mixed emotions. Sheeria smiled and waved him over to embrace and welcome him back and see for the first time the scars on his face; Keppal wanted to leap forward and tear his throat out but now knew there were too many present; and Acarlie felt angry with him still and spoke her heart's truth.

"What did you think you were doing, Val?" She jumped up and slapped his shoulder, her back flared up again but this time she gritted her teeth and ignored her pain. Sheeria quickly turned back to her and laid her back down gently.

"You knew you shouldn't interfere, Val! You knew and you still did it! Why!?" she screamed at him. The last thing she remembered was briefly seeing him there with Felix.

Val couldn't let everyone know what was happening to Acarlie; if word got out that Acarlie was as dangerous as a nuclear bomb they would have her executed. The only person who had seen Acarlie's true power was Vix, and he'd made sure she would be quiet and given her a mountain of lies and promises to keep her mouth shut. She was good about it though, with Sharcole dead she was now the C.E.L. champion and forgot quickly and turned her attention to her own success, only making Val promise to protect Acarlie. He didn't know what Sheeria would do so thought it essential to not let her know and take the fall for this.

"I had to cancel the event, I had the cameras turned off so the fighting elementalists would not need to fight and kill themselves any more. I ran in knowing I shouldn't and I evacuated every elementalist there."

Acarlie didn't know if this was true or not. In her memory he *was* there and this did sound like something only he would do. She didn't see this as a heroic act though but instead a violation of her wishes as an elementalist.

"You shouldn't have gone down there, Val! I told you before about following my instructions! You are a guide, Val! You're supposed to act like one!"

Val took her every attack on the chin and looked down.

"I know, Acarlie, and I'm sorry." He hung his head.

"We have been through this over and over again, Val! I know you're new to Sphere and its customs but that's not an excuse any more. Your childish and imprudent decisions are costing people's lives now, Val. Felix followed you down into the C.E.L., didn't he? He died because he followed you. You killed Felix!"

This one touched a nerve for Val; Felix had been his friend, "I did *not* kill Felix!" He pointed an angry finger down at her; even Sheeria had to push him back now.

"Calm down you two!" she tried to shout and ease the situation.

"Yes you did, Val. Felix's blood is on your hands!"

"If you want to blame someone for the death of Felix and Electra–"

"–Don't you dare say Sharcole!" she shouted back, and would have jumped up out of bed if Sheeria had not been there.

"I wasn't going to. The blame falls at the feet of the tigian who arranged for the death penalty on your arrival to the C.E.L.!"

This cut Acarlie's words short. "What do you mean? Who ordered the death penalty?"

"Take one guess who ordered it," he said patronisingly.

"Don't talk to me like that!" she bellowed.

"Calm down you two!" Sheeria now screamed to the both of them.

"Maybe we arrived at the wrong time, Zoudiva," came a

familiar, welcoming, strong voice, breaking up the argument.

Everyone stopped and turned to see both Raiden and Zoudiva standing at the door where Val had stood previously. The last of Acarlie's guides had returned, the reunion was complete.

Keppal was standing embarrassed during the whole argument, like a guest at a friend's home made to sit through a domestic, and just wanted to leave now the largest of the group had arrived. Now, murdering Acarlie was completely out of the question and so he stepped back and sat down and just watched the reactions of these terrorists in action.

Raiden and Zoudiva both stepped forward into the room, "Is everything okay in here?" Raiden said. His large presence and deep voice dominated the room instantly. It was remarkable, Keppal thought, Acarlie was the elementalist and therefore should have the authority here but it was clear to everyone that Raiden was the alpha here.

The first person he saw to though was Sheeria, standing there between the two hot headed humans.

"Raiden," she said and reached up to wrap her arms around the back of his mane. She seemed more relieved to see him than everyone else.

He squeezed her in his arms lightly, wincing in pain as he did so, and when he let go he held a gunshot wound on his side, Acarlie noticed.

"What happened to you?" she asked from her bed.

"Apart from being shot, nearly dying and being saved from the very creature that was created to kill me? Nothing," he lightly joked and winked down at Zoudiva.

"You were shot?" Val asked, feeling the same concern as everyone else in the room. Raiden looked over to Val and instantly fell silent. He didn't answer but stepped forward and reached out to lift Val's face to look straight at him. This was the first time he saw Val's scar. He sighed in pity but also in relief. He paused while inspecting it, running his finger down the river of tissue around Val's face before finally smiling.

"Now you look like a leo, Val."

"What?" Val asked, stunned.

"You have the leo's mark now, just like King Kerry has."

Val remembered the bear of a man known as King Kerry. King of Racoves, trained as a leo just like him by Raiden's older brother, Valadad. He remembered the scar Kerry had across his face, it was a common sign of being trained as a leo.

"But I thought the leos had to make that mark."

"Well, normally they do but who am I to scar your face more than it already is?"

He let go and now turned his attention to the sweet girl lying down and knelt down and hugged her, gently so as to avoid the injury on her back as well as his own wound. This was his way of letting her know she was still important to him. At first it felt like he would never let go. Acarlie closed her eyes and buried her head into his fiery red mane as if it were a bed of soft straw.

Zoudiva walked up to both Val and Sheeria, nodded and waited for them to greet him too, when Raiden finally let go of Acarlie and stood up. He could see that she was still upset with Val but with both Raiden and Sheeria now standing beside her, optimism, relief and even some happiness started seeping through her. Stress was leaving her like steam and she laid her head back down on the pillow against Sheeria's hand and took Raiden's in hers. It looked like Val was the only one here who was disturbing her calm right now.

"I'm glad you're safe, Raiden, and you, Zoudiva," she

said. She looked up and caught Val's eyes then instantly looked away so as to avoid further conflict.

"And I you, Acarlie." Zoudiva nodded and gave her a warm smile, almost croaking with his deep voice.

The tension was slowly dying now but Raiden still needed to cut it more.

"Well, I am fine, Acarlie, except for the unknown amounts of kingnine blood I now have circulating through my body."

Zoudiva knew Raiden's intention here and didn't take offence and instead followed on the banter: "Ha! Think of my shame knowing that my blood was wasted on reviving the last Leo. I could have let you die, my name could have lasted for thousands of years among my kind."

"Oh, your name will last longer than that, Zou', I assure you of that."

Val smirked much like everyone else in the room then. It was great to see two previous enemies now sharing banter like brothers. He noticed Keppal still sitting in the corner of the room.

"I am sorry that you had to watch this, Keppal."

Even as he spoke Acarlie seemed to flinch with anger again but held her tongue and let him continue.

"How is Dusty?"

Keppal blinked, his memory flashed again of the moment when he murdered him, blood staining his hands, blood that since then he had felt not washed away.

"Dusty fell in the attack in Donolan. He was killed by the army led by Feydon."

Val stood stumped; he knew Dusty better than anyone here and saw him as a friend, but when he knew of the ursa's death a new responsibility was immediately appointed to him.

"Oh, I see, in that case I feel I have a promise to attend to."

He stepped forward to leave but before he did there was one last thing he had to do. He turned to Acarlie and bowed his head.

"Acarlie, my elementalist. May I be excused?"

"Where are you going?" she asked. There was still ice in her words, she was still angry and unfinished with him, but she didn't hate him.

"I made a promise to the ursas that I would speak to the councils of the great cities on ending the divide between the humans and the ursas. Since the Senate is here this is my chance to fulfil my promise since Dusty cannot be here for himself. I will return afterwards."

He spoke the whole time to the floor to avoid the accusing stare in Acarlie's piercing eyes, but eventually looked up to bite the bullet he was taking for her.

This was clearly what was needed right now. While looking into Val's eyes Acarlie knew she was still too stressed to look more at him right now and needed the time with Sheeria.

"Okay then, Val, you may go. Please return once you are done though."

Val nodded.

Raiden looked from Val to Acarlie, then looked over to Sheeria, who nodded in approval as if she could see what was in his mind and agreed with him.

"I shall come too, Val. I think we need the time together anyway. This will be the perfect time for everyone to cool down a little."

He walked up and rested a hand on Val's shoulder. "Ending a divide, Val? Very noble of you. Come on then, let's go make history."

13

Rezosa was in the Scarlet Arise in training still with Mitis. Since the ship was docked and the crew dispersed it was now the quietest it had been. Only Zahied was also on the ship, all the way down at the other end studying the map they had recovered and making a copy to present to the others when they returned.

Mitis stayed quiet and together they used this quiet time on the ship for some undisturbed training. Mitis was slowly getting used to the handling of weapons and slowly her legs and back were getting used to the stances and postures.

She hit the ground over and over again, every time thudding against the floor while Rezosa showed her technique after technique, reverses and throws in a catalogue she made Mitis memorise as well as patterns and katas. Rezosa still didn't understand why Mitis was so persistent sometimes and often admired her spirit. Mitis had been through a lot here and no matter how she tired her out, bruised her or trained her until her muscles ached and seized, she never gave up; there was a strength in Mitis and she respected it.

Mitis charged at her, guard raised, and lifted her leg to thrust into Rezosa as she'd instructed. Her kicks could now reach up to Rezosa's chest and Rezosa caught her foot and pivoted around and sent Mitis to the floor to slam down again and this time twisted her ankle in a lock that would break it if she applied pressure.

Mitis cried out and tapped the floor and afterwards Rezosa showed her the technique and how to apply it.

Mitis was now red faced from exhaustion, her long, soft, blonde hair now stuck to her head and face by sweat and her fringe now almost covered her emerald green eyes. She nodded when she was showed and grunted and huffed when she picked herself up again and leaned against one of the plaster walls of the ship to catch her breath. Rezosa finally saw her legs and arms were shaking now. "I think that's enough for today, Mitis. You should rest. I heard the others have caught up with us now. You should probably go and see them. The leo might have a few things to teach you anyway."

Mitis still panted and was rubbing her shoulder, leaning into the wall, "Okay. Maybe this is time too for you to go and speak to him."

Rezosa was picking up her weapon from the floor. "Who?"

"The mute."

Rezosa rolled her eyes when she heard. Not this again.

"Look, Mitis, I've already told you, I'm just not interested in Monkey and he needs to learn to just get over it and carry on. This isn't my problem, it's his and he is dealing with it. It's your interfering that is making things worse."

Mitis finally straightened her back and looked over at the tall, dark beauty. It was no wonder that the mute was infatuated with her with her large dark eyes and sharp eyebrows. Her hair was a dark shade of auburn that glimmered red if caught in the right light, the colour of caramel to match her tanned skin. Her figure slender and toned, her hair long and soft; if only she were as beautiful inside as she is outside, Mitis thought.

Maybe it was because Mitis never had the attention Rezosa had when they were younger, Rezosa thought briefly. Mitis was a pretty girl and there was no denying it, but her beauty was softer and not as piercing as Rezosa's; she was a small girl, almost petite, with small shoulders, soft, elegant hands and glowing with grace, but with uncertainty. Her real strength came from within. Maybe she was larger when she was young, Rezosa thought. Maybe she was jealous of the attention Rezosa received.

"Things will only get worse if you keep him at a distance like this, Rezosa. All you need to do is talk to him and clear this mess up and he will be fine."

She was naïve, however, Rezosa thought to herself and tutted away her suggestion.

"No, Mitis, trust me on this. If I start being nice to him and give him more time he will only see this as a wrong sign and be filled with false hope that will only hurt him more later. I've seen this before. His heart needs to break if he is to become stronger; we have all been through this, Mitis."

"You know that's not true, Rezosa," Mitis said coldly now. She was beginning to tire of Rezosa's stubbornness.

Rezosa, however, was also just as done with Mitis's meddling with her affairs and snapped back at her.

"That's enough, Mitis. I'm done with this. You want me to speak to him, then fine."

She threw her weapon, Hevana, down onto the floor in her temper and walked out of the room, shut the door and locked Mitis inside.

"I'm going to go and tell Monkey what he needs to hear!"

"No!" Mitis yelped out as soon as she heard the door lock. She tried turning the handle and after she realised she was locked in the room she slammed onto the door and listened to the sound of angry footsteps walk away from her until she was left in silence. She fell down to the floor with her head in her hands and cursed both herself and Rezosa. After the tension died down and she realised it had been ten minutes and still there was nothing but silence she reached down for Hevana and began to practise.

Prime Minister Tigian Cecil Vurbute was talking quietly to the porcus prime minister, Lucdear Enzo, in the Senate.

"So how do we know the Elemental Lord will be true to his word?" Lucdear asked.

Cecil Vurbute held down on the wheels of his wheelchair, turned around, rolled over to the end of his desk and pulled out a letter, showing it to him.

"The words of the E.L. will be solid, I promise you that. He had already predicted the arrival of Elementalist Acarlie, which should be enough to believe that he speaks the truth."

The porcus read the letter then quickly burned it away, holding it over a candle on the desk. "But if this is true then–"

"Are you having another meeting without the rest of the board?" the human prime minister said as she walked in.

"Sarah Celadore, what a pleasure it is to see you," Cecil declared and bowed lightly from his chair.

"Spare me the false pleasantries, Cecil, we both know you would rather govern these races yourself sometimes."

She smiled as she entered the room with the aeomon prime minister.

Cecil smiled politely and went to open his mouth, when she continued.

"And lying would only further the insult, Cecil." She sat down at their table. "Now then, I'm sorry for the hasty discussion here but I have very important matters I wish to present to you all. A short while ago I heard that the head of the elder council passed away. The cause was unclear, even to us, and we have been told that all of the High Elders have now passed away in an accident that recently happened in their temple."

Lucdear gasped and Cecil, having been a little annoyed by her last sentence, now listened with wide eyes and open ears while she carried on. Only the aeomon beside her, whom she had told a few moments ago, was unscathed by the news.

"This is terrible news," Lucdear announced.

"Yes, indeed it is. But I do have some hopeful news though. I have four people with me today who are essential to this table right now and bring hope to these dark days."

Cecil folded his arms, unsure of how only four people would be able to turn this around; without the High Elders there was no one to represent them in the Senate or to lead their kind.

"Now firstly I would like everyone to remain calm here…"

With a sentence like this everyone now sat in suspense, even the aeomon prime minister was unaware of where Sarah was going with this. They all turned as Sarah gestured in two figures. One they instantly recognised as the young human guide to Elementalist Acarlie and the other figure walked in beside him. Both the porcus and the aeomon jumped out of their seats in shock as for the first time in their lives they saw a leo armoured in glistening leoium alloy armour walk proudly into the hall, towering over his small human companion.

Cecil was dumbfounded. "A leo?" He turned his chair and wheeled himself toward the furry giant.

"If I could jump out of my chair in shock I would. I thought the leos were all extinct."

The leo bowed to them all. "No, tigian, however, I am the last of my kind. There are no other leos any more besides myself."

"Surely this should mean you should be given a sanctuary. A species like yours and its history in Sphere deserves the chance to repopulate," Sandchi Oshea, the aeomon prime minister, suggested. He walked up to Raiden and held out a hand. Raiden shook it firmly with a polite smile.

"Finally, after ninety eight years since the Leo Divide started, we have a leo here with the council. Now I feel the council is finally complete once again."

"Actually you are mistaken there, Sandchi," Sarah said and stood up from her chair and walked over to them. "Young Val here and Leo Raiden have some important issues to discuss with us and so I also have the other two guests with me who will help with their plea."

This was new to both Val and Raiden. They had previously spoken to Sarah Celadore about this matter but had no idea that there would be another two guests with them.

Once again Sarah gestured with a hand over to her side and welcomed them in.

"Now I should say that the words spoken before about Elementalist Acarlie's journey are true and both Val and Raiden here are key members of this special crew and their progress so far has been of great interest to the planet and to the elders."

Val's ears pricked up and he looked over his shoulder to see who these two new guests were.

"And so I have with me today both the old, recently re-instated High Elder of the Elder Council, Elder Amber Pulaguy, from the small island of Walton in Racoves, and the Ursa Representer, Tiffran Arnill."

Once the old, wrinkled elder whom Raiden knew from home had slowly hobbled in holding her cane beside her and wearing a warm smile for him, he knelt down on one knee. She was still dressed in the common cotton robes and silks of the elders and the colours she wore suited her name. She reached down and gently touched his shoulder.

"Hello, my dear Raiden. It's so good to see you."

"Elder Amber? What brings you this far away from home?" Raiden asked.

She gestured him to stand back up on his feet. "I have heard about the progress of your mission, Master Raiden," she glanced over to Val, "and young Val. I knew you would eventually be here in Chippenham and so I packed some bags and started travelling here with the hopes that I could assist you once more in our most significant mission."

"I still don't understand, Elder Amber. You have been retired for years now. Why return here?"

Beside Amber the last guest walked in, another familiar face for Val. With chocolate brown fur with wisps of white and grey streaming from his nose to the back of his head the elderly ursa stood proud and wise. Val recognised this ursa from the council he had to speak to when he visited the Ursa Village; it was his idea to send Dusty the ursa with him on his journey, still not aged enough to need to support himself on a cane but old enough to show a history of memories in his eyes and an encyclopaedia of knowledge buried in his mind.

Elder Amber continued, "I have been given regular updates of your mission, Raiden, and it was when I discovered that you and Val would be visiting the elder capital that I decided I would travel here. I knew of your help from the ursas and so took it upon myself to arrive in the Ursa Village outside Toshiro first so as a civilised council we could end this petty divide once and for all."

The wheelchair-ridden tigian, Cecil, raised an eyebrow and glanced over to the porcus prime minister, who understood immediately what this could mean.

"I...well, it would be an honour to discuss these matters. Now we truly do have a full house of the different species here in this council once more." The aeomon prime minister stuttered at first but welcomed the ursa.

Tiffran Arnill had been the spokesman of the ursa race once long ago before the forty-seven year divide between the humans and ursas started. Since then most ursas had hidden themselves away in their own little communities and distanced themselves from the world, and he was no exception. He wore black silks and linen similar to the elder and the tigian; having a full pelt of thick, dark fur he didn't need tailored clothes like the humans did.

He walked past slowly at first and sat down at the table. It was clearly important to him that the ursas be re-instated back into civilisation and he needed to present himself formally and assertively if he were to succeed.

"It was my understanding that another ursa under my command would have originally been here representing the ursa race." He spoke softly but dominantly and turned to Val.

"Where is Ursa Dusty human?" he croaked in the deep voice of the ursas.

Everyone now was stepping back to the table to take a seat except for Val himself, who stood stricken and lost for words. This ursa did not know of Dusty's death yet and he didn't know how to break the news to him. "I'm afraid Dusty fell, my lords and ministers."

The ursa Tiffran Arnill's eyes glazed over as he remembered the strong, black furred fighter, before nodding. "Well, I hope his death will not be for nothing."

Everyone was now seated except for Val, who stood back a few paces as before, and Raiden, who had to kneel down when presenting himself at the table of species since there was not a chair for him.

"Well then. I guess we should decide on this matter of the ursas first since we are all here now before moving on to the topic of the elders," Sandchi suggested, pressing his elbows into the table and locking his fingers together.

"The divide was the idea of the humans, my friend," Cecil added suggestively. "It was when the Leo Divide ended that Sarah's predecessors decided on dividing with the ursas for their 'indecisive, neutral actions' during the world's last great divide."

He aimed his words carefully and precisely at Sarah. The olive-black skinned prime minister saw through his attempt and tried to avoid an argument.

"Yes, I agree, Cecil that the actions made by humans towards the ursa race over the present years have been rash and, frankly, unforgiving." She nodded her final word to Tiffran himself, who also saw what was going on between the tigian and the human.

"I would like to add that over the years of exile my people have endured I admit that I grew somewhat to despise and even hate your kind Human Prime Minister. We were friends and were betrayed only because we chose not to fight against the leos, but now all I desire is for my kind to live alongside the rest of this world."

This sentence now called the attention of Raiden himself. "And as the only leo of Sphere left I too must admit the same sin, ursa."

Val looked shocked hearing this and Raiden looked over to him, feeling his stare, and finished his sentence.

"The Leo Divide saw the near extinction of my people. The leos ruled Sphere for a very long time…"

"Three thousand and forty-one years to be precise," Lucdear added, "and another two thousand, one hundred and thirty-six years of a golden age of peace of all races before the Leo Divide started."

Sarah was beginning to tire of the word arrows all aimed at her. She was supposed to be the highest in command of this council since humans currently controlled the majority of the world and she wanted to remind them all of this but bit her tongue and let the leo continue.

"…Yes, thank you, porcus. My kind were wiped out due to war and divide and I confess my own heated feelings towards humans sometimes, but I know these are selfish thoughts and share the desire of the Ursa Prime Minister."

He looked across the table at the noble, elderly ursa sat upright, as tall as himself, and nodded. "On behalf of the leo race, I thank you, ursa, and stand by your side in your re-insertion to Sphere's community."

The ursa smiled and nodded. Too many words could be said now but he knew only a small gesture would be enough; he was grateful. He turned back to Sarah and spoke formally, straightening his back.

"Prime Minister Human Sarah Celadore. You are the highest in command on this table and represent the race who divide us. I vow for all my kind to never bring these actions of yours up again in these meetings in exchange for an end to our little divide. I do, however, have some conditions I hope you will honour. First of which is an apology to be broadcast so my ursas all around the world can know it is over."

Sarah now felt silenced. She looked over the table to see every eye was now on her. Humans ruled Sphere and had done since the end of the Leo Divide forty-seven years previously. Apologising to the rest of the world would strike up countless debates about the humans' control over the world as well as her own human councils debating about her own integrity, but she knew what must be done.

"Very well then. I shall see to it that the ursas are welcomed back into the world once more. Now, what were your other conditions…?"

Rezosa stormed through the ship stopping briefly when she found Zahied and asked where the mute aeomon was. Kaza and Midia were now also here on the ship with a tigian who explained he was Sheeria's brother. Kaza was showing him the weapons on the ships after he had been informed of the deal she'd made with her brother. She quickly acknowledged them before walking off again and going deeper down into the bowels of the ship to where they said Monkey was usually hiding. She was still infuriated by Mitis's meddling with their affairs and now only wanted to find Monkey and straighten this mess out. The planet was in danger, Zane was off somewhere causing as much trouble for them all as possible, Acarlie still had a few more elemental battles to fight but Monkey thought it more important to think about his manhood and cried when he couldn't get his way. Monkey was not her problem and the sooner this was all sorted out, the better.

She nearly ran down the metal steps, her feet tapping loudly on every step and clicking as she hastily walked down the narrow corridors until she came to the room they told her he would be in.

She reached for the door but before she did took a quick breath and calmed herself down before opening it. Sure enough there he was, holding onto a supported wooden beam above him and pulling himself up in exercise.

Once he heard the door he dropped down, seeing her, and reached for an old jumper, which he threw over his head and dressed himself.

"Monkey," she began. "We need to talk."

He hesitated at first and slouched forward a little first and nodded, waiting for her to continue.

She took another breath, wondering how to break this subtly before thinking to herself, *No, this isn't about me. This heart needs to break if he's to move on. The longer I leave it the worse it will be. It's half my fault it's got this bad. I should have done this sooner.*

"I want you to know that I appreciate you helping me…" *that's too easy, it needs to be harder…* "but I want you to stay away from me."

She looked into his eyes the whole time. At first his eyes shot all around the room avoiding hers, but after she said this they fixed on her. She could see the pain in his eyes now, and confusion, especially since he really didn't deserve this. He had stayed away from her just like he should have done, but it wasn't enough.

Damn you, Mitis!

"All the while we are on this ship and on this mission I want us to keep out of each other's way, you got me? I want you to forget me and understand that I don't like you. You're too whiny, it would never work between us so drop this whole brooding, pining nonsense now. I don't want you near me, okay? Get it in your head that I don't like you."

She stood after her speech and waited for his reaction. He still stood as silent as ever, his head dropped towards the floor and he didn't even nod. She knew he understood though.

She took a step back and held onto the door, wanting to finish it off but thought otherwise, she had said enough. She closed the door again and left him there and walked back down the ship before turning a corner and falling against it and sitting on the floor.

She didn't hate Monkey, how could she? He came back for her when she was captured in the Feydon camp. He was there when she needed him and it hurt her deeply to be the one to break his heart. Mitis was right, Monkey was a fragile thing, unstable and unpredictable. When this was all over she vowed to tell him the truth. She sniffed as her own emotions got the best of her and covered her face as she sat against the wall. She started to hear the sobs of Monkey as he cried in his room and started crying herself; her eyes brimmed with tears and she quickly wiped them away.

"I'm so sorry, Monkey," she said to herself, "there was no other way."

She sat and listened to him crying in the distance before standing back up and gaining control of herself again.

"Damn you, Mitis."

The council meeting went on for another fifteen minutes on the topic of the ursas before both Sarah and Tiffran were satisfied. The vote was unanimous and after forty-seven years the divide between ursas and humans was over. Some things Sarah was not too keen about, like the apology and announcing this moment as the ursas' 'victory over the humans', but with all the other species around her she had no choice. It helped greatly that even a leo was there, since the Last Divide was primarily between the humans and leos. Raiden stressed the fact that the ursas should not have been divided in the first place for staying out of the affairs of others. Val listened intensely to the history lesson from a sideline and learned that the timeline of all Sphere was set between different divides. He learned that the leo timeline started in 00 LW (Leos' World), which was a leo-made divide that lasted over three thousand years. In 3041 LW the divide ended and so started 00 UTS (United Time of Sphere), which lasted another two thousand years – golden years of peace between all species. This lasted until 2136 UTS (98 years previously), when the Last Divide (at the time called the 'Leo Divide') started and lasted for fifty-one years until 2187 UTS became 00 ALD (After Leo Divide), the timeline they were in now.

Immediately after the Last Divide was officially over (only announced when they believed the leos to be exterminated) the humans called for another divide on the ursas and Val himself saw the end of that forty-seven year divide and brought himself back to the present, 47 ALD.

Sarah had no say in that matter except to agree with the rest of the Senate that the humans had wronged the ursas and signed a written document with promises and vows of how they would amend their wrongs. And just like that, it was over. A historical day for all of Sphere. The word was sent out immediately, even before the meeting was adjourned, and Tiffran Arnill had a welcome spot in the Senate as important as everyone else's.

"And so may I ask that we move onto other pressing matters, Prime Minister Sarah Celadore?" Aeomon Sanchi Oshea asked. He turned his attention to Elder Amber Pulaguy. "Like what is to happen with the Council of High Elders?"

Amber smiled and nodded gracefully and spoke in her usual soft, formal voice, "I heard of this unexpected and tragic news of the deaths of the High Elders when I arrived here and was immediately approached by the other elders of our great city. Many still do not agree with my coming out of retirement but the vote was in my favour and so it is my duty to not only represent the elders in this Senate but to also become High Elder of Chippenham again. I have requested for my old supporting elders in my council to stand by me once more but have only been given a new council."

"A new council? So quickly?" Sarah asked.

"Could a new and inexperienced team govern the elders as before?" Cecil asked.

"I admit my new council is made of younger elders than before, still brash sometimes and power hungry, but I assure you all that as long as I stand at the head of my council and all of my race the old ways of the elders will be sustained. It is unfortunate, yes, but soon we will have everything back to normal. Once I find another suitable team of wise elders I will reorganise another successor, as I did before. My main issue though for coming here was of course to speak with both Master Raiden and Master Val."

Raiden now looked intrigued. "What is it, elder?"

"It is my understanding you travel with a young human elementalist who is searching for some very important items that will help us all against the black hole."

"Not this again," Cecil complained and sat back in his chair.

"How do you know this, Amber?" Val asked now, walking around and kneeling beside Raiden.

"You should know by now that we elders have ways of communicating with the planet and each other. I spoke to a certain elder named Vanslow from Selodia not long ago and he informed me that this elementalist travelling with you is also searching for more elemental schools that are outside the normal circuit of schools on her pilgrimage."

Raiden remembered Acarlie mentioning this and became excited. "You know of them?"

Amber smiled. "Yes, of course, these were schools that over the years had been forgotten or banned from the pilgrimage, back when even I was young. The first is a cold school in the mountains of Glacias Terras – they train there in the Element of Ice – and second is an underwater city just north of the Amburn Sands. There they teach the Element of Dimension."

"Amburn? That's next to the Anglish Desert," Raiden mentioned and mentally noted.

"Are there any more, elder? More schools I mean," Val asked.

"Well, no one can be certain, Val. The elementalists are an ancient race just like the rest of us and so have been pilgrimaging for many, many years. I think it's certainly possible that there could be more but no one can be certain. I think if there are more then they would possibly be tombs by now. These are the only two of which I know. If your Acarlie wishes to finish her pilgrimage and defeat Lord Zane then these elements would be useful for her."

This now made Cecil Vurbute sneer, "No one can defeat Lord Zane, Elder Amber, he's the greatest elementalist that has ever walked Sphere."

To which Amber politely countered, "True, but he will only be the greatest until the next elementalist defeats him."

Edwin Townsend finished another mundane shift at the warehouse where he worked, finished the same routine of cleaning down as before, said goodbye to his managers and left the building feeling the usual sense of relief and freedom being away from work gave him. He walked down the streets alongside the same faces as before, past the broken window scattering glass over the roadside, past the deathly smell of the same take-away bin left rotting outside, and boarded the same dirty, rusted old tram. He sat in the same seat with his head pressing against the glass window staring into his reflection watching the street lights pass over him rhythmically as before.

He sighed as he stepped off the tram and made his way to his apartment again, looking up into the black void above his head and wondering if it was day or night above him in Hiro. He turned a corner and saw his apartment. The blue light from his gran's room still flickered and made him smile briefly. He was already planning his night of speaking with her then heading out to the bar again with his friend Jacob, when he looked and saw Jacob was already there on his doorstep waiting for him.

He was sitting on the patio step with a small, black, plastic ball, bouncing it and catching it. Jacob had a strange fascination with that ball; it was small enough to put in his pocket and so he took it everywhere. He often called it his 'lucky ball'.

He looked up and caught the ball, stood up and slipped it back into his pocket.

"There you are."

"Why didn't you wait inside? Gran would have let you in," Edwin asked, stepping past him and opening the door. They had been friends so long they really didn't need to say hello sometimes. They had always been thick as thieves and used to act like them when they were kids.

The door creaked when he opened it and immediately the warm, cosy smell of home wafted past him and out into the street.

Jacob stepped in and headed straight for the kitchen. "I was only there for like five minutes. I knew you wouldn't be long so I didn't want to get your gran to come all the way down just to let me in."

He picked up an apple and showed it to Edwin and after Edwin nodded in approval he bit into it.

"Oh, thanks. I'm going to check up on her."

"I'll get the TV on."

Edwin nodded again and walked further into the hallway, hung his coat up, took his shoes off and headed up the stairs, rubbing the tiredness out of his eyes and clearing his airways and throat. He heard the sound of a male news reporter from her room and sighed, the news always unsettled her.

He opened the door and sure enough there she was still lying on the bed with the television on in front of her. She said nothing but he didn't mind, she often was asleep when alone, or sometimes she was so enthralled in what was on that she blanked off sometimes.

He walked past her to the television and only heard the words '*Ursa*' and '*Divide*' and '*come to an end*' but again took no notice and turned it off.

"You know you shouldn't watch the news, Gran. It's always morbid you keep saying, remember? They never have anything nice to say."

He stepped back around the bed and sat down again. "How are you anyway today, Gran?"

She didn't reply, sound asleep as always.

Edwin smiled. "That will be the news again, boring

voices send you to sleep."

He didn't want to wake her but reached out and touched her hand. Her head was facing away from him, as if looking out of the window opposite them. He noticed her hand was colder than before. He frowned at first, worrying about the heat, and reached out with the back of his fingers to touch her forehead, again cold to the touch.

"Gran?" he asked her gently and took her chin and turned her to face him to wake her up.

"Aren't you cold in here tonight?"

Only when he turned her head he saw her ice blue eyes were half open and staring out straight through him and into oblivion.

"Gran?" he asked again. His heart now beat like a drum, her touch was so cold, her stare so vacant, her chest was so still.

He let go and looked down at her, a sudden loneliness cast over him and suddenly the room became so much darker, light faded around him and he closed his eyes and inhaled the cold, empty air around him.

He'd known this day would come, he'd known it was only a matter of time before he was all alone but this still didn't help ready him for the shock of finding out. He choked and held his hand over his eyes.

He didn't make a sound until he whimpered out and a single tear trickled down his cheek. He wiped it away and stepped back downstairs where Jacob was watching the news.

"Good news, Ed. The Ursa Divide is over. They announced it earlier today. Looks like we'll have ursas back down here."

He smiled over his shoulder to see Edwin standing at the door, supporting himself against the frame and standing like he was lost in his own home.

"What's wrong with you, ya big bastard?" he joked, but

once he looked into Edwin's teary eyed stare he looked briefly up to the ceiling where Gran slept, the smile wiped from his face; suddenly this was no time for friends to jest. Jacob suddenly changed into the serious friend needed. "I'll call an ambulance, you sit down, here. I'll turn the TV off. Just sit here, take a breath." He sat Edwin down and ran off into the kitchen to call for an ambulance.

The ambulance came and went, carrying Gran's body away, and Edwin insisted on going with her. Sure enough Jacob went too with moral support for his friend.

A day passed and her death was confirmed. The doctors said she died peacefully in her sleep, age was the killer and that she had lived to a grand old age considering she'd lived all her life in True Hiro. None of this meant anything to Edwin though. He knew she'd died peacefully, he'd known this day would come soon and he'd been waiting for it, but he still felt empty, alone and lost without her. She was like a mother to him and without her he felt he had no direction any more, no stability. In a way he was now free but his freedom was a dark bottomless pit. Everyone around him was still celebrating the end of the Ursa Divide. There were parties in the streets, even though there were no ursas down there. True Hiro looked for any reason to celebrate sometimes and the end of a divide was always a global deal that connected everyone.

It lasted two days. He didn't show up for work and hid himself away in his dark apartment. She had always been upstairs bedridden so he had always had the space anyway, but even now it seemed empty without the occasional call from her or the constant sound of the television coming from her room. He cried, he drank until he passed out and when he woke he cried again. His gran was gone and now there was no one in his life apart from his best friend,

Jacob, who was good enough to give him a couple days of space to mourn in private but soon enough the silence of his apartment was broken by the sound of the same four taps on his front door, Jacob's knock.

Edwin poured some liquor down his throat and stumbled to the door to see Jacob there.

"Hey, how you holding up?" Jacob asked quietly and carefully.

Edwin swayed a little at first but eventually nodded. "I'm okay."

"I'm glad to hear it...she was a good person, Ed. I'm sure she's back with the planet now."

Edwin nodded again and thanked him for his compassion.

"Anyway while I'm here I have to show you something. Something *big* has happened!"

"If it's about that stupid Ursa Divide I don't care, Jacob," Edwin warned.

Jacob shook his head. "Nah, everyone has already forgotten about the Ursa Divide. Something else has happened. Come quickly, there's a big broadcast in the streets."

"Why? What is it?"

"There's been a leak of information from Chippenham, something bad is happening."

"Another city invaded?" Edwin asked but Jacob didn't answer, instead pulling him away from the door. Edwin quickly locked it behind him and dashed after his friend until he found himself amongst hundreds of other people. A grand screen used to broadcast E.B.s above them was displaying a news report that people gathered around to watch in shock and horror.

"Quit stalling, Jacob! What's happening?" Edwin asked, tired of the secrecy.

Jacob pointed up to the screen and said the sentence that was on everyone's lips. "The world is ending!"

The news continued on a loop telling the crowd and all of the world about the black hole. Pictures were drawn up to present to the world what was now lying outside its atmosphere. It reported that this news was 'leaked' from Chippenham after reports that the High Council of Elders had all passed away and a new council had been appointed.

The people screamed in shock and wonder when they heard. Many thought it was some sick joke, many didn't believe what they were hearing and the more stubborn believed they did not have to worry after it was announced that the Elemental Lord himself was currently working on finding a solution to this potential global disaster.

Edwin stood dumbstruck when he watched a representation of what would happen once the black hole approached. Suddenly his mourning for his gran had gone and he felt scared and suddenly small and helpless, even a little happy she died when she did because she now wouldn't have to worry about this. Jacob was right, he thought, this was big. The world was ending, and they were all trapped down in this forgotten city.

The broadcast finished and started again on its loop and when everyone had seen it they suddenly became panic stricken and immediately took their families away from this crowd of people. Then the police arrived to disperse the crowd.

Edwin stood feeling his soul was now hollowed out; first his gran died and now this, what was the point of going back to work now? What was the point in anything if they would all die soon?

"Everyone go back to your homes!" he heard a distant cry from the police.

He heard screams and cries of people around him and suddenly a crash behind him. A window was smashed and the villain pounced on by the police.

"This is some heavy shit right, Ed?" Jacob asked from behind him. "What are we going to do?"

The smashed window was part of a kiosk, a spirit merchant, and people scrambled in to steal the spirits and run away with them. Some were caught, pounced to the floor, where the bottles smashed and the unbroken ones rolled down to Edwin's feet.

He felt himself come back to reality when a bottle touched his foot and he picked it up, thoughts and ideas rushing through his mind like a waterfall. He looked to see a parked M.V. close by and walked over to it, picking up a rubber tube some villain had left on the floor while the police beat him down.

"What are you doing, Ed?" Jacob asked and had to run to catch up with him.

This was all too much for him. Edwin knew this wasn't right but with his life already ended with the death of his gran and now the end of the world coming he had nothing left to lose. He twisted off the lid and drank some of the spirit straight before pouring the rest away, put the tube into the M.V.'s fuel tank and started transferring the fuel into the bottle, and in a quick moment he had made a Molotov cocktail.

He stood on the M.V. and quickly glanced over at the people now screaming and running around. More windows smashed and the police now stood as a wall with their electric shields activated, glowing light blue like sapphire in the darkness of this city. He lit the bomb with a lighter and screamed out at the top of his lungs, letting the world hear the pain in his heart, everyone's attention now on him as he threw the bomb at the police line. The bottle lit up the night around them, all eyes watched the flaming bottle fly towards their oppressors, the fire itself lit a spark in the eyes of the beholders and became a symbol of freedom. As the bottle smashed, the fuel exploded fire as well as the imagination and ideas of the people witnessing it, taking their cold souls into its warm embrace and danced a dance of imitation and retribution. Thus the riots began.

14

The blue sky over Racoves was littered with thin clouds. The sun was high and burning down bright and warm over the green meadows and fields leading into forests and distant farm lands. A peaceful, light wind brushed over a large tent fit for a king which was set up away from any civilization next to a single manned skyship. A small dead deer was carried over the shoulders of the tigian and when he reached his temporary home he flung his bounty on the floor ready to skin.

Zane had been waiting days for word now and used the time to sit back and wait for his plans to take effect. He had a monitor set up inside his tent and had since kept a keen eye on the world news. He watched the C.E.L. matches and witnessed as much as the rest of the world of Acarlie's progress and was disappointed when the power cut out and the broadcast was cut short. He did, however, hear of her in Donolan from Miles's report and could only guess that she was the reason for the premature ending of the games. He grinned as he took out a knife and began skinning the deer while thinking about this elementalist and her broken conditioning. He needed her dead if he had any real chance of completing his mission, but her being alive was also of great use to him if he carried things out accordingly. He had been around for a very, very long time now on Sphere and had learned many things about tactics and time. Time especially. Sometimes he would try to remember previous lives he had lived. He tried and failed. Faces would blur into a shadowy darkness, voices would blend into his own mind's inner monologue and some memories were nothing but a black void like a drunk's night out. Smells, however, lasted longer; a long forgotten perfume or the smell of cooked meals would sometimes awaken lost memories; he liked remembering things. He would often close his eyes and go back and remember all he could but mostly the memories were like pictures. He could see them but their edges led nowhere but back into reality.

Some faces would never leave him though, some very few individuals had made such an impact on him that he could never forget them no matter how old he was. The first was his own appearance, the one he was born with, and second would always be his first parents. Then there was the young woman, dressed in clothes people wore no more, light brown hair, amber yellow eyes, plump pink lips and a name that echoed all through his incredible time on Sphere. Sometimes he would still dream of her, his beautiful Asta.

There was also a man from his first life, a strong man with a bushy black beard, strong posture, almond shaped eyes and wit as sharp as a razor. Ezique was the last person he ever saw in his first life and he would always be one of the most important. He also briefly remembered a tall lean man with gelled black hair and a strong, piercing stare, but he too was eventually fading over the millennia.

There was something in Acarlie that brought up memories millions of years old. He had witnessed so many things, he had seen creatures evolve from single celled organisms to become great monsters and eventually die out and become extinct; he had witnessed every divide that history told of, and Sphere was so very, very old.

He tried not to think about them and cut out more meat from the deer and threw the pieces into a pot he had filled with water and placed sticks under it. He gestured his furry orange hand to the sticks and conjured fire to light them and began boiling water, then sat down and admired the blueness of the sky today and listened to the boiling water begin to bubble.

"Excuse me, Mister," a young voice said from behind. He raised an eyebrow and turned around to see a young aeomon child, his hair strawberry blonde and his tail not yet fully grown.

"Would there be any left of that deer once you're done?"

The boy looked skinny, weak and probably was used to begging; he probably was a wildling, forced out of the village he was born in and made to hunt for himself; and from the look of him he hadn't mastered it.

*The young and foolish...*Zane thought to himself. He wanted to turn the boy away, any other Elemental Lord would have had a most pampered life, but he was different.

"Sit, join me." He gestured a hand downwards and let the young child sit beside him. He cut out some raw meat and with his control of fire cooked it in his hands and offered it to him.

The boy gasped in wonder. "Wow, are you an elementalist or something?" He took the meat. "Thank you."

Zane smiled. "Yeah, something." The boy ate like he hadn't in months, still blissfully unaware he was dining with not only the Elemental Lord but the very being who wished to kill him. Zane liked that; ignorance was bliss sometimes.

Zane heard a beeping noise and looked at his arm to see that there was an incoming message on his receiver. He opened it and pulled the flexible screen up and turned it on to see the face of his wife before him.

"Hello darling, how are you? I'm here just like you asked," she asked sweetly.

Here we go, it looks like we can finally get this plan moving.

"You took your time."

"Yes darling, I had to make a little diversion for Miles..."

Good, just like I wanted.

"…and secondly, I needed some parts delivered from Alpha. I needed, however, to make another change of course to acquire them."

Hmmm…

"What was that then, my queen?" he asked carefully.

Queen Angel smiled, her beautiful, long, thick brown hair shimmered in the light and her large, sapphire blue eyes with long eyelashes opened with excitement when she continued.

"Proto-Weapon is finally complete. I'm sending it into Chippenham."

Zane now scowled and narrowed his stare as he contemplated before finally deciding he didn't care, but she wasn't to know this.

"Proto-Weapon is and always will be unstable, Angel. It is a disaster waiting to happen."

He knew his plan would work – tell Angel not to do something and that is exactly what she will do. He had said this a dozen times now when sending her concubines but she would always have them executed when she was bored or disappointed with them. He really was waiting on Proto-Weapon and waited for her to disobey, which she most surely would.

"But darling, Proto-Weapon is the tool we will use the acquire what we need. Once you have destroyed the black hole and I have what I desire we can finally live together forever in each other's arms. Sphere will be ours to share for eternity."

Sphere already is mine, Angel. Since it's mine I have the right to do what I want with it.

"As you wish, my Angel. So be it, send in Proto-Weapon and I will make my way forward to destroy the black hole. Soon it will all be over and you can share this immortality with me."

Zane noticed the little boy beside him was looking up

while still eating his free meal. His eyes stared more at the device on his arm and Zane could see words like *Proto-Weapon*, *black hole* and *immortality* were alien to him.

Angel kissed her fingers and pressed them against the screen. "Yes my love. Please don't be too long. I will have our ticket soon. I love you."

Zane gave her a comforting smile and touched the little fingers with his own; he turned off the connection and immediately dialled in another with the touch screen and waited until another face appeared before him, a soldier. He wore civilian leather clothes and had black hair with streaks of grey, a wrinkled face and a crooked nose.

"Yes, my lord?" the man asked.

"Queen Angel has just arrived on the outskirts of Chippenham. Is everything in position?" Zane asked.

The soldier saluted. "Yes, my lord. Everything is just as you left it. The charges are still in position. I have the detonator ready."

Zane grinned and nodded. "Detonate it. Good work, soldier, I'm sending your payment. Everything that I promised and more." He pressed another button on the screen and waited to see the reaction of the man. His eyes looked like they were popping out of his head.

"T...thank you, my lord."

"Now remember, not a penny of that will go through until you press the detonator. If I were you I would do so immediately and escape that city as soon as you can."

"Yes, at once, my lord. Thank you."

The connection was cut again and Zane lifted his head to the blue sky and sniffed the air, he smelt victory was so close now and so easily taken. He arched his head to the distance of Chippenham and felt he could almost hear the explosion; but of course that was in a different country and completely untraceable. He cut more meat from the dead deer and again handed it to the young aeomon and began dining in the sunshine with him.

He smiled. "There is going to be a lot on the news in these coming days, son."

"I don't have a television, Mister."

"Of course you don't. Now why don't you grab some wine from behind you and two glasses and tell me a story," Zane smiled, relaxed back into the chair and faced the blue sky.

"What do you mean a '*leak*'?" Kaza asked, astonished.

Kaza, Zahied, Midia and Mitis were all in a council in the Scarlet Arise. The day previous they had witnessed the broadcast of the discovery of the black hole, and now the world knew about it. Acarlie and the guides were still around the hospital, and Dude kept to himself in his hole and was watched by Mitis with care and enough distance that he was unaware of it. She herself had no more to say to Rezosa after what she said to Dude but now after this broadcast she didn't know if it even mattered any more.

Zahied had finished making a map for the crew when he first heard and called the Captain and his second in command.

"It was broadcast late last night. Someone from the Senate must have leaked this information. I was there when Acarlie mentioned it, they were the only ones who knew."

"What will this mean?" the long haired pirate Midia asked. She stood wearing boiled brown leathers with a black, short sleeved shirt underneath, her hair tied back with a single dreadlock strand hanging down her right side.

Kaza already knew what this meant and struck the table before him with his finger in his irritation. "It means riots. True Hiro was the first to spark them off. It's been going on all night apparently. You can't look at the media at the moment without hearing about it. All day now they're saying it's nothing to worry about, that the black hole will just pass by without harm."

"Denial?" Zahied suggested.

"No, just bullshit. Only problem is that True Hiro is one of the cities that doesn't believe it."

"Okay, but why does this affect us?" Midia asked again.

This time Zahied answered in contempt. "Because we still have to go to True Hiro."

"We do?"

"The items, remember? In each elemental school. True Hiro still holds an item that Zane hasn't reached yet. That gives us a chance to snatch it before him. Only thing is, now we've got another obstacle in the form of a massive pissed off city before us."

"Maybe we can actually use it to our advantage though," Mitis suggested optimistically. Since she had not trained today she had dressed herself in a rose red kimono with white, shaded flowers reaching from one sleeve to the other, matching the white centre piece, and tied with a black ribbon. "We could use the riots as a distraction and get Acarlie to the school before anyone knows we're there. Dude can help us. He's from the city, right? He will know the short cuts."

This much Kaza couldn't argue with. The mute aeomon had already taken Kaza and his men across the rooftops of the city once before; he could do it again.

"I think Mitis is right," came a voice from the door behind them. Rezosa and Major were walking into the conversation; they each understood the problem and Rezosa knew Mitis was right.

"I also think it will help the little guy, not only will we take him home but he can also prove to us and himself that he is useful in this cause."

No thanks to you! Mitis wanted to shout out. Rezosa walked up and looked over to Mitis.

She wore a frown as if she knew what Mitis was thinking and didn't want to bring up an argument, but instead talked about what the real issue was.

"Is he safe now though? We all know what happened at Donolan. Can we trust him?" Zahied asked.

"Monkey is safe for now, I can guarantee you that much, but he is not suited for these missions any more. I think we can all agree that he will be safe once he is back home where we found him."

The small discussion was suddenly cut short as an explosion erupted from within the city. The floor shook lightly and everyone quickly sprinted for the cockpit, where they saw the two pilots Dillon and Smythy peering out of the window and into the distance.

"What was that?" Kaza asked, pushing Smythy out of the way.

"I think it is the Elder Temple, Captain," Dillon said, running his hands over his bald head.

"The Elder Temple? Who would…?" Zahied began but the name popped up in his mind immediately: "…Zane."

Kaza pushed back past the people and pointed at Zahied, Rezosa and Major. "Go and get the elementalist and the guides back here on the ship, we're leaving!"

Rezosa and Major immediately nodded and started to leave but Zahied knew there was more to add. "But what about the elders? Destroying the temple is a pure act of divide! If we leave immediately then we're the priority suspects!"

"Screw the elders, damn you, caster! Get the elementalist back on the ship!" Just before he left Kaza quickly called him again and threw him two arm communicators he had brought previously, "Here, take one and give the other to the leo! Just in case."

Zahied left the ship with Rezosa and Major and made his way to the hospital to find the others. Mitis still stood at the cockpit and watched as another explosion detonated. She froze in fear and wondered what was to happen now.

Val called his staff. The long, six foot metal staff appeared as it always did and he charged his opponent with a feral war cry. He named his staff '*Staff*' back when Mitis first introduced herself to him back in the Toshiro hospital before it fell to the storm. It wasn't the most creative of names but it suited the staff well.

He dived forward, Staff in hand, and swung to one side aiming for Raiden's skull. Raiden ducked and blocked, lifting his arm, and used the metal plate attached to his forearm to take the impact of the staff.

Raiden still wore the leo armour of his deceased brother, Valadad. His armour was a large, shining, metallic blue plate that covered his chest and was attached by leather to his shoulders. Extra pieces stretched down his arms and covered his forearms and down his legs, over his leathers, and protected his shins with armoured pads. Val, now having his purple traveller's cloak off, was fighting in his old lizzier skin armour, using his electric shield whenever he needed. His armour still wore like leather clothing but the skin of the lizzier was tougher and had seen him well through his journey so far. It was attached to him with buckles and clips and covered his front and back, straps with small pads reaching up to his shoulders leaving his arms completely free for movement.

They practised and sparred with Zoudiva watching from a sideline until Val was out of breath and defended while Raiden swiped and dived for him. Every time Raiden caught him he would open his mouth to pretend to bite down on Val, who would chuckle and laugh and push him away. They fought like pups with Raiden still teaching Val how to fight like a leo and teaching him manoeuvres and throws. Val was becoming a better fighter. Raiden was pleased with his progress but reminded him that no matter what, they were both Walton Warriors, protectors of the small island of Walton back in Racoves.

They finished their training both smiling, feeling well exercised. Raiden took off his armoured chest piece and put on his green waistcoat, completely sleeveless, and over that his light brown cloak. Since his accident at Donolan and his journey on the train, his cloak had since taken wear and tear. He always liked his cloak and so cut it down to half its size and still wore it over his shoulders. It still reached down his back and tied at the top making an upside down V shape across his chest. The sleeves now showed the cut stitching of where the rest of the cloak had been and now only reached to his elbows. He wore it well still.

Val was throwing his same old purple cloak over his shoulders when he turned back to Raiden.

"Raiden, about Acarlie."

Raiden brushed off the dust from his knees and lifted his armour and bag and threw it over his shoulder. "Don't you worry about Acarlie, Val. I spoke to Sheeria and a reason why we needed to train now was so that I could speak to you about her, and she could about you."

"Look, I don't want Acarlie to ban me from the pilgrimage. I know I messed up but…"

"No one is banning you, Val. Acarlie may be the elementalist but she will listen to Sheeria when necessary."

"This is true, Master," Zoudiva said. "She will not abandon us from her pilgrimage. She may be upset right now but she will understand."

This wasn't all Val wanted to say though; a truth struggled deep inside Val's chest, and he had to let it out.

"Raiden, that's not all I need to say about Acarlie."

Raiden tilted his head slightly to his side and looked down at Val wondering what he meant.

"What is it, Val?"

Raiden was Val's best friend, and one of his only friends. He knew what he had to say would be hard for the leo to hear but he thought maybe now Raiden would understand.

"There is something I need to tell you, Raiden. Something is happening to Acarlie. Please sit down and hear me out."

Raiden nodded and sat down beside Zoudiva and let Val continue. At first Val struggled with his words but eventually spat them out. Raiden was surprisingly patient while Val told him about the elementalists' conditioning, how the elders have always been afraid of their power and so gave them boundaries by walling them in with customs and teachings. The news of Acarlie breaking these mental barriers and turning into a white eyed creature of great power was unsettling for him, however.

Zoudiva, having heard this news, told them too of her first experience when she changed when she fought Khan back in Selodia.

Val felt he had to leave out what Miles did to Acarlie. As much as he wanted to tell Raiden this he simply couldn't find the words to tell him how he had failed and Acarlie was raped. He paced up and down as he told everything he could. Once he finished he stopped and spoke over his shoulder. "So you see why it is hard for me to tell you this."

Raiden nodded slightly while thinking and taking in everything he heard. "Does Sheeria know?"

"No, I don't think so. I think Acarlie is keeping it quiet and not wanting to worry her."

"Good, I don't want Sheeria dealing with any more stress than she already has." He stood up and took a couple steps forward. "Thank you for telling me this, Val. From what you have told me, it sounds like Acarlie has this switch inside her that only switches on at an emotional level."

"What do you mean by *switch*, Raiden?"

"So far every time you have seen Acarlie change has been when she was faced with a dramatic, or emotional moment. When she first changed in Selodia she was lost and thought all her guides but Zoudiva had died. She was faced with death from a superior elementalist and turned in a moment of desperation to survive. In Donolan, you were fighting Miles; she was scared and turned again to try and save you. The third time was she was faced with losing you to the Bastard Camp and so turned again, and finally after she witnessed the death of both Electra and Felix she must have felt despair and anger and turned again and took her rage out on Sharcole. This time even fighting you in a moment of frenzied emotions. So far it only responds to Acarlie's negative emotions. I think it would be safe to presume that you should stick by her at all times. She may be angry with you at the moment but if she lost you again she would turn. We all need to keep her from turning into whatever the elders have done to her."

Hearing Raiden speak of his masters like this surprised Val. Raiden stepped past him and holding onto his armour said, "Come on, Val and Zou'. Let's get back, you can tell me more on the way."

"But that's not the point, Sheeria," Acarlie argued with her closest friend. She was now back on her feet and dressing herself back in her tight black shorts she battled in and her dark grey vest. Sheeria gently helped her into a sky blue and white sleeveless waistcoat as her back was still sensitive and she wore long, black, leather boots she tied up. She stood up and ran her fingers through her silky black hair, pulled it back and tied it into a pony tail, letting small wisps of her fringe hang down over her brow. She finally put on her black cloak with the red and white lines and patterns decorating it over her shoulders with the hood down. "Val still goes against everything I tell him. He's supposed to be my guide and abide by the rules of my pilgrimage."

Sheeria was wearing her brown, leather shorts, reaching down to her knees, and a buckled lizzier skin half vest that only covered her breasts and ribs. Her cloak was made of tigian velvets the colour of blood; they were wrapped around her neck and hung down over her and a hood hung down behind her head. "Acarlie, you must understand that Val only acts as he does because he cares for you. You should be thankful for that. You wouldn't be here now if it wasn't for Val."

"I know but it still doesn't excuse him from constantly breaking vows he took when he became my guide."

"We both know this isn't your ordinary pilgrimage any more."

"Yes, I know, but whether he likes it or not, it still is my pilgrimage. I can't have him constantly putting my pilgrimage at risk."

"Even if it meant saving your life?" Sheeria asked now.

Acarlie had rarely seen this side of Sheeria before. Sheeria was always behind Acarlie's decisions; this was the first time ever she had sided with Val.

"Why are you defending him, Sheeria?"

"Because without him we wouldn't be having this discussion, child. At first I cared very much for your honour and pilgrimage and would have sat down and watched you die by the Elementalist of Lachine. I now only care for you, Acarlie. I thank Sphere every day that Val is different and doesn't care for the teachings as much as most people."

"What are you saying?" Acarlie asked.

Sheeria moved away from her at first and looked out of

a window to see the blue sky above them. The day was warm and bright and Sheeria felt comforted by it, also being back with Acarlie and seeing her safe made her realise now what had been bothering her for some time now. "I'm saying I don't want you battling any more Acarlie. I have lost too much in my life to lose you because of what your pilgrimage wants."

This shocked Acarlie beyond words. Val told her at Donolan about the elders' conditioning, she knew she had broken this conditioning and now from the look of Sheeria's face, she had too. Sheeria always used to train with her and helped in her upbringing and was as strict on the rules as Acarlie. This really was Sheeria's pilgrimage as much as it was hers.

"Don't you trust me, Sheeria?"

"Of course I do, Acarlie, I have never had any doubt. It's everyone else I don't trust – first the fake elementalist in Lachine, then the elders in Selodia; then the deception of the C.E.L. and let's not forget Zane. Everywhere you go, Acarlie, people are desperate to stop you. I want to see you become the Elemental Lord, you know I do, but I fear I myself will step in on the next battle if things carry on the way they are."

Acarlie looked saddened by this news. "I'm a little disappointed in you, Sheeria. These are not the words of an elementalist's sacred guide leaving your mouth."

"Maybe not, but they are the words of someone who loves you," Sheeria reminded her then. "As do Val, Raiden and Zoudiva. You have to remember we are only thinking of your best interests. Would you rather die and leave us alone on Sphere without you just for the honour of your name?"

Acarlie shook her head and now felt ashamed of herself, confused and now with a loss of cause. "Then why do I persist on this pilgrimage if not to become the Elemental

Lord and bring honour to Eloma?"

"Because you have to defeat Lord Zane. Remember the black hole, Acarlie. There is more at stake now than the pilgrimage. If we don't defeat him then there will be no pilgrimages any more. If you fight for honour still, remember honour will be restored when Sphere is safe."

"I guess so," Acarlie agreed just as Raiden and Val entered the room. Zoudiva entered too but sat down at the door and began licking his paws, cleaning them as all dogs do.

She turned to see Val before her. Raiden pushed him a little in front of her and took Sheeria away to let them have their moment.

They were both hesitant and quiet at first.

"Are you still angry with me?" Val asked carefully.

Acarlie shook her head and looked up to him. He looked into her dark brown eyes, deep enough to drown in, and saw she wasn't mad. She herself looked up past his scarred face and into his hazel eyes and told him, "No, Val."

Val reached out, placed his hands on her shoulders and rubbed her arms to comfort her all he could. She reacted positively to this simple gesture and stepped a little closer to embrace him.

Sheeria was right about Val. He may not have been the strongest, tallest or even the smartest, all traits Miles outshone him with, and now his heavily scarred face took away his gentle looks, but Val was there for her, that much she was grateful for.

She looked over to see that Raiden and Sheeria too were sharing a moment. Val noticed it too. Raiden had Sheeria in his arms, he had her furry head between his hands and lifted it slightly to see the smile on her face, something of joy. He too smiled in a way that they had never seen before; it was a smile of content. He thumbed the fur on her cheeks backwards and she too held onto him tightly around his waist.

"What's going on with you two?" Val asked and started walking towards them.

They quickly let go of each other, shifted uncomfortably and fumbled with character as though they were acting. "Oh…nothing, Val…nothing," Sheeria said quickly.

Acarlie had known this part of Sheeria before and knew there was more to it. "What is it, Sheeria?"

"We're just…happy to see each other, that's all, Acarlie," Raiden confirmed.

Acarlie raised an eyebrow at Val and grinned but before she could interrogate the two felines a loud explosion rang out from the city. Instantly screams filled the air with fear and confusion.

The floor rumbled lightly, Raiden's smile was wiped from his face. He ran to a window and cursed.

"Sphere's divide!"

"What is it, Raiden!" Sheeria asked.

He looked back over so they could all see the smoke leaking from the city vertically like a black snake. "The Elders' Temple!"

"What? No!" Acarlie gasped.

Val knew immediately what this must be. "This has to be Zane; he's up to something again. We have to get out of the city. We found the map so there is nothing more we need from here."

"Agreed, I think we should rally back to…" Raiden began but was silenced as another explosion from the temple detonated and more wild screams ringing out from the streets.

They all began to exit the building and made their way into the street. Screams of confusion and panic cluttered the city now and people were all rushing past to see the great black snake of smoke in the sky.

"Look!" people screamed and pointed to a distant dot in the sky, flying in from the horizon. Raiden had stopped in the middle of the road to drop his half cloak and re-equip himself with his armour, when they all pointed to the sky.

"What is it?" he asked while throwing his armour over his head and attaching the buckles and straps.

"I don't believe it," Val said as he too witnessed it. "It's Feydon! Their ships are entering the city."

"What? But why? Zane was already here?" Acarlie pointed out, but Val's observation was correct. Feydon skyships began to slowly enter the city the moment the Elders' Temple exploded sending everyone into a wild panic, running around and screaming of another attack.

"We have to get back to the ship before the fleet arrives!" Acarlie commanded but of all her guides present it was Sheeria who was hesitant to leave.

Acarlie noticed her flinch at first and asked, "What's wrong, Sheeria?"

"Acarlie, please, child. I cannot leave without my brother Audie."

"Is this really the time for family matters?" Zoudiva asked over the sound of the confusion.

"I have left him once before, Acarlie, you know that. I will not leave him behind again."

"What's that!?" Zoudiva pointed out, cutting off Sheeria's conversation.

They all looked into the distance as something fell from one of the distant ships. It was so small from where they were it was hard to make out: a large, cuboid shaped, metal box fell from the ship and to the ground.

"More cannon fire maybe?" Val suggested, but Raiden dismissed it.

"No, there is no explosion. It looks like they are dropping something into the city."

"Maybe it is a part of the ship, maybe they're already retaliating?" Acarlie said.

Zoudiva sniffed the air and quickly turned, seeing Zahied and two more members of the team sprinting up in the distance.

Zahied ran as fast as he could in his clothes and blue and silver cloak but still trailed behind the two soldiers before finally reaching Acarlie and the others. Raiden was still finishing putting his half cloak back over his armoured shoulders when he arrived and passed him one of the arm communicators, panting, "Here, Kaza wanted you to have this and wanted everyone back on the ship."

Raiden took the device and fitted it comfortably to his left forearm with his padded, metal armour gauntlet over it.

"We are going, Zahied," Acarlie told him. Again Sheeria wanted to speak her mind but Zahied surprised them all.

"In that case you'd all better get going. I'm going to stay here."

"What? Why!" Acarlie asked.

"Blowing up the Elder Temple is serious. This will mean war and divide, no doubt about that. I don't know what the elders will do but we have to make sure your pilgrimage is left unsoiled. I will stay here and represent your progress with the Senate and the High Council of Elders. Their temple is destroyed, they won't like that, and we leaving so early will not look good on us. Hopefully Elder Amber is safe. She can vouch for us but we will still need someone to speak to them and keep them informed before they too start coming after us, blaming us for this divide."

Acarlie's eyes widened; Zahied was absolutely right. This was now a delicate situation: if she was blamed for the attacks then her pilgrimage would most certainly be over and she would be hunted down and executed. With all this now swimming in her mind she was speechless.

Raiden, however, was better prepared for such news and agreed. "Yes Zahied, you're right. We have already been blamed for the destruction of the C.E.L. No doubt the blame will fall straight on us unless we prove them wrong, but we have to make our way to the next item. True Hiro is the closest. We should make haste there."

"I can't go!" Sheeria now shouted hysterically. She had had enough of her voice not being heard. "Not without my brother!"

"Sheeria, please. We can send for Audie while on our way," Acarlie tried to convince her but Sheeria still protested.

"Acarlie, you don't understand. I have already left my brother once before. I have only just got him back after not seeing him for a century and now you ask me to leave him again. Please, Acarlie, please don't make me leave my family again."

Acarlie was stumped, but made up her mind quickly. "Okay, we'll wait until Sheeria gets her brother on-board the Scarlet Arise."

"I don't think we have time for that," Val countered and pointed again to the sky and the distant fleet of Feydon skyships.

"No, you're right, we don't," Raiden confirmed and stood tall and assertive, pointing at Val. "Val, you and Zoudiva get the elementalist to True Hiro. As soon as you acquire the next item you are to wait there. I will accompany Sheeria and Zahied to the Senate. We will find Sheeria's brother and get the first skyship to meet back up with you."

Acarlie looked over to Sheeria and couldn't believe what she was hearing. She had only just got back her dearest friend and now was being forced to leave again. She wanted to order Raiden as wrong but Sheeria turned to her, held

Acarlie's little, fragile hands in her large paws and pleaded, "Please let this be so, Acarlie, my elementalist. I know I am to follow you everywhere on your pilgrimage and I know I haven't been there as much as I have wanted to be, but please don't force me to leave my brother again."

Acarlie wrapped her hands around Sheeria's neck and consented. "Okay, this won't be long though, okay? Find Audie and get back to the airport. I will wait at the ship."

Val stepped forward to speak up but was silenced by Acarlie. "No, Val, Sheeria only needs to find Audie, we will bloody wait at the ship!"

"We don't know how long we will be, Acarlie, it's too dangerous to keep you here any longer," Raiden pleaded.

She stepped back and separated again from her two guides, all while the city still screamed, and ordered again, "Just find him quickly, Sheeria! I'm not going to leave without you."

Val took Acarlie's arm and they began to make their way back when Raiden shouted over to Val, "Remember what we spoke about, Val! Keep her safe!"

Val replied with a nod and a wave, wishing them good luck, and together they began their way back to the Scarlet Arise.

"What about you?" Zahied asked Rezosa and Major.

Rezosa looked back toward the skyship where Monkey would be and decided, "It's probably better if I stay away from the ship for a while anyway. I'll stay."

Major, however, did want to stick close to the others; as he had always stuck close to Rezosa, being the only person he was close to, he decided to stay and help.

The large, rectangular, metal prism smashed down on the ground after being dropped by the skyship. It tumbled over and over itself down a small hill before landing against a little road busy with people. People close enough to witness it crash down stopped and drew closer like flies. One male tigian stepped close and reached out to examine the strange alien metal cuboid. Before he could touch it the cuboid reacted. Pressurised steam whistled as it was released in jets into the atmosphere and little metal arms began poking out from all of the rectangle's sides. Poles pushing into the floor started raising the metal cuboid up until it rocked slightly and stood upright.

The tigian jumped at first at the sight of this near impossible contraption but stood in wonder watching it slowly stand upright all by itself.

"What is that thing?!" someone called out.

"Who cares what it is! Run away!" another cried and escaped. The tigian, however, was brave and curious.

He saw small lines reaching down the face of the cuboid. Once all the poles retracted back into it he saw it was a box of some kind.

The bottom opened an inch then, more jets of compressed air escaped and frightened more people. A strange bright green, jelly-like substance began to gush out of the bottom as the door lifted itself up. The tigian now jumped back so as to not let it touch him and more people ran away. Now only a select few stayed and watched as a figure began stepping out of the box.

Its first step almost seemed to shake the ground. A large, furry, cream foot stepped out. Its claws looked to have been removed and, instead, great metal claws seemed to have been hammered into the bone with grotesquely dried blood around them. They scraped against the concrete as it took another step. The tigian now gasped as it looked upon the beast that now stood among terrified people, towering over the humans and towering over the tigians. Its flesh was furred and cream coloured but it was armoured with metal on its chest, like it had had flesh and bone removed and replaced with metal plates and wires. Its shins, forearms, chest, back and shoulders all shone a metallic silver. It stood breathing heavily, its huge chest extending and retracting smoothly. It had a thick, red mane from the top of its chest that reached over and around its head but had been cut away for a metal helmet to cover its eyes. Its eyes shone out red like a kingnine's. More wires emerged through the top of its head, ran down behind its ears like hair then ran back into its body, covered with its shaggy, red, horsehair-like mane. The teeth it showed were like its claws and nails: metal replacements. Dried blood had hardened over parts of its body where it had been worked on. It stood terrifying and hideous, dangerous and monstrous. It looked no more than a machine, but it breathed, it saw.

The tigian could hear deep puffs of air entering and escaping out of the mouth of this terrible beast. He couldn't work out if it was dead or alive.

"Sphere's divide!" the tigian cursed.

The metal beast heard, its ears twitched and its head jerked with quick mechanical sounds like metal turning, its blood red eyes fixed on him immediately.

The tigian fell back in horror now and tried to turn and run, when the beast let out a digital roar, like its lungs were still working but it sounded like a computer making the noise. Before the tigian could turn the beast was on top of it. Its huge, razor sharp metal claws reached down and pierced the tigian's diaphragm and gripped the inside of its ribcage. Blood instantly spat out of the tigian's ribcage and he immediately projectile vomited more blood as the claws dug in. The beast had a grip like a vice; once its claws had dug in there was no escaping.

Everyone now screamed and ran away in every direction, as fast as their mortal legs could carry them. With another computerised bellow of what should have been a roar the beast ripped upwards, grabbing the bottom of the tigian's ribcage and ripping it out; bone snapped and crunched, blood sprayed and entrails fell around the instant carcass. With everyone scattered the beast let go of the tigian's bones and tissue it still held and lowered its head and peered out into the city, listening and breathing deep, angry breaths; growling with every breath, energy and violence seeping from its aura.

Proto-Weapon stood waiting...

15

The team were wrong in their blame for the explosion at the temple. As soon as the elders caught sight of the fleet of skyships, Feydon was immediately blamed and the elders were called to arms. They lined up in front of the temple and raised their hands to the sky. Instantly a purple dome was set over the temple. It glowed like the electric shields and made an impressive shield, only there were no more attacks to follow after the first two explosions. Another two lines of elders stood outside the energy shield and raised their hands and, with perfect timing, jets of glowing red and white energy fired from their hands and snaked across the sky to the distant fleet and fired upon them. The people ran screaming from the city as war had now been declared.

The city now was a grid of screaming people running down and away from the temple, over the dusty white concrete and past the windowed buildings of bricks and plaster.

Raiden and the others sprinted through the mass crowds like fish swimming upstream in a river before they reached the bright purple dome protecting the sacred elder temple. They were stopped when they arrived by an elder dressed in a dark green uniform, a turban covering his eyes and a conical, straw hat on his head. He was a military elder in charge of defending the temple.

"You must stop and go back! The temple is now off limits to any creature other than elders!" He called to them over the swift, zipping sound of more projectiles escaping from the hands of the elders and speeding towards the skyships, leaving a trail of red and white mist behind them.

"We are only trying to find my brother, elder. He is

Tigian Audie Katsan, leader of a settlement of tigians in Rowsena," Sheeria tried to explain.

"No one can enter the temple!" the elder ordered this time and pointed to Raiden. "Leo, do as I command and take these away from the temple!"

Like he had his own conditioning Raiden then bowed and reached for Sheeria's shoulder. "Come on, Sheeria, we will have to find another way to get to him."

"Raiden! Leo Raiden!" called a voice from behind them. They turned to see the wheelchair bound tigian Cecil Vurbute calling them over from a neighbouring parliamentary building.

They rushed over; still there was no other attack from Feydon but instead silence. No one or nothing made a sound and suddenly everything stopped.

"It is a miracle I saw you when I did. You are a Senate member and must be kept safe from this fighting. Come with me in here," Cecil called back to them over his shoulder and entered an office to his right.

Zahied was the first to enter, asking the question that was on everyone's mind: "Please tell us what is going on, Prime Minister Vurbute."

The tigian wheeled around to the end of his desk, "The elders have declared war on Feydon. Already Magna has called enforcements from Angland, Calmeron and Racoves. They hope to keep Feydon at bay for as long as possible. President Orion of Magna himself is on his way here with what is left of the army from Toshiro to help in its defence against Feydon."

Sheeria shook her head. "That is not going to work, Prime Minister. Feydon will have left the city before your enforcements arrive and even if they do, remember Feydon has already invaded their cities and Magna stood back and allowed this to happen. King Kerry is a noble human and so might offer assistance but I couldn't say as much for President Sarauami from Calmeron. Please, Prime Minister, we are only here to find my brother, Audie Katsan."

Cecil lifted an eyebrow in thought and nodded as he realised she was right. "Yes, I can understand what you mean. The elders, however, will find this a little harder to digest though...." He rubbed his chin while he tried to think of a solution.

"How is it though that you know Feydon will only stay briefly?" he asked.

"Because that is what they have been doing in all the other cities. They have been targeting the elemental schools."

"But we have no school here," Cecil stated bluntly, correcting her.

This clicked for Raiden. "He's right, there is no school here, no items."

"Items?" Cecil asked but was only ignored as Sheeria too realised what this meant.

"But if there are no items here then why are Feydon even here?"

"We are here for you, my darling," said the sweet, womanly voice of a human from behind them.

Cecil was the first to see. "Queen Angel. What is the meaning of this? Is this your fleet that stands outside our city?"

Queen Angel walked in elegantly and beautifully. She wore a long white dress that hung down and reached her ankles, with short sleeves to reveal her slender white arms, her hands covered in jewellery.

Raiden and the others were lost for words as she walked straight past them and up to Cecil, still seated behind his desk.

"Get the elders to call off their attack, Prime Minister

Vurbute. I am no threat here. The attack of the Elders' Temple was not my doing."

"What? Then who is responsible for the attack?" Vurbute asked.

"I have no doubt it was my dear husband; the reason for this though eludes me. I am here only for one individual." She turned and pointed to Raiden. "Him."

"I will not be going anywhere with you nor anyone else, Queen Angel. I have been given a sacred task by Elder Amber and intend keeping it."

"You misunderstand my reason for being here, my darling. It was by coincidence that I found you here. I came to order Cecil Vurbute to contact the elders to stop their attacks on my ships or I will be forced to defend myself and strike back. I came here for you, leo, and I have sent in only one to retrieve you. I am not asking you to come with me."

Raiden couldn't help but smile. He stepped forward and towered over the sweet, beautiful woman. "You forget, you are only one Angel and I am a superior being. I could snap your spine now and be done with this whole attack."

"Do leos always have to resort to violence and threats?" she asked, looking up at him, her sapphire blue eyes gleaming more than the diamonds hanging around her neck.

"Raiden is right, Angel, whether it is you or Lord Zane's doing you both represent Feydon and therefore are charged with war crimes against Magna as well as Racoves, Calmeron and Angland. Raiden, please seize Queen Angel and escort her to the elder temple, where she may wait her trial."

"With pleasure." Raiden reached up but his hand went straight through her as if she were a ghost.

She only stood there mockingly looking up at him.

"You're a caster?" Zahied asked, realising first what she

was doing.

"It astounds me how you all could believe I would walk by myself into this city just to demand this." She turned back to Cecil with a more demanding tone. "Cecil, call off this attack."

Cecil made not a sound but sat in decision and narrowed his eyes into hers, warning her away.

She understood what this meant and accepted his proposition. "Very well." She turned to her side and spoke to a phantom beside her that no one could see. "Send in the troops, Alberto darling. We shall not leave until either the leo is on board this ship or the city is on ruins." She finally turned back to Raiden and concluded, "Remember, leo, this war is not your fault but can be stopped by only you. Proto-Weapon is on its way to you now. You are to be taken by him. You will not resist or you will be killed and taken on board our ship."

"That will not happen, Queen Angel. Raiden is the last leo. This may be a war but even the elders will not forfeit by sentencing the last leo left on Sphere to death," Cecil finished.

"Then get ready, Cecil, and warn the other Senate members. I am sure Sarah Celadore would love to hear of how you refused to end this fighting."

As quickly as she came, she vanished, as though she was never there to begin with. The dust particles holding up the apparition suddenly fell to the floor. Immediately the distant ships opened fire. Missiles and explosives were fired at the city and, more specifically, the temple. Suddenly the giant purple mass of energy doming over the temple started taking heavy damage and hits. The elders, however, stood their ground and fired back at the ships.

"So, Feydon breaks the universal treaty of using forbidden weapons? Sphere hasn't seen a battle such as this for over a century." Cecil spoke to himself as he turned his chair around and faced the window to see the battle now commence. "We must warn the other Senate members immediately." He wheeled back around and to a side drawer in his desk. "I fear my legs do not work, can I possibly ask you to run this note to Prime Minister Sarah Celadore for me?"

"I'm sorry, Prime Minister, but I cannot. I am here only to find my brother as I have mentioned before. Myself and Raiden are still Acarlie's guides and must re-group with our elementalist once I have found my brother," Sheeria insisted.

"I will go." Major now stepped forward. He approached the desk and watched Cecil open his drawer and pull out a letter, already written and sealed, waiting for him.

"Feydon will be tracking our radio messages and so it will be safer contacting them the old fashioned way. In this letter is a code to a destination that only we Senate members will understand. Under no circumstances are you to open this letter and break the seal. If Sarah Celadore is handed this message with the seal tampered with she will be forced to believe that the message has been tampered with also. Do you understand me?" He held the letter and waited for Major to reach and take it. He held onto the letter as soon as Major's fingers touched the paper and continued, "Whatever happens you must keep the Senate members safe, else we risk another divide. You will find Sarah and the rest of the Senate members on the edge of the parliamentary district. I have no doubt that they will be advising Elder Amber since she now will be trying to resolve this issue rationally. I myself will go to the position now. I shall not say where though, that is for Sarah and other Senate members only."

"I understand, sir," Major said, taking the sealed letter and putting it in a pocket in his jacket.

"If we are to find the quickest and safest route we should go around the back of this building and away from the cannon fire. No doubt we will also encounter ground troops on our way too. We should hurry," Zahied said, while looking back out of the door.

"Good. As for you, leo and Sheeria," Cecil began again, "I suspect you shall find the tigian from Rowsena and his porcus associate with their zeppelin. No doubt they too will be trying to flee from this city. Since the zeppelins are aeomon-made I doubt they will have radios such as more modern ships', however."

"If that's true then how are we to contact them should they be on board?" Sheeria asked, trying patiently to take the details.

"There is a communications tower in the port. There they will have enough implements for contacting with aeomon technology. You all should hurry now, Feydon will be upon this building in minutes and I cannot move with such haste as the rest of you."

Before they left Raiden was the one who poked his head back around the door and finished with saying, "Thank you, Prime Minister, and thank you for sticking up for the leos too. As the only speaking member of the leo race, I appreciate the help from the tigians."

Cecil only nodded silently and waved him away since he still had to escape too.

Raiden and Sheeria departed from Zahied, Rezosa and Major and made their way back across the city now under siege. Raiden quickly found two dark green lizziers and mounted one, Sheeria did too and together they rode across the city with haste, hoping to find her brother before the Scarlet Arise had a chance to leave. They reached the terminal and felt relieved when they saw the Scarlet Arise was still docked in the distance. The terminal was nearly all glass, with wide open spaces and plastic chairs all mounted on a cream, marble floor in rows. Some travellers and staff were still scattering from the terminal and the rest had seen the dangers of the city and now ran through to their ships or had already escaped. The public transport skyships, however, were all cancelled and so left travellers looking to other places for escape.

"Oh, Acarlie is a good girl. She is making the captain wait for us like she said," Sheeria said while opening the first door and going into the terminal. She could see straight through to the other side and saw the Scarlet Arise and, more importantly, the communications tower on the other side of the runways. There were many, many obstacles to pass through before they could reach them.

"Security will not allow us to pass straight through, Raiden. What are we going to do? We must be quick."

"Of course they will, Sheeria. We came on board a privately owned ship each. You yourself arrived on board the zeppelin we are searching for."

They passed most of the public with no distractions but found it would be difficult to get past Security after it was established they had no paperwork. Sheeria tried to explain they were guides trying to get back their elementalist but still the security officer took them into an examination room where they would be properly interrogated, which was exactly what they had been worried about. They knew this might take hours. Raiden followed the tigian security officer, wanting to just punch him and make a run for it but luck was on their side as suddenly the whole station rumbled. Distant windows shattered and fell and voices shrieked in terror and despair. Something had attacked the station and now suddenly the security officers had no choice but to dash off, leaving only one behind to look after Sheeria and Raiden.

After the last security officer was left unconscious in a nearby room Raiden and Sheeria had access to the rest of the station, dashing past more Security, all running down to where these screams came from.

Their hallway led them into another terminal. They were the only ones in there now; most of the ships had departed and many bags and suitcases were left circling on the conveyor belts. They stepped in seeing out onto the runways of parked skyships, out into the large open space, when another large, tumbling sound came from where they had come from. They stopped as they could hear roars and screams getting louder as they approached. Running footsteps and cries to "Run!"

Before they could leave the survivors to their fate the body of a tigian was thrown through a plaster wall separating them from the screams. The body tumbled over itself and lay in a twisted heap, bloody and twitching. The two guides stopped as another cried in agony as it too was thrown, crashing through the wall and revealing to them the reason for the screams.

It walked with armoured pads, metal claws covered in sticky red fluids and two tigians grabbing onto its back trying to force it to the floor. It just straightened its back and reached over its shoulder for one tigian, flipped it over and onto the floor then repeated the action on the other, immediately grabbing the throats of the tigians and ripping them out and roaring in its feral rage.

Sheeria immediately saw the wires hanging out of its head and going back into its body and stood in shock of what she was seeing. "What on Sphere is that thing?"

The metal berserker growled and breathed like it was being caused agony, like it had a pain in its head that only violence could cure. Once it saw them its eyes locked on

Raiden. Screaming out again it began approaching them.

Raiden stood also in a frozen wonder, his eyes widened and his voice suddenly blunt. "Sheeria, I want you to run to the communications tower and find your brother," Raiden spoke unusually coolly given the situation but had a sense of immediate urgency to his words.

"Raiden, I can't leave–"

"Sheeria, do as I say," he commanded. "I will deal with this and get to the Scarlet Arise. Find your brother…I will deal with mine."

All the while he spoke he never took his eyes off the red bulbs that were on the plated head of Proto-Weapon, who also stood waiting now, staring straight into Raiden's eyes and breathing heavily.

Sheeria took a step back and left Raiden there, standing strong against this metal monster, hearing, and realising, what he just said.

"Wait, what? What did you–?"

"Sheeria!" Raiden demanded once more and cut off her sentence. She left him and started running for the tower across the tarmac and concrete.

Raiden stood still, facing Proto-Weapon. Its fiery mane matched his own but was torn and cut making it look scruffy and feral.

"What have they done to you?" he asked the creature, but really it was a rhetorical question. Proto-Weapon stood taller than Raiden, its claws sharper, its muscles larger, but even after all the work Feydon had done he still saw the same face. A tear appeared in Raiden's eye. "I cannot let you pass, Valadad, my brother."

16

The streets had emptied once the public caught sight of the Feydon forces now marching through their peaceful city. The tall human-made buildings of glass and concrete reflected the sun down onto the markets and bazaars in the centre. People were expecting the buildings to fall and gathered their families and escaped as soon as they could. Word had already reached the city about Feydon and their march through the cities of Donolan, Toshiro, Mecroyles and Hiro and now they believed it was their turn and, taking no chances, they ran as soon as the ships were seen and the Elder Temple burned and smouldered. Sirens were crying from ambulances and armed forces like they were flying past towards the marching army. The elders called to arms and tigians, humans and aeomon alike were now hastily equipped with electric shields and a melee of weapons ranging from short swords to long spears; bastard swords to war hammers; crossbows and bow and arrows. Their armour was all black metallic plates over dark green lizzier-skin leather that fitted each species differently, attached tightly with Velcro and small plastic clips and buckles. The humans wore plated chest pieces matching the aeomon's with similar helmets reaching around to cover their whole skull with a mouth piece feeding oxygen in like a pilot's mask and leaving their eyes exposed. Tigian helmets were larger and shaped differently, their ears were spiked up and left their face exposed so their teeth could be used as weapons, their metal chest pieces were carved to match their muscular body and gave them durability. Finally the elders wore not much metal armour, nor needed helmets, but instead glowed with an aura of blue and violet over their shoulders and down their arms and covering their bodies, only thick leather and cotton, dark green garments. Their bodies and legs were also covered in their own protective aura, metal armour would only slow them down. Their heads were covered in turbans masking their faces apart from their eyes and over their heads they wore straw, pointed conical hats. Their real armour lay in the aura, a small protective shield that covered their person and provided defences similar to the electric shields. As for weapons, the elders would use their mastery of planet's energy or *Spirit* to conjure knives to their hands that would cut the skin and evaporate back into air. Mostly the elders were archers and healers. They could shoot energy across their city against the Feydon forces.

The Feydon army, however, still wore their light green metallic armour made with a light and flexible metal that left nothing exposed, their helmets were masks and even their eyes were covered with small red bulbs. Their electric shields were large and rectangular, different from the oval shape of the rest of the world's and they carried everything from staffs to hammers; lightning rods that shocked their enemies; rifles, pistols and even cannons on the ships. The soldiers armed with forbidden weapons wore extra webbing with many large pockets with clips of ammunition around their waist. They were the more advanced army, their weaponry easily outmatched everything Chippenham had to defend with. This time, however, Feydon was not on the war march as before but was instead only marching through, not a shot was fired, not a building was fired upon; at least until the Chippenham defences were face to face with them.

Chippenham were the first to attack, still believing Feydon to be responsible for the destruction of the Elder Temple, with a charging assault, screaming down the empty roads with the tall human-made buildings looking down at them. As soon as Feydon was encountered, so did they defend themselves and suddenly shots fired out, echoing around the city, followed by wails and screams of victims.

Zahied ran, pulling his blue cloak close to him but still

trailing behind Rezosa and Major as they made their way around the back alleys of the city, trying to keep away from the panic and excitement of the battle. They were, however, beginning to fall behind the enemy lines. Their route led them behind the embassies and temples and into the outskirts of the city's parliamentary district until they had no choice but to enter a human-made, tall, glass skyscraper. This building was where Cecil advised them to go and so they forced themselves through the doors. Security had already been attacked, their bodies lay bloodied around the floor and leaning up against the welcome desk.

Zahied stepped forward and squatted down to inspect the bodies.

"What happened here?" Major asked, rubbing his bald head in concern and unease.

Zahied reached down and touched the small, still bleeding hole in the human's chest.

"This man was shot, forbidden weapons it looks like."

He looked around to see behind the desk and there was a single Feydon soldier lying strangled, his killer was the corpse dead on the desk from the look of his hands. Zahied picked up the small firearm still in the corpse's hand and checked its chamber. Only a few bullets remained but the corpse's webbing provided him with sufficient clips. He stole the weapon and took the clips for himself, just in case.

Maybe I'm picking up a few bad habits from Kaza, he thought to himself while he filled his pockets with the heavy metal.

Rezosa and Major didn't seem to mind though. "Why was there a soldier here?" Rezosa asked. "I thought they are only here for Raiden."

"I'm not sure, maybe they sent a single squad to reassure the Senate to not attack. Queen Angel herself already tried to ask Prime Minister Vurbute to call off the attack. I guess this only means that there may be more here though. We should be careful. Come on," Zahied said as he walked past them and opened a large glass door into a well-lit cream corridor, holding the pistol out. "Sarah Celadore and the rest of the Senate are here somewhere. We have to find them."

"Are you sure you can use that thing?" Major asked following close behind him.

"I don't know yet. I'm a caster, I'm not a killer but if it means ending this battle or even war then I'll do what I have to."

He crept with his back against the wall, the metal in his pockets slowing him down even more until he had to take off his blue and silver cloak and leave it in a bundle on the floor and carry on walking in his white silk, collared shirt with a black waistcoat, black leather trousers and black shoes.

They soon could hear the voices of the Senate members. A loud human male voice was now screaming angrily, which caused Zahied to run to the situation. They found the Senate members all in a large hall with marble floors, a great window looking out to the city and decorated with elder glyphs and human-made chandeliers. Aeomon cog-powered moving pictures circled the room and large tables of the finest porcus delicacies, fruit dishes and carved ice swans sat at the side of the room. Tigian gauntlets of metal claws hung on the walls and various spears used by both ursas and tigians alike. This was one of many rooms of the Senate that reflected something of every species.

The Senate members were all stood together, their hands raised as a Feydon soldier had his arm raised and aimed a pistol to them. Only Elder Amber wasn't present, a male elder being in her place. He wore white silk garments with pearls around his wrists and neck, his hands were raised just like the rest and showed his three fingers, that all elders had. His face had a large rounded nose, beady black eyes and thin gaunt cheeks; his long stringy black hair he had tied back. Their security officers also all stood in front of the crazed Feydon armed man, his mask dropped on the floor so they could see the importance in his eyes.

"If you will not call off the attack then I've been given orders to force you to by pain of death!" the armed man shouted.

Zahied crept up, hiding behind the table of fine porcus food, and listened.

"Please, sir," Sandchi Oshea the aeomon started in fear, "we do not have the authority to call off any of the forces in this city. We are Senate members, it is the High Elder and the President of Magna who have the authority to do so. Amber is insisting on the security of this city and President Orion is on his way here now from Toshiro."

The man screamed wildly, waving his arms around. "Don't give me that. I have been briefed and Amber Pulaguy is a member of this Senate and so through *you*," he pointed to the elder present, "this fighting can be stopped. Find her and get her to call off her troops."

"What are we going to do?" Rezosa whispered to Zahied behind his ear as they listened in.

"Whatever we must to prevent any more bloodshed," he replied and pulled back the hammer of the pistol, turned off the safety lock and crept forward.

"Sir," called the elder. "If you will calm down and cooperate we can try and get hold of Amber soon. Just please put down the forbidden weapon before somebody gets hurt."

"My friends are dead! We only came here on peace terms but you insisted on attacking us! We were forced to fire upon you. This is your doing!"

"Peace terms?" the brave aeomon now asked. "Feydon has been attacking cities and leaving them destroyed, marching where they please and taking what they want. You came here and suddenly the elder temple is destroyed and you expect us to believe you are here on peace terms?"

"Right! You die first!" the man screamed and pointed the pistol to Sandchi's head. A shot fired and the Senate members screamed but the aeomon didn't fall but froze and tensed expecting the worst.

The soldier suddenly collapsed and fell face first to the floor. A small hole pierced his skull behind his ear and the exit wound on the other side had blown his head wide open and brains and skull lay on the floor around him. Zahied stood behind him with the chamber of his pistol smoking, the smoke vanishing in the air.

Sarah Celadore suddenly lowered her hands. "Thank you, Zahied. It's safe now, everyone, the threat is over now."

"You know, I was beginning to believe this was all more human mischief if I can be honest, Celadore," Ursa Tiffran explained as he lowered his hands and walked over to the fresh corpse. "But since we were saved by humans I guess I have to apologise. Thank you, human."

He looked at Zahied but Zahied's eyes were glazed. He stared down at the first man he had ever killed, the body still warm and spilling a puddle of black and red around him. His hand shook at first but he eventually inhaled and calmed his nerves.

"I am not supposed to kill," he explained. "I am a caster, my work is to supposed to help and heal, not this."

"Don't feel ashamed, Zahied. You saved us all, you are a hero right now," Sarah reassured.

"Why are you here though?" Porcus Lucdear now asked.

Zahied blinked and shook his head, snapping back to reality and remembering why they were all really here. "Oh yes, of course. Sarah, we came to deliver a message. Major if you would be so kind as to pass the Prime Minister the letter."

Major nodded, took out the letter and stepped forward,

his hand raised to pass the letter over.

"This message was sent by–"

"Seize those humans!"

Everything stopped. Once again Zahied felt a familiar entrapping sensation and felt he was frozen to the spot. His lips could not finish the sentence and he could see that both Rezosa and Major were caught in motion, suddenly frozen in animation. Out of the corner of his eyes he could see small blue candles burning at the edges of the room – *Suggestive Oil! But how–?*

"Don't let that letter be delivered!" came the voice again.

"Cecil Vurbute! What is the meaning of this?" Sarah asked.

Cecil appeared, wheeling past Zahied with two elder soldiers and a tigian security guard with him.

"I have heard information from an inside source that Queen Angel and Sarah Celadore are working in partnership. Bring me that letter and do not let loose the humans carrying it."

"Partnership? This is absurd, Cecil!" Sarah now protested. "Let loose these humans immediately. They have just saved us from a hostile presence and should not be treated in this manner."

"I will do no such thing, bring me that letter."

The tigian with him walked over to Major, his hand still held out with the letter in it, the very same letter Cecil himself gave them to deliver, and took it and handed it to the wheelchair ridden tigian.

He opened it and read. "It is as I thought. Senate members, I am sorry to say but this has all been a ruse set by Queen Angel and Sarah Celadore. Guard, seize Sarah immediately."

Every ear now listened as Sarah was approached by the

tigian. She stood proud and offended by this accusation but allowed the tigian to hold her skinny arms behind her back while Cecil continued.

"Please explain what is going on here, Cecil," Porcus Lucdear asked.

"Gladly." He held up the letter and showed them all. "This here is a letter by Queen Angel herself addressed to Sarah Celadore. It reads of the murder of all the Senate members present and even old Elder Amber. It looks like the plan was for Angel to first send in her forces to scare us then Sarah's humans would save us from their own kind and force us to believe her intentions to be noble. This letter then reads that she was to bring us all to a building close to the temple where the two armies were at battle and kill us all, blame it on an accident and take over Chippenham for herself. An attack was made on the Elder Temple and the High Elder Council was previously killed so as to not stop their takeover."

"Is this true?" Sandchi asked Sarah, still with the tigian standing behind them.

"Of course this is not true. This is all lies made up by Cecil!"

"But I have proof right here, Sarah, the letter is signed by Angel herself." He held up the letter and showed it to the Senate.

"A common forgery! I am appalled with this ridiculous attempt to blame the human species! You think I want Chippenham for myself? I already am the highest member of this Senate!"

"Yet it is a known fact that a human's lust for power exceeds the porci's love of food," Cecil countered while the rest of the Senate all read.

Zahied was screaming in his mind while frozen in animation, *No! Cecil gave us that letter. This is all lies! All lies, you cannot believe this!*

"Actually, the signature looks authentic enough. Queen Angel's hand was at the end of this pen," Lucdear confirmed, briefly looking up at Cecil and giving the smallest of smirks and turning back to Sarah.

"How do you explain all this, Sarah?"

Sarah scowled at Cecil, her eyes now sharper than any knife. "I explain that Cecil has had this planned out all along. Release the three human messengers and let them tell the truth."

Cecil countered quickly and calmly, "But these messengers will be working with both Angel and yourself. You have already told them exactly what it is you want us to hear. Now they will only back up your claim. Am I right?"

"If that's so then this calls for a trail. If I am accused of treason against the Senate then I am to receive the same treatments. I demand a trail."

Cecil's eye caught that of the tigian standing behind her. "No, I'm sorry Sarah but I have just proven your guilt to the Senate itself. You can cry and bark all you like but it is clear now to every other species minister that whatever power the humans receive they only want more. I sentence you to an immediate execution for the treason against the Senate. Guard!"

The guard quickly pulled out a knife and reached around Sarah's throat.

Zahied saw the whole thing, Cecil sat in his chair smirking the whole time. Sarah stood so strong and innocent, she finally pulled away her eyes from Cecil and looked towards Zahied. She could have cried and begged, instead she only told the messengers, "I don't blame you…"

The knife cut, her throat opened, blood sprayed staining down her dress and she dropped to her knees. She still didn't make a sound until she gurgled when she tried to breathe, spat out blood and gasped. She hit the floor face down and stayed there in a fresh red puddle.

Everyone stood as frozen as the messengers. Sandchi sighed and stepped forward and knelt down to touch her back. "Your methods are too harsh, Cecil. Sarah could well have been innocent. An execution this early will now never confirm her innocence."

"That letter is all the evidence I need," Tiffran the big black ursa said.

"And I," Lucdear concluded. "So what happens now?"

"Now, since Sarah cannot sit at the head of the Senate, I call for a vote for the leadership of the Senate."

So this is what this is all about! Cecil and his own greed! Zahied screamed in his mind.

"As our saviour today I vote only for you, Cecil," Lucdear started.

"I also vote for the tigian," Tiffran said.

The elder glanced back out of the window at the still smoking building of the temple. "On behalf of the elders I can only vote for Amber. She is the smartest and wisest here and should be the one to lead."

Sandchi stood up. Everyone was waiting for him to reply, especially Cecil.

"Sarah was a fine prime minister, the humans did well in leading Sphere for the last hundred years. I vote for Sarah's successor."

Cecil scowled but grinned as the numbers still added up. "And I vote for myself and accept, and for my first act as head of the Senate I call for an immediate *divide against the humans!*"

Now every head turned, to kill a senate member in such cold blood was one thing but this now turned into something new altogether.

Cecil continued, "For too long the humans have

ruled. It is now the tigian's turn to rule Sphere. Send out an immediate message to the whole of the world. Every human world leader is to stand down and hand over their country to the highest tigian political leader in their respective countries. If the humans refuse then the tigians are to take the country's arms and force them. Tell King Kerry of Racoves he is to stand down. President Orion of Magna will stand down for myself as the new President of Magna and President Sahota of Angland is to stand down and Audie Katsan will be given the Anglish army for the takeover of the country. This also goes for President Sarauami of Calmeron, President Shuian of Isolies and every other world leader of Sphere."

"This is very serious, Cecil," the elder warned. "Are you sure you want to exclude the humans from the world? This will be no small divide like the ursas'. This will be global, it has been ninety-eight years since the Leo Divide, the last great divide, and now you wish to make another? Amber will have something to say about this."

Cecil scoffed. "Amber will have too much time to protect and deal with her precious temple. As President of Magna, Chippenham now belongs to me and as head member of the Senate I will have the last say on divides and right now I say the humans have gone too far and will be forced from their power of the world and be made to live as they forced the ursas to live. Take the messengers away, guards. They will be sentenced and tried for treason, then imprisoned or executed. Right now I have many issues to discuss with my senate."

Zahied, Rezosa and Major were all taken away back outside the building and into the streets by the two elder guards. Zahied still tightly gripped onto the pistol in his hand since they all moved like puppets being controlled by the elders.

He wished for some sort of miracle. There was now no way out of this and he needed a distraction. A new divide had now begun, now every city would be a battleground since armies led by the tigian world leaders would be forcing out every human. Millions of deaths would be confirmed in a matter of months now and together the three of them would be blamed. Prison would mean death.

Luck smiled down on him as they walked further into the street. In the distance he could see the port for the skyships and in another direction he could see the Feydon fleet firing in all directions in anger. Angel must have just found out about the failed attempt to stop the fighting and now had to deal with her own country being taken over by tigians. Explosive cannons now fired toward the city everywhere, aiming for the port and parliamentary district in particular. He saw in the distance the communications tower being pelted with cannon fire, break away and begin to crash down in chunks, roaring like thunder. A nearby projectile crashed over their head and sent rubble to fall and clatter around them. The guards immediately dropped their concentration on the prisoners then and, just like Kaza did previously, Zahied wasted no time and shot the two elders immediately.

Once they fell Rezosa spoke up. "What are we going to do? We can't stay here now. We have to warn the elementalist."

"I think it's too late for that," Major said and pointed to the Scarlet Arise that had been unable wait any longer in the port and had risen from the ground in its attempt to escape.

"If the elementalist is escaping I guess we have to regroup with Sheeria and Raiden if they are still here. They are tigian and leo and will protect us from the armies and divide now. No doubt Feydon will still be searching for him though so we will have to be cautious," Zahied explained.

"This is so messed up, so now a new divide stands?" Rezosa asked.

"Yes, and with forbidden weapons back in the world, ursas taking sides with the tigians and no leos left at all it doesn't look good for us humans."

17

Sheeria dashed up the spiralling staircase of the communications tower. She had had to leave Raiden to fight the metal monster and all she could think about was his last words: *"Find your brother...I'll deal with mine."*

That monster, that thing. I don't know if it's dead or alive. That's Raiden's brother! Valadad brought back to life as a mechanical feral beast sent to kill Raiden. What madness is this? Why would Feydon stoop so low as to disrespect the dead and turn them into whatever that thing is?

She could not get out of her mind the horror of the idea that right now Raiden was battling the only other leo left on Sphere and, more importantly, his own flesh and blood. Raiden had loved his brother and regretted his death and now was having to face a metal demon in the desecrated remains of his body, animated once again. But soon the thought of his brother made her think of her own and she charged as fast as she could to get to the top of the tower in order to contact Audie.

The tower was empty save for a few workers who sat at the top in a windowed cylinder having a view of the whole airport and aiding ships to make their escape. Once they saw her there they approached.

"I'm sorry, tigian, but you are not allowed up here, this is for staff only."

Sheeria was panting and out of breath, leaning on a desk. "I beg your pardon, sirs...I have been given permission by Prime Minister Vurbute to come here and contact the aeomon zeppelin still stationed here...This was the only place where I could contact them."

The worker only nodded and ran to his superior who

approached and again Sheeria explained her situation.

"Yes, of course you may, tigian," the head of the tower told her and escorted her to a small radio. It was nothing more than a wooden box with a receiver wired to it and a circular speaker protected by a wire gauze on the centre. A simple pin switch needed flicking on and instantly she heard the radio's static. A small, round, metal switch needed turning for her to tune into the zeppelin's radio output. She picked up the receiver and spoke clearly into it.

"Hello…? Hello…? I'm trying to reach Audie Katsan of the zeppelin stationed in this port…"

There was no reply but the whirling static. She turned the dial gently once more until the static turned to a steady silence; she knew she had found them.

She repeated her words another three times before she finally got a reply.

"*This is Audie Katsan. I heard someone was requesting me on this frequency. Who is speaking?*"

She nearly cheered, she had finally got hold of him. "Brother! It is me, Sheeria."

"*Sheeria? What are you doing up there in the communications tower? Shouldn't you be with your elementalist? The city is under attack, my sister.*"

"I told you once I wasn't going to leave you again. I have come here to try and get you. Please come with me aboard the Scarlet Arise. We have to go to True Hiro but I couldn't leave without you again."

On the zeppelin everything was now beginning to look ready for departure; they were only waiting for Audie to finish his conversation with his sister.

"Sister, I thank you for your concern but right now I feel we have to escape. If you are all the way up there you should come down. It looks dangerous up there."

"*Just promise me that you will meet me outside Audie. We can all board the Scarlet Arise and be gone from this place.*"

"Sir, everything is ready for take-off. Waiting on your command," a tigian pilot told him from his seat. Audie was about to try to convince Sheeria once more when another voice from the other side of him shouted out.

"Dire news, sir! Sarah Celadore has died and Cecil Vurbute has been made head of the Senate and had ordered a divide against the humans!"

This news suddenly took priority for Audie. He quickly said into the receiver, "Hold on a moment, Sheeria. Something has come up…"

Sheeria was listening the whole time on another radio in the tower. Every worker there suddenly gathered around it. The truth was confirmed. A new divide had begun, one banning all humans from civilisation.

Sheeria felt wounded then and screamed back into the receiver for her brother again. This time she could hear the voices in the background telling him the news.

"*Sir, Cecil Vurbute has ordered President Sahota to cease control of all of Angland and pass it all on to you. You have just been declared the President of Angland. Congratulations Mister President!*"

Her world shook when she heard the news but she didn't know what this meant for her brother and her any more. Years ago she wouldn't have believed it but now she didn't know him. He was a good leader but had never thought he would suddenly have these responsibilities.

Another report came in in the background and she listened as they spoke to her brother. "*Sir, I have been informed that the Ex-President Sahota is refusing to give up his seat as President and is on a skyship here now. The whole Anglish fleet and army is now at you command. What is your order?*"

Her breath stopped, she wanted to scream loud into

the receiver for her brother to hear but she knew it would never work. She waited until she finally heard the words she thought her brother wasn't capable of saying.

"*Command the army to seize the Ex-President. If he shall not stand down then he shall be executed on sight.*"

"No." Sheeria shut her eyes tight, hoping that when she opened them she would be young again and her brother young and full of life and energy, her old life would be returned and she would be reunited with her young husband and child once more. But she opened them again only to the heartbreak of reality.

Audie's voice appeared on the receiver again. "*Sheeria, I'm sorry but I now cannot come with you. I have just been made the President of Angland and have a host in my country refusing to stand down.*"

"I know, brother, I heard everything. You shouldn't do this. This is not you. You have a wife and family."

"*I also have the lives of every tigian in Angland and, more importantly, Donolan to think about. The humans will try and kill us all in order to terminate the threat. I mustn't allow that to happen and must strike immediately. I am going to Donolan to take control of the country.*"

"*Actually, sir,*" came a voice in the background, "*there is an Anglish ship docked here in the port. I have a visual now on the Soaring Grace. Since you now own the entire fleet, that ship is now under your command and can get us across the ocean faster than any other vessel.*"

Sheeria looked down and saw the ship mentioned. Raiden and Zoudiva had arrived on this ship and it had since been stationed where it landed.

"*Excellent, we'll depart immediately. Sheeria, meet me outside, come with me.*"

She wanted to say yes to travelling to Donolan with her dear brother but instantly thought of Raiden and Acarlie.

"I can't, brother, but wait for me. I will be down as soon as I–"

A scream from behind her filled the room. Her head swivelled and she instantly saw a human fly into a window, smash through it and disappear as gravity's toy. Another human fell with a bloody gash across his chest and suddenly she saw a tall, black hooded creature attacking the humans.

It wore black silks tightly and wore its hood up so close she couldn't see its face, but while it swung two curved knives she saw it had cream coloured, furry hands. It also looked to wear a long skirt, with added material between its legs and arms. It restricted its movements but it still slaughtered the defenceless humans, leaving none untouched. Sheeria froze in terror at first and was forced to watch the workers here now being slaughtered by this creature, its movements so quick she couldn't even discern the technique. It slashed, jumped on desks, flipped and stabbed the humans around it. Its movements were perfect, it was clearly well trained. In only a few seconds they were all gone, lying around or thrown through more glass. The hooded creature stood strong and caught its breath back.

Sheeria slowly tried moving out of sight where she could possibly sneak away but the creature suddenly pounced on a desk and ran along it, jumping from one to the other. Sheeria screamed as it pounced high with strong legs. She tried to turn and run but the weight of this thing was suddenly upon her. She lay on the floor next to a great window looking down at the terminal below her. The hooded creature pulled its curved knife and held it to her throat.

"Where is the leo?" it screamed.

She looked straight into its hood and now could see cream fur covering cat-like features. It was female with eyes as yellow as the burning sun with a long, horizontal black pupil in the centre. A large cat nose with whiskers matching her own and teeth as sharp as hers, its bow elsewhere but the ice-axes still attached to its wrists. This was no tigian and that only meant one thing.

"Impossible," was all she could say while looking into the face of the hooded creature, but the female hooded assassin screamed again.

"I said, where is the leo?" She held the knife tighter to Sheeria's throat and growled, waiting for an answer.

Sheeria began to cry. Her apple green eyes were moist and a tear ran down her orange cheek.

The Archer sniffed twice and on the third time looked down slightly and narrowed her eyes, looking straight into Sheeria's and releasing her grip of the knife slightly, but still waited.

Sheeria didn't want to say anything but also knew she had to escape. She didn't know why she did but she turned and looked down at the Scarlet Arise, hoping her dear Acarlie and even Raiden was on board.

The Archer took this as a sign and saw the ship. "So, he's on the ship is he?"

She immediately released Sheeria and sprang up and dashed away. Sheeria gasped for breath and got to her feet and tried to catch The Archer, when the distant Feydon fleet suddenly fired in all directions. Cannon fire pelted the communications tower and the whole thing shook, the floor quaked and even The Archer now lost her footing and slipped in her escape.

Part of the floor broke away from under Sheeria's feet and she screamed and dived forward. The floor creaked and moaned as the metal girders supporting it leaned and snapped to one side, half of the floor fell from behind her and now the strong wind from outside blew in. Gravity claimed everything behind her, which all disappeared in a scream of wind and breaking rubble. She quickly looked behind and felt vertigo as the floor way below her called her name.

More of the floor cracked and Sheeria dashed forward as more tiles began to fall away with not much more to support it from underneath. More cannon fire hit the tower again, this time cracking the whole cylinder in half. They were in the weak half as it now slanted aside with a great moan like the building itself screamed in agony. The Archer jumped and dived from different platforms before climbing up and reaching the safer half while Sheeria trailed behind.

"Stop! Don't leave me!" she called after her. The human corpses now slid down and to the open space and fell to the floor like the rest of the equipment. The Archer's way was clear and she was about to leave when she turned back and looked down at the helpless Sheeria, who was unable to climb as she was. She stopped for a moment and growled in contemplation before finally walking over to two tables and desks that still stood between the two levels and kicked them down. As they tumbled, the floor shook again but they fell on top of other office-ware and made stepping stones for Sheeria to climb up on and escape.

She reached the top as more of the floor gave way and she sprinted back down the corridor out of the room and into the spiral staircase. A large hole had been opened in the wall, which The Archer was now climbing up to.

"What do you want with Raiden?" Sheeria called up to her.

"None of your damn business!" she called back as she got to the top of the broken wall.

Sheeria could not climb like The Archer could and suddenly remembered, this was what Keppal was talking about. This was the murderer that he apparently killed.

"At least tell me your name!" she called up.

The Archer stood up and faced the outside and looked down at the long drop below it and turned around to see Sheeria once more.

"My name is Umbra Tenebris!" she snarled, flicked her hands to one side and as the ice-axes attached by string flicked out she caught them with perfect technique. She leaned forward and fell from the building and she was gone.

Umbra fell leaving the female tigian to try to chase her down the stairs. It was a long, deathly fall below down the tall, conical tower. She, however, wasn't afraid and instantly opened her arms and legs revealing an extension in her clothes. Knowing she would need a quick escape she wore a wing-suit over her normal black silks, something she wasn't keen on trying but knew she had no alternative. From her arms to her hip and from one ankle to another were thick materials that caught against the wind as she fell and slowed her down by wind resistance. She flipped in her fall to face the wall and dug her small axes into the building. They scraped and screeched as she fell but slowed her down more. She concentrated on her arms and pressed as hard as she could, digging the axes into the concrete. The building was beginning to cone outwards and soon she even used the claws on her feet. She was coming to the floor soon and her claws felt like they were about to split open so she released and fell more but held onto her axes as best as she could. She was soon near the floor and let go. It was a hard fall but she slowed herself with enough force to not completely break her body when she finally struck the floor.

Umbra rolled when she hit the floor and kept rolling for another ten yards. She screamed when she stopped and lay panting and looking up at the sky. The cylinder top of the tower had now broken away even more on the opposite side and rained down concrete rubble. Her feet were bleeding and she looked at the damage she had done to her axes and promised herself she would sharpen and fix them. She looked up to where the hole was in the building. It was a tiny black hole in the building from where she lay. This was by far the worst stunt she had ever pulled off and she grinned and thanked Sphere she was still alive.

She slowly climbed to her feet but her arms ached and her feet were raw and bloody. She fell at first but grunted and endured the pain and ran back to the tower. Hidden away by her was her backpack, bow and arrows. She equipped herself with them again and looked back to the ship the tigian was looking for.

It still sat there waiting to take off so she pulled the backpack across her back and started limping toward the ship across the tarmac.

18

The year was 2135 UTS: The place, North Angland and the sky was bright blue with white clouds cluttering the sky slowly, peacefully. The wind was gentle and the meadows Raiden stood in were a perfect green and as far as his young eyes could see were green meadows with white and red flowers. Hedges cut into the horizon turning green to blue and birds sang songs of hot summer days. He was four years old, young and full of life and energy. He loved to play out in the fields under the sun and play at war with the shadows. His head was bare and cream, his mane had not yet grown and he wore small leather leggings. The air was hot since they were only a few hundred kilometres from the Anglish desert. He lived out here away from the rest of the world with his brother and father in a small community with other leos. He was too young to understand the start of the worldwide slaughter the humans were beginning against his kind. He was younger than his brother by several years and so often took to playing by himself. He never knew his mother, he was always told by his father though of how she had given her life back to the planet in exchange for his. He never told the details; only that the humans were involved, and in particular a human named Osiris. Whenever he did mention his mother though his father called her a strong, proud and beautiful leo who was a hero and his love.

This was a peaceful and happy place his father took him to to get away from the terrible humans who were killing leos with weapons that could *bang!* and shoot a proud leo warrior from a hundred yards away. There was no honour in war any more. The young Raiden snarled and jumped while in the field and dived on an imaginary human. He was Sphere's last hope of saving all the leos from the evil humans. The imaginary human screamed mercy but he was a proud leo warrior and killed the human to face the rest of the evil army before him under the blue sky and warm sun. Every leo in the world was cheering his name as he ran and dived on more armies of humans, their numbers were in their thousands but he was a powerful leo warrior. Their bullets bounced off his skin and his small squeak of a youthful roar made the world shake and the humans fall. He tripped as the imaginary human army shot out a thousand cannon balls which blackened the sky like an eclipse. He crouched down and shielded his head, using his strong arms to deflect the cannon balls until they were all around him and he was unscathed. There was a button before him, a button to kill all the humans in the army and end their evil intentions once and for all. He was so close too, but the army charged seeing how close he was. He squeaked again with his mighty roar and ran. They were so close, just metres away, but he jumped high into the sky and landed on the button just before the thousands of humans could reach it. He pressed it and the sky lit up so bright it was white and yellow, the fields burned and were set ablaze in a wave of fire and energy like a nuclear bomb and the humans all fell, screaming for surrender. It was over, young Raiden jumped to his little feet, every leo in the world was cheering him again. He saved the world, he was the greatest leo ever. He ran under the sun with green grass and soft soil under his paws, with his hands held high, cheering and commentating his success.

"And the crowd goes wild! Woooo!"

"Raiden! Raiden!" called a voice from the end of the field he knew all too well. "Father says dinner is ready!"

Valadad was twenty years older than little Raiden. He

was twenty-four but still very young for a leo. He stood tall and proud, he shared the same red eyes as Raiden; they were their mother's eyes, red like rubies, their father used to say; however, Raiden always did have a dash of brown in the likeness of his father in his. They too would one day share the same red mane as their father but Raiden's fur was a lighter shade of golden cream than his brother's. He took his mother's fur while Valadad took more of his father's darker shade for his own.

"Come on, Raiden, don't make me come and get you!" Valadad called from over the field.

Raiden stopped running around and dashed to his older brother, his arms held out and panting, smiling the whole time.

Valadad crouched down and caught his younger brother in his arms and lifted him up. "You're getting heavy, Raiden, and strong. One day you're going to have to lift me up."

"Spin me!" Raiden cried, still too excited from his worldwide victory to think about dinner.

Valadad laughed, his voice echoing into the wind and forever in Raiden's memory. "Okay champ, hold on."

Valadad lifted Raiden over his shoulder and he held on. He playfully growled and spun Raiden over his shoulder in the bright sunshine and gentle breeze.

Raiden cried and laughed as the world around him spun so fast he couldn't see, but he held tight onto Valadad's fur. He loved his brother with all his heart and knew from then he would never stop laughing.

Raiden crashed through the glass window of the terminal. He hit the floor and grunted in pain. His armour clanged against the tarmac and he turned over to his front to pick himself up. Proto-Weapon had just picked him up, spun him and thrown him through a window leading into the runways of the airport and followed him out.

Raiden gasped and moaned in pain but had forced his arms to press into the floor to push himself up when Proto-Weapon reached him, grabbed the back of his head and slammed it into the floor. Raiden turned on his back as Proto-Weapon lunged in, his bloodied metal teeth ready to rip flesh but instead bit into Raiden's gauntlets made of leo metal as Raiden lifted his arm to protect himself. Proto-Weapon's teeth were only of human steel and fortunately for Raiden could not bite through the superior metal. Metal scraped against metal and a single spark jumped into the air. Raiden struggled and held his left arm out while his reanimated dead brother tried to bite down through his arm.

Eventually he gathered his strength and pulled to his left side. Proto-Weapon's head flung to the side and Raiden used the opportunity to punch him in his jaw with his right. He felt like he punched a wall, his knuckles cut and bled under his gauntlets but the attack stunned Proto-Weapon long enough for Raiden to get back to his feet.

"Brother! Please listen to me. Valadad, it is me, it's Raiden, your brother. Please, Valadad!" Raiden tried to get through to his brother, he hadn't seen him since he left for Decrenia, for Osiris, a year ago and now what he saw before him was an abomination of life. He wanted to cry seeing his brother like this, all grotesque and morbid. Metal was plated under his skin, enforcing the bone tissue with the stitching marks still present. His dark cream fur of their father was stained red and black with dried blood. His mother's ruby red eyes were now covered by its helmet and glowing bright red like a kingnine. Thin plastic wires connected to his brain looped out of his helmet and ran past his ears and back into his body to connect to his spine. His shoulders were enforced and the skin was stretched until it began to tear from within, showing scratched silver and black metal, stained in blood.

His words were all in vain as Proto-Weapon jerked his head back. Raiden could hear the twist of wires and metal under his skin as he moved. His proud family roar of the Teleskys now was a digital cry. Raiden could not hear the same scratchy growl Valadad used to share with his father any more. He was gone and it broke Raiden's heart to see what Feydon had done to his beautiful brother.

People from the rest of the terminal started to pop their heads around the corners, seeing the horrors of the metal monster plaguing their port but they each took no notice. Proto-Weapon snarled and lunged forward for Raiden again, who caught him this time and swung him back over to crash through the broken window and back into the terminal. Leos never really used weapons, it was seen as a weakness for something so strong to resort to killing something with anything other than the teeth and claws that Sphere had blessed them with but Raiden was now past worrying about shame and picked up a metal pipe that had broken from the building. He ran up and, roaring, swung with both hands and all his might as Proto-Weapon got back to his feet and struck his head hard enough to knock it off any normal being. The metal clanged and echoed over the terrified audience and Raiden let out a cry and released the bar. It dropped to the floor and echoed and rang, the shock of the attack nearly breaking his hands. He could feel them tense from the impact, sending the shock up his bones and weakening him. Proto-Weapon, however, took the impact and fell sideways, its head dented.

From the runway behind him Raiden suddenly heard a distant crash and turned to see the communications tower being pelted with cannon fire from the distant ships. The circular disk at the top started to break away and crumble and fall in large chunks of shrapnel.

"Sheeria!" Raiden gasped in shock. She was still up there and instantly he turned his attention to the tower. He began to run but felt a metal vice against his leg, scratching his greaves and yanking his leg back and throwing him back to the floor where Proto-Weapon was on top of him again, pressing down with his immense weight against the armour that used to belong to him.

The year was 2139 UTS: The place, North Angland; and now Raiden was eight years old; Valadad, twenty-eight. Raiden still had not a single red hair grown yet for his mane but now his cries and screams were no longer of joy and happiness but now of horror and disbelief. A terrible divide had been declared three years previously between the humans and leos. The slaughter of the leos had now turned to a worldwide extermination and the Leo Divide (soon to be known as the Last Divide) had begun. The leo population was now nearly extinct but the human forces of the whole world still were, with contempt, exterminating them. The news came slowly over the three years that one by one the leo villages and settlements were being destroyed by firearms and a new sub-species of the leos was being genetically engineered by the humans, called kingnines. His small village community was now one of the last leo havens to be mowed down. At first they came under a red, morning sky, marching across the field Raiden once played in; they were less than a hundred though, unlike the massive number that he once imagined.

Raiden was sitting on the floor at the time with his legs crossed and looking up at the manikin before him wearing his father's armour. Valadad came into the house fresh from hunting and saw his little brother's interest in the shiny, metallic armour and went to him.

"Hey champ, what are you doing?"

Little Raiden looked over his shoulder, his ruby red eyes gleaming with youthful inquisitiveness. "I'm just looking at Father's metal. I like it, I want to wear it one day."

Valadad smiled. "Oh don't worry, champ; you'll have your own one day. You don't have to worry about Father's smelly old armour. When you come of age you'll get your own like mine. Check it out."

Valadad held up his arm to show young Raiden his gauntlets, a pair he would wear one day. "They're made of leoium alloy."

"What's that?" Raiden asked and ran his tiny fingers across the gritted texture of Valadad's forearm.

"It's a metal stronger than steel. They say that once, long, long ago the leos found a mine where there was a ship. In this ship was how we all first came to Sphere."

Little Raiden now looked confused. "But I thought we were born here?"

Valadad smiled gently. "Well, we were, Raiden, and so too were the leos who found this ship, but long before that, before we could walk and talk, they say we came on a ship with humans and all others creatures from a far, far away land."

Hearing the word *humans* suddenly made Raiden not like this story. "Why would we go anywhere with humans? This story is stupid. The humans are stupid."

Valadad chucked again. "I know Raiden; this is only a legend and is not to be taken seriously, it's like a fairy tale. Anyway, on this forgotten ship they say the leo adventurers found a compartment with metal like Sphere had never seen before, stronger than any steel and shining blue. They say they used this metal to make all the leo armour and even weapons and together the leos used this new finding to win Sphere from the elders and humans."

"Back in the Golden Age?" Raiden asked with wide eyes. He was always told of this 'Golden Age' where the leos took

Sphere from the humans and ruled for three thousand years. With no forbidden weapons nor kingnines to kill them. Often Raiden wished he had lived in this time and wondered what it would have been like. A world where the leo was the boss and the evil humans would run and hide from the proud, honourable and strong; he liked that idea.

Raiden stood up and followed his brother into the kitchen. The red morning sky was beginning to brighten up. He knew it would be a sunny and hot day today and had already planned to play on his own again once Valadad had cooked breakfast for him.

Valadad slung his game on the table, a dead fawn with a slit throat. Valadad was good enough to let it bleed out first, their father had often disciplined him for getting blood everywhere around the house.

"Yes, Raiden, back in the Golden Age. Long before this accursed divide."

"Will it ever be over?" young Raiden asked. He stepped up to reach for the lip of the table, only the top of his head could see over it. He stood there looking over the dead fawn at his brother at the other side.

Valadad smiled when he looked at his cute little brother trying to see over the table and turned to find a knife for the fawn. "Yes, Raiden, one day. We all just have to make sure we all grow strong and stay together. Father will be there to protect us though."

A leo scream sounded from outside and their father charged though the door startling the two boys.

Their father was a tall and particularly strong leo. He stood eight feet tall with a shaggy, fiery red mane that grew long and he plaited the hairs under his chin. His eyes were brown like his father's before him. His name was Degnaler Telesky and he was the source of Raiden's dreams; he was everything he wanted to grow into.

"Val!" he called to Valadad.

"What is it, Father?" Valadad asked, rushing past little Raiden.

Their father stormed through their house to where his manikin was, picked up his armour and threw it over his shoulders and started to put it on.

"I want you to take Raiden and go upstairs, climb up to the attic and stay there until I come and get you, do you understand?"

"What's happening, Father?" Valadad asked. "Have the humans arrived?"

"Just do as I say, Val, and get Raiden upstairs!" Degnaler ordered as he hastily put on his armour.

Little Raiden, small and vulnerable, ran up and clutched onto his father's leg. "What's happening Father?"

He could hear the shots being fired now. He already knew the answer. His heart jumped and tears crept into his eyes: the humans had arrived. His father knelt down with his large hands against Raiden's little furry cheeks. "You be a good boy, Raiden, and go with your brother, okay? Daddy has to go outside for a while, but I'm coming back, I promise. Just stay with your brother."

"Come on, Raiden, let's go upstairs," Valadad said and took Raiden's arm and pulled him away from their father.

Their father ran to the door and looked back at them. "Whatever happens, Val, look after Raiden."

"No, Father! Don't go!" Raiden began to cry but his big brother picked him up.

"Come on champ, we're going to hide in the attic."

Raiden always remembered this moment. He remembered crying while being carried over his brother's shoulder. He remembered hating his brother for hiding like a coward. Leos didn't hide, they were strong and didn't fear anything and so had no need of hiding. Their attic was cold, dark and silent with wooden flooring, and cobwebs and dead spiders everywhere. Raiden used to love coming up here and pretending it was a vast tomb full of treasure but now he kicked and screamed as Valadad carried him up and threw everything in there over the hatch to barricade themselves in.

Raiden was still weeping when Valadad was done. He hugged onto his little brother and shielded him from the cries, shots and roars of the massacre outside. The village now screamed as one, fires broke out, familiar voices of neighbours shrieked and cried and the floor rumbled as they could feel neighbouring homes being destroyed.

They both could hear the mighty roar of their father while he fought to protect them but Valadad covered his little ears, whispering, "No, champ, don't listen."

Even through his big brother's hands Raiden could hear his father being slain. He cried out and buried his head into his brother's mane and wept. He remembered his father's last words to him. His father never did keep that promise and now he knew his whole world was his big brother protecting him from the evil outside. He clutched onto him tight and wept tears into Valadad's mane.

Proto-Weapon clutched onto Raiden as he tried to break his neck. Raiden's head buried in the shaggy mess that used to be his mane and pushed as hard as he could against the metal chest trying to break free from its vice grip arms. When Proto-Weapon felt Raiden was pushing hard enough, it let go and allowed Raiden to fly back and crash onto the floor again. The audience had now all fled apart from the tigian Security, who tried to close in on Proto-Weapon to get Raiden away from it. They tried getting long tasers used to shock tigians but found that even though Proto-Weapon was plated in metal, electricity had no effect to him. The tasers sparked and shocked it but only caught the attention of the mechanical leo. It left Raiden on the floor as it sprang on the tigians around it in a berserker rage, slashing with its claws, grabbing flesh and tearing. After two fell they retreated, calling for the injured leo on the floor to run away.

Proto-Weapon eventually snorted in frustration at their pitiful attempts to defeat it and turned its back to them and walked back over to Raiden struggling to his feet on the floor. He lay on his front, his armour now weighing him down, his arms pressing into a dent on the ground where he fell and grunting as he pushed his chest off the floor.

Proto-Weapon stomped up behind him, his long, black, metal claws still covered in dry blood scratched across the cream marble tiles. He reached down and took a handful of the red mane he shared with Raiden and lifted Raiden's head up before smashing it back down on the floor. The world spun for Raiden as he was suddenly blinded with pain, his senses all numbed in a confused mess and somehow felt he flew and tumbled even further into the floor. In reality, after Proto-Weapon smashed his head into the floor he immediately grabbed the back of his armour, picked him up and threw him again across the terminal to land onto the conveyor belt and tumble over it and land back on the floor.

He gasped for breath, rolled onto his front again and pushed himself up, bringing his knees up to force himself to his feet but staggered at first. He could only hear an echo of the digital roar as his hearing was still a high pitched ringing behind his eyes numbing out all other noises and he spat down blood near his feet.

"Valadad...," he said in his stagger. "Val...brother...."

He felt a presence upon him but still could only see a spinning world in his dizzied state. He felt a hard knee against his armoured chest that jogged his system and shook the air out of his lungs and suddenly he heard glass smash again. The world spun more, over and under; colours blended into a blur and just as it started it stopped, with him lying back outside staring up into the sky again.

Proto-Weapon stepped through the broken window, picked up its target again and lifted the limp leo and forced him to his feet and up against a brick wall. It punched the armoured chest twice. Still it could not dent the armour even with the metal under its skin but could attack the fragile flesh and bone of Raiden's head. It only needed to strike his chin once against the broken wall to daze him again and then backhand with the same fist. It held Raiden's head up and aimed another for the tip of his nose when he was disturbed by the brave tigians again, this time throwing anything they could to get his attention. Their plan worked and he let go of Raiden again, who dropped to the floor face down, and chased after them.

Raiden's eyes were sore, his jaw felt swollen or even broken. He breathed with his chest against the floor and could slowly see his cut and bruised hand in front of him under the metal gauntlets. He moved his index finger a little and slowly his hand turned back into a fist.

The year was 26 ALD: The place, a small town on the outskirts of Hiro in Racoves on a dark and grisly night. Raiden was now eighty-two years old, a prime young age for a leo to be. His red mane had now fully grown and so had he. Strong and broad he stood with great arms, large hands and still a youthful fire of anger in his eyes. An age where he believed he knew everything. He was young, but not too young, and stronger than in any of his previous years, if a little naïve still. It had been twenty-six years since the Leo Divide had ended and twenty-six years of his new life of being of an endangered species. For the past twenty-six years it had been known as the Last Divide and the wise and old humans were apologetic, remorseful and even pitiful towards him. He didn't mind them so much but it was the young and stupid he had no patience for. The ones who saw the massacre as *winning* and mocked him through his childhood and forced him to build himself strong just to protect himself when his big brother wasn't around. Valadad himself had gone from his life and had been absent for the last twelve years. Raiden travelled and took it upon himself to avenge his father and his people in the only way he knew how.

The wooden back door of a small tavern in the middle of this town broke open as Raiden crashed through it and fell down on the stony concrete floor. He managed to get away with only a cut lip and grazed knees.

"You think that's going to stop me!" he shouted in his anger as he got to his feet and faced his attackers.

Three young humans and two tigians stepped through the doorway. The leader of the pack was actually the shortest, a small human was a buzz cut hair cut and round nose. "I think we're gonna finish what our dads started," he said, referring to the Last Divide in a lazy slang.

The slang of this short human only wound up young Raiden even more, "You talk like a moron. You!" He shouted and pointed to the tallest and broadest tigian there. "You're first!"

The group laughed and stepped forward, Raiden smiled and tensed his shoulders and arms, showing them all his broad chest and pulsing biceps, his claws for show to the tigians and a look of war in his eyes. He wasn't a murderer and had never killed anyone but he loved a good fight. He heard the wives and girlfriends of the group try to pull them away and the landlord calling the police, which only made him smile. He didn't have long but long enough to teach all these ignorant bastards a lesson or two.

He couldn't wait to see the look on their faces when the police arrived after he beat them all up. Everyone would tell of how he arrived quiet and reserved in this bar and was confronted by this group and forced to defend himself. Even after he'd beaten them all up there was little the police could do since he was of a very select few leos left on Sphere and so the elders and world leaders gave him a kind of pass against most police arrests, as long as it wasn't too often and as long as it wasn't too bloody. Raiden loved taking advantage of this and would go from bar to bar and innocently provoke the youths and when they attacked would fight them all. He took a beating every once in a while but learned everything he would ever need to defend himself.

The tallest tigian moved the short human out of the way and cracked his fingers in his fist.

"You should really think about where you choose to drink, leo."

Raiden smiled and growled, waiting, but an old voice stopped the violence instantly.

"One against five? Are you okay there, champ?"

A second, even taller and stronger leo stepped past the broken door and twisted the tigian's arm behind his back and threw him back against his companions.

"Beat it!" Valadad ordered the group.

With two leos present the fight now looked one sided. The group knew their handicap now and retreated with abusive calls and hand signs.

Once there was silence again Raiden wiped his cut lip with the back of his fist and looked up at his older brother for the first time in twelve years.

"Where have you been?" he asked coldly.

Valadad turned from the door to his young brother still

full of hate and aggression and slapped him upside the back of the head. He stood a foot taller than Raiden, had twenty years on him and was stronger than he ever would be.

"Never mind about me. What have you been doing? Did you start these fights? Looks like I came at the right time."

Raiden spat down at the floor. A small puddle of blood sat in this phlegm. "I could have handled myself. I have done before."

"Is that what you have been doing all this time, champ? Fighting petty bar fights?" Valadad's voice was a deep base that dominated Raiden's; he spoke like a warrior.

"Don't call me that! I'm not a kid any more," Raiden ordered.

Valadad folded his arms, straightened his back, looked down at his bruised little brother and said nothing. His last question was still unanswered.

Raiden stared up at his brother. His ruby red and brown eyes almost mirrored Valadad's. He looked so much more like his father than Raiden ever did.

Eventually Raiden caved in on his stare-out. "I only fight when I know I can win."

"And you think this is what you should be doing, Raiden?" It was different when he called him Raiden. It felt like a lecture and Raiden wasn't in the mood right now for one.

Raiden avoided Valadad's disappointed look the best he could. "What do you want?"

"I *want* to come and see my little brother. Is that too much to ask?"

"You left that a little long, don't you think? Sphere's divide, Val."

"Mind your tongue, Raiden. Father didn't like it and neither do I."

"Yeah, well, Father's...." He looked up but couldn't finish his sentence. He looked straight back down at his feet once he saw a flare of anger in his brother's eye. Valadad, however, was mature and could handle his anger and breathed and calmed instantly. He stepped past Raiden and pointed to a walkway across town away from the tavern. "Walk with me."

He started his walk and got to the end of the walkway before his angry little brother caught up.

They walked past a dark green field and down a road of brick houses before finding an open field of farmland with a small pathway outlining it. They walked under an overcast, gloomy sky and a spit of cold rain began to fall around them. The rustling of the wind in the trees surrounded them until Raiden spoke up.

"So are you going to tell me why you're here, brother?"

"I came here because I heard of a leo abusing the immunities the law gives us by constantly being found in the centre of bar fights. I came here and have been following your trail before coming to this place. Are you going to tell me why you're doing this, Raiden?" he asked while they walked in the brisk cold night air. "The divide is over now. You don't need to keep doing this."

"Damn it, Val. You disappear for twelve years to find your own life and return and lecture me on mine? What business is it of yours why I do this?"

"You're my brother and my responsibility, that's why. Father told me to watch over you and that's exactly what I've done. I went twelve years ago to try and find a new life after this divide. I went travelling, I admit I fought a few fights. I even took a human as a protégée. There is a young prince called Kerry who will soon be king who will be trained as a leo."

Raiden forgot the name instantly. "Why would you want to keep a bloody human as a pet, Val? They're all scum who wiped out our kind."

"No, Raiden, they're not all like that. This is what I came to teach you. You can't go about life hating the race that killed ours. Fighting constantly, thinking you're avenging the dead, because you're not and you'll only end up joining them. The divide is over and you should be looking, like me, for a new life now. Go out there and find a wife, damn it."

Raiden snorted. "Find a wife? Where brother? We are the only ones left or haven't you noticed?"

"We don't know that. And if we are then we'll find another way."

Raiden almost laughed now. "Like what? Marry a tigian?"

Valadad shot an angry stare at his brother. "You sound as ignorant as those animals in that bar."

"Don't compare me to them!" Raiden snapped back and pointed back at the tavern. "I'm nothing like them! They killed all of our family, all of our friends, they destroyed everything we have and left us with nothing!"

"You're wrong, Raiden. They didn't take from us. Their parents and grandparents did."

Raiden shrugged off this counsel. "It's the same thing."

"Well, regardless of what you say. I'm here now and plan on staying for a while. Now why don't you show me where you're staying, champ? It's getting cold out here."

Raiden spat down at the grass again and walked ahead, "Don't call me that." He walked on ahead with Valadad behind him.

Raiden stumbled as he tried to flee with Proto-Weapon behind him. He held his hand out to stabilise himself against the wall of the airport. He looked out onto the runway to see Feydon had fired again. Cannon fire smashed into more of the city. The terminal and more of the communications tower crumbled and the whole of the top of the tower fell and crashed down into smoke and dust to clutter and poison the air. He, however, had far worse problems now as the tigians managed to distract Proto-Weapon long enough for him to get to his feet and try to flee. His feet ached, slowing him down. He reached out and gripped onto the corner of a wall, turning right, and fell into the wall as his knees twisted. He panted in agony but couldn't get up and turned to sit against the wall and breathe deep heavy breaths. He waited a few minutes before gathering his strength to pick himself back up. In the distance he saw the Scarlet Arise slowly ascend from the ground and thanked Sphere. Acarlie must have tried telling Kaza to wait for them, she was a good girl. The ship slowly turned trying to avoid Feydon's ship-fire. One cannon, however, smashed and exploded into a nearby zeppelin, which he recognised as the zeppelin that Sheeria and Keppal had arrived on. The whole thing ignited in the sky as the explosion lit the hydrogen in the blimp carrying it and suddenly a whole new sun beamed in the sky, blinding everyone, black smoke quickly followed and where the dark black cloud went one way the debris went another and fell down raining fire onto some small distant figures on the tarmac. He hoped Sheeria wasn't there and finally forced himself back to his feet. He still had to escape himself. It felt wrong fleeing. He remembered a time when he was young and being carried up the stairs in the arms of his brother and felt the same anger and pain but knew survival was paramount over a leo's honour. Sheeria was still out there too if she wasn't either in the Scarlet Arise or in the fallen tower but he needed to lose this metal creature first. He couldn't fight it as much as it pained him. He staggered again as his knees felt loose and felt so shamed, weak and vulnerable; he felt like prey and didn't like it. He could hear the mechanical noises of Proto-Weapon walking fast trying to catch him up. His snorts of rage and heavy breathing soon filled his ears; he felt scared, terrified even. His own brother was going to kill him, rip him into pieces, the very one who had saved him a dozen times would now take his life.

His legs weakened again and he fell to the floor and panted, his other hand under his armour holding onto a previous gunshot wound which now opened again, his kingnine blood now leaking over his hand. He feebly tried getting back to his feet but fell to his knees again and gasped for air, praying for strength. He had never felt so weak and defeated.

Proto-Weapon approached and finally caught him, reached out and grabbed the lip of his armour and wrapped his arm around Raiden's neck and squeezed. Raiden couldn't even lift his arm to attempt to fight back and choked, his eyes bulged and soon closed. He fell limp in Proto-Weapon's arms. All was black.

"I still don't understand why you're doing this, brother," Raiden said as he watched Valadad climb onto a great, dark green lizzier.

The year was 46 ALD (one year previous): The place, the coast of Racoves on a cold day. Wooden seaships were loading their cargo and assembling their crew while waiting for the winds to pick up and set their sails across the waters. Raiden had now just turned one hundred and seven. Much wiser now than in his previous years but still strong for his age. Valadad was one hundred and twenty-seven, past the youthful years of his life now but still with character, wisdom and even some strength left in him. His voice had grown deeper with age now, still not quite in his twilight years for a leo but old enough to know a thing or two.

They were waiting for the okay from the ship's captain to take Valadad away and he had packed supplies in his lizzier's satchel and mounted it and sat on the saddle of the great horse-sized, two legged lizard.

Raiden was seated on his own lizzier, Bluey, and pulled the reins to face his brother. "Decrenia is a long way away, brother. Are you sure it's wise to travel there just for Osiris? It's only a small town. Let Feydon have that whole country and let's just get on with our lives."

Valadad gleamed a smile at the white, cold sky. "No, it's more than that, Raiden. I have to go."

"Was it not you that said we should stay away from the world's violence, Val?" he asked.

"Yes, but you must understand why this is different, Raiden."

"Enlighten me."

Valadad sighed a great deep breath as though he had had it stored within him all his life and let it go free into the sky above him, "Did you know Osiris was a man, Raiden?"

Raiden looked puzzled. "Father told me once of a man named Osiris. What of it?"

"Osiris was one of the Ultra Soldiers originally created to wipe our species out before the kingnines were around. His original name was a number, he was called 051715, later to be known as Osiris. Once the kingnines arrived they made the Ultra Soldiers obsolete. Osiris was supposed to be put down but instead built an army of his peers and fought against the humans and triumphed over them with the help of the leos. After the fighting he made his own land on Decrenia and named it after himself."

"This still doesn't explain anything, Val," Raiden complained.

Valadad smiled and explained, "During the fighting Osiris found a leo he was supposed to kill, a leo named Degnaler."

"Father?"

"Yes, Father helped him, and so did Mother and even I. I was a little too young though to be any help. Even little you were there."

"I was?"

"Only a suckling pup, but yes. On the year you were born this took place. Osiris was even there on the day you arrived."

This was now beginning to sound very personal. Raiden looked a little sad. "Where is this story going?"

Valadad continued, "One day, during the fighting, Mother and little you were left behind as the enemy advanced and forced the lines to retreat. Father begged and cried to return but the army would not allow him nor me to return. Osiris, however, turned back on his own and headed back into the enemy territory. He returned two days later with only you in his arms. He told of how Mother had died protecting you."

Raiden sat silent on his lizzier, Bluey. "Why was I never told this?"

"I'm sure Father would have told you the story eventually. I, however, have always found it difficult to talk about it."

As he spoke Raiden remembered his father and he could see him through Valadad. Only the plait under his chin was missing, preventing Valadad from looking identical.

"Osiris was there for our family when we needed him. He couldn't save mother but he saved you. Osiris may have been dead now for years and years but his children still live on. His family now needs the strength of the leo and I aim to answer just like he did for us."

"Do you really think it matters, Val? Going to Decrenia is a one way trip."

"I may be old, Raiden, but I am still a leo like you. We are leos, and leos have honour. I'm going to fight for Osiris and protect his family as he did for us and that's the end of it."

"In that case I should come with you." Raiden tried to order but Valadad countered.

"No, Raiden, I'm sending you on a different ship, to Walton."

Raiden appeared confused again and looked across the waters in the direction of the small island.

"Walton? It's only a small farming village island. Why are you sending me there?"

"Because I know you will be safe there, that's why. I have already spoken to a human named Theydon. He says he needs a leo like you to help with thieves attacking the village. It's good work, you'll be given a good home in a safe community and all the freedom you wish with the forests surrounding it. A haven for leos like us. At least there I know where you will be and feel stronger knowing that you're safe there."

"I'm past a century now, Val. You don't have to keep looking out for me," Raiden reminded him.

"I know." Valadad turned his lizzier around and faced the seaships on the coast. "But I want to. Please do this for me, Raiden. Please go to Walton and stay there until I return."

"How do I know you will?"

"You have my word," he smiled. They could hear the horn of the ships, they were ready for departure.

"That's what Father promised, Val," Raiden said as they made their way down.

"I know, but I'm not Father." He punched Raiden's arm playfully. "Don't worry, champ, I'll be back, I promise…."

19

Keppal heard the commotion from the cockpit of the Scarlet Arise while he walked along the wooden floors of the hallways of the great skyship. He wore black, short leggings of cotton and a large dark green tigian shirt. Its buttons only went down three and were more for show. He left them unopened and wore his old police issue sleeveless stab-proof vest over it, dark blue; the colour of the ocean by night. He jumped when he first heard the cannon fire from the Feydon fleet and made his way to the captain of the ship to see what the commotion was. As he got closer to the door he heard the heated arguments of Captain Kaza and Elementalist Acarlie. He speeded up his pace to a run until he reached the door.

Acarlie was standing with her hands out to each side preventing Kaza getting past. Val stood in front of him by the door and only the two pirate pilots, the bald Dillon and the messy black haired Smythy, were present.

"Standing there like a scarecrow isn't going to change anything, Missy!" Kaza wasn't impressed with her impersonation.

He stood wearing ripped brown boiled leather three quarter-lengths that reached to his shins, the knees were torn and had holes in them from wear and tear. He wore no shirt but let his golden brown tanned skin show, only wearing a black webbing tightly, he only used it for the convenience of the large pockets across his chest. Both wrists were still decorated with coloured metal bangles ranging from gold to copper and woven, plaited string bracelets that looked so worn they were about to break; on his left forearm was the communication device attached to his arm like a large rectangular watch. He took off his glasses and hooked them onto his webbing and ran his fingers through his short, ink black hair in frustration with Acarlie.

"We can't leave just yet. Sheeria and Raiden are not on board!" Acarlie tried calling back.

"What's going on?" Keppal asked as he stepped past Val, trying to ignore him completely.

Kaza looked back hearing, "Missy here thinks she can stop me from leaving port with my own ship."

"We just have to wait for Raiden and Sheeria. They won't be long, Kaza, I promise."

Neither Raiden nor Sheeria are on the ship? Maybe this is the moment I have been waiting for? He thought and remembered the mission Lord Zane gave to him. Another shot from the Feydon fleet fired across the sky and crashed into the communications tower. They all rushed to the windscreen of the ship to see a large chunk of the circular disk at the top begin to crash down.

"Right, that's it!" Kaza called and stormed back to his Captain's Seat and ordered his crew by pressing a button on the arm and shouting into the attached receiver.

"Crew! Feydon is attacking. I want all hands readying the ship for evasive manoeuvres. We're using the thrusters so strap in! That goes for you guys too," he ordered the people in the room with him.

"Aye aye, Capt'n!" the two pilots acknowledged but Acarlie still refused.

"No you can't. I am the elementalist–"

"And I am the captain of this ship!" Kaza finally silenced her, "and I'm not staying here and risking my ship and crew for two individuals. They know where we're going, they can catch up, now get with the rest of my crew and strap yourselves in else you wanna be flung into the walls?" He looked from the stubborn elementalist to the back of

Dillon's bald head. "Dillon, lift the ship!"

The ship waited for its crew to assemble and as soon as it was ready the ship lifted off the ground. More cannon fire now fell around them and they had no choice but to attempt escape. Val and Keppal took Acarlie by her hands and took her away to safely sit with the crew and Kaza buckled himself in as the ship ascended from the ground.

In the distance they could see the Feydon ships. Small circles of smoke appeared and instantly they could see the projectiles falling like heavy rain around them. They watched and saw the aeomon zeppelin begin its flee attempt, when it was struck. The projectile missile exploded and ignited the hydrogen in the zeppelin's giant air bag above it and suddenly the sky lit up. Instantly the zeppelin exploded and rained down fire and debris onto some small figures running away on the airport's tarmac down below.

The ship turned and once Kaza was informed that his crew were ready the ship's thrusters started up and shot them out of the city in the direction of Hiro.

Once they were safely out of the way of the attack the thrusters were powered down and the crew were ordered to go about their duties again. Acarlie was still upset about leaving her guides behind and ordered that she be taken to the captain again, but was instead ordered to her quarters like a disciplined child. She tried screaming and throwing her position at Kaza once again but he banned her from the cockpit and cut off the communications of the ship. He had more important issues to worry about than an elementalist's tantrum.

Val eventually calmed her down and escorted her to her quarters, when Keppal stepped in and offered to escort her himself.

Acarlie was still a little upset with Val herself and accepted Keppal's help, ordering Val away for now. She did so as calmly and politely as she could. Val understood and gave her a small kiss on her cheek before leaving her in the hands of Keppal. This was exactly what he was waiting for. He finally had the elementalist all to himself, just her and him, no one around, no witnesses.

He led her down to the bowels of the ship until only the ship's engine could be heard droning away. The sound of the crew's voices was completely drowned out. The soles of her shoes clanged down the metal staircases rhythmically and then tapped on the brown, polished floor as she followed Keppal to the depths of the ship.

"Why are we down here, Keppal?" she asked as he led her as far away from the crew as he could.

"I know it's noisy here, elementalist, but I thought it would be best if we got away from the crew and had a little chat, that's all. Maybe I can calm your stress a little." He smiled a genuine smile and looked over his shoulder at the small human. She agreed and thanked him, which was the part that hurt. He winced without her seeing and finally found an empty room.

"In here." He opened the door and held his arm out to welcome her in.

As she walked in she walked past his elbow and instantly he had her in his arms.

His lock was perfect and he had her throat tightly in his grip. He reached with his other hand for support and tensed his biceps, cutting off her oxygen.

She couldn't even gasp for air, within five seconds she was limp. "I'm sorry, human," Keppal whispered to her as she fell unconscious.

He picked her up and closed the door with his heel and walked to the end of the room and laid her down.

Here she is, I did it. I completed Lord Zane's mission…

He sighed and lowered his head at the crime he had

committed and waited in silence for something to happen but when after another twenty seconds she was still lying before him he knew it was over. Silence surrounded him but the air screamed 'murder'. He closed his eyes to try and block out the guilt in his mind. She was only a sweet, young thing, but this had to be done.

She breathed, a small breath in her unconscious state, lightly. He saw this and suddenly wanted to cry; he would have to do this the hard way.

"Why?" he asked himself and tensed a fist in frustration, when he opened it his claws extended. He raised his hands and begged for forgiveness.

"You!" screamed a voice and suddenly something pounced on him. He tumbled over and felt a sharp knife's tip at the base of this throat.

"Where is the leo?"

A face was before him, covered in a black silk hood. A furry, whiskered face and yellow eyes glared down at him. He couldn't believe what he was seeing.

"Impossible! I killed you," he said in disbelief.

"I have you now. Back on the ship to Donolan I was forced to let you go but not this time!" Umbra punched and punched him until his large black tigian nose was bleeding. She turned the knife around and struck him repeatedly with the pommel, picked him up by his stab proof vest and tested it for him three times.

He screamed something fierce and tried to grab her but she was too fast and agile.

She grabbed his hand and twisted it an unnatural direction and threw him past the human on the floor.

"What do you want?!" Keppal cried. He half knew the answer. This was the archer that he had tracked down a year ago in Toshiro, this was the killer that trapped and ate its victims. Songs and legends would tell the stories of this hooded creature, stories to scare the children around warm fires on cold nights; none of them would ever tell the truth of the story, however.

"What do I want?" Umbra repeated in her fury and drew both her knives now from sheaves on her chest. "You killed my husband!"

Husband? The thought terrified him when he imagined it.

"You killed my Venator!"

So it wasn't you! It was your husband. There were two of them! "I'm sorry!" he cried and reached out from the floor in his pain. "I was only doing my job, your husband was killing people and–"

Umbra screamed and dived for him again. "We were surviving! We were doing what we needed to survive. We killed, we ate, but we survived. Until you came along and killed my husband and ruined my life. Now tell me before I kill you, where is the leo?"

When he didn't answer she began to assault him until she struck his head hard enough to knock all sense out of him.

"No!" she cried and took hold of his white and black, furry head and began slamming it against the floor. "You're not getting away that easy! I want retribution!"

She slammed his head on the floor loud, his head thumped and shook the ground loud enough that she didn't hear the other person behind her.

She felt hands grabbing her back and threw her off Keppal skidding across the room. She flipped back on her feet and stood to see the tip of a red katana pressing into her throat and an aeomon at the other end of it.

Dude didn't know what was happening, why the elementalist was down here laid out on the floor, who this hooded creature was nor why the white tigian was bleeding out.

All he knew was that the bowels of the ship was his space and this murder wasn't going to happen on his watch. The black hooded cat glared daggers at him. "Get out of my way, aeomon…." She could tell only from his smell that he was an aeomon but looked for his tail and sneered. "… Sorry, aeo-*man*," she corrected.

Dude poked her in the chest and pointed with the end of Fireshaver as if to say, "*Get lost.*"

Umbra, however, looked over her shoulder at the door and back at him. "I'm not going to do that. Why don't you try asking?"

Dude scowled now. She was new to this ship otherwise she would know he was mute. He shook his head and repeated his pointing to the door.

Umbra took his silence as a rudeness and pointed to the white tigian. "You can keep the human. I only want the white tigian. It looks as if he was about to end her anyway."

Dude's eyes left the hooded cat's and looked down at Acarlie. As soon as he did Umbra struck, knocking away the tip of his katana and slashing with her knives.

Dude jumped back and slashed Fireshaver. Instantly the blade lit up and sparked fire, lighting up the room. Umbra jumped back now seeing this wonderful weapon of sharp metal and burning fire.

"Stay out of my way, aeomon!" Umbra ordered but Dude shook his head and bravely stood his ground. Her ears twitched under her hood as she heard footsteps running down the metal staircase; someone had heard their commotion. Her eyes widened as a fear crept into her mind, the white tigian would have to wait. She tried to escape but the silent aeomon was still standing his ground threatening her with his fire-blade. She frowned as the hastening footsteps drew closer; she now was out of time. In a flash she jumped, slashed away Fireshaver and grabbed the aeomon, gripped his mouth to make no noise and took him away with her.

Val appeared in the room, a small party of the pirates with him. He instantly saw Acarlie on the floor and ran to her. The crew went to Keppal.

"What happened here?" Rocco, the silver haired mechanic, asked seeing his cuts and bruises.

Val inspected Acarlie carefully. There was no damage to her, she was unharmed. He instantly realised what must have happened to her.

She's had another episode, she must have turned and injured Keppal.

"I don't know," he lied but picked her up and held her in his arms. "But at least it's not too serious. Take Keppal to the infirmary. We'll ask them when they wake."

Umbra found her part of the bowels of the ship and threw the aeomon inside first. He scraped his knees and his metallic red katana clanged on the ground and skidded across the floor. He stood up to face her, scared of what she was going to do. After a short stare-out Umbra finally sheaved her two knives. This wasn't how she'd planned her mission; she wanted to stay out of sight of everyone but now had no alternative.

"Okay then, tell me and I'll let you live, aeoman. Where is the leo that travels with this crew?"

Dude stood silent and strong in his resolve to bring down this hooded killer. He knew she would pounce if he again went for his blade, she was faster and stronger than him.

Umbra waited and became frustrated by his silence. "Answer me!" she barked.

Again he stood silent. Umbra was beginning to now wonder, "Can you even talk at all?" she asked once she realised he had not made a single sound yet.

The silent aeomon frowned when she asked, he didn't like anybody mentioning his handicap and shook his head.

"Why?" she asked again. He opened his mouth wide to show her the severed tongue sitting right at the back of this mouth. The tongue didn't even reach his glands and sat like a tiny, dark red slug below his tonsils. She stepped forward and now reached out with her furry, golden hands and took his cheeks gently and inspected his handicap. Suddenly she felt sympathy toward him but also noticed he still needed some council.

"So you have no tongue? It doesn't mean you can't talk. Now tell me, talk slow and look at me when you do, try to pronounce things as best as you can and be patient with me."

She let go and stared down at Dude and started with the basics. "What's your name?"

Dude felt stung. *This is stupid*, he thought. She wouldn't be able to understand him, no one did.

"Yhou whown urherha," he said gravely.

"Try me," she snapped back.

Dude looked up with a gasp; she understood. Never had anyone understood him, never.

For the first time since he was cut he could have a spoken conversation with someone, only now he didn't know what to say.

"What's your name?" she asked again.

He remembered trying to pronounce Dude to Rezosa and only saying "Oooh" which is why she called him Monkey. As much as he loved her he didn't like that name and didn't want a repeat. He remembered a long forgotten name some doctors and nurses called him a long time ago but decided against using it.

"I haf eyo eyame," he told her.

"Don't give me that. Everybody has a name, aeoman. What's yours?"

He suddenly wanted to smile, to laugh and jump. She could understand. He felt emotion overwhelming him, a foreign and alien energy of happiness took him, his hands twitched and so did his lips, something that hadn't happened for years and years. He wanted to say more.

"I...mouh people hall me...oooh," he slowly tried to pronounce the Ds as best as he could.

Umbra saw his struggle with the Ds and understood but need clarification, "Are you trying to say Doo?"

"Oooh...OooH." He tried again trying to pronounce the last D clearly.

"Dude?"

"Hei!"

She nodded and almost smiled seeing his face light up like this, "Well...that's a stupid name," she cut off. He didn't care, she could say whatever she liked because she could say it to him and he could answer back and so would she.

"So long as you won't tell me your real name I'm going to call you Mute, since you choose to be so quiet to everyone all the time."

Mute was still smiling, it was a name that reflected his handicap but still he didn't care because as long as he was speaking to her he wasn't a mute any more.

"O-hey..." He wanted to ask her now and moved his lips first to show her he wanted to speak. "Wassh eyor eyame?"

"My name is Umbra Tenebris," she confirmed. He almost squeaked with excitement. She now could even see the excitement and moisture in his eyes.

"You haven't spoken to anybody in a long time have you?"

He shook his head.

"No, don't do that," she ordered and continued looking down at him. "Tell me, no more sign language."

"O-hey. Oh."

"When was the last time?"

"A yong hime a-ho. I wassh eyihal."

She nodded and finally calmed down. This aeomon was enjoying her company, a first for her since her husband's death.

"Okay then, Mute, listen to me. I'm looking for the leo of this team. I want you to tell me where he is?"

Mute looked unsettled now. "Rhayhen ish hor here. Haphin effe wivouel hir."

She was hoping he wouldn't say that. She cursed and grunted in frustration.

"He's back at Donolan."

"Hei, we're hairhing for Hiwo. He will fowow an mee uh hair."

She sighed and flung her back against the wall and sat down. "Shit!" she cursed.

After thinking she looked back up at him. "I don't want anyone knowing I'm here. Can you keep quiet about me to the rest of the crew?"

Mute almost laughed at what she was asking. "Hei, I ha heep whouoir."

"Good." she looked around and asked, "What about food? Can you fetch something to eat?"

He nodded again then remembered what she had said about signs from now on. "Hei, weigh here."

20

With a new divide only recently declared Chippenham turned from an elder city scarred by attack to a desperate mass gathering of fleeing people, most of which were humans. The word got around within the hour, Sphere was witnessing another great divide. Only a few days ago they were all celebrating with one another and now a time of great fear swept the world like a plague. The humans took no chances and trusted no one, gathered their families and fled as fast as they could to leave the rest of the creatures to suffer the aftermath of Feydon's attack. All of the other creatures, now hearing about Sarah Celadore's false plans all feared the humans and also tried to leave the city. So much confusion filled the wild streets, humans fled down them like water rapids, people were trampled, left behind and lost or even mugged by opportunists as they made their escape. Chippenham wasn't the only city at war now, the divide spread around the world instantly. As soon as the word reached, the tigian leaders of each country took control of the corresponding armies and marched them through each capital fearing the human world leaders would strike first and repeat the massacres they committed before the Leo Divide. The tigians were smarter than this and instantly knew to seize control before things got out of hand. As the hours passed the reports soon started coming in: President Marshal Sahota of Angland had been killed defending his home in Donolan; President Orion of Magna had had his skyship shot down while trying to enter the city and President Sauarami of Calmeron had fled his home and surrendered his country. President Shuian of Isolies had been thrown off his towered home in Lachine.

King Kerry of Racoves was currently defending his large pyramid palace in a siege against his own army led by tigians of Racoves. Only Queen Angel got off lightly; she had instantly lost the whole of Feydon and Septura but it was known that Lord Zane would be crowned king when he returned. Since she was married to him that gave her control still of the Feydon army. Many wondered if this was her plan all along; either way of the divide she would have lost nothing but gained much more.

Zahied, Rezosa and Major now decided they would find out on behalf of the human species why Angel was doing this, why she wanted Raiden so much, and try to bring her in to prove to the Senate that neither she nor Sarah Celadore had anything to do with the new divide and this all was the result of the evil plans of Cecil Vurbute. To do this they had to run through the city and to the skyships. The Feydon army though was now in battle with the defending Magna forces. Zahied ran around the two conflicting armies, using his skills as a caster to slip past them, seemingly invisible to them, while Rezosa and Major followed closely behind.

Feydon had again changed their tactics and had now landed their ships on the dusty concrete floor and set a perimeter of soldiers in a large circle around them that made a radius of three blocks of the city. They used the large human-made skyscrapers as a means of protection and the ground fleet now only stayed within their perimeter and fought defensively. Magna now had circled around them and surrounded them, seeing their strange new tactic and needed not to send in melee combats but shot with arrows and projectiles. The Feydon ground soldiers huddled in as close as possible and turned their large rectangular, glowing blue electric shields to the sky and turned themselves into one large shell that deflected everything Magna threw at them. Behind them was a line of their own marksmen and archers, who fired back.

Zahied ignored the Magna troops, who only saw them as civilians and let them be, and ran as close as he could to the ships until they were in plain sight. He peered around the corner of a tall building of brick, concrete and plaster with another twinned right next to it making a narrow alleyway with the fleet in an open square just past it. The street opened up with roads going in all directions and footpaths beside them. Glass windows at the bottom of the neighbouring buildings had been smashed through but the buildings themselves were not looted; Feydon was not here to rob and pillage. Their lines had a narrow opening that would lead them to the stationary skyships. Rezosa peered around Zahied's shoulder.

"Why have they landed?"

"I guess that they intend to stay for a while this time. They don't want to waste fuel. Angel said she wasn't here because of the items this time."

"She's here for Raiden," Major said from behind them.

"That's right, they must be waiting for him. She mentioned a single operative being sent out to capture him. They're waiting for him here so they can make a quick getaway."

"This is all an extreme way of capturing a leo," Rezosa pointed out. "Why do you think she wants him?"

Zahied rubbed his bearded chin. "Well, Raiden is the last leo alive. Maybe she's after the glory of hunting down the last surviving leo and putting an end to the race altogether."

"I can't believe I used to work for them," Major said guiltily. He crouched down and checked the straps and ties of his armour.

"Me neither," Rezosa followed and reached around her

back for her weapon, Hevana, when she realised she had left it with Mitis back on the Scarlet Arise. She cursed again and asked Zahied, "So what do you think we should do?"

"Considering we know that they are targeting Raiden, I'm thinking we board the largest ship there," he pointed to a ship to the left of the others. It looked like the flag ship of the whole fleet. Only seven of the ships were stationed in this part of the city, all were large men-of-war of the skyship kingdom. All were large, brown metal monsters, narrow in design but bulky with circular thrusters on either side. Cannon ports lined each side and none had wings like the Scarlet Arise but instead the propellers were built into eight shorter wings on each side and would face down to the ground, which would help with stability once lifted. They looked heavier and more sustainable of damage. They needed their powerful thrusters to lift them off the floor and sail the sky. The largest, in the centre, stood like a mammoth to its subordinates. Its cannons stuck out of its side decorated with gold plate line work around them, like rose stems, and it needed an extra two propellers on each side. Its cargo doors were left open for the army to retreat if need be.

"Raiden will most likely be taken to that ship if he's caught. We can stay hidden there until he arrives then help him escape. If the Magna army does finally break their defences we can always slip back out of the ship. Also, while we're there we can find Angel, bring her to justice in front of the Senate and put an end to the divide."

"I like it," Rezosa smiled, "it will be known as the quickest divide in history. What could possibly go wrong?"

"Don't say that," Major complained.

Zahied pulled out the pistol and cocked back the chamber and took a breath to calm his nerves, "Okay then, so long as we don't make a sound nor touch anything I can get us through the ground defences. Remember this is only an optical illusion that will make us not unseen but unnoticed. Once we're inside, there will likely be cameras, the illusion is for biological eyes only, mechanical eyes such as cameras will see us. This will also mask our heat signature so kingnines and soldiers who see in infra-red will see straight through us."

"We shouldn't be here," Rezosa confessed. "This is too dangerous. To try and infiltrate this skyship while the ground fleet sits outside seems like a suicide mission."

"Well, we've not got too much choice, Rezosa. Raiden and the others could be in danger and we have the time and power to stop this attack."

"Isn't there anything else we can do though?"

"Is that fear I hear in your voice, Rezosa?" Major asked slyly.

Rezosa sighed and peered out past the defences. "Maybe. This just doesn't seem like a tactical plan of action, more like a desperate bid with a small chance of success."

"You mean like the same plan you had to run across the battlefield in Donolan with bullets flying over our heads?" Major countered wittily.

Rezosa smiled and pulled the hair back from her fringe over her ear. "That was different."

"Relax Rezosa, you underestimate my abilities," Zahied reassured them, stretching out his hands and remembering the trick.

Zahied had used this elder trick before back in Lachine and remembered the hand gestures to complete it. Within a minute they were all creeping down the alley and soon were almost touching the soldiers in their bright blue shell. Arrows and elder projectiles fell around them but they kept silent like Zahied said and thus made their way to the largest skyship without incident.

"At least tell me your name!" she called up.

The Archer stood up and faced the outside and looked down at the long drop below it and turned around to see Sheeria once more.

"My name is Umbra Tenebris!" she snarled, flicked her hands to one side and as the ice-axes attached by string flicked out she caught them with perfect technique. She leaned forward and fell from the building and she was gone.

Sheeria tried to stop her knowing the fall would be too severe but within a second the hooded archer was gone and only she was left in the communications tower. The ceiling shook and plaster fell around her. She didn't stay any longer and dashed back down the winding stairs.

Once she reached the bottom, the sky screamed above her and heavy chunks fell. She screamed and covered her eyes and ran as fast as her legs could carry her. The top of the tower now tilted and broke away from the foundations holding it and fell to the opposite side of the tower to her. Smaller chunks of bricks, concrete and burning metal fell around her, dented the tarmac and shook the floor. She heard a male roar and ran toward it, her eyes blinded by the thick, hot dust engulfing her, choking her.

She ran into an embrace. Furry arms took her and a figure shielded her from the dust and gave her a moment to clear her lungs.

She gasped and spluttered, opening her sore eyes to see it was her brother, Audie, clutching onto her, and a large crew of tigians were around him.

"We have to get out of here, Mister President!" one of his subjects shouted over the confusion.

"Audie…?" Sheeria asked, still shaken from shock and confused by what was happening.

He stood her up. "It's okay, Sheeria. I'm here," he

tried to calm her but her head was spinning, her heart pounding from the excitement. She looked back to see the communications tower was only a long, narrow neck that stood out of the ground now, its disk shaped head had fallen down now and entombed the poor souls underneath it, crushing a smaller skyship; a thick grey cloud of dust and ash floated around it, impossible to see through. She blinked and blinked again, she had hot ash in her eyes, and continued coughing and rubbing her eyes until they were red and moist from her tears.

"That's okay, Sheeria, take your time," he said and rubbed her back.

They led her away from the dust to breathe in the clean air and gave her, and themselves, a few minutes to recover.

Once her lungs were finally free again she looked around. They were still standing on the airport's tarmac, closer to the terminal again now. She heard a familiar engine and looked to see the Scarlet Arise ascend from the ground, so too did the aeomon zeppelin.

"Look!" one of the tigians shouted and pointed to it above them. They all witnessed the blinding view of the zeppelin exploding and lighting up the sky. The bang it released was deafening. Instantly afterwards, they all realised the horror they now faced as the whole thing began to fall down like falling stars.

They all screamed, Audie grabbed his sister and they all ran in every direction. Fire fell around them once more as the aeomon craft of flaming hydrogen crashed down onto the ground. Its black cloud swallowed the sky into the colour of death and only the flaming, twisted skeletal girders of the zeppelin stood. The blazing inferno cooked the air around it and entombed the poor aeomon souls of the aircraft forever. They would each join the song of fire, adding their ash to the chorus.

Sheeria found herself spread across the floor; she could feel the heat of the flames on her flesh, as horrifying as it was the heat felt warm but burned her eyes to tears. The air stank of death, oils and fire. She picked herself back up and tilted her head to the sky. The Scarlet Arise was escaping, beyond the reach of the black shadowy ink that now drowned the sky with long fingers, like death itself was claiming everything underneath it. She had been left behind, Acarlie could wait no longer and had fled, leaving her to burn in the dust and ash. She wasn't angry though. *At least she's safe*, she thought.

She heard a voice beyond the screaming of grief and despair of those who had witnessed the explosion from the terminal. His voice was comforting and again her brother was there to pick her up from the floor.

"Are you okay?" he asked.

"I hope so." A sudden fear took her and she checked her body to see if anything was broken or worse. She was relieved to find nothing amiss save her confidence.

Audie helped her to her feet and went to help the rest of his people, the rest of *her* people. She saw a figure walking along the hallways of the terminal. She recognised it immediately as the metal monster Raiden called his brother. But she wasn't sure, her eyes still blurred with a burning pain and her head spun.

"Valadad?" she asked herself but she knew her answer when she saw that it was dragging something by its feet; its metal, clawed, large hands gripped around the golden ankles of a leo. Raiden was not moving but being dragged by his feet on his back across the terminal by the victor of his fight.

"No!" she cried in despair and ran towards him. She instantly felt tears form, fearing the worst, and heard her brother scream again and chase after her.

She reached the broken windows, now just glass shattered on the floor around them, and passed the tigians in the terminal and chased after Proto-Weapon.

She turned the corner Raiden had previously fallen into; she could see the red stain of where he fell and sat against the wall to catch his breath and witnessed the zeppelin fall. Proto-Weapon was at the end of the hallway, Raiden, on his back, behind him, his eyes closed, his arms reaching back.

"Raiden!" she screamed and charged after him.

Proto-Weapon heard, its ears twitched and its head jerked and it looked over its shoulder to see the crying tigian following him, her brother closely behind. It dropped Raiden's feet and turned to face its new opponent.

Only it didn't move. It bent its legs, spread out its chest and opened its hands and its black, metal razors for claws gleamed in the sunlight. It stood breathing deep, heavy, painful breaths like it was forcing oxygen out of its body manually but it didn't move. Sheeria stopped before it and saw the look of fire in its glowing red eyes and waited for its first move, but it never made it. Instead it seemed to power down. Its horrifying breathing pattern slowed down instantly, its shoulders slumped forward and its head lowered.

"Sphere's divide, what is that thing?" Audie said when he first saw it.

"I…I don't know," she answered and waited. Half a minute passed while she waited for it to move.

"What's it doing?"

Sheeria plucked up some confidence and stepped forward. It didn't move, it didn't even notice her. It was like it was suddenly inert.

"I think it's stopped."

"It?" Audie asked seeing what it was. "It's a leo? But what has happened to it?"

Sheeria now was right in front of it and knelt down to look into its eyes. She waved a hand in front of it, the eyes didn't even flinch. It still breathed, however – slow, light breaths – but everything else was dead.

"I know of this leo. This was Valadad, Raiden's brother. He died at the Battle of Osiris last year. Feydon must have taken his body and turned him into…this."

Audie scowled and stepped up to inspect the wires reaching out from its brain and snaking down into its spine.

"Humans are monsters, Sheeria. Look at what they are capable of."

"No," she said and blinked slowly. "Not all humans. My Acarlie would never do this."

Sheeria went to Raiden and checked his pulse while Audie went for a closer inspection of Proto-Weapon until he was almost touching noses with him. She heard Raiden breathing and picked up his arm to wrap it around her shoulders.

"Please, Audie, help me carry him. I don't want to be here when this thing wakes up."

Zahied and the other two ran across the hallways of the skyship. They made it past the soldiers outside and now knew it was only a matter of time before they would be spotted and so took no chances. The hallways were painted white with a brown, wooden skirting lining the top and bottom, the floor garnished oak and circular lights above them on the ceiling. Cameras were at the end of every hallway and soon saw them infiltrating through the ship. Soldiers were sent out and soon they had no choice but to fight their way through.

"Well, this was a good idea!" Major shouted over Zahied's shoulder sarcastically. They all hid round a corner. To their left, soldiers were firing down the corridor. Zahied leaned out and fired back with the pistol he had. One soldier made his way down the corridor behind them trying to flank them and pointed a rife at Rezosa, who acted fast, pushed the barrel of the rifle away and flipped the man over her hip, took the rifle from him and struck him with the butt of the weapon until he stopped moving.

The rifle was a wooden, long barrelled, bolt action rifle. The Feydon army was using weapons like these since Zane seized the factory where they were being manufactured illegally in Toshiro. Rezosa and Major had each seen and fired these before. The weapons were strong with excellent range and accuracy but in narrow corridors with many enemies were not so effective.

She looked around to see a door and grabbed Major's shoulder. "Quickly, we can't take them on with these weapons. We need to lead them into a small space where they can't use these weapons and are forced the resort to melee weapons!"

Zahied followed after sending two more rounds from his small pistol down the hallway at the armed guards. Rezosa had no idea where she was going and ran from one room to another. Soon she found a large, thick door with a push handle and opened it. The room was like a laboratory. The door behind them could be locked and barricaded so they each took everything they could and barricaded themselves in. They thought they were alone and could give themselves a minute to decide what they would do when Zahied turned and saw a figure sitting in a chair. He froze at first believing they had been discovered but calmed down when he saw the figure in the chair was blinded and strapped in. It was a tigian; a metal device was covering his head and his arms and legs were tied to the chair; he looked asleep. The chair was wired in and connected to a monitor. Zahied stepped cautiously past the tigian in the electronic chair and glanced into the monitor to see a familiar corridor back at the skyship port's terminal. There was clearly a camera back there which this monitor was displaying but Zahied felt something was different, it was not like a normal camera with a person filming nor a stationary security camera, but instead appeared to be looking through the eyes of something there.

"What is this?" Major asked and stepped forward.

Zahied inspected the monitor and saw a familiar face on it.

"That's Raiden!"

They saw he was correct. The monitor showed Raiden being strangled from behind by whatever was showing them this image. They then watched as this thing grabbed Raiden's ankle and began dragging him away.

"What on Sphere is this thing?" Rezosa asked, just as horrified as the rest of them.

The door banged behind them. The other soldiers had caught up with them.

"This must be what Angel was talking about," Zahied pointed out. "She said she was waiting for Raiden to board this ship and has sent a single agent to recover him. This thing here must be what she meant."

He looked back at the tigian in the seat and looked at the metal contraption on his head, 'Proto-Weapon' was engraved on the top of the device and masked the tigian's eyes completely.

"He must be controlling that thing out there. This… Proto-Weapon."

"How is that even possible?" Major asked. The door banged again, louder this time.

They looked back at the screen, when they heard a scream.

"*Raiden!*" screamed the voice of Sheeria. The monitor

turned and they saw the tigian charging after it and saw it, from its perspective, jump back and wait to attack her. From the corners of the monitor they saw this mechanical beast spread its shoulders and open its hands and stretch out its dark metal claws.

"It's going to kill her!" Rezosa shouted.

Zahied understood immediately and quickly pulled out his pistol and pointed it at the head of the tigian in the chair and fired. The bang shook the room alerting the soldiers outside. An immediate silence consumed the room with the three still in shock from Zahied's rash thinking. Zahied's hand was shaking still when the jingle of the falling bullet case hit the ground and rolled away. Blood trickled down from the mask like red tears; the tigian died instantly. Zahied understood what was going on but felt himself almost have a panic attack. Now there was another death by his hand and by this forbidden weapon. Thoughts of his Caster's Pilgrimage filled his mind but he forced them away, now was not the time for regret. They still were all in danger and needed him to keep his composure.

"They were waiting for this thing to arrive with Raiden," Zahied explained as he again put the pistol away. "Quickly, destroy this chair and all the machinery. They will leave once they know they can't have Raiden!"

They started immediately, the dead tigian was removed from the chair and the wired mask helmet was pulled and ripped apart, the wires connecting it to a computer cut and the computer shot and destroyed. Soon only the image on the monitor was left of Sheeria and her brother standing before them. She waved her hand in front of the screen as if testing whether Proto-Weapon was active.

The door banged again, this time moving the barricade and again nearly smashing open the door altogether.

"What now?" Major asked.

Rezosa cocked her rifle and shot at the door. "Find another way out!"

Major scrambled through the room finding another door, yanking it open as the other door was finally crashed through and a flood of soldiers piled in.

Rezosa could only shoot one of them when they reached her. She turned the rifle around and began striking them with it as a club.

Zahied blindly shot behind him as he reached Major. He turned to see Rezosa suddenly look overwhelmed by enemies, even with all her training. "Rezosa!" he cried back but witnessed the tall dark haired beauty suddenly take a knife in her belly.

She screamed in agony and despair, punched the enemy away, ripped the knife from herself and threw it down, but she was piled onto by another three soldiers. Zahied tried to run back, was taken by Major and shoved through the door. Zahied knew to leave her, she was already dead. Together the two of them knew to escape as quickly and quietly as they could but were forced to leave their companion behind.

Rezosa lay down, bruised, cut and lying in blood. The soldiers all stood towering over her as she struggled to breathe. A tall and familiar man looked at her. He was a Master Sergeant in the military camp in Racoves. Rezosa remembered briefly speaking to him when she first met Monkey. His name was Spencer, a tall man with a buzz cut, trimmed black hair who wore his uniform neatly, unlike the rest of the crew.

"What are we going to do about Queen Angel's weapon, Sergeant?" a soldier asked while looking down at the broken machinery of Proto-Weapon.

Spencer turned to address him. "They may have broken the manual control of the weapon but not the weapon itself. It still has an A.I. function built in that will re-operate the weapon. It was built as a safety feature in case anything happened to the pilot. It's dangerous though, all they've done is exacerbated the situation for the target. Inform Queen Angel though, the ground fleet will have to be called in. The target will have to wait."

"What are we going to do with her, Master Sargent?" another asked, referring to Rezosa bleeding on the floor.

"I know this woman, she escaped from the camp in Racoves. She's a strong fighter..." He knelt down over her. She wanted to spit but hadn't the strength to. Her lungs hurt when she breathed, the wounds in her body were becoming too much to bear. Her eyes began to feel weighted. Her vision blurred and her breathing feint, finally her hearing faded. All she could hear was, "Take her...I want her for the Angel Project..."

Her breath stopped, her last thought was not the divide, nor the mission that she failed; instead she saw the tears of the broken heart she condemned an innocent aeomon to. Monkey would cry, he would hurt himself and tear his heart apart, and it would be her fault. The broken heart of the innocent aeomon whom she owed her life to would be her sin for all eternity. With her dying breath she silently pictured his face, the final tears he shed for her and wished she could apologise and end poor Monkey's torment.

Rezosa died.

21

The year was 45 ALD: The place, a green hill on the outskirts of Decrenia in Septura. A great Cedar tree sat on the top of the hill, its thousands of needle like leaves were a shade red as autumn overcast the bright green scenery and decorated the floor with its leaves. The sky was a burning orange with long clouds spreading out across the distance. The fields were infinite around it.

Lucinda was a young and beautiful lady. Her hair, of golden blonde, reached down her back like golden silk. She decorated her hair with a circlet of daisies she picked from the floor around her. Her dress was red and shades of pink with white flowers all over. She lay, relaxed in fatigue, looking up at her fiancé, Axel, who stood up to put his helmet over his head. They had just finished making love in their favourite place, under their Cedar tree, with no one around for miles. This was their spot, this tree was the symbol of their love. Axel was soon to be leaving to add his help to his country. It was rumoured that Feydon was marching on them, something to do with Osiris, but he didn't ask too much. She hated that he would leave soon to fight but Axel was as stubborn as he was loyal and honourable. He looked to be struggling with the metal helmet that covered his eyes. She stood up and went to him to help.

Her eyes were dark and deep, the way he liked them, the dark hazel in her eyes were so dark sometimes he didn't know where her iris ended and her pupil began. She reached up and helped him with this helmet until it covered his face perfectly apart from an opening for his mouth.

"Just promise me you will come back, Axel." Her voice was soft and sweet, to match her slim figure, gentle, delicate hands and loving nature.

Axel straightened his back to address his uniform. This would be the last time he would see her until the fighting was done. He had already said goodbye to his family, only his love was left to leave for the girl in his life. This wasn't permanent, however. "I promise, Lucy. I'm sorry again for putting you through this but–"

"Shh…." She held a small finger to his lips and kissed them. She had known this day would come and had already come to terms with his absence.

"Do you know how long?" she asked.

"I don't know, Lucy. It could be anything from a few months to a year…maybe more. Just promise me you will wait for me."

She smiled sweetly and stepped forward. "Okay, but in return I want you to promise me you will keep your helmet on…all the time, I don't want your pretty face being messed up."

"And then what happened?" Rod asked.

Axel grinned and reminisced. "She kissed me one more time, as well as some other oral activities that you gentlemen have no right knowing."

The men around Axel laughed. They had been stationed in a small fortress of wood and rock surrounded by forests and distant cliffs for the last four months. The only way from Feydon towards Osiris was through them. Their mission was to stop Feydon from passing their perimeter. Axel always did tell the best stories; it was well known by the band of brothers that he was the best story teller as well as boasting of his beautiful wife-to-be back at home. Their platoon was of forty but together their squad was of five:

there was Axel, the faceless boast; Rod, a ginger mammoth of a man; Jim, the youngest and smallest of the group; Crain, a tall and greasy sell-sword whose best pastime was to sharpen his knives; and finally Miles.

"Why is it that your stories always end with her lips around your pecker?" Miles asked cheekily, looking toward the other soldier.

"Why don't you try saying that to my face?" Axel countered.

"Well, take off your mask then and I will, pretty boy."

"Oh no, I'm not going to fall for that, Miles. My Lucy said–"

"My Lucy. My Lucy," Miles mimicked mockingly. "It's all I ever hear from your mouth."

"Well, at least I have someone waiting for me when I get back."

"Yeah, come on, Miles. Tell us. Why are you here?" Jim asked. Jim was another soldier who, like Axel and many others, refused to remove his helmet. He wore it all the time and tightly like a dignified soldier.

"Me?" Miles asked and turned from where he stood and stared out into the forests around him and drew his sword. "I want to kill people."

"Ha!" Axel laughed. "You're like a common faceless murderer, Miles."

"Is that the only reason?" Crain asked now while he slid his knife down his whetstone.

Miles stopped now for a brief moment. "I have my reasons."

A shout came from the gates of the fortress, the large wooden gates opened and a militarised truck drove in with new recruits. They and the rest of the platoon were all called to attention. They all lined up immediately in a drill they knew all too well to wait for their platoon commander to address them all and introduce their new brothers, here to help protect their fortress.

Lots of new faces appeared before the platoon adding another twenty to their numbers but the very last was a furry giant who took everyone's attention.

"What on Sphere is that?" Rod asked. He had never seen such a beast before.

"It's a leo, dumbass," Axel whispered back so only Rod heard.

The leo was large and with dark fur, a red mane and red eyes. He walked forward and thanked the platoon leader before addressing them.

"Hello, soldiers. For those who don't know, I am a leo and have opted to lend my strength to this company on behalf of the people of Osiris. My name is Valadad and I wish only to fight beside you against Feydon."

There was a silence. Any other soldier might have been mocked but the size of this beast was something no man could mock. He would surely be a great help in their defence.

Valadad continued, "I may be here to help but I have made no pledges nor oaths and so am technically not a part of this army. The platoon commander said he would send me to a squad he saw fit but I have requested that you all be asked first. Is there anyone here who would accept the help of a leo?"

There was another silence. At first people didn't know what to think but finally Miles stepped forward.

Miles opened his eyes from a dream of a memory. The world was dark now and he sighed as he remembered all the faces he had fought with in the Battle of Osiris. He remembered the slaughter that they had then been only a couple days from. A siege that took many lives but luckily none of the lives of his squad. They all died later when the battle began: Rod, Jim, Crain, Valadad the Leo and even the faceless boast Axel. He was the only one who remained. His scars were more carved in his memories than on his skin. He sat up from his bed and heard a groaning next to him as the woman he slept beside began to wake too.

She reached up and rubbed his head, smiled and reached up to kiss him. As she pulled his head down the other girl beside him also woke and reached too for the back of his head and suggested pulling him back down to snuggle with the two girls.

He, however, sighed and got out of bed.

"The money's on the side," he told the two prostitutes and walked towards the bathroom. "I'm getting in the shower, you two better be gone before I get out."

The bathroom was old, dark and murky with water stains and grunge staining the dark, cracked tiles. The shower was filthy and the hot water didn't work too well. The soldier stood in the shower with his head bowed as he felt the warm water's pathetic attempt to try to shower down but which instead drizzled down over his head. His master had left him here for days now and so he had taken it upon himself to find some local prostitutes and entertain himself. He did, however, miss his Angel. He had been with many women in his past; a tall and good looking traveller such as himself found no difficulty in seducing women; he had even seduced Acarlie back at the start of her journey but he admitted to himself that Queen Angel was beginning to get under his skin, even if it was only a little. He didn't know how to feel about this emotion he was feeling. He wanted her there in the shower with him and felt alone when he realised he was miles and miles away from her, but he thought maybe this was just because he was accepting his orders – Lord Zane did order him to sleep with his wife and even love her – but he didn't know for sure. He always knew Acarlie was a pretty girl, but she was a little too skinny for him, her features too plain and small. Angel, however, was beautiful. He finally snorted and smiled at himself when he realised how he was feeling and continued washing himself.

He walked back into the small hotel room in the darkness. The two prostitutes had gone, had taken the money and left quietly, as he had ordered.

He walked to the window of the dark city; a distant woman screamed and a bottle smashed, the scream stopped suddenly. People walked aimlessly below him as he peered out of the window and the city's lights decorated the scene and stretched out far and wide. Dank and dark as this hotel was, it was actually one of the nicer hotels in True Hiro.

Another high pitched female wail rang from the streets followed by a primal scream and the sound of charging men. He was beginning to tire of the sounds of the riots. They had been going on for days now, it was now beginning to become a war. He dressed, equipped himself with Razor and headed to the door.

Edwin Townsend was standing beside his friend Jacob in the cold, wet streets in the centre of the riots and watched as the men of True Hiro charged down the streets towards another line of police officers, all standing strong with glowing blue electric shields and metal truncheons. The thugs and thieves carried whatever they could, threw Molotov bombs, bricks and stones and slashed with knives and broom handles. The dark streets now came alive in a blaze of fire and rang with the clashing sound of metal and screams of punctured men. In the first night there was terror within families, people expected pillaging and raping, but there was none. No pedestrian was killed, no civilian was mugged nor raped. It was hard to believe that the rioters were coordinated. The riots were not about selfish desires but quickly became about the city itself. The people didn't like the thought that the world could very well end and they would all die hidden underground by the 'perfect city' above them. They wanted more than that and so they found a leader to lead them to take the city for themselves so they could die with dignity or live free from the darkness. That man was Edwin Townsend.

"Do you think the police forces will pull back yet?" Jacob asked his friend as they watched the charging army now crash against the wall of officers in a terrifying scene of violence. Jacob was still bouncing his lucky black ball and catching it.

"Soon they will have no choice. King Kerry will have to send his army down soon. Even some of the police forces are beginning to change sides and are siding with the rebellion, and more and more civilians are joining our cause. Soon we will be an army ourselves and take this city for our own. Only then will we be given our freedom and challenge King Kerry to give us our precious sun back."

The rioters fought with passion and ferocity, while the police fought with honour and strength; however, soon the police had to fall back again leaving their wounded to be taken by the rioters and brought back to their leader.

"More captured!" one of the slum folk shouted and the wounded officers were thrown at Edwin's feet into small puddles on the stone and concrete.

The men were bloodied and bruised, weak from fighting and could only lie before him trying to pick themselves up, only to have their ribs kicked by the rioters.

"That's enough!" Edwin barked to stop his men and stood forward to see the faces of the officers and noticed how pale their skin was.

"You're all from down here. Not one of you is from Hiro above us." He knelt down and took off the helmet of the man closest to him and lifted his head to look into his eyes. "Don't you see we are fighting for your freedom too? Do you not want to see the sun? To raise your family in a place where we can grow our own vegetation and live with the rest of the world the way we were born to?"

He waited for an answer from the scared and wounded officer. "I…I am only here because I am ordered to be. I have a wife and kids…"

"And you are only trying to provide for them, correct?"

"…Yes."

"Then fight with us," he suggested. "All we are doing here is fighting for freedom, so we may live a life without the True Hiro Sickness, without oppression by the rich people who have stolen our sun away from us and cast us to live our entire lives in the darkness and damned, to be swept under the carpet, forgotten by life itself."

Edwin blinked as the face of the old woman he loved dearly appeared in his mind. He closed his eyes and let himself remember her smile and advice before the memory turned bitter and he remembered what her fate was. "No one should be made to live their entire lives here. Do you even know what a flower is?"

The officer now blinked and stared blankly. "Of course I do."

"Have you ever seen one, in real life I mean? Or the ocean, do you know the sound of the tide when the ocean meets the shores of land?"

This time the officer's eyes twitched. Edwin knew he was right.

"Fight with us, and I will give you the ocean. The sound of seagulls, the smells of spring as trees and flowers bloom. I will give this whole city its dreams back, a life to live, not just to survive."

"Jack, no!" one of the wounded officers called from behind and was silenced quickly by a boot in his ribs again.

"No sir," he called back to him, "this man is right. We have been given a bad deal all our lives here in True Hiro. It is a hard city, maybe even the hardest city on Sphere. I…I will fight with them. He's right…" the man shook his head as though realising that Edwin spoke the same words that had once echoed within his mind years ago when he was young and the world seemed so unfair. "Please sir, forgive me. I want only what's best for my family."

"No!" called his superior again. "What about your honour? Your oaths you made to our king? King Kerry will bring his army down here and tear this rebellion into pieces."

"We both know that's not true, sir. King Kerry is too busy right now fighting off the tigians to send his men down here. Don't you understand that we're the only ones left?"

This was news to Edwin. "What did you say? Why is King Kerry fighting off tigians?"

"Didn't you know? A new divide has started. Prime Minister Cecil Vurbute has declared a divide against the humans. King Kerry has been stripped from his command and now a tigian called Zaro Ashmere has been named king."

Jacob, behind him, laughed and clapped loudly. "Ha! There isn't even a king upstairs to fight against any more. You know what that means, Ed? You've won. Tigians won't give a shit about us leaving. You could even strike a deal with them and bring down King Kerry in exchange for a life up top."

The rioters now even began to whisper and murmur when they heard the news. King Kerry right now was in a siege in his palace and would not care about the rebellion. This was what they had all been waiting for.

Edwin stood up and faced the rioters. "No Jacob. If I leave then everyone here leaves with us. This isn't about me, this is about True Hiro."

When the rioters heard they lifted their arms and cheered. They cheered his name over and over until someone called out, "To the Slum King!"

"The Slum King!" another followed.

"The Slum King!" echoed through the ranks over and over again.

Even the beaten and wounded officer climbed to kneel on one knee, bow his head and say it before Edwin, who only stood dumbstruck.

"This will never last!" called the officer from behind, still on his knees.

"You will bow to your new king!" shouted one of the rioters and kicked him down to the floor again but the officer pushed himself back up.

"There is only one king! He is in danger now and we should be all up there defending him! Instead you all play this stupid game calling yourselves kings! A divide has begun! That means we're all in danger from the tigians with power! If they wanted they could blow up the supports holding up the city and we would all die!"

He was finally silenced with a punch to his jaw forceful enough to break it. His head hit the ground and broke his teeth. He spat blood down onto the floor.

Edwin held up a hand to stop the beating. "Please sir, you are a strong and honourable man, Sphere knows that. But your honour is only doing you wrong. Fight with me, we are both from this city, I am more your brother than King Kerry ever was."

"I will never call you my king!" he spat back and tried to hold his dignity.

Edwin sighed and thought for a moment and asked the

rest of the prisoners, "Are there any more who refuse to fight with me?"

One by one the men answered, seventeen in all, and six sided with their superior officer and stood their ground.

Edwin nodded mournfully. "Okay then. This is the choice you all made, I salute you all for your honour."

He looked to one of the leaders of his new army and paused before saying, "…Execute them."

The men didn't even scream when taken away but Edwin still closed his eyes and faced away so as not to see the faces of the men he had just sentenced to death.

How did this change so much so quickly? Only a few weeks ago I was mopping floors and now they call me king? I don't know what's going on. I wish Gran was here…I miss her.

"You okay?" Jacob asked, waking Edwin from his thoughts. "You look troubled. Come on pal, you have just been named king, Sphere's divide, Ed, you should be happy."

Edwin wanted to answer but couldn't. Jacob just couldn't understand what was actually going on here. From nothing Edwin had suddenly been given the power over a man's life and chose to destroy it for the safety of so many more. He wasn't used to this.

"Hey, what's that?" Jacob asked again and pointed to the dark sky above them.

Edwin looked up into the black abyss above them, past the giant stone pillars, and saw the large circular elevator that was the only means of travel from one city to another begin to depart from the black ceiling above and make its way down to the floor.

"More of the King's reinforcements?" Jacob asked.

"Either that or the King is retreating, why would anybody want to come down here, especially in a time like this?" Edwin said. "We should send men over there in case anything happens."

The air was still, stale and stagnant, the air he remembered. The deathly silence was broken as a rumbling from a train high above shook the hallways of his old apartment. Mute walked broken, his heart heavy, his mind cloudy. His smile brought about by remembering Umbra was wiped clean from his face a day later once he heard of Rezosa's death. He was silently sitting in the shadows of the ship when he overheard the crew chatting. Once he realised what had happened he hid once again to endure the agonising defeat of his broken heart. Umbra disappeared for the rest of the journey and so he took it upon himself to disappear once the ship landed. He slipped away from the Scarlet Arise and decided to run back home where he belonged. It murdered his soul to think that the last time he saw the woman he adored, she had expressed her hatred for him before he had had a chance to redeem himself in her eyes. Now she was dead and her hatred would follow him to his grave. The sharp and long knife of guilt and sorrow stabbed through his heart and left splinters to fester and infect his already broken self-love and poison his mind once more with dreams of the impossible. All he wanted to do now was find his old apartment and sleep; sleep would bring relief and hope of a new day. This was his only sensible choice of action, the only other way he thought to end all this was by an unspeakable absolution he forbade himself to choose. The block of flats was how he remembered them, brown but water stained, the ceiling stained to a urine yellow from smokers, brown carpets with clutter and rubbish swept to the side rather than cleaned. He had no idea what would become of the rest of the team but now he decided he didn't care. He wasn't like them. He wasn't like anyone. He was alone. His contribution only brought hassle and inconvenience to them. He would be more useful staying away, and so he slipped back into the shadows of the dark city to disappear back to the brooding darkness where he could hurt no one, where he belonged.

He stumbled as he walked; his mind tortured him with the repeating sound of her final words and the look of her beautiful, hating eyes towards him. He fell against the wall, his eyes burning, his chest convulsing, his heart stretching and his tears flowing down his reddened cheeks. He wondered how long this would last for; grief was known by some to last for years, five stages he knew he would pass through; denial, anger, bargain, depression and acceptance. He knew not where he stood now in this upcoming torment but he knew he would miss her, which either meant he had already missed the first stage of grief or that he wasn't grieving at all; he didn't know.

He stumbled down the hallway he had been in for what felt like all his life to find the same old door to his old apartment. He didn't have the key any more and wondered what might have happened to it, but found the door was unlocked and allowed him to push it open. A waft of warm stink filled his nose. The room had been lived in but stank of chemicals, sweat and urine. A whispering came from within and he silently slid back into his home and closed the door. At first he stood breathing deeply, closing his eyes and listening to the voices on the other side of his door leading into his lounge. Anger and fear filled him. Someone was here in his home. He drew Fireshaver still with flashes of Rezosa in his mind clouding his judgement. He became scared, not knowing what he was now capable of. A single tear rolled down his cheek and dropped from his chin. He gripped tightly onto Fireshaver and kicked the door before him. The door slammed open and he heard voices shriek. Sitting in his home, on his floor and on his old, comfy sofa were seven homeless humans. Five males and two females, each skinny and clearly drug addicts.

One of the females was asleep on the sofa with pale, skinny white legs spread open from a recent drug induced fornication and the other was lying drowsily against a far wall. The five males were sitting on his floor now gaping in fear and shielding their eyes from the aeomon. In the centre of them were spilled ashtrays and beer bottles lying around. It looked like they had all lived here for months, since Mute had been forced to leave, and had taken full advantage of the empty shelter he had left.

"Wha…who are you?" one stammered in fear. His arm still had a needle hanging from his elbow that he quickly pulled out and threw down on the floor but could not get to his feet; another jumped to his feet and stood with his arms out.

"Hey, look now friend. We…we mean you no harm, okay? Whatever you want just take it and go." His voice woke the others up, who all staggered in fear of the metallic red katana the silent stranger was holding.

The man looked terrified and wouldn't take his eyes off Mute's sharp weapon gleaming in the pale light. Mute didn't move but stood there inert, his mind racing so fast that he couldn't move, everything was happening too fast for him to grasp the situation. These intruders were in his home, taking drugs and destroying everything he had left in his life. Rezosa still screamed in the back of his mind, "*Stay away from me!*" and his self-inflicted wounds began to burn brightly. His grip on Fireshaver's hilt now began to burn his fingers and soon the blade began to burn blue. At the sight of this the first man finally jumped to his feet in shock and yelped in fright.

The female on the sofa began to wake now. Her hair was as pale as her skin and theirs. She looked gaunt and starving but with dark black bags under her eyes. As soon as she saw what was happening she sat upright on his sofa and let out a scream in terror, waking the other female, who lent her voice to the chorus.

The scream rang in his mind, he wanted to scream and everything flashed. He felt himself jolt forward and soon the screaming sound began singing and repeating like a high pitched droning sound in his mind. He felt lost but his heart drummed in his chest with fear, adrenaline and excitement but everything was dark for him. Only the now distant screaming rang louder until he came back to his senses and found himself looking straight into the eyes of one of the humans. The man struggled to breathe and spat out blood. Mute looked down and saw Fireshaver had found its way through his chest and pierced him against the wall. The screaming now filled the room and rang in his ears like a horn he couldn't turn off. He felt two hands grab his shoulders and yank him back into the blackness. Everything became silent. Mute stumbled, Fireshaver was gone, his flat was gone, the seven humans were gone, and nothing but a black, cold void consumed him. He felt emotion driving him, blood pulsed through his veins and he felt his muscles tighten until he felt cramped. He couldn't open his eyes, they were sealed tight. He felt his body dance uncontrollably, his voice felt hoarse and strained, like he had been shouting for hours. He felt like he had suddenly become nothing but emotion itself; alarm, anger, rage, envy, frustration; guilt, sorrow, grief, love, hate. Everything blended in his mind in a flash of yellow and red fire. The screaming still rang loud until it suddenly stopped and everything fell abruptly silent. His heart still raced and he felt he couldn't breathe. His chest hurt like his heart had exploded within. He felt himself slow down and soon his eyes opened to see a massacre in his apartment. Blood smeared and sprayed all across his walls, his hands were soaked and dripping a sticky red.

The red steel of Fireshaver seemed to drink the blood and had now burned down but was dripping as much as his hands. The room was silent, the seven humans were spread across the room, limbs scattered and torsos hacked and chopped and leaking black blood onto the dark carpet. His hands began convulsing when he realised what had happened and he dropped Fireshaver to the floor and he dropped to his knees. He stared at his shaking hands. They were so red. What had he become? Murder was an understatement of what he had done to these people; they were barely recognisable. Now he felt his heartbreak and frustration finally soothed by pouring murder over it. With him sitting in the middle of a crime like this he knew then all his previous problems were inadequate. But what would happen to him, he wondered, the law was right now all facing a rebel army, the king was fighting against a divide. This crime would go unresolved. He stood up and slowly paced over the corpses and to his bathroom and began undressing to wash himself. Even as he washed he felt he couldn't turn his mind off, his head felt empty apart from a giant question mark floating around. What was he? Why was this happening? What will he do? When he dried, he dressed again in new clothes and re-entered the red room. He felt loss of cause now. Rezosa was dead and he was a murderer; Val and Acarlie would be better off without him. The city was warring in both halves and he was stuck in the middle. He was no use to anyone any more and he felt an urge to walk up to the top of the flats and take the quick route down. He sat down with wide eyes in deep thought. He was a monster, a murderer; the only thing he was good for was killing. Fireshaver still sat silently on the ground before him; this was his only friend now; his only companion. No other knew his pain and with that train of thought did his answer finally come; killing was all he was good for. The city was now at war, criminals roamed the streets, fought against police who had turned from the law and decided on their own punishments, like chopping off a poor aeomon's tail instead of arresting him. This city, his home was evil, and now its most dark and forgotten resident had returned in the shape of a monster. Everything now became clear in the lost and clouded mind of the poor aeomon who bent down and picked up his Fireshaver, his only remaining friend and his tool for atonement. He searched in his cupboard for an old, long, dark overcoat he used to wear and threw it around his shoulders and stowed Fireshaver under his arms to conceal it. He marched out of his home, never to return, and climbed out of the flats like he used to. He climbed out of a window that overlooked a lower platform he had to jump down to. Once down and back outside he walked across and to a drain pipe he always used to climb. He liked climbing, he had always felt like climbing when he felt nervous or lonely when he was younger, he yearned to climb sometimes. He felt like every time he climbed, he climbed away from his problems, reaching the top and looking down on the world below him, everyone getting on with their lives and leaving him up there. There was comfort he found in being alone high up. Like his problems couldn't reach him if he climbed high enough. When he reached the top of another building he walked to the edge and looked down below at the city's lights and let the wind blow against him, blowing the bottom of his long overcoat. Fires burned and screams and yells of the riots were still ringing strong. His city of sin, his home, now looked infected to him and the city's cure was the burning steel he now held tightly in his grasp once more. He was already dead and so he felt he had nothing to lose. His love was gone now, and so was his home and everything he owned and finally his sanity. He vowed to punish life itself that had taken everything from him; he finally accepted what he was: a monster.

22

Val yawned as the floor of the city of Hiro became the giant lid of the underground city True Hiro. He had recently lost hours of sleep after taking the unconscious Acarlie back to her quarters on the Scarlet Arise. He still had no idea what had happened to Acarlie and Keppal and once she woke Acarlie could explain nothing when Kaza and Midia asked her what had gone on. All Acarlie could tell was the events she remembered: Keppal led her downstairs to a quiet part of the ship and to a room, then everything went blank in her mind and she woke a day later in her bed. She was, however, concerned for Keppal and asked the captain what had happened. Kaza told her Keppal had been taken to the infirmary on the sub levels of the ship and since had not woken from his injuries. Acarlie did not know really what had happened with the mute and Umbra, who had stayed silent for the rest of the flight and took upon herself the blame for Keppal's injuries. Val had stayed by her bedside while she recovered and hadn't said a word that might have upset her more. Two days later and they arrived in Hiro. The news of the new divide had spread across the world by now and so the crew had to land in the city's docks with caution and care now that tigians were in control of the upper city. Since the elementalists were of a separate species Acarlie was given passage so the crew were allowed to explore, the only rule being that King Kerry's palace was now out of bounds since it was currently under siege still. When Acarlie explained that they only were visiting True Hiro underneath, the tigian security guard only laughed and wished her luck, showing them to the elevator.

Val had been on this elevator once before back when he first arrived in Hiro and stepped on board the large circular disk with Acarlie, Zoudiva and Mitis. Kaza remained back in Hiro to refuel the ship and so his men could rest.

Val stood on the end of the elevator and looked down on to the distant, cold and dark streets of True Hiro. Half a mile down, it looked to fall for forever. Small pinpricks of lights glowed up, as if he were looking at the stars but looking in the wrong direction. Soon he felt the chill of the draft and, above him, Hiro's floor became distant and sound from neither cities reached their ears and condemned them all on the elevator to a void of darkened silence. He still worried for Acarlie and now mourned the recent death of Rezosa. Dude had gone missing again and now he thought he understood it a bit more. With Dude missing, Mitis now began to show signs of fatigue and wariness due to stress. When he tried to ask her about it she remained silent. He stood almost swaying in his fatigue and yawned again and felt the heaviness of his eyes, his vision blurred slightly and he wiped them and gripped tightly onto the railing.

Acarlie stepped up behind him; she had said nothing all day or the day before but now chose to end her silence towards him with small talk.

"I've never been to True Hiro…"

She spoke softly, he felt a small pulse in his heart and breathed a deep breath of sorrow. He felt a little relieved that she was at least communicating with him and these were the first words to leave her mouth which didn't come with a command or quarrel. He, however, reflected on the way they spoke now. They had become distant, a simple conversation seemed a chore for her, but she was trying.

He said nothing but waited for her to step forward until

she was beside him. She waited and stared over at him seeing how tired he had begun to look.

"Are you…okay?" she asked carefully.

Val forced a small but genuine smile for her but again held his silence. He knew to be careful around her now; it now had become that he didn't know what to do or say that would make her feel better.

She finally looked down over the edge of the elevator. "I was always told by my elder, when I was young, about this city. The Sky-less City some people called it, or the City of Twilight. When I was a child I used to imagine what it would be like to live here. At first it seemed appealing, like the night life of a city, with so many interesting people and things constantly happening. But as I got older I began to understand what really was happening here. The drugs, the prostitution; the overlooked crime, the violence and constant sickness, and I felt sorry for anyone who lived here. But now I am entering this city at a time of war, riots and divide…" She paused, trying to think how to continue her sentence.

The tiny lights, still far away, started to slowly shape and make neon colours of the shops and streets and the flickering red and yellow of raging fires, the tips of buildings began to form out of the darkness below them.

Val finally glanced over to her. "Are you scared?"

She looked back and caught his eye and turned away to face the darkness again. "I…I don't know how I feel any more."

"Don't be scared," he reassured. "You have myself and Zoudiva here." He paused and rubbed the back of his head. "…I know I haven't been the best guide lately, but I'm not going to abandon you."

She nodded silently. "Yes, I know, Val. You just have to understand how hard it is for me right now with Sheeria

383

and Raiden being gone again. You keep on disobeying and breaking the rules, Val, but you do it because you care, that much I have to be grateful for."

Again Val fell silent, still very careful of what to say and how to put it in case she responded emotionally with a flair of anger; she might even turn into the white eyed monster again. She was delicate right now.

However, he knew this was probably the best time as any and asked, "Can I ask you something?"

She looked back at him, saying nothing but waiting for his next question.

"When…you…," he tried searching his mind for the right words before spitting out all he could find, "…black out. The parts you can remember…" He again looked down at his feet in an uncomfortable fidget while he tried asking a different way. "What do you feel? I mean, do you know anything is going to happen or…?"

She stopped him there and let him listen instead. He thought his questions would be in vain and didn't expect an answer.

"All I can remember is this deep cringing feeling that feels like my whole body suddenly shakes. It's like when you feel a chill or when someone walks over your grave. My blood feels cold all over and a sadness consumes me. I am starting to feel like this every day," she finally confessed. "It started back in Selodia when I first thought you were gone, every time I used to think about you it would hurt me physically. These small moments, these…shivers would happen multiple times a day, each one would make me feel I was dying a little more each time."

Val still said nothing and waited. She opened her mouth, still searching for the words to continue. He stood there in the cold silence watching her, a gentle but cold breeze took a few strands of her hair to blow them gently backwards. She squinted slightly when she continued as though she herself was only just realising. "But when it happens, the second before I feel this quiver in my heart, there is…an energy to it. Like a powerful energy that I feel, if unleashed, could level a building or more. When I saw you fighting Miles in Donolan I felt it then, like my whole body just exploded in a blinding white light. I felt that energy like never before but instead of it becoming a small shiver or chill followed by a moment of gloom and sadness it was instead all I could remember. I woke with you beside me, it was the same when Electra died…"

She closed her eyes and squeezed them hard together and wiped a tear away when she remembered the last image of her friend's head falling to the floor before the rest of her body.

Val looked gravely at the floor. *So it is as Raiden suggested. It is a switch on an emotional level, I guess I have to make sure she stays safe without myself being the one to make her turn.*

"If I was the cause for it in the first place then I want to make things right. Please allow me, Acarlie. I feel this is all my fault."

She shook her head. "This isn't your fault, Val. Miles attacked you in Toshiro causing you to be in the hospital. Miles again tried to stop us from leaving Donolan and Sharcole was the one who killed Electra."

But it was I who made you promise…It was I who made you break your programming. None of this would be happening if I hadn't made that promise, he thought silently. He kept those words to himself though.

With another small gesture he finally moved his fingers slightly to where hers were on the railing. Slowly and gently he touched her hand; she responded by opening hers and he reached across and held her hand, feeling her warm palm in his. She stepped closer and leaned her head against his shoulder, still angry with him but also too troubled and depressed to argue any more. Val, who just felt relieved, now rested his chin against her head and closed his eyes and remembered how relaxing it felt to close your eyes when tired. He wished he never had to open them again.

Mitis was standing on the other side of the elevator looking over the side as more of the underground and troubled city slowly appeared in the abyss below. All she could think about was the mute aeomon and how he had disappeared again. She was in the cockpit when they first heard the news. Zahied called Kaza telling of how both he and Major escaped from the Feydon ship and were trying to escape through the city where they would find refuge and safety away from the Anavrin forces. However, Rezosa was left behind. Mitis blamed herself entirely for this but remained silent about it. She was only trying to help poor Dude and now things were worse than ever. Rezosa had been killed and Dude had disappeared; she knew she had to make things right. She took it upon herself, once they landed, to join Acarlie and her two guides in coming down to True Hiro, where she might be able to find Dude again. She had learned that he lived here and thought he would maybe run home. She closed her eyes and breathed in the cold, stale air of the city below and clutched tightly onto Hevana, Rezosa's double sided, spring powered spear; she had left it behind and now Mitis, vowing she would make things right, claimed it for herself.

"Lady Mitis?" the deep, husky voice of the kingnine asked.

She looked down to see Zoudiva looking up at her. "You look troubled."

She sighed, "I'm fine, thank you, Zoudiva."

He looked at the weapon she held in her hand and

recognised it as Rezosa's, then saw the stress and mourning stare in her eyes.

"This mission is now taking its toll on every member here." He looked back and gestured with a simple nod at his master and elementalist standing with each other on the other side of the elevator.

"Even my master and elementalist are looking too tired to carry on...I worry for them."

She turned to see Acarlie standing against Val; him resting his chin on top of her head made her remember her deceased lover and how he used to comfort her like that. The thought led to a train of faces and memories of him, how she felt after Val first broke to her the news of Mecroyles's destruction and how she still grieved for him now. The thoughts then reminded her how Dude would be feeling now, guilt again stabbed deep in her chest and the responsibility of ensuring his safety now became paramount in her mind again.

"Zoudiva, I must find the mute aeomon," she confessed.

Zoudiva looked back up and remembered the quiet, troubled aeomon. "Ah yes. The one who prefers solitude, or maybe the one who is bound by it, cursed by it. I heard it was you who saved his life in Donolan."

She instantly remembered the night, the feel of the heavy rain slamming down, its constant raging showering noise was deafening, the clashing of lightning and the water instantly soaking into her bones and freezing. At the top of a building with gravity whispering in his ear Dude stood, Raiden and Mitis chased him through the streets and cornered him upon a high building. She closed her eyes and remembered his fragile defence of drawing his sword and pointing it to his friends in a moment of desperation...

"Why do you feel you need to find him?" Zoudiva asked,

breaking her thought. "Is this not his home? If I recall the story correctly as my master tells me, the aeomon was brought upon this mission only by chance of the unlucky. I remember seeing him as a burning corpse slowly dying on the North Anglish Desert. Maybe now we are back in his home city, we can at least save one life here and let him find his home again, and forget all about the burdens of our venture."

"No," Mitis said in sympathy. "This is not the burden he carries. I think I understand him. His bane is his own heart and he punishes himself for the acts of others." Hearing herself say these words brought her more guilt. "I think I am the one who brought him his misery, and because I have seen what he is capable of once his emotionally wounded self is broken more, I feel it is my responsibility to help him before he does something that no one can save him from. You are wrong about bringing him here, Zoudiva. He has no home and so bringing him back here will only torture him the more so with nostalgic visions of the person he once was. He has changed now, he is a stronger person but bringing him here will weaken him. I fear he will be tempted to fall back to his old self, like leaving a recovering alcoholic in a wine factory for a night, this city will consume rather than nourish him."

Zoudiva sat patiently listening while Mitis spoke and soon the elevator reached the floor.

"I am here to find him, Zoudiva, and I don't expect anyone to stray from the mission to help me."

Zoudiva, however, stepped off the elevator to follow his master and spoke over his shoulder to her as she followed. "I understand. However, I and my master will not leave someone as delicate as you to fend for yourself in this city at war. I will speak to him and ask to be your guardian, at least until my brother and Sheeria return."

He spoke with a dominating responsibility that

convinced Mitis there would be no arguing with him and remained silent. She didn't want to stay in this city alone any more than he wanted to leave her, but she still had to find the mute before he did something he would soon regret.

The smell of fire first greeted them as they stepped off the elevator and onto to the cold, wet, black concrete of the City of Twilight. Val remembered stepping off this elevator once before and knew the area a little. The urban concrete wilderness now grew taller than they could see and welcomed them all into damp arms and bitingly cold drafts. The streets still hummed with echoes of distant shrill voices, buses and M.V.s; distant crashes of broken bottles were followed instantly by a glowing flash of red and orange like lightning, reflecting in windows and over the shoulders of the neighbouring buildings.

It was Val who was the first to step off and was greeted by a dark man holding a metal pipe at hand with two more guards behind him.

"State your business here! By order of the Slum King!" he ordered.

Acarlie wanted to step forward and present herself in the manner she was accustomed to when entering a city but this time was held back by Val.

"I'll handle this," he quietly whispered and waited for her nod of approval before facing the guard.

"My name is Val Blank and I represent the Elementalist Acarlie of Eloma. I have heard of your war taking place and want to state that we stand on no one side or another. We are here only for a short errand that will take us to your city's elemental stadium."

The man looked unscathed by this news and questioned Val more. "The stadium is above us, Val. You have no business here, and as I recall...," he looked over Val's shoulder and saw Acarlie standing behind him, "...the Elementalist Acarlie has already fought her battle here and should be somewhere else on her pilgrimage."

"The stadium we are here to visit is the ancient one in this city. The reason for this is our business and doesn't concern you," Val stated.

"Anyone who comes down from the city above for whatever reason concerns me," the man countered and pointed his metal pipe at Val.

"In that case, take us to your Slum King. If he is truly a king than he will receive an elementalist who is visiting his city," Val finally pointed out. This at last the man could not answer.

"Fine, follow me."

Val smirked as he saw the back of the guard and led the party after him.

Acarlie seemed a little impressed and walked beside him. "Well done, Val. I didn't think you had it in you to talk us into an audience with their king; this will save time."

Val smiled. "Thanks. Maybe I'm learning a few more formalities from hanging around you. How did I sound?"

"You sounded...okay," she confessed. "But please do me a favour and let me do the talking when we meet him."

Edwin and Jacob were consorting in the lobby of an abandoned hotel with Edwin's close and loyal supporters who now called themselves '*generals*' once they established that this was not a riot any more but a war of freedom.

The fighting had since died down, the freedom fighters were celebrating another victory of winning the space of another two blocks of the city and pushing back the police forces. The men all sang drunken songs of sex and violence in the streets outside while Edwin and his generals, with no celebration whatsoever, went straight to the prints of the city and were deciding how to next win more of the city.

Edwin was leaning over a map of the city laid on a wooden table with his hands stretched on either side and glaring at the streets, the lines he had won and the lines of the enemy. They still surrounded him on all four sides and only needed a few reinforcements to overpower them; this he knew and needed another victory to gain more ground. He had six men, all standing around him, and Jacob standing against a wall at the back of the room and bouncing his lucky black ball.

"I'm telling you, Ed, if we mean to win this war we need to starve them out. We need to win the elevator, there is a food drop off point there where they send down food supplies and rations. If we win the food supply, in a matter of weeks we can starve them into submission."

"No, no, no!" said a tall and bald man named Marlock, the second general to Edwin's army, second only to Jacob. "You have no experience in this field, boy. I have seen a couple of wars in my time and know enough to know that if we take the elevator then it would only take one reinforcement drop from above to have them within our perimeter. A single strike then and we would not only be surrounded but be fighting within our own territory. I say we make south to the walls of the city, there we can at least put our backs against the wall and have a stable start to fight against."

Another man, tall, darker and younger, now spoke up. A man they called Scar as a nickname for the terrible scar upon his face where someone once took a knife to either side of his lips. "The south is too close to the police station. If they have had any reinforcements there then we should avoid that place as best we can. Let's not forget that they are all trained in combat, and these drunk fools outside are all we have and we need to rely on them to win our freedom."

The men all argued still; all the while Edwin remained silent staring at the map before him, wondering how he could possibly win under siege against an army of trained officers, when one of his guards walked in.

"Sir, these are the ones that came down on the elevator. They say they are not from Hiro, one is the elementalist who fought Logan a few months ago."

Everyone stood silent and Marlock quickly pulled the map off the table. The young and pretty elementalist walked in wearing a black cloak, decorated with red and cream lines crossing one another and a man wearing a purple cloak stepped behind her, his scarred face looking worse than Scar's. A kingnine followed him and finally a young, slim and petite blonde woman.

Edwin stood up in shock, confusion and a little star struck when the elementalist revealed herself and bowed politely to him.

"I never thought I would see the day where Acarlie would bow to me," Edwin said and bowed himself. "I remember your battle like it was yesterday."

The young elementalist smiled modestly and bowed again. "Thank you, sir. I hear you are the king down here in True Hiro. I come to offer my congratulations and to ask only your permission to walk your streets to the old elemental stadium for an errand myself and my guides are on."

This time it was Edwin's turn to modestly wave away the formal pleasantries. "Please, elementalist, call me Edwin. As much as I appreciate the support of the men and women outside who support me in our cause, I am no king, only a man fighting for what he believes in. I thank you, however, for coming here, for your own safety. The police forces currently still have the elevator under their control. It's lucky one of my men came to you before they did. I doubt very much the police would warrant an elementalist down here at this time of war. Especially since there is currently a murderer stalking the streets."

"A murderer?" Acarlie asked, shocked.

"Yes, only a few hours ago it was reported. I've only just been informed of it myself. Seven humans were massacred in a neglected flat not far from here. The people of the streets say they were slaughtered and decapitated by some guy with a sword."

Mitis now flushed hot and cut in before he could continue. "Has anyone said anything else?"

Edwin shook his head. "No, there were no witnesses. They say there were barely any of the victims left, that they had to pick what was left of them up into plastic bags. The victims, however, have been said to be local drug users, homeless folk. No one is sure of the cause or anything about the killer but know he's still out there. No doubt the police will try to stick this on me, probably call it a trick I conjured to take their eyes away from the riots. Anyway, this means that the police have called for a curfew tonight of the whole city, which of course I am not partaking in. You say you need to visit your old museum...?" He looked over to Jacob still standing at the back of the room and bouncing his ball seemingly not paying attention at all. "...Jacob, please take Elementalist Acarlie and her guides to the museum. Take them the back ways and stay away from open streets."

Jacob looked up and brushed his hand through his thick black hair to spike it up again. "Sure thing." He stepped forward and put his ball back in his pocket. "But if we're going it should be now. I don't want to miss anything."

"Miss anything?" Acarlie asked and looked over to Edwin, who now just rubbed the back of his neck and stepped away in silence and walked away. He reached

393

the door with his generals behind him, when he looked back. "Tonight is still young, elementalist, and the night is eternal in this city. I suggest you hurry on your errand and exit True Hiro before you get caught in anything. The fires will burn bright tonight…"

Jacob took them from the hotel and down dark, wet and smoky alleys. The cold air bit deep into exposed flesh, turned cheeks rosy and froze ears. They each walked in single file following the young freedom fighter as he took them down deserted roads of black concrete littered with black puddles. Moss and slime grew on the corners of the buildings around them, reaching up as tall as a person on some walls, and reminded them not to touch anything. They didn't say a word at first. Jacob walked fast like he didn't really care for the others behind them and wanted to only walk them so far that he could point out the museum and be done with it. Mitis trailed the rear in deep thought about the nameless mute. She knew he must have been the cause of these murders; more blame and guilt piled on top of her when she thought that now at least seven people had lost their lives because of her mistakes and knew not how to feel about Dude any more. She knew he was in a bad place mentally right now but he being the one murdering these poor people hurt her. It, however, made her realise she was wasting time now. How many more lives would be taken tonight? If Edwin was true to his word then more riots were only a few hours away and if Dude was the cause of these murders then he would likely strike again when the violence hits the city. She stopped walking when she reached the end of her train of thought. Only Zoudiva noticed her trailing behind and walked back.

"Something wrong, Lady Mitis?" he asked. She remained silent and lost in thought, debating when was the right time to leave the current party and continue these dark and dangerous streets alone, and didn't even notice Zoudiva standing there at first until he repeated himself. She looked down at him like she had just woken up and returned back to reality. She was about to lie when he continued, seeing her thoughts behind her eyes.

"You think the aeomon is the cause of the murders?"

She nodded.

Zoudiva looked back to his master, understanding Mitis's dilemma.

"Okay, wait here," he croaked and trotted over to Val.

"Master!" Zoudiva called from behind. They were currently walking through an abandoned basketball pitch when Val heard the call. Mitis was standing a few yards back in silence and Zoudiva was trotting to catch up with him.

"What's wrong?" Val asked.

They all stopped now, including Jacob. When Zoudiva approached he quickly said, "A minute of your time please…" He looked past his master and elementalist and over to their guide and continued, "…in private."

Jacob waved and took his ball from his pocket again and took a few steps away until he was out of earshot.

Zoudiva pitched the dilemma to both Acarlie and Val then took them back to Mitis to explain in full about her reason for coming down to the city and her concern about the silent aeomon.

"You think Dude did that?" Val asked when she mentioned the murders.

"I do, yes. I think also that if Raiden were here he would agree with me. He was the only one to see him that night in Donolan. The fear and desperation in his eyes, he nearly killed both Raiden and I."

"So what do you think is the cause?" Acarlie asked.

Mitis shied in guilt at first but continued, "Rezosa. We both knew he was infatuated with her, only she couldn't return the feelings. I tried convincing her to speak to him to clear things up but she was content on telling him straight."

The realisation hit both Acarlie and Val instantly: Rezosa was dead and Dude was now all alone with his heartbreak, probably blaming himself with no counselling to ease his torment.

"Why didn't he say anything?" Val asked, rubbing his eyes, now understanding.

"Is that a joke?" Acarlie snapped at him and turned back to Mitis. "I understand your situation, Mitis, but is this really your responsibility? If he really did commit this crime then it's beyond our help. He needs psychiatric help."

"No, Acarlie, we can't abandon him now when he needs us the most. If we leave him now then there's no telling what he could be capable of."

"She's right," Zoudiva added. "The Silent One is still a member of the group. We all know he has played an important role in this, especially when rescuing my master from the Bastard Camp."

Val nodded. "Yes. He was there for us, I can't let him down."

Acarlie, however, was the elementalist and had the final say. "Let's not forget though how his actions led to the team being split back in Donolan. I want him safe too but he's becoming a liability to our mission. I'm sorry but I can't put it off again while we look for him."

"I understand, Acarlie, I only want your leave to search for him myself," Mitis requested.

Acarlie frowned, it was a hard decision. "If you can't find him in time then I can't wait for you, Mitis."

Mitis knew this would eventually come and lowered her head. "I understand."

"Well, I'm not okay with Mitis going around on her own in this city," Val pointed out. "She doesn't know the city and with the riots going on it will be dangerous. Also, I should point out that if Dude is *not* the cause of the murders then you will be putting yourself in danger in looking for a killer."

"This is where I come in, Master," Zoudiva said, but now turned and looked to his elementalist instead of his master.

"My elementalist, since you have the final word on this matter I will ask for your leave to protect Lady Mitis and help in finding the Silent One. I would like to add that both my brother and Sheeria will be travelling here and so we will need someone here to meet them and bring them the news of the next item in case we get lost. I nominate myself."

"You are too noble sometimes, Zoudiva," Acarlie said and knelt down to stroke the top of his metal plated head and rubbed his furry cheeks before giving him a final hug.

"Okay then, look after Mitis, Zoudiva, and find Dude. If, however, you don't manage to find him by the time that Raiden and Sheeria return to Hiro then you are to abandon seeking him and return to me. That goes for you too, Mitis." She looked up and saw Mitis nod.

"It's settled, then," Zoudiva said, letting Acarlie stand back up, take Val's arm and begin to walk back to Jacob.

"Good luck finding him," Val said. "See you soon."

Zoudiva nodded. "Yes, Master."

Mitis waved and waited for the three to carry on to the museum before Zoudiva looked up at her.

"Well, this is a strange one for a kingnine. Usually a kingnine stays by his master for life. It would be uncustomary for a kingnine to walk around without a master but since this is only temporary then I am stuck on what I should refer to you as. Technically you would be my master until I am reunited with my old master."

"How about you call me what you always have?" she suggested.

"Lady Mitis? No, it doesn't sound right. Too formal."

"How about just Mitis then? Or Lady?"

Zoudiva thought for a moment. "Lady? Yes, My Lady shall suffice." He smiled up at her and brushed his bulky, furry body past her legs and took a few steps back. "So where will we start looking for the Silent One, My Lady?"

"Well, the only ones who would have more information would be the police. I was hoping to find them before more fighting starts."

23

The air was still and silent when their guide, Jacob, finally turned a corner in the silence of the Sky-less City and pointed out to them the old abandoned museum. With only a waved gesture to Acarlie's thanks Jacob said nothing but turned and disappeared back into the darkness of the city. Both Val and Acarlie remembered Kaza telling them about this ancient old elemental school now turned museum back when they were last here after the Battle of Hiro. Dude and the crew of pirates had all been here and successfully managed to prevent an explosion which had been planned by Lord Zane. While the battle raged above their heads Zane sent secret operatives to infiltrate True Hiro, plant bombs in the school and after the explosion Zane would have walked down here and collected the item while all eyes still looked upon a decoy invasion above in Hiro. A cunning plan but thwarted by a pirate and his crew, a silent aeomon and a mob of upset residents of True Hiro. A single head still rested upon a spike above the metal shutters of the entrance and stood as both a morbid trophy of the strength of the city and a warning to future trespassers.

Acarlie stopped and sighed when she saw the sign, without one of its Feydon armour helmets to disguise his face the head was slowly decaying; long greasy hair hung down and blood stuck it to the spike. Its eyes were pecked at by birds that managed to fly down from the city above.

"Why only when people gather together do things like this appear? They could at least honour the dead by burying him."

Val glanced up and ignored it. "Don't worry about this, Acarlie. We're not here to judge these people. Just to grab whatever the item is below and get out before we are caught up in the riots."

"But do you think if they knew we were here we would share the same fate as him?" she asked. A distant fire exploded and an echo of distant and violent cheers reached them. The black sky above the shoulders of the buildings behind them illuminated orange before black once again commanded silence and consumed the light under it.

"We haven't much time," Val said and turned back to the metal shutters of the museum. There was only a small lock placed to close the door. He called Staff, which instantly appeared into his palm, and he began moulding it quickly into a small crowbar, which he then used to force the lock open, lift up the metal shutters, and then he waved Acarlie in.

Once inside they passed a small, old and empty, dark reception, down a single lonely corridor passing ancient pictures of old elementalists who once trained here. Acarlie walked slowly down this corridor to look at every picture and canvass while Val looked for some lights. He eventually found that some still had working bulbs that flickered a little less than others but still only really gave off a dim light and a slight buzzing noise.

"I have never heard of these people," she confessed.

Val caught up with her and continued on straight past her.

"These are all ancient elementalists. Their stories have all probably been lost in history. Come on, I think it's through here."

He opened one final door which led to a large open room; more lights shone down revealing a giant pool of calm water. Fifty metres wide and one hundred metres long the pool sat menacingly and colossal, bringing wonder to the both of them. This was once a world class stadium and fighting ground for the best elementalists of their days but now only remained like a small lake forgotten by its people since the stadium in Hiro took its place. Stadium seats which once encircled it were now only a semi-circle and a wall had been put up on the right side with more canvasses of ancient elementalists. In the distance another distant shutter door remained which had been recently forced open but again shut by the people of the city and was now barricaded with pallets and heavy wooden objects. Val again found the lights and the room was illuminated bright yellow. The water looked murky but untouched. Parts of the floor were still bloody with smeared, stained reds. Still uncleaned it remained as another warning to them. Val remembered the story Kaza told of when they were last down here. The shutters on the other side had been forced open by the soldiers and they were confronted by Kaza and the pirates; now only their blood remained. The pool, however, was untouched.

A clear metal sign was posted at the foot of the pool warning of the dangers of its depth: *Warning: Unknown depth. Do not swim!*

Acarlie walked up to the sign and passed it, taking down the rope that encircled the pool, separating it off from the public, knelt down to the water and peered down into the deep, dark blue abyss. Only yellow orbs reflected from the lights above looked back up at her as she tried to peer down into a depth so deep that since it was created no one had ever known how far it went. The only one out of the team who could have told them stories of this pool was Dude, who once learned to swim in this lake-sized pool. If he could have spoken he would have told them the stories of how children once drowned in this pool and have never been recovered because it was simply too deep for anyone to descend to the bottom.

She reached down and touched the cold water and shivered, watching her face now distort in the ripples she created. "Do you think it's down there?" she asked Val.

Val read the sign. "I would think so. Only somebody who could manipulate water could possibly venture deep enough to find out. I don't know how you're going to do it though."

She stood up and thought for a moment, measuring the pool and deciding the best way it could be done. "I guess I could make the water under my feet solid and make a staircase down. I would have to do it on the outside walls of the pool, only once I'm too far down I won't be able to concentrate on very far behind me. I would be left in an opening of water."

"But wouldn't that cut off your oxygen? You might go too far down and find you're too far to get back."

She nodded silently, understanding but realising there were not many alternatives. "That's right. I would be left dry but in a descending bubble, oxygen won't appear the deeper I go. I can separate the water but I can't add any oxygen to it."

"Then maybe we should wait and think of an alternative, Acarlie. This sounds too dangerous," he suggested.

She replied sullenly, "We don't have time, Val. I can make sure I control my breathing but once it's gone there won't be much I can do but hope the ones who made this have prepared something for me."

This was not the answer Val had been hoping for and he stood awkward and fidgeting with worry but could think of nothing he could provide Acarlie with that could aid her.

"I guess I have to go down," she said quietly after a deadly silence.

"Do you want me to come too?" Val asked.

"No. There will not be enough oxygen for us both."

She stood up and took off her cloak and stood wearing her black leggings, dark grey cotton vest and a sky blue and white sleeveless waistcoat. She reached into her pocket and took out a small hair band and tied her black hair back leaving only her fringe to hang down to her eyebrows. "I can't concentrate with two people anyway, I am still a little weak with the Element of Water."

She gave her cloak to Val to hold and before she turned back around she leaned toward him and gently kissed his cheek. "Please don't leave me down there, Val. I don't know what's down there nor how long I will be."

"I'm not going anywhere," he reassured her as he took her cloak and folded it over his arm.

She turned back to the pool, closed her eyes and concentrated with her hands out to the water. As she did so the water began to obey her commands and began to morph into steps that went horizontally across the side of the pool as they descended. She took her first step onto the watery staircase she had formed and began walking down. When she reached the corner of the pool the steps turned and continued down vertically.

Not wanting to spoil her vital concentration Val remained silent and could only stand and watch as the first steps began to rise up again and back into the watery substance where her concentration could reach no more. As he looked down on Acarlie's back as she stepped deeper and deeper down the length of the large pool he noticed how far her concentration reached and how big the opening she made for herself. Right now she appeared to have at least forty metres of air before the steps way behind her began rising up to conceal her beneath the water. He stood in silence and did not take his eyes off her until the last step rose up and the pool was as it was before. Acarlie had now disappeared into the dark and deathly pool and it sat there silent as if it had consumed her completely. No air bubbles appeared, however, which afforded him slight relief knowing that none would be wasted, but now Acarlie really was alone, in a depth so dark, cold and with vital oxygen limited that he feared he would never see her again. Val sighed as he was now alone with only his thoughts and concerns. He could do nothing now but wait and he proceeded over to the wall to inspect the canvasses and look at the pictures.

Mute finished what he'd started. He lay down on an old bed in an abandoned room; an old friend he once knew had lived here, a child who gave him the name Dude before dying of the True Hiro Sickness when Mute was young. His room became one of Mute's favourite hangouts and hideaways of this city. People seldom came down, deep underground the city near the sewers, the place stank and was infested with rats and vermin and was forever dark save for the candles he stole but it was the safest place for him to come when he needed space and to cry. Soon after his friend's death Mute took this for his own, a fortress of solitude and a place for his broken soul to weep and despair.

The moment it was over he was glad rather than relieved, this used to be fun for him but now he only saw it as an inconvenience and doing this only dealt with these emotions and desires, if only temporarily. It also now brought him shame and self-pity knowing he was at this age now and still needing to resort to this. He closed his eyes and enjoyed the fatigue hoping he would fall asleep and forget all about who he was, to dream and cast aside the cold truths of reality, to return to the kingdom of freedom before he was condemned to wake and face the malice of truth once more. Maybe he should cut them off he thought, they only brought him pain, dissatisfaction and depression, at least then he wouldn't have to deal with the mental torment any more but he was like every other male and instantly dismissed the idea. He was mutilated enough as it was. He felt he was at war with himself whenever the temptations began, he hated the idea of every time knowing he could never fill this empty cup of desire and instead felt he would rather just get it over with. It never took long and every time he could carry on pitying and hating himself all over again like an excruciating repeating record, filling his ears with the constant drone of the unfulfilled. He stood up when he felt he could lie down no more and stood like a broken man, still feeling his body was disconnected from his mind. He wavered at first and staggered before making his way to a small shower room to clean. The water was at least warm down here and he clothed himself in his trousers, a warm black jumper and his long overcoat still feeling anger, shame and even embarrassment for himself. Before he left he stood before the bathroom sink and peered into the mirror which was only made of one large shard of an old mirror, it spiked at the top but served its purpose still. He looked into his eyes as if he were still trying to find himself, to order himself to come out of hiding from within his mind and face the consequences of being himself. He became lost in his mind and remembered an elderly woman once giving him some advice: to smile. He smiled into the mirror until he could see the whiteness of his teeth. His cheeks began to burn as they stretched and he forced his eyebrows up and widened his eyes. He felt he looked like a puppet with his teeth still clenched together, his lips began to twitch but his eyes still stood in their depressive resolve, cold and dry they became like they refused to blink when commanded, only they spoke the truth under the lie his face was portraying. His head began to feel heavy and tilted slightly to his left shoulder. As he stared into his forced smile all he could see was how fake it was, and how insane he was beginning to look. He thought he was even looking a little scary to anyone else who might look upon him now. He released his smile and, like elastic, his face sprung back to the way it was before. He didn't know where this old woman was now and wished he could see her one more time so she could maybe counsel him on what to do. He was now a murderer, lost and tormented by even himself; only Fireshaver, the sword that caught his eye in the corner of the dusty reflection, comforted him now. Like it was motivating him to push forward through this darkened tunnel of time and promising him help in his moment of need.

Time to go, it seemed to whisper in his mind, *Time to go. Time to go.*

Its voice only brought tears to his eyes. He shut them tight and sighed. Hearing his sword? Now he truly was insane. He pressed his hand tight against his face wanting to scream but controlled himself.

He turned and picked up Fireshaver and strapped the red katana under his arm and around his chest so as to hide it within his overcoat, flicked up his collar and blew out the candles in the room before leaving in the darkness once more.

Time to go...

Keppal's head pounded with a splitting headache when he woke. He found himself sitting upright in a white bed, pillows had been set up behind him giving him a relaxing sleep and he had been kept warm. A human head passed his vision and shone a small but bright light in his eyes. He briefly heard the dark, bald man say, "He's waking up, there looks to be no real damage here save his pride."

"Good," said another voice. "Report back to your duties, Roscopp. Leave us here."

He groaned, wanting to rub the mist from his eyes while he remembered the last thing that happened but found he couldn't lift either of his hands. They were both tied to his bed. When he realised, he woke up to see Captain Kaza and his quartermaster, Midia, standing before him.

"Welcome back," Kaza said with his arms crossed. The ship's medic, Roscopp, walked out of the room and left the three of them together.

"Why am I tied?" Keppal had to ask, feeling slightly annoyed but more confused as to why he was suddenly being treated like this. Kaza, however, wasn't in the mood for answering questions and instead snapped at him.

"I'll ask the questions, Keppal. What happened with you and the elementalist?" Kaza stood stern and pelted the question at him like a bullet from a gun. Keppal felt stunned, his blood froze.

"Nothing...I–"

"Don't give me that, tigian," he snapped again cutting him off. "Two days ago you were found beaten and bloody next to the unconscious body of the elementalist. Now I am going to ask you again and this time I want an answer..." He stepped forward and pressed his hand down against a wound on Keppal's ribs where Umbra had previously stabbed him, which caused him to flinch in pain, "...What happened?"

Keppal tried to thrust himself off the bed and away from Kaza's hand pressing down on an agonising wound and instead let out a yelp but still could not escape from the bed; he was tied down tight.

Kaza let go and stood over him with folded arms again, this time he remained silent and waited for an answer, glaring down at him.

"I was taking the elementalist down to the lower decks of the ship so she could find some quiet after the dramas at Chippenham, Captain," Keppal finally explained. "We were attacked by a hooded figure."

"Bullshit!" Kaza shouted and again pressed down on his wound causing him to cry out and spasm again. "Try again!"

"I'm telling to truth!" Keppal cried. Once Kaza let go again he took a few deep breaths to calm his rage and began, "Acarlie was found with bruises on her neck and throat and you were beaten to a pulp. You think I don't know what happens on my own ship? I don't know whose side you stand on but you're not going to sabotage this mission on my watch. Don't think I've forgotten about the events of Donolan either," Kaza barked at him. "You were left with the ursa and in a moment of coincidence he ends up dead when you're the only witness and now this coincidence repeats itself this time with Acarlie, only now I believe you underestimated Acarlie when attacking her. I know her enough to know she wouldn't attack you unless she had reason to. You attacked her, didn't you? You led her down to the bowels of the ship to lure her into some trap, only she fought back."

"No, of course I didn't!" Keppal cried in defence. His eyes widened in horror though when he realised Kaza was now heavily onto him, his mistake had now jeopardised his whole mission. Kaza was only speculating, however, there was still a way out of this.

"Just listen to me for a moment," he shouted and sat upright as far as his bindings would allow him. "A year ago now there was a killer in Toshiro! He was hooded with an arsenal of weapons ranging from poison arrows to knives made of leoium alloy. I killed him last year, at least I thought I did..." He panicked a little under the pressure remembering Umbra and her devastating attack on him. "...Well, I did kill him, but–"

"Get to the point!" Kaza warned again and pressed his hand down again on Keppal's wound.

"There was another!" Keppal cried out in pain. "There was another, his wife! We at the police force all thought there was only one. I killed him but I was wrong, she survived and has been following us. She struck me in surprise and put Acarlie into a sleeper hold. When Acarlie was on the floor I tried to protect her but the attacker got the best of me. She kept screaming, 'Where is the leo!' and the last thing I remember was her beating me and stabbing me. If it was Acarlie then how would I have received this wound you seem so eager to press?"

Kaza still stood adamant before him like a statue of stone with a look of impatience in his eyes, seeing straight through Keppal like clear water. It was Midia, however, who spoke up in Keppal's defence.

"That story does concur with Zoudiva's, Captain. There was some hooded stranger who had been tailing Raiden, also Acarlie would not carry a knife let alone resort to using a weapon if attacked."

"I know that, Midia," Kaza finished sharply, still staring down at Keppal.

Keppal knew he was half right, Midia saying this gave him a slight edge he felt he could use.

"Acarlie, the elementalist...is she...okay?"

He knew this would be the antidote, the innocent question that would show his concern for her. Why would the guilty man ask if the victim was okay?

Kaza replied down at him in words as cold as ice, "The elementalist suffered serious choke burns on her throat... She later died in the room beside us. Raiden and Sheeria still don't know but Val is livid. He wants revenge."

Keppal's heart sank. He felt his stomach drop, his chest felt hollowed out. Acarlie had died, his mission was a success. But this only made him feel worse; she had died by his hands but it still felt terrible, like murder all over again.

"I...I am sorry."

Kaza's eyes didn't move, he studied Keppal's reaction, staring down at him like a puzzle he was solving in his mind. Keppal noticed him squint and realised what he was doing. This situation now became like a game of chess.

"Val, where is he now?" Keppal asked. "And the hooded killer?"

"I have never seen nor heard of any personnel on my ship apart from the current crew, Keppal. Like I said before, I am the captain of this vessel and know the comings and goings of its crew. If someone was on this ship then I would have known about it. Two people had mysteriously died on your watch, Keppal. You're a detective, you tell me what this looks like."

Keppal stammered, "I...I didn't kill her, Captain. You have to believe me."

"Well, unfortunately the elementalist isn't around any more to back your claim up, Keppal. It's been hard enough as it is to keep Val away from this room to stop him from throttling you in your sleep and you still have Sheeria and Raiden to answer to when they arrive."

This now scared Keppal. "No, please..." He thought quickly how he could maybe mend this. "Where are we? We are docked, right? Maybe I can find this hooded killer and bring her to you. I found them once, I can do it again."

"You're not going anywhere, Keppal. I'm not letting you get away." Kaza finally stepped back now and walked back over to Midia, who also stood with the face of a blank sheet. A poker face they both shared. She didn't even flinch after Kaza's lie of Acarlie's death but stood resolute beside him, silent as death.

"We are stationed in Hiro. There is currently a siege taking place in the heart of the city. Divide has caused the tigians to rise against King Kerry and below in True Hiro a rebellion has caused wars and riots. If I let you go now you will only run to the tigians. This I cannot allow."

"I don't care for the divide, Captain. I just want to find this killer so I may prove my innocence. Your quartermaster has already said my story concurs with another of the crew's. Let me prove my innocence. If Acarlie is dead then my life also hangs on this, don't let two innocent lives be taken."

All the while he protested Kaza and Midia stood staring, calculating his words, every action he portrayed seem legitimate. He honestly did look remorseful for Acarlie and his fear was as honest as a dog's love.

Finally Kaza said nothing but pulled Midia away and left the room.

"What was the lie about, Captain? I thought you were trying to find out if he was lying or not?" she asked.

Kaza looked back to Keppal's room, still not convinced by his story. "I thought I would test his reaction to knowing of her death. If he really was planning to murder her then at least some relief would show in his mind knowing his deed was done."

"And what did you see?" she asked.

"He seemed...remorseful, this may be, though, all an act. He was a police officer, I'm sure he has seen the ways of lying to others."

"He looked pretty convincing to me, Captain. Even if he did attack her he seemed pretty damn horrified knowing she died."

He grumbled in thought, "But maybe that's only because he knows he's caught."

"But by doing this you have given him an opportunity to seem innocent. He's going to find out sooner or later that you lied to him. His natural reaction would be to confront you about it, confess he worried about her and you lied to him. Also, what if he *is* telling the truth? Keeping him tied up, lying to him and blaming him will only force him to act against us."

Kaza still grumbled and gritted his teeth realising she spoke true. Finally he nodded. "You're right. Go and release him. He is still, however, to remain where I can keep an eye on him. He may not leave the ship and let him know that I am still onto him."

Wendy was a young and naïve, skinny woman. Her hair was dark blonde and thick like wire, tied up in a bun behind her head. She lay down fatigued after a recent fornication and watched her lover stand up and dress himself again. This was not love, however; she often slept with this man but it was business only and she thought of him only as a means of paying her bills and delivering food to her table later that night. The room they were in was no larger than a small studio room. The walls were dark cream and stained yellow from her smoking habit. She herself picked out a cigarette from her packet and breathed in its sweet toxic scent and enjoyed the fatigue brought on after her work.

"That will be fifty currents," she said. 'Currencies' was the currency of Sphere. Each country had their own and named each one as their own but like every other country, the Racoves Currencies were later slanged and abbreviated into 'currents'. "Just leave it on the couch as you leave."

The client, however, was more selfish and violent tonight, maybe a fight he had had with his wife earlier on, she didn't know nor care, she felt a little sore but cared little so long as he paid her.

"I'm not paying you shit, whore!" he declared spitefully while pulling up his trousers and tying his laces on his shoes. "Johnny tells me you only charge him thirty. After he told me this I thought I should at least get one on the house."

She wasn't expecting this and got to her feet quickly. "Fuck you, Levi! Johnny only pays thirty because he buys me dinner. The deal is fifty. Otherwise I can't eat." She quickly grabbed her clothes and dressed quickly. It looked like tonight would be another violent and painful night and a day afterwards of tending to bruises. "I'll tell Jerry. He'll come down here and beat your ass and leave you in the gutter."

This time the drunk laughed and spat at her. "Jerry? Your fictional pimp?"

She suddenly stopped in fear of him finding out.

"Yeah, that's right. Didn't think I would find out, did ya? I've been asking around and I know you work for yourself. There is no Jerry and never has been, just a scare tactic to make chumps pay. Well, I know the truth now."

He stepped forward and slapped her across the cheek. She yelped and fell to the floor, her face stung and her eyes began to fill with tears in a moment of desperate fear knowing tonight was going to be worse than usual.

"And besides," he sneered down at her, "there's a riot going on outside or have you not heard the streets? Even if Jerry was true then he would more likely be out with the army than listening to some whore's bullshit."

He spat down at her and turned to leave her room with her sobbing in a heap on the floor. Anger, fear and desperation pulled her to her feet. She couldn't let him get away with this. She really would starve tonight if she couldn't get anything out of him. She knew the riots were on going and so knew this would be her only chance.

"No!" she screamed as he went through her door. She ran to her kitchen and grabbed the nearest heavy item she could find, which was her iron. She tied the cord around her wrist and flew through the door in a blaze of desperate and horrifying anger and pelted the iron around his shoulders. The moment she struck him her strength failed her and again she only quailed in fear seeing him only take the blow as an annoyance and stand his ground.

They now stood in the cold and dark alleys of True Hiro. The streets were lonely and her scream would have alerted anyone close by, if there were any ears to hear. Unfortunately for her the only ears that heard were his and hers, and one other's…

Levi stood and wiped the blood from the back of his neck and looked back over at the poor, desperate prostitute now staggering back in horror of his oncoming wrath.

"You bitch!" he cried and pounced for her.

She cried, closed her eyes and swung again but this time he caught her hand and swung it aside and with all his strength punched her to the floor. She began to weep in terror as the floor met her like another fist across her brow, cutting above her eyes. He reached down and grabbed a fistful of her hair. She screamed and wailed more but could stop nothing as he threw it down to the floor.

She felt her face instantly bruise. She kicked and swung her arms, desperately attempting to escape and hoping he would let go.

After another three punches the drunk stopped suddenly. She gasped and cried, closing her eyes tightly, and covered her face to protect it from harm. She heard him give out a shrill cry, she felt a shower of hot liquid fall over her. When she looked she found herself covered in blood. She looked up to see the drunk now with a blade cutting through his chest. Blood started spitting from his mouth and he was thrown to the side of the alley by a stranger in a long overcoat holding onto the bloody katana.

"Thank you!" she wept and staggered to her feet. "Thank you, thank you."

She felt so relieved she felt she couldn't breathe, reaching out for the figure standing before her like a darkened hero, a liberator of the weak and a true vigilante. She reached him and threw her arms around his shoulders. He was an aeomon, standing stern and surprised that she would thank him. Never had she felt so relieved, she still could not stop her weeping and clutched onto her hero in a fit of tears.

She felt his hand raise to her shoulder and suddenly push her back against the wall, her back slammed against it and took the wind from her. Before she could realise what was happening the sword that took her attacker's life found its way through her chest. She stopped, she was so confused as to what was happening. She was staring into the eyes of her hero but found no dreamful saviour, no man here to help her in her moment of peril, but instead his eyes were dark, almost lifeless, like he didn't even know what he was doing. There was no remorse, shame, anger nor sorrow in his vacant stare, it was as if he were not a man at all but a shadow controlling the body of an aeomon like a puppet.

She tried to speak but he silenced her more by forcing his blade further into her chest. She jerked in recoil and lifted her hand feebly to try to push him away but instead could only softly touch his face and stain his face with her bloody fingers. He never moved.

She died there against the wall at the end of his blade. The aeomon withdrew his katana and stood silent watching the whore fall to the floor beside the drunken attacker and listened to the night around him.

Two more lives spared from the peril of the city, two more rats cleansed from the dirt and grime of his home.

He listened to the rumbling sound of the distant roar of the riots and wars while the cold wind swept the souls away and left him lingering in the brooding silence.

Time to go...

24

The sound of the engines of the Soaring Grace was a smooth light humming, the room was warm and the air was conditioned. The lights were bright and windows either side showed bright blue sky. A small, black, disk-shaped oil diffuser burned and scented the room with an aroma of bluebell flowers. With all of these factors there was only one that made Sheeria sit in patient silence, fear stricken and sick from anxiety until it felt like something was pressing against her epigastrium; the steady beeping of the heart rate monitor next to Raiden's bed.

It had been a day and a night since the ship had left Chippenham. Her brother had managed to get both herself and Raiden aboard the Soaring Grace leaving the hideous monster Proto-Weapon in suspended animation. Since then Sheeria had not left Raiden's side as he slept soundly in the ship's infirmary. Again Raiden had taken a severe beating and been left in a sensitive state. He had lost blood and suffered cuts and bruises the ship's medic had managed to bandage up but since then he had not woken. There was no leo nor kingnine blood available on the ship and so the medic had had to resort to letting him rest. Sheeria reached out and took his large, golden hand in hers and sat in silence gently stroking the fur on his thumb while lost in a train of thoughts and worry. The ship was crossing international waters now and heading for Donolan. After a heated argument Sheeria had had with her president brother about taking her and Raiden to Hiro to catch up with Acarlie, with him refusing, she stormed out of the room and ever since had been by Raiden. The thought of knowing they were now heading away from

Acarlie and leaving her in a city under siege now brought Sheeria to tears. She desperately wanted to contact them somehow but the only means of communication she had was the device on Raiden's arm. She, however, did not know how to work this device and could only wait until Raiden woke up.

Raiden will convince Audie to take us to Hiro, she thought. A gleam of sunlight caught a single tear that fell from her eye and ran down her orange cheek like liquid crystal. *Please wake up, Raiden. I know now how stubborn I must be sometimes, seeing my brother like this, how all tigians must be. To think that we have declared divide against the humans and my own blood is one of the leading tigians in the movement. I want no part of this, I want no part of any of these dark days. I just want you to wake up and Acarlie back…I want…my family back…*

Again these thoughts brought a pressing pain against her chest. She had closed her eyes and bowed her head to allow the thoughts to pass over her when she felt a small buzzing coming from Raiden's arm. It was the communicator; someone was trying to contact him. The thought of Acarlie suddenly made Sheeria jump and grab Raiden's arm and fumble with the clips, trying to pull out the flexible screen before it was too late. She was careful and clipped the screen up while holding Raiden's arm steady and pressed the flashing button gently, hoping she was doing it right. Suddenly before her eyes the screen lit up and the face of Zahied appeared before her. A wave of warm relief rushed through her. "Zahied! Thank goodness!"

Only when Zahied opened his mouth she realised there was no sound on this device, he was talking but completely silent.

"I…I can't hear you, Zahied," she said while trying to gesture her hand to her ear. She tried looking on the screen and the rest of the device for a button for volume but feared turning it off or breaking it somehow.

Zahied realised what was happening and first tried pointing at Sheeria trying to guide her through what to do but it felt hopeless, Sheeria was terrible at these hi-tech human-made contraptions and since Zahied only appeared in the screen made it difficult for him to guide her. Eventually he pulled out a small device from his pocket and showed it to her silently and then pointed to Raiden. She recognised it as a small port that was attached to the device. She gently removed it, unfolded it and showed to Zahied. He then proceeded to show her the button to turn it on then put it in his ear. When she followed his instructions she put the small device to her ear and heard a small fizzing and cracking before finally; *"Hello? Sheeria, can you hear?"*

"Yes!" She finally smiled. She watched the face of Zahied light up when she replied.

"Thank Sphere, these ear pieces are the backup way of communicating through these Wrist-Communicators. Remember how it worked, Sheeria, because if anything should happen–"

She knew the lecture he was going to give her. "Never mind about that now, Zahied," she cut in. "How is everyone, please tell me you have spoken to Acarlie."

"I have, she is fine."

Sheeria sighed out loud as though a great weight had lifted from her shoulders.

"She is aboard the Scarlet Arise with Val and the others. I just spoke to Kaza and told him the news. He informed me that both you and Raiden have been separated again."

"We have. We are currently aboard the Anglish ship the Soaring Grace with my brother, Audie. He has been made the new President of Angland. We are destined for Donolan at the minute but I am trying to convince my brother to take me to Hiro."

The news seemed to unsettle Zahied slightly. When

Sheeria looked around his surroundings Zahied looked to be sitting in a war-zone; a broken wall was behind him with unwanted sunlight beaming through jagged holes of concrete onto a dusty floor with desks and tables turned over and a barricaded door to his right with wooden cabinets. She also began to notice that Zahied looked injured, his clothes looked tattered and loosely worn, his head bruised and cut and he breathed heavily like he had been running.

"*Yes, I heard about your brother's promotion, Sheeria. It is something I wanted to speak about.*"

"Zahied, are you okay?" she found herself asking.

Zahied nodded and waved with his other hand. "*Yes, Sheeria, I am fine. Listen, I have to tell you what I told Kaza. While delivering the message for Prime Minister Tigian Cecil Vurbute we were set to take the fall for his treason and the murder of Prime Minister Human Sarah Celadore. Myself, Major and Rezosa managed to escape but now have been made fugitives.*"

"Sphere's divide!" she cursed. "Is everyone okay? Does this mean that Acarlie–?"

"*Please just listen, Sheeria. I may not have much time here to explain and I think you need to know this,*" Zahied cut in quickly. Sheeria held her breath, now expecting the bad news to present itself.

"*While aboard one of the Feydon ships we intercepted an assassination attempt on Raiden. I believe you were there too. Something called Proto-Weapon.*"

Sheeria gasped and sat up instantly, her back tensed and she felt she missed her breath but remained silent and let him continue.

"*Proto-Weapon was something that was being controlled by a pilot in a special room in one of the ships. We saw in a monitor through its eyes and saw you and Raiden and managed to destroy it before it could attack you...*"

That would explain why it suddenly seemed inert. I hope this means that Valadad is now truly dead, for Raiden's sake, she thought and bit her lip, still eagerly waiting for Zahied to finish.

"…However after we destroyed the machine we were overrun with soldiers. Myself and Major managed to escape but Rezosa lost her life…"

This was the first of the bad news she was waiting for. Rezosa was a good soldier and now she became another one of the poor souls who lost their lives to this cause, like Ursa Dusty and Human Zack, the archer from Plainess. She closed her eyes to picture their faces but already they seemed shadowy and distorted; she couldn't think right now.

"We have been running all night, Sheeria. We thought we were free once we were out of the ship and back with the Magna army. Only when we tried to speak to them they chased us screaming our guilt for treason, they think we are the reason for the current divide. We have been going from building to building trying to find some sanctity but found none. The Feydon army has left the city but that has only given Magna more time to scout out their fugitives."

"This is terrible, there must be something you can do," Sheeria said. "Maybe you can find Elder Amber of the Elder Council. Surely she can vouch for your innocence."

"She possibly could but what choice do we have? If we hand ourselves in, the wrath of the army could kill us both and the truth will never be told. We are currently trying to find our way out of the city and make our way across the ocean to Hiro, if not to group up with yourself and Acarlie then I think that at least King Kerry will hear our plea."

"But Zahied, King Kerry has now no power in Racoves. He is currently under siege in his own city. Even if you make it to Hiro there is a strong possibility that you will have tigians to answer to."

She saw a look of defeat in Zahied's eyes then, a plan already blown. "*They're coming!*" shouted the voice of Major. She saw Zahied nod to Major, who ran to the barricaded door.

"*I don't have much time Sheeria. What about your brother? Can you speak to him? Maybe we can find some sanctuary in Angland.*"

"I will try, Zahied, but right now I can't even convince him to briefly fly to Hiro to let me and Raiden meet up with Acarlie. It will be tough but I will keep on it. I promise."

She heard the door slam behind Major in the corner of the small monitor's vision and Major cry out as he threw his weight behind the crudely-made barricade. Zahied exchanged a worried glance before turning back to her.

"*One more thing, Sheeria, before I go. Last night, when the last of the Feydon ships fled the city we witnessed a small scout ship land in the airport where the skyships were docked, right where the communications tower fell. I believe they were picking something up. You should be careful. If that thing is active again then I have no doubt that they will be looking for you again.*"

Sheeria's heart felt it skipped a beat and the face of the hideous monster Proto-Weapon now filled her mind with razor sharp teeth and a look of war in his dead, red eyes. It would be coming for Raiden.

"I will, Zahied, but please, run away from where you are. You must escape and find somewhere to hide until we can prove your innocence," she tried to convince him.

"*I'm afraid we have run out of time and energy to run any more, Sheeria, this was going to be our last stand before we collapsed.*" Loud banging began on the door and the items that were holding it shut started to be shunted away. Major was screaming, trying to push them back. "*If we don't make this then please let the elementalist know that I cannot be there when this is all over.*"

Sudden fear now shook Sheeria as she realised that these could be his final words. "No, please, Zahied. You're a caster, there must be something you can do to mask yourself from them!"

"*These are elders, Sheeria, there is nothing I can do.*" There was bellowing and screaming as the door was forced open and Magna forces swept in like a tide of malevolence. "*Sheeria! Get to*–" were his final words when he was struck and tumbled to the floor, the communication was broken and Sheeria was left crying into a black screen, still holding onto Raiden's wrist. Zahied was gone, Major with him, left all alone in the destroyed city fleeing the wrath of a misguided army filled with erroneous malice brought about by the deceptions of politicians and their greed. Alas for Zahied; poor gentle Zahied for whom now Sheeria could only pray to Sphere for the mercy of his captors and that he would be given a trial rather than, by a rash decision, be left hanging by his neck; that is if it hadn't already been removed from his shoulders. Sheeria embedded her face into Raiden's chest and wept, wrapping her arms around his neck and hugged onto him willing him to wake up. However, he stayed in his dreaming resolve until her eyes dried again and silence filled the room, a deathly silence surrounding her with darkness; but through this tunnel of gloom was a spark of optimism; the steady beeping of the heart rate monitor next to Raiden's bed.

An hour passed with Sheeria staying by Raiden's bedside. She had left to go to the ship's canteen and brought herself back a mug of coffee; she remained in silence sitting beside the sleeping Raiden, with both hands wrapped around her mug sipping the warm, milky coffee not daring to leave his side.

Audie, the new President of Angland, walked down the halls once he heard of his sister's stress and left his crew to continue flying to Donolan, where he would talk to his people of the country and try to iron out this mess as best he could before many lives were lost unnecessarily. He knew his history and knew what the humans were capable of and remembered the fate of the leos better than most. Right now an entire country of lives rested upon his broad, furry shoulders, his wife and children were probably worried sick and he had his newly found sister to deal with too. After the last argument in which his sister stormed out of the cockpit after he refused to take her to a city like a taxi service when he was needed more in his country's capital, he reflected. He couldn't let his dear sister down and decided to give it a couple of hours before facing her again.

His footsteps echoed on the oak flooring with the tips of his claws tapping against the laminated wood as he made his way down to the infirmary, where he knew she was. He reached the door and leaned against the frame, when he saw her there sitting in silence next to the only leo left in the world. He waited in silence at first, watching his sister now just stare at the injured leo and sip her coffee and wondered what she even felt for her own family any more.

"Sheeria," he finally said in a tone as low as a whisper.

He watched her ears twitch hearing her name and then her shoulders slump forward like a child awaiting a lecture.

"Yes, Mister President?" she said, still not taking her eyes from the leo.

Hearing her say his name like this made his heart sink. "Please, sister. Call me as you would your brother. I may be the President of Angland to the people of our home country but I will always be family to you." He took a step away from the door and stood behind her.

"As you wish, brother," she said, but still he felt she was defeated in this moment and only conforming to his wishes since he was the President. He sighed seeing his sister like this and reached out to gently rub the back of her neck.

"Sheeria, it breaks my heart so see you like this. I never asked for this divide, for this sudden responsibility of being President, but I feel I am losing my sister again so soon after finding her."

He waited for her reply but she did not speak, only sat staring at the leo beside her. Audie looked up to see the sleeping Raiden. He had heard the stories of this leo from Sheeria previously. A strong and noble creature who has journeyed with his sister and now was taking her away from him again, he needed to remind her who she was.

"Sheeria, I know you. I have known you since I could not walk or talk. I grew up knowing my sister to be gentle and fun, always putting her family before anything else in this world, with not an ounce of selfishness in her. This was what shocked me when you first left all those years ago. When you absconded you fled your family, leaving us, and now you have returned with this...false family, taking a human for a daughter and a leo for a–"

"Please do not finish that sentence," Sheeria suddenly finished, reaching out again and taking the leo's hand. "You know nothing of what I have been through this past century and especially since the start of Acarlie's pilgrimage."

Hearing her speak to him like a spoilt child made him flush with anger then, "Sheeria, you are a tigian. You are of a proud, strong and intelligent race that now controls the power of the world, and you stand as the sister of one of the leading members of this new world. This is your life, Sheeria, you have always been a creature of family but now you forget who your family really is. I am your family, Sheeria, I have lost you once and I am not going to just give up and let you go when you have only just returned. I beg you, sister, leave this pilgrimage and come back to your family. You may love these people, Sheeria, but remember what you are – tigians are not humans and do not just follow their hearts but instead rely on logic and reason."

Sheeria remained silent all the while he spoke, her eyes closed, gripping onto Raiden's hand.

"This Acarlie is not your daughter, Sheeria, nor your sister. She is only a friend and a friend will understand that you have to leave to re-join your family and become what you were meant to be."

Still she remained silent but he knew she was listening. "You can still help her, Sheeria, but not like this. Back at home you will have resources to help her along her path to become the Elemental Lord and to destroy this black hole."

"No," she finally whispered. "I will not abandon her." She paused and straightened her back. "I abandoned whom I loved once long ago, it was something that cursed me and followed me all through my life. Too many years have flown by leaving me to reflect on a wasted life because of my naïve cowardice and deafness to reason. I know now what I have done and I am sorry, brother, but I cannot make this mistake twice."

"But by leaving with these people you will be, Sheeria. You left, you returned but now you want to make this same mistake all over again. This I cannot allow you to do."

Sheeria now understanding her situation now felt like crying all over again, she felt like she was split in half and put her face in her hands and slumped forward.

"Please do not make me do this, brother. I love these people as I love you but you're forcing me to make a decision I cannot make."

He knelt down now and held her shoulders. "No, Sheeria, I am not forcing you to make a decision, because this shouldn't be a decision. This is as clear as fresh water. This leo, these people; this whole pilgrimage is not your problem, Sheeria. Your place is in the tall halls of Donolan, where I can find strong tigian suitors for you. You can find yourself a new husband and start your family again in the safety of the tigian world."

"I don't want another tigian, Audie," she almost snapped.

He remembered what happened at the airport and brought up the hooded archer. "I hear there is a hooded creature looking for the leo, a female one…"

This made Sheeria open her eyes. She remembered this Umbra Tenebris, she remembered the burning lust for finding Raiden.

"She was not a tigian," Sheeria said out loud, more to herself than to Audie, realising what this must mean.

"You see, Sheeria, if she is not a tigian then that means she could only be…"

"A leo."

Audie waited in silence; he could feel the air around him become cold. He sensed Sheeria felt it too, she understood what this meant.

"That's right. We all thought this Raiden was the last, but we were wrong. The leo species has a chance to continue through these two. Let him go, Sheeria, Sphere calls for these two. If you love this leo then you will let him go and find this Umbra and let his race have another chance. This is the logic you must see, let the leos go with the leos and the tigians with tigians."

Sheeria began to shake when he told her this, like she was finally beginning to understand. "I know you're right, brother, but still I cannot leave him here like this."

"Sheeria, might I also remind you of the dangers we are all faced with? Would this Raiden want you to continue on with this mission or would he rather you remain somewhere safe?"

This she knew the answer too easily. "He would want me safe."

"Then he will understand, and so will Acarlie," he finished and stood up, standing dominant and proud. "I don't see anything on the other side of this debate to level your decision, sister. I promise when we land that I will send Raiden back to Hiro, where he will find Acarlie, Umbra and Val. They will continue on with their pilgrimage and you will return with me where it is safe and you can start a new life before it is too late. Once their pilgrimage is over you will see them again and none of them will think any wrongly of you. You will have your family returned and a fresh tigian family to nurture in the safety of every tigian in Angland. The leo species will again flourish after Umbra finds Raiden and Acarlie will become the Elemental Lord since her pilgrimage can still continue as she still has three guides. This is the tigian logic."

She wanted to argue with him and defend her loyalty to both Acarlie and Raiden but she knew her brother was right. He would not lie to her, he was family and cared for her. Tigian logic was something harsh but fair. Apart from her own selfish desire to be beside Raiden there was no reason to stay; it really was the right option to go back home after so long, where she would be safe and could bring up children in a safe world away from the war and divide. She finally reached out for Raiden's hand one more time and understood. "I know, brother, I understand. I am being greedy and selfish. You're right, Raiden should go with this Umbra, that way the tragedy of the Last Divide will not consume the leos and render them extinct." She paused when she remembered. "I remember once telling Acarlie to leave Val behind, how it was the right thing to do and now it is my turn to listen to reason." She stood up and leaned over Raiden, kissed his brow and stroked the top of his mane. "I'm sorry, Raiden, as much as I want to stay I must go if you leos are to have a fighting chance."

She felt herself hold back a tear which she eventually squeezed from her eye and let fall to his chest. "Please understand why I have to do this. This is for the best, this is for the leos."

"Come on, Sheeria, let's get you away from here." Audie helped her stand and held gently onto her shoulder as he escorted her out of the room, before she left she took one more look at the sleeping Raiden before leaving with her brother.

"It's going to be okay," Audie whispered comfortingly. "This is the right decision, now let's get to the top deck. You have a room there, I will have Raiden watched twenty-seven hours a day, okay? I promise he will be safe."

With all his reassurances and promises of safety Sheeria still felt no better, but she at least understood her decision. Audie walked Sheeria up through the Soaring Grace until they came to one of the top levels. The blue sky now filled the large windows on one side of the hallway. The day seemed warm and loving, forgiving even to Sheeria right now, who remained silent as though she was still trying to decide whether this was the right or wrong decision, but every time she thought of Raiden she only thought of what he would say. He would want her safe, more than anybody else would. Acarlie might be different though, she still didn't know. But Sheeria promised she would tell her; Acarlie would understand, she had no doubt about that. With all these thoughts going through Sheeria's mind she totally forgot about the warning she had received previously and couldn't warn her brother until it was too late.

As they walked along the corridor the ship suddenly

jolted violently as if it had been hit with a giant rock. Their feet failed them and the two of them were thrown up against the wall.

"Sphere's divide! What is going on?" Audie cursed as he helped Sheeria to her feet.

Suddenly all the tigians aboard were rushing around the ship. As soon as they saw their president they rushed to him.

"Mister President, we are being attacked! We must get you to the emergency vessel and off this ship before we are shot from the sky!" they said and began bundling around them. Sheeria was separated from her brother at first and looked back down the hall and thought of Raiden. This was what the attack was for, Raiden was in danger. She started to walk back when a hand grabbed her wrist. She looked to see her brother had fought through the crowd of tigians to get back to her. "I wasn't lying when I said I wasn't going to lose you again, sister. I promised you safety and that's exactly what I intend to give you. Come with me."

"Brother, it's Raiden they want!" she called over the commotion. A window smashed behind them as a cannon ball was shot into the ship shooting large splinters of wood and glass through the air.

"He will be safe, Sheeria! I promise you. Please come with me!" He held tight as the other tigians began taking them to the escape ship docked at the port side bow of the ship. More attacks began shaking the ship and throwing its crew across the floor to jump back to their feet and scramble around to their stations. Sheeria caught a glimpse of the skyships in the distance; most were too far to attack but one small ship armed with cannons was firing upon it, climbing into the sky and firing down. The Soaring Grace was not yet ready for battle or even for evasive manoeuvres and needed to send its priority passenger away before it could attempt escape before the rest of the fleet came in firing distance.

"The Feydon ships are after the leo!" one of Audie's advisers called to him while they sprinted through the hallways of the ship.

"I am very aware of that!" Audie called back in his stride.

"If that is so, sir, then maybe you would entertain the idea of–"

"Of what?" Audie suddenly snapped. They came to a corner and this time he stopped and stood with his sister behind him to stare at the tigian.

"I'm suggesting that maybe we shouldn't be heading for the emergency vessel, sir, but should instead load the leo on board it. Having the leo aboard it we could send a message to Feydon that their target is no longer on our ship and that will give us time to escape ourselves."

Audie answered only by slapping the tigian across his cheek, a slap that made Sheeria look to her brother lovingly. This was the brother she remembered, strong but always with a right sense of justice as well as tigian logic.

"I will not send the last leo off in a state such as his to face the wrath of this army while we flee like cowards. That's not the tigian way!"

"We must get you off this ship then, sir. You are too valuable to all tigians to stay aboard this ship."

"I understand that. Myself and my sister will be leaving in the escape vessel. Where is the closest land to us at the moment?" he asked.

"Right now, sir, we are over international waters but soon will be closing to Racoves before we reach Angland. If you depart now your small ship will see you safely to the ground. We can out manoeuvre the ships then turn and receive you."

"But what if Feydon sees this as a decoy and decides to

not give chase?" Sheeria pointed out. "We should try to outrun them now. If we're quick we can reach Donolan before, or even Hiro if it's closer."

Hearing this made Audie's ears twitch. "No we will not head for Racoves. Set course for Donolan. Once we are close enough I want a radio signal sent to the city to ensure this ship lands safely and to send out the army to look for us."

Another shot fired into the ship, and this one felt like it cut the whole ship in half. Down from the corridor they saw what had been fired on them in a blaze of fire. A large, metal, rectangular cuboid set ablaze by its impact. Its door exploded open and immediately out stepped the armoured vision of Sheeria's worst nightmare. His figure stood a foot taller than any of the tigians there, his body covered in black and silver, scratched metal and long teeth and claws soaked in blood. Proto-Weapon stood in the corridor behind them in a blaze of fire. His old, red mane now fully ablaze like a halo of fire leaving black smoke in its trail as it approached them menacingly. Its fire mane now reached high and touched the ceiling as it passed the inferno around it filled with rubble and smoke. Valadad's old deceased body now slowly burned away leaving only the metal skeleton to protect the organs inside. His eyes also seemed to catch fire from under its helmet and leave small black snakes of smoke to trail upwards from its eyes and join the black mist around it. Proto-Weapon, with its giant stature, evil eyes, sharp teeth, claws and its burning aura of red and orange now looked the picture of rage and wrath.

It arched its head back and roared out in its digital cry of rage and malevolence that seemed to shake this ship. Sheeria fell back in fear with Audie grabbing onto her shoulders and picking her up.

"Raiden!" she screamed.

25

The world was dark around her, cold and lonely. Acarlie left the world of Sphere and walked deeper down into an abyss that had forgotten the most important things in life and existence – light, heat and sound – many years ago. Nothing was here with her but the little oxygen that followed her as she descended deeper and deeper. Space, time, air; all things that we all take for granted were now the only things in the world she wished for. Everything was so dark and silent that her slow, controlled breathing pattern became everything in the world to her. Her large bubble of oxygen was beginning to feel smaller and smaller now that carbon dioxide was beginning to fill it instead, a substance she could not breathe. But now she had long passed the point of no return. She was far too deep now to attempt to reach the surface, especially if she decided to swim. A single moment became like an hour, every breath was rationed. She kept her eyes open but in a darkness so black, her eyes were useless and in a deafness so silent her ears were pointless. This was death, a taste of a reality she would soon face, but still she descended, every step down a step further away from existence, away from Val. She kept her thoughts to a minimum, pessimistic thoughts would lead her faster to death and every sigh waste precious oxygen. She descended; faces and lives became distant to her. Objectives, feelings, light, warmth; thoughts, time and love all disappeared. Breathing became her only reality, life became her world. Death crept closely behind her with a bag of poison air to suffocate her with. He whispered the song of impending, eternal silence in her ear and promised her an easy passage. Her ears, however, were deaf to the world and her eyes were blind to his taunts and persuasions. She saw nothing; nothing, but a dim light... As her eyes flinched the world opened up again. Thoughts, personality and desires came gushing back to her after she saw this was no hallucination. Suddenly the black void spat back Acarlie into the world of the living once more, optimism and hope wrapped their arms around her. Thoughts came flooding back in an echo in her mind; these thoughts, however, were not hers but were the thoughts of instinct – *Light! Hope, chance, air; reach, walk, swim; light, reach, reach!* As quickly as they came, though, the thoughts of instinct changed. Seeing this light brought her excitement, her heart raised, she panicked and dropped her concentration, the bubble popped.

Air! The thoughts suddenly screamed in her ears as the water thumped her and consumed her instantly. She flapped and squirmed in her watery tomb while her precious oxygen now escaped her and ascended to the surface leaving her behind, *Air! Air! Air!* Instinct screamed and screamed, *Light! Reach! REACH!*

Instinct became her master and she its puppet. She turned in the water, kicked her legs and stretched out her arms to swim through the darkness, the dim light her goal; fail...and die. The light grew as she approached, every stroke felt harder than the last. Every inch she moved the water felt thicker until she felt she was swimming through jelly. Her lungs burned and screamed, begging to breathe but she dared not open her mouth. The light grew slowly until her last stroke hit the wall, the light before her eyes. A sign, a bright gel in a tube, glowed upon a small door. She reached and lifted a simple lock that opened a small compartment built in the wall, wishing, praying, panicking and on the verge of convulsing. Once the compartment opened a small item began to float out. She grabbed it regardless of what it was and felt with her fingers since her eyes were blind. The item seemed to be in three parts. The left and right parts felt like two bicycle handles, only two inches away from each other, and connecting them was what felt like a rubbery mouth guard. She had no time to decide nor think what it was, only instinct ordered her to put it in her mouth. She forced the silicone mouth piece between her lips and bit down hard, holding onto the two handles now on either side of her lips. *This is it*, she thought. *This is where I live or die.*

Breathe! Her lungs screamed so loud she felt she was going to explode. She had to, there was no denying this. Her lungs began to spasm, she arched her head back and finally caved in to her body's deepest desire. She breathed. Air came to her, sweet air, and with air came everything else, hope, life, Acarlie.

She didn't move but kicked and kicked against the water and took the time to breathe in through this strange contraption she had now fallen in love with, her saviour. Like a fish's gills it took the oxygen from the water around her and fed it to her for her to breathe. She promised in that moment she would cherish whatever this thing was and keep it forever. As she breathed out the gadget forced bubbles of carbon dioxide back out through its end. She now had time to look at the sign and read the illuminated words displayed in bright florescent yellow gel. The sign pointed to a large lever, which she pulled down, and also showed her some brief instructions of how to wear the 'rebreather', something she had already worked out. Pulling the lever down started what sounded like a distant machine behind the walls, which began to vibrate. The walls shook lightly and a few metres below her, under the compartment she had previously opened, an elevator-type door opened. She swam down to the new space, which was already filled with water, and entered it. Once again with only the glowing gels to see by, she found a small button. She pressed it, which closed the doors and trapped her inside. Still in the darkness and breathing only small amounts through this rebreather she wondered what was happening when suddenly the water fell from above her as if suddenly sucked from under her. She struck a metal grated floor and was left in a vacuum. Under the grate a metal surface slid across and closed the gap between her and the water and small lights flickered and turned on. Again she panicked as her new device was now useless. This thing could help her breathe underwater but in a surrounding vacuum it was useless and she would again suffocate. However, once the lights appeared in this elevator she noticed there was a diver's tank in the corner with a mask attached to it. She didn't need instructions to know how this would work and applied it to her face, slowly turned on the gas and again breathed air. She now sighed the sigh of relief she had been waiting for. She took deep breaths and felt her body go limp with exhaustion; she sat down on the grated, metal floor and took a moment to herself. The machine behind the wall was still droning away, and she now guessed what this was. Like the previous two elemental schools she had visited, the room holding the item below needed to be quickly cleansed before she went down there, the vacuumed room would need to be pumped with fresh air from the surface, the vents would need to be bleached in case any undiscovered forms of life managed to grow and mutate down there and contaminate the air. After a few minutes, however, the vibrating stopped and the elevator began descending. Beside the tank she found a plastic note, picked it up and read:

Acarlie: If you are reading this you found the elevator, congratulations.

How does it know my name!? she thought but continued reading.

You must understand, however, that you are not safe yet. The rebreather is a device that extracts oxygen from water, but the air you breathe is 78% nitrogen. Oxygen on its own is actually a poison. This is why this tank was left for you. Even so, the air in this tank is millions of years old to you and could potentially be poisonous too, it has been kept preserved perfectly but still could be dangerous for you. You must understand that this is the best we could do for you to survive. If you are the first here then your prize shall be waiting for you.

As the ancient elevator made its long descent Acarlie sat in silence with the mask around her face feeding her air to breathe. After a few minutes the watery darkness outside turned to complete black. She knew she was now below the water line and under the giant deep pool, but still the elevator kept on descending for what felt like miles below.

Val was sitting in boredom next to the silent pool. He had looked at the board of ancient elementalists until he felt he had memorised their faces and names, jogged up and down the length of the pool to warm up and used the time to exercise with his usual regime of push ups, sit ups and practising the katas that Raiden had taught him. But still after all this time Acarlie had not returned and now Val sat down, tired, and waited. In the silence of solitude he had time now to think and listen. The city sounded quiet but with a sense of impending energy, like a calm before a storm. He sighed and brought his knees to his chest and rested his chin on them.

I hope she's okay, he thought, not taking his eyes away from the pool, which still stared back at him mockingly, knowing it was now far too long for Val to do anything about it. But thinking about it would only make things worse. His mind wavered and he instead began to think of himself again. His identity was still a mystery to him; he knew he was the reincarnation of a deceased solider, but who? What happened to this mystery man who had died against a tree on the small island of Walton so close to a skyship crash wreckage? Why is it that Sphere chose this man to become the tool it would use for its survival? Did he have family? Parents, siblings, a wife, children? Were they out there missing him? Would they even recognise him? It was a big world out there and even if he searched for his whole life, all the while he was Val he would never know anyone but the friends he knew now and would not even know where to start looking. Eventually he realised it was pointless to think about, there was nothing he could do about it: whoever this man was, he was dead now. The pool stirred and a large bubble rose from the depths and popped when it reached the surface. Val jumped up and ran to the pool. He knew exactly what this bubble meant, something had happened to Acarlie, she had lost her concentration for some reason and now had no oxygen. He wanted to dive in hoping he would find her but his sense persuaded him not to. For one, she was still far too deep down to save, and secondly, if she was down there then maybe she really did need to concentrate and him disrupting the pool would only exacerbate her danger.

"Acarlie?" he whispered. The word left his mouth almost trembling. He stared down into the depth below not seeing anything but his own scared reflection staring back at him. His reflection looked just as concerned and as though it was about to jump up from the water into reality to try to save its own Acarlie. Val couldn't move, fear and concern froze him. *Maybe she is swimming back, in which case I need to stay here, ready to save her*, he thought and started taking off his cloak and lay it beside the pool readying himself for a cold swim.

A scream from the city rang like an alarm and something crashed down in the street close to him with a mighty *thud!* Whatever it was it shook the floor and nearly tipped Val into the pool. Another scream, "*FIRE!*" reached his ears and another projectile was thrown, this one smashing into the stadium. Val fell back in horror as the metal shutters on the other side of the pool smashed open leaving large metal shards to scatter all around as a large chunk of metal shrapnel was thrown through. It rolled into the stadium seats and destroyed them before it rested. Val dashed to the open shutters now and saw the black abyss was now lit up orange and yellow. Screams of war and the scraping clatter of clashing metal now swam through the cold air. Distant wooden catapults slung burning shrapnel soaring into the black sky. The fire, bringing with it terror and malevolence, lit the darkness around it. A line of fire followed each projectile and snaked the sky, scarring the void above like a whip wound. They each thumped the buildings around Val, crashing through walls and extinguishing lives, leaving only the crackling of fire, cackling evilly in the aftermath. Val blinked feeling the burning air now dry his eyes. Instinct ordered him to flee but his promise to Acarlie shouted louder, he couldn't leave her behind and he stepped back in silence, hidden in the ancient stadium in the centre of the Battle for True Hiro.

26

Zoudiva was dashing through the streets as fast as his four legs could carry him. The damp concrete was cold on his paws and in his kingnine vision he now felt blinded by the bright morphing heat of the fires around him. He turned back to see the cowering coloured shape of Mitis behind him but had to walk back to check. Usually he relied on his nose when speaking to people he knew but now all he could smell was smoke and burning steel.

"Hurry, My Lady!" he called back to her.

In the cold darkness around her Mitis glowed purple and blue, her face yellow, her cheeks red and nose blue. Over her shoulders and behind them were the white fires burning hot and looking brighter to the kingnine, who could see only heat. He could even see some of their footprints behind them, something she would be blind to, and finally with smoke all around them he could see far down the streets to witness the police battling the rioters.

Mitis fell to the floor and screamed with fires all around her when Zoudiva caught back up. She could hear the screams and fighting but could only see bright fires and smoke around her, fogging her vision. Zoudiva could see straight through smoke, it was his sense of smell that it blinded him to.

"I'm scared, Zoudiva!" he heard her call, covering her mouth from the smoke around them.

"We shouldn't stay here, My Lady. I can guide us through the smoke and fire but my sense of smell is numbed by all these burning scents around me. I need to get away if I am to find the chief of the police in finding the Silent One." He looked back and tried sniffing again but coughed in failure. He felt her hand reach up for him and pull herself back to her feet.

She also coughed and held her arm over her mouth.

"Okay, Zou', lead the way."

Windows still crashed and smashed around them. The battle seemed to echo from all around with cries and clangs of weapons. Distant catapults launched burning debris into the sky to crash into their targets and set the sky-less city off into an urban wildfire. With all the child screams around her Mitis was reminded of the Battle of Donolan, and the Feydon solders who chased her and would have raped and murdered her if it hadn't been for Dude. She kept a hand on Zoudiva, hoping not to lose him.

Eventually Zoudiva rounded a corner and found himself at a lonely crossroads of the city, one side was dark and black and the other side glowed orange and white. Now he could put his nose to the sky and sniff.

Mitis finally let go and gave him a moment. She walked to a public seat close by and sat down to catch her breath. Zoudiva ran to the highest, central point and put his nose to the sky. Two minutes passed while Mitis caught back her breath. "Can you smell anything?"

"Apart from the fires behind us, there is a large group of different species fleeing east of us and a smaller group to our north are heading toward us. The north group don't smell as bad so I'm guessing they are the ones we are looking for. They must be the police reinforcements."

Mitis brushed her hands through her blonde hair. "Okay, let's try them."

Zoudiva sniffed again and squinted his eyes. "There is no need, My Lady."

Mitis looked and saw the first few uniformed humans appear, marching down the streets dressed in dark blue riot gear, helmets with plastic visors and bright blue electric shields, and equipped with batons and truncheons. They marched down the roads before them and stopped when they reached the crossroads, blocking off their way down.

"Excuse me!" Mitis called when she saw them.

"Halt where you are!" one called back. They suddenly all grouped together and locked their shields and shouted over to them.

"Cease and desist, rioter! You are right now breaking curfew and are under arrest!"

"Humans!" Zoudiva roared dominantly, pouncing from behind Mitis and instantly scaring a few of the humans. "I am Kingnine Zoudiva! Sacred guide of Elementalist Acarlie of Eloma! We are not residents of True Hiro but tourists here on an errand. We ask only to speak to someone who is in charge!" He barked his words so as to not start bartering or haggling with them.

The police remained silent at first.

"We are unarmed civilians!" he barked again to the dark blue shapes before him hiding behind the glowing dark red shields.

"Please, sirs! We mean no harm and are only here for some information," Mitis tried but was suddenly silenced as a brick was thrown from behind them and cracked in two when it hit the floor.

Zoudiva quickly turned and saw from the bright white aura behind them a large group of red and yellow human shapes now also marching upon them, their hands held out and hurling abuse at the police.

Mitis froze in fear when she realised they were now in the middle of two armies facing each other.

"Civilians! Get behind us!" one of the officers called. Their wall opened up for them to let them through with two men holding their shields to one side. They both hurried through and made their way through the streets with what looked like a hundred officers all standing shoulder to shoulder awaiting their impending battle. When they found themselves on the other side Mitis asked to speak to someone in charge and was finally pointed to a decorated officer at the back, standing proud with a short moustache and a riot helmet over his head like his comrades.

"Whatever it is I don't have time for it. We're just about to war with half the city and I don't have time to give tourists directions," he said to them sarcastically.

"We only need to know if there is any information regarding the killer who slaughtered those people earlier tonight," Mitis said. The rioters behind them began shouting more as they approached the wall of officers on the crossroads.

"There have been a lot of murders tonight, madam, you'll have to be more specific," he said, again trying to hurry the conversation along. His eyes kept looking past them and at the back of his comrades' heads.

Zoudiva now took over, growling his husky voice. "A sword killed a group of homeless people earlier this night. We believe we may know who this person is and are trying to find him."

"Look around you, we will make hundreds of arrests tonight. Anybody who carries a sword will likely be our suspect. Likely it was just one of the rioter's tactics to pull our attention from the city tonight."

A scream yelled out and the rioters began hurling bricks and Molotov grenades at the police, knowing they could not charge them, their defensive stance now turning to a burning furnace of burning flesh and screams. The officer pushed them aside. "I don't have time for this. If you find your friend, you better make sure you catch him before we do or you'll likely be attending his funeral." He turned back to his men. "Men, charge!"

His cry was echoed with screams and charging feet as the officers broke from their wall and, like a wave of war, charged into the ranks of the freedom fighters. They met their battle in the crossroads with the burning city before them. Noses were broken, as were arms and legs, faces slashed, bricks thrown, feral roars of tigians instantly followed by wails of pain and grief of victims. Spines snapped, flesh tore, fires burned, war raged.

"What do we do now?" Mitis asked, as she started to tremble again.

Zoudiva looked around. "It's getting too dangerous here, My Lady. We should get back to the ship." Only, when he looked to the tops of the dark buildings he saw a quick flash of yellow and orange, a familiar scent following it as it dashed from the rooftops to the battle.

"Wait here!" he ordered and suddenly dashed ahead into the battle.

"Wait! Don't leave me here!" she called after him and chased him down the streets and to the crossroads. Before she could catch him a figure pounced down onto two fighting humans, his sword burning fire so bright she couldn't see his face before he turned and slashed it into another fighter. There he was before her, flying through the battle with his legendary weapon, cutting through flesh like soft butter. He fought for no side but his own and the police and rioters both fell from his red sword as he ran through in his blinded rage of adrenaline and confusion. Wearing a long overcoat that seemed to sway like a cape as he turned to face one enemy after another, he murdered everything around him.

"Dude!" she cried in vain over the other sounds of the battle. But when she saw his face he looked different, a fiery war seemed to glow in his eyes. He was quicker than anyone else there and his weapon far outmatched anything it faced. The brighter Fireshaver seemed to burn the easier it cut through flesh, and the more Dude seemed to scream in his wild rage, the brighter Fireshaver burned, until he looked to hold a star in his hands that blinded his opponents before decapitating them. Tears streamed from his eyes as he cut more and more down, using his aeomon agility to dash from one to another and looked to try to stop the fight himself by killing everyone there. Out of instinct she pulled Hevana out from behind her and tried dashing for him. The moment she did so she was faced by one of the police officers now seeing her as an armed rioter and going to attack her. She screamed at first and ducked his first attack but when he swung again the training Rezosa had given her kicked in and, like a reaction, she blocked his arm and twisted it, kicking his ankle and throwing him to the floor. He feel with a thud and an "Ooof!" and stayed down to tend a bleeding nose. She stood dumbstruck, she had never thought of herself as someone who could put a man to the floor as she just had but, not waiting to find out if she could kill a man, turned and ran for Dude. She found he was cornered by five rioters, who now tried over-powering him with sheer numbers. She screamed his name again and ran towards him as they began to pounce on him, holding his arms down and kicking him. She reached the first man and threw him off. When the second man let go of Dude's arm he reached out for her. Again she remembered Rezosa's training, grabbed his arm, twisted him over her hip and struck him with the blunted Hevana.

Once Dude's arm was free he threw the other man off him, picked up his sword once more and began blindly massacring the rioters around him, totally ignoring his female saviour and only concentrating on his vengeful rage. One by one they fell around him in a pool of sticky liquid claret; in his darkened mind he saw nothing but void and emptiness. His senses were all gone, as was he. Only a familiar cry of his false name seemed to echo all around him; the name brought with it memories and faces and finally ripped Dude back into reality.

"Dude!" Mitis screamed before him. She dared not step any closer to him in fear for her own life. Dude stood still, slouched forward holding the burning Fireshaver, now dripping with fresh blood, with both hands. His teeth gritted and he breathed heavily like a beast, tears still snaked down his cheeks like two tiny rivers and his face was hidden by the blood smeared all over it. His hands were shaking and stained dark red too; his dark cloak now covered in his opponents' blood, sweat and tears.

"Dude!" she called again, hoping he would finally hear her.

He stirred and looked up, blinked and looked around him confused as to where he was and why he was so out of breath.

She called his name one more time and finally he twitched and looked up. She finally saw the lonely aeomon in his eyes; he looked scared and confused. Fireshaver stopped burning and now only shone metallic red in the reflections of the fires around it. He lifted one of his hands up to look at the bloodstains and the carnage around him and began to tremble. She tried to approach him but another rioter suddenly screamed and pounced for him. In a move of instinct Dude lifted Fireshaver and blocked the wooden weapon he carried, spun around and drove his sword into his opponent's side, who, with a shriek fell, holding a wounded side.

"Stop, please!" Mitis called.

Dude stopped, hearing her voice, and looked over again and finally recognised her, and looking down at the weapon in her hands, suddenly his heart broke again. At first Mitis didn't understand but Dude backed away in fear, not taking his eyes from Hevana, Rezosa's old weapon. Tears began to build in his eyes again and gleam from the fire around them. The weapon instantly reminded him who he was, of his failures and his lost love.

He looked up at her one more time, this time in fear. He met her eyes but he didn't see Mitis standing before him.

"Um orry Weohoya!" he cried. He dropped Fireshaver and fell to his knees, pressing his hands into his eyes in despair. She stepped forward to comfort him, when she was knocked down herself. The rioters now saw her as an associate of the crazy aeomon and tried to kill her too now. She screamed and knocked her head against a wall and fell down covering her head as someone reached for her. She took a punch across her cheek and began to cry, holding her hand up begging for him to stop when she heard Dude scream again.

Dude disappeared into his darkened mind once more and let his feral emotions take over, picking up Fireshaver and slashing everything around him once more.

With Mitis cowering on the floor he completely missed her and dashed off again to his next kill. She cried and wept, holding a bruised cheek. Her weeping was muffled out by all the other war cries all around her, the sirens of more police reinforcements arriving and the chopping propellers of small helicopters in the black sky above them. Bottles smashed over heads and still more and more fires burned, consuming all and eating the oxygen around them.

"Zoudiva! Help!" she cried and forced herself to her knees. "Zoudiva!" Only she looked to see Zoudiva a few yards away now battling seven rioters. They all pounced on him and dragged him to the floor, he yelped like a beaten dog as they began to punish and beat him.

She wailed and reached out for poor Zoudiva, tears now streaming down her face, "Zoudiva!"

Her screams now alerted five more rioters, who pointed to her and began to run for her. Fear and horror chilled her blood as she now jumped to her feet. She left Hevana on the floor and Zoudiva to fate and just desperately ran away in the safest direction she saw. The five gave chase.

27

The creaking elevator descended further into the sphere. All Acarlie could do was rest and breathe through the mask connected to the air tank. In a vacuum with total darkness outside the elevator she felt like she was being transported into another dimension. If she left this small elevator she would perish and never be found again. All she could do was sit and breathe and hope there would be no further issues. *Val is somewhere up there waiting for me*, she thought. She looked to the ceiling and wondered how far she was from ground level. Hiro sat half a mile above True Hiro and she was far below True Hiro now, beyond the deepest pool ever created of which no one knew the exact depth. Now she was so far down she wondered if she was even on Sphere at all. How many miles down was she? She remembered her schooling back in Eloma and remembered a fact: Sphere was nearly four thousand miles deep before reaching the planet's core. She thanked Sphere she wasn't that far down but became concerned about the pressure down there. If there is water then what would she be facing? She kept breathing; soon the tank would run out and when it did there would be no escape for her, she could only hope the elevator would hurry up so she could grab this item and continue on.

After another five minutes the elevator stopped suddenly. The floor shook and jogged the mask from Acarlie. She quickly put it back on her face and waited for the door to open. She could still feel droning sounds of distant engines working and fans turning somewhere behind her but could hear nothing, in a vacuum everything was silent. The door creaked and opened, she closed her eyes and waited for a gush of water but instead felt the cool, relieving air touch her face, blow her hair gently and chill the blood behind her ears. She ripped the mask off her face and inhaled hope, relief and life once more.

"Fuck!" she finally said, panting. She was never one for swearing and profanities and thought the word leaving her lips sounded strange but if ever a time was needed for swearing, this was it. She heaved and panted loudly, finally filling her lungs with something other than limited air, pure oxygen and ancient air left in a tank for millennia. After a moment she finally pulled herself back on her feet and looked out. Before her seemed to be a watery tunnel. The floor was a smooth silvery metal connected to a domed long corridor of the same substance, except above her head and just where the ceiling began to dome the corridor had two shoulders either side of small fountains. Each fountain let out a tiny amount of water that ran down the metallic walls and into tiny canals either side of her feet as she passed. It gave the illusion that the walls were each made of running water stretching down with small layers of rippling liquid. She walked down the corridor and shivered as she still was damp and cold from her watery experience, her clothes hugged tightly to her skin and chafed while she walked. Her hair also was loose again and hung down in large, sticky clumps. She quickly pulled her hair back again and took off all her clothes just to wring them out while she still had a moment. After she dressed herself again she proceeded down onto what would be her next watery trail. At the end of the lonely corridor was a curtain of falling liquid, lit by a neon pink light colouring the water as it fell and concealing from her what was beyond. She had no intention of getting any wetter than she already was and held her hand out to order the falling liquid curtain to open to let her pass. She stepped past and gasped as she took in the view.

She now stood in a glowing cave filled with water features all around her. The walls way above her glowed purple and violet. She recognised it from the underground monastery in Aragorth. Water flowed all around her in many different fashions. Just like the metallic corridor there were large metal spheres with a small fountain at the top to flow water in a thin layer around them, each one lit in a different colour – aqua blues, yellows, reds, pinks and greens. A similar feature was to her side but was a glass wall with water running down it, lighting up in different colours as it fell, the specks of light flowing on the ever dynamic motion of the water like dancing diamonds of changing colours. Water fell from the curtain behind her like a small waterfall. All around her, echoing around the watery tomb, were drips from other features gently falling into small contained pools. Two giant cylindrical containers a few feet before her slightly apart were filled with water. They each looked ten feet wide and she could only guess how deep. When she stepped forward they seemed to react. A small jolt of static electricity reacted with the two cylinders causing the water in each to jump and, before Acarlie's eyes, the two cylinders became connected by the water in each. Like a watery bridge, from one brim to the other, the cylinders were now connected, allowing Acarlie to pass. She still concentrated on her first step onto the water, solidifying it under her feet and reaching the snake-like watery bridge, passing the second cylinder and stepping back onto the glowing rock of her last trial. A staircase stood before her leading up to a large crater with a sphere of bright blue water at the top. She opened the water again and this time saw a bridge had been set for her inside this sphere. She stepped inside and allowed the door she had opened to close again, which left her inside this aquatic bubble. Flowing water all around her still glowed in different bright colours. Bubbles rushed all around her and the water rippled and shook from the vibrations of the droning sounds way below it. It was beautiful for Acarlie, who just stood now and witnessed the amazing phenomenon and wondered why this elder trick had been kept so secret. Bubbles of air danced all around her in the fluorescent luminous lights the inside of the crater gave off and in the centre of the rock bridge was her prize. Only it wasn't a chest as with the other cities but instead looked to be a small fountain containing two weapons. She recognised them instantly as a pair of sai, sitting across each other, with each finger facing down into the small fountain. She stepped closer to examine them and saw that each one was tinted blue from the handle down but saw that the fingers seemed to disappear into the water, as though each sai was part of the watery pond it rested in. She reached out and took each handle, feeling how cool they were to the touch, and lifted them up. As she lifted them they seemed to take more shape and also seemed to drain the small pool they sat in, like each one was drinking the water, until she held one in each hand and the water was gone. Suddenly the large sphere of water also disappeared and fell around her into the crater until the waterline was level with the bridge she stood on. Suddenly the room became still, every water feature around her stopped; it was like the two weapons were the key to the water in the room: once they were taken out everything stopped. She looked at the weapons in her hands, each one shining metallic blue in the light around her. As she looked closer she saw each one had tiny bubbles inside it, like they were each made of glass and filled with bright blue water. At the hilt of each handle sat a small blue marble. She had no idea what it was she was holding and now felt confused.

"These can't be what I am looking for," she whispered to herself before the room stirred again. From under the crater and up through the water something emerged. The fountain before her now jerked back and allowed a casket made of stone to appear before her. She stood in silent wonder while it slowly ascended from the depth below, touched the skin of the water and rose up to face her. Before her lay a stone figure of a woman dressed in robes, her hood pulled tightly over her head concealing her face from Acarlie and across her chest she held two stone sai. In stone at her feet was written: *Here is the final resting place of Alixia Laguna. The forgotten saviour of Sphere and her two prized possessions, Aqua and Hydro. May she rest peacefully.*

Acarlie was stunned now by what she was seeing. *Who is this? What's going on?* She didn't move, not knowing what she had to do now. She hoped she didn't have to open this casket and thanked Sphere when she noticed something else was on the stone carving of this ancient warrior. Just under the carved stone weapons was a small box. Acarlie took it and opened it to reveal a small laminated piece of paper. She sighed in relief and unfolded it to see the next piece of this ancient puzzle:

163 Long W

She closed her eyes and sighed, instantly memorising the information and folded up the laminated paper and put it away in her pocket. After only a moment of her taking the small container away, the mysterious stone casket stirred again and, now having fulfilled its purpose, started slowly descending back into the bright blue watery tomb, the ancient heroine being laid back to rest and Acarlie alone. She knelt down and watched the stone figure distort in the water until she became a darkened blur once more. Acarlie took one more look at the ancient weapons in her hand before thinking out loud.

"Thank you, whoever you are. Here." She handed back down the pair of sai back into the water and watched them instantly evaporate and turn back to water. "I believe these were yours. I cannot take them for they do not belong to me."

Once the weapons were back in the water the whole room burst into life again, every feature now began flowing with coloured water once more, all except the watery sphere. Now she had the item Acarlie turned and wondered how she would be able to escape…

The city still buzzed with excitement. Val remained hidden in the old elemental stadium and stood close by the large metal shutters now smashed open and leaving a large hole in the stadium. He enjoyed the feel of cool air on his face but the noise was unsettling. Distant cries still lingered in the air, some cries were of women who sounded as though they were being raped and some children cried like they stood over deceased parents' bodies. Val could not check any of these suppositions though and he kept an eye on the pool. These people needed his help but he could not abandon Acarlie, he had made a promise. The pool lay undisturbed since the last bubble appeared and another fifteen minutes had passed. Val could not stop himself worrying. How long would she be down there? How long would he wait before it became obvious she would not be returning? Days? Months? The thought instantly depressed him. He sighed and wiped his cheek, feeling the scar tissue down his face; his hands were warm.

"I don't care," he said to himself. "I don't care how long she takes. I don't care what happens, I'm not moving." He looked back at the silent and still pool in the hope that his declaration would somehow make the pool answer him or his words would make her arrive back now. Instead the pool gleamed up at him, reflecting the lights above it, seeming to sneer at him.

"Why don't you jump in and find her?" the pool whispered in his mind. Val instantly bit his lip, turned away shaking his head and almost laughing at himself for suddenly being stupid. "That's enough of that," he whispered to himself. A quick dream of Val waiting at the pool for years and years, turning mad and talking to the pool and becoming the city's crazy, homeless bum made him smile. It also made him realise that if that is what it took, that is what he would do. When he realised that he came to the realisation of what Acarlie really meant to him. He looked back at her potential watery tomb and remembered everything he had done for her. He had risked his life jumping into an Elemental Battle for her. He had run, whilst severely injured, through a storm that destroyed a city to get back to her. He had infiltrated a camp of crazy psychopaths, rapists and horrific murderers on his own to save her. He had taken the blame for the destruction of the C.E.L. He had even gone against his own promises for her and now he was willing to risk his sanity and his life in just waiting for her. He wondered if she knew all he had done for her.

A familiar cry broke his thought. His head jerked to glance down the dark streets still glowing from distant fires and he saw someone with a familiar face running down the street with five rioters chasing her desperately.

"Mitis!" he shouted suddenly and jumped forward. She could not hear, however, she was too concentrated on desperately trying to escape the band of rioters, drunk on violence, chasing her.

"Help me!" she wailed to anybody. Only Val heard her call though.

Val's heart stopped when he realised his sudden conundrum: he couldn't leave the pool to help her. Acarlie hadn't arrived back yet.

"Help!" she wailed again.

Val reached back and touched the wall, his hands shaking and his legs trembling, wanting to dash forward; he could not take his eyes off her.

"Mitis!" he tried calling again, but failing; she still could not hear.

They suddenly caught up with her, grabbing her arms and pulling her. She shrieked and grabbed her wrist and tried to pry it back from one of the attackers, when the others arrived and instantly overpowered her to the floor.

"Please, no!" she screamed, kicking desperately.

Val still didn't move, he couldn't watch what was about to happen but looked back to the pool. It still laughed at him silently.

"What are you gonna do?" it laughed.

Val closed his fist until his knuckles cracked and turned back to Mitis now being held down by four around her.

Mitis cried while they held her down, each man grabbed an arm and leg and held her down tightly while the fifth crouched down over her. Her tears now drenched her face. "Please don't," she tried to plead.

He laughed while looking down at her. "And what about our friends that your monkey boyfriend killed? Well?" he slapped her across her face. "Where's your monkey friend now, bitch!" He backhanded her across the other cheek. She closed her eyes and wept, smelling his hot sticky breath against her neck and wanted to bite him or spit or head-butt, anything that would get him off her, and now remembered Rezosa's advice from when this had happened to her.

"It doesn't matter how strong you are in a situation like that," Rezosa stated. Her eyes glazed over as she remembered herself being

raped by this army. Mitis knew about this but chose not to answer
and let her continue. "The fact is that if you would have fought in
a situation like that it wouldn't have made a difference. There were
just too many of them."

Still she cried, her cries now only became another voice
in the chorus of various screams on this dark night in
the forsaken city. The man reached down and groped
her breast before running his fingers down her belly and
towards her navel. The others holding her down taunted
and cheered him.

"Now let's see how this bitch fights," one said.

"I call seconds," declared another.

"Over my cold corpse, faggot!" a third shouted.

"Shut the fuck up!" the first, leaning over her, ordered the
others. "You're spoiling the moment for me and the lady."

His hand reached further down before he was suddenly
thrown off. A metal staff swung and smacked into the head
of one of the men to her left holding her leg; his head split
open spraying blood over all of them and they fell instantly
silent.

Val appeared before her, kicking the other to her left
off her. The others let go and jumped up to face their new
opponent. Once she was released Mitis crawled to a nearby
wall and curled into a ball, shivering from shock from the
experience, closed her eyes and wept in despair.

Val remembered all his training from Raiden and
showed no pity nor mercy towards these four rapists. He
swung Staff to each one hoping for the same result as in
the first one, now bleeding on the floor. Since they were
unarmed and now faced with a screaming man with a
hideous scar down his face, fighting with a weapon, skilled
and facing them like a leo would, two of them fled. The
one previously on top of Mitis jumped up and pulled out a

small knife, pointing it at Val.

"Come on then, you ugly son of a bitch!" he taunted and slashed the air with his knife. With him taunting Val the other edged slowly behind him waiting for a signal from his companion to grab Val from behind. In one swipe Val knocked the knife from the attacker's hand and in the same circle of momentum cracked Staff over the top of his head. The sound *clanged* and the man's legs caved in instantly. Remembering the last man behind him Val dropped his weapon, turned and dived on top of the final man and began biting and punching him like a leo would. The man screamed as this sudden hero became a wild animal, scratching and screaming, picking up his head with both hands and smashing it down to the floor in a feral rage. The man kicked him off, picked himself up and fled as fast as he could. Val did not give chase.

"Val," Mitis finally said, her voice still trembling and reaching up for him. When he heard her he ran over, knelt down and embraced her.

"It's okay, Mitis, it's over now."

Feeling the sudden warm comfort and safety of Val, Mitis's emotions built up again, she held tightly onto him and cried. Val gave her a minute but soon looked back over to the museum. He held her head up to look at him.

"Listen, Mitis, I can't stay. I have to go back to the elemental school. Acarlie is still waiting for me. Come with me."

He helped her to her feet.

"No, I can't, Val. Dude is still out there, also," she said, still shaking but straightening her back. "I have to go back for Zoudiva, I left him behind. I think he needs help."

Hearing this made Val worry; he was still waiting for Acarlie. "I...can't go with you, Mitis."

"And I can't leave Zou'," she countered.

Val wanted to make her go with him but the thought

of Zoudiva being alone in the city surrounded by war persuaded him otherwise.

"Are you sure you can go on your own? Look what *just* happened here."

"I know what just happened, Val. But if I don't, then who is going to help Zoudiva?"

"Okay, hold on a minute, let me think." Val paced around now before the answer came to him. "Okay, we'll swap. You go and wait for Acarlie in the museum, it will be safer there, and I'll go and find Zoudiva."

"No, Val. I'll go, this was my doing, and besides, I know where Zoudiva is, you could be looking for too long and get lost yourself."

"I can't let you go back out there alone, especially after what has just happened," he protested.

"This is the only choice we have, Val, I don't like it either but I'm not leaving Zoudiva behind. Dude still needs help too, he's become like a serial killer, Val. I've seen it, only I think I'm the one who might be able to get through to him. He knows I am here to help, he might attack you, and, no offence, Val, but I've seen what he is capable of now. He might kill you without even thinking. It has to be me that goes."

Val hated choices he didn't want to take but bit his lip and handed her his staff. "Take this." As he handed it to her he walked past and quickly turned around before running back to Acarlie.

"If anything happens though you run straight back, okay?"

"Okay!" she called back to him and watched him sprint back to the museum. She took a breath then turned back to the city before her; only before she left she walked up to the man still crawling on the floor, dazed and holding a bleeding head wound. She clutched onto Val's metal staff and finally found out that night if she could kill a man. She was happy with her answer.

Acarlie felt she had been swimming up for hours. The rebreather was feeding her oxygen but was now beginning to make her feel light headed. She realised this was what the sign in the elevator was talking about, too much oxygen was actually harmful for human lungs and so she decided to try to slow her breathing down. However, this proved an impossible task whilst swimming. She kicked through the dark water constantly, her arms also continually cut through the water in large strokes that expanded her chest and began to tire her. Soon, however, on the edge of the pool she saw a metal pipe that climbed vertically upwards. She swam towards it and used it to help her climb up. She found pulling herself up on this was much quicker and easier, so long as she kept up the pace and didn't stop. Lights began to appear at the surface. She felt like she could laugh in triumph when she finally saw them – the surface was in sight. Her head was beginning to feel lighter, however, and now she felt drunk on the high levels of oxygen but kept her mind on her hands reaching up one by one in rhythm. The lights became brighter and larger until finally her hand shot out of the water followed immediately by her head. She yanked the rebreather from her mouth and breathed in the sweet atmosphere all around her. The poor, dirty True Hiro air had never felt so clean and rich. Nitrogen, oxygen, argon, carbon dioxide and all the other gasses that made up the atmosphere. She welcomed them all in one loud gasp before reaching out and touching the edge of the pool, hugging to it tightly; she crossed her arms and planted her head safely between them and took a moment to herself. *Never again! Never ever again!* she thought between her heavy breaths. She was from Eloma, a school of wind: air was everything to her, she never wanted to leave it again.

She heard the footsteps of Val walking over to her. He knelt down beside her. She felt his hand reach down and touch the back of her head.

"Let go of her!" she heard Val scream, but from somewhere else.

The hand gripped onto her wet hair and yanked her head back; she was still too exhausted to fight and only opened her eyes to see the villain before her.

"Where were you, Val? I've been waiting!" Miles called back to Val, having Acarlie's silky black, soaking wet hair tightly in his fist.

"Shut up, Miles!" Val warned. He wanted to summon his staff but remembered Mitis still needed it. "Here's what is going to happen," he pointed to Miles. "You're going to let her go and I'm going to let this one go and not murder you here and now and throw your corpse in the pool!" His blood still raged from his previous encounter, anger flared through him. Miles, however, only laughed at Val's attempt to threaten him and countered, "No, Val. You have very poor powers when it comes to reading the future. Here's what is really going to happen." He reached down and took the item in Acarlie's pocket and held it up for Val to see.

"I'm going to walk straight past you and you're going to get wet."

"What?"

Miles sneered before Val could work out his meaning and slammed Acarlie's head against the pool's side. Her head bounced and she instantly disappeared back into the water. Val's only reaction was to sprint to the pool, straight past Miles, who stood up, and walk straight past and dive into the deep pool. The water met him with a slap. *Maybe it wanted me to chase Miles*, he thought ignoring the pain across his body and swam down. Acarlie was right before him but sinking down into a depth no one could save her from if he wavered. He grabbed her arm and pulled her towards him and swam back to the surface. He returned to the surface with an unconscious Acarlie in his arms and pushed her up from the water before climbing out himself, quickly laying her out before him and checking her breathing. He panicked when he found she wasn't and began pressing on her chest and blowing air into her lungs. He didn't know how he knew this technique, he didn't know how he knew it would work but he continued anyway. After a moment she stirred and coughed, spluttering out water that spat up at him. He quickly turned her over into the recovery position and fell back himself in relief when she started moaning and breathing deeply.

He closed his eyes in relief – she was alive. The sound of her crying convinced him of that. Her head was bruised and swollen terribly, blood ran from her eyebrow and a small river of red ran behind her, into the tiled groves of the pool before meeting with the rest of the water. Val finally rolled over and took the weeping Acarlie into his arms only to have her suddenly scream and strike him in her fit of tears.

"You bastard, Val! You said you would wait here, you promised you would wait and you didn't! You nearly killed me! You promised!" she cried, striking him over and over again. Val didn't say anything but remained silent. Tears began to fill in his own eyes, he wanted to put her right and tell her that Mitis had been attacked and needed help but couldn't. He just held her in his arms, safe from the world around them. His beautiful, wounded Acarlie was safe at last. It broke his heart to hear her cries. She finally stopped hitting him and buried her head into his chest and fell limp and shuddering from her tears.

"Why, Val?" she cried. "Why did you leave when you promised you wouldn't?"

A tear now fell from Val's eye. Why was he the bad guy here? He had only left to save Mitis and now he was the villain.

"I'm sorry, Acarlie. I had to leave, Mitis was in trouble. I only left for a minute, I promise. I couldn't stand here and let her..." He couldn't even finish his sentence but felt like crying himself. "I let it happen to you, I couldn't let it happen to Mitis too."

Acarlie still cried in his arms, it was like she didn't even hear what his excuse was. "You promised, Val. I am your elementalist and I needed you then."

He remained silent and held her tighter while she wept and blamed himself over and over again. He took every insult, he took all the blame and just sat where he was and let her finish.

"I'm sorry," he finally whispered down to her, wiping the blood from her brow and pulling the wet hair from her face.

A few silent minutes passed. Acarlie asked one more time why and he explained to her his side of the story. She didn't like his explanation but didn't blame him, she just lay in his arms in silence.

"Miles," Val finally said. "That bastard has the part of the map."

He didn't expect an answer from Acarlie. He spoke more to himself so was surprised when she finally answered.

"So do we." She turned in his arms and looked up at him and wiped her face. He could still see the severe disappointment in her vacant stare. "It was a coordinate, I memorised it. 163 Longitude West."

"How did he know we would be here?" Val asked again. "We could have been anywhere in the world and he knew we would be at this stadium."

When Acarlie thought about it the answer was quite clear to her. "Zane told him. He's probably been waiting for us for days here. Zane knew where we needed to go and so he sent Miles here while he probably went…" The thought hit her like lightning. She suddenly sat up, how could she miss this? "Home!" She broke from Val's arms.

"What's wrong?" he asked.

The sudden thoughts broke Acarlie into tears again, the realisation brought her to her deepest fears. "Eloma! Zane went to Eloma. He sent Miles here while he went to Eloma. Master Argo! I have to go back, Val."

"Wait, hold on," Val said trying to calm her down. "There is still so much going on. Mitis, Zoudiva and Dude are still out there, there is still a war going on that we're stuck in the middle of. Also, Raiden and Sheeria still need to meet us here."

"No, Val. Eloma is my home. Master Argo is like my father…Barry!" she suddenly cried.

"Wait? Who's Barry?"

She buried her face in her hands when she realised. "He would be the High Elementalist of Eloma…When Zane would arrive at Eloma…I have to go back, Val, I can't wait! I'm sorry but I can't!"

Her sudden fear started to scare even Val now, who stood up and tried to comfort her, only for her to push him away.

"Whoa, okay. You win, we'll get back to the ship and go straight to Eloma. Screw Miles for now, he can have the item this time."

He quickly ran to their cloaks on the floor and picked them up. He threw both her cloak and his over her shoulders to keep her warm. He felt he could deal with the wet and cold. He took her still shaking hand and escorted her back through the fiery war zone of the city hoping he would never have to visit this damned place ever again.

28

Val sat silently in thought. The Scarlet Arise was back in the air as soon as Acarlie stepped foot on board. Zoudiva, Mitis and Dude were left behind by order of his elementalist, who suddenly seemed to forget everything and everyone around her and only wanted to reach her old home above all else. She was at that moment being treated by Roscopp, the ship's medic, for the bruises and cuts and being checked for oxygen poisoning. He sat in the ship's canteen alone, all the pirates were at their work stations and so gave Val the large room to sit and brood. He hated leaving Mitis and Zoudiva behind, he hated how there was no word on Zahied, how Raiden and Sheeria were miles away and he especially hated the way Acarlie looked at him now. He was finally beginning to waver in his resolve. He had to save Acarlie from herself and her teachings but now it seemed more of a task than saving the planet itself. He buried his face in his hands and tried massaging his eyebrows, his fingers meeting the scar tissue at every stroke. His soul weakened and his blood shivered cold, time slowed and he sighed, filling his lungs with the dry, stale air. The room would have been silent but for the low droning of the ship's engines, distant voices of working crew members and the approaching clicking of someone's heels from behind him.

A bowl of steaming hot, creamy porridge was thrown on the table before him. It rattled against the small, black, circular, wooden table; the spoon fell beside it.

"Eat."

Val looked up to see the ship's captain had joined him. Kaza wore his leather sleeveless coat with a black vest underneath and brown, tattered and torn trousers. His metal bangles hung from his wrists and still his woven, beaded necklace hung around his neck. He was never one for rings, however; he always used to say rings only hurt and broke his fingers when he punched someone.

"I'm not really hungry," Val said looking down at the poor excuse for sustenance before him.

"It wasn't a request," Kaza said again in a tone that forced no argument and pushed the bowl toward Val. After smelling the porridge before him did Val remember that he was in fact hungry and picked up the spoon. Kaza put his elbows on the table, locked his fingers together and rested them against his chin.

"She told me everything that happened down there. I can't say I'm happy about what has happened about Zoudiva and the young nurse but at least we have the information gathered from the school."

Val said nothing but ate the porridge a spoonful at a time. Kaza stared at Val, analysing his mood and the way he slumped forward in his chair before continuing.

"Listen, kid, I know she's giving you a hard time right now, she can be a real spoilt brat sometimes. She's actually asked me to use the ship's thrusters and get us to Eloma as soon as we can."

"She has?" Val asked. He knew what this meant, the ship was the fastest in the sky but only used the thrusters in emergency evasive manoeuvres and could not handle a long distant dash like that.

"Of course she did. Little Missy doesn't understand what fuel is. She's so wrapped up in her own issues that she forgets the world around her."

Val wanted to defend her but kept silent; not that he agreed but he just didn't have the energy for it.

"I heard about what you did," Kaza said again and noticed Val twitch and listen. "Don't take any notice of what she's like at the minute. You made the right decision. It cost her a heavy bruise and a near death experience but even she would agree...eventually...rather that than the alternative. Mitis is a good person, maybe the only innocent one here on this mission. She doesn't deserve all these problems. You saving her may have also saved both Zoudiva and that bloody mute."

Val looked up now. "You don't like Dude?"

"Like him? He's a fucking liability! Always crying and brooding down in the bowels of my ship. He depresses everyone around him. More than once now he has had members of the team split up and put off the mission just to find the little shit, only for him to run off again. Now, I will admit, he's handy in a fight and is a useful member when he wants to be. I don't think we could have acquired the first three items from the Feydon base in Racoves without him but all of a sudden he turned into a moody teenager."

Val smiled a little now. As much as he liked Dude, Kaza was right there.

"It's the reason I wanted to come here and give you a pep talk, you sitting here all miserable and depressed. You're starting to remind me of him."

Val's smile grew. "Maybe so. You can't blame him though. Mitis told us what was wrong with him. Apparently he was pining over Rezosa."

Kaza sat back in his chair and crossed his arms and put the facts together. "So that's his problem? I really wish someone had told me this earlier. If he was just having some rejection issues I would have bought him a whore. It would have put a spring in his step."

Val continued with his porridge. "I don't think that would have worked, Kaza. Remember, he was from True Hiro, he would have been surrounded by prostitutes. Even if you offered I don't think he would have accepted it."

"Nah, that's what they all say," he dismissed and waved the statement away. He thought about the timing of the events and realised, "He went missing after the news came out about her death…"

A few seconds passed silently. Val looked up to see Kaza was thinking, finally understanding what Dude's issue really was and realising maybe he was being a little judgemental about him, but then realised… "Then that means he's sort of responsible for her death in the first place."

"How so?"

"I ordered Rezosa and Major to return to the ship after they found you guys. Zahied wanted to stay to represent us in front of the Senate but I guess she wanted to stay to be away from him. If he hadn't made her leave, she would still be here. I'm telling you that's the answer to his problems, whores."

Val was done with talking about Dude. He looked back down at his porridge and decided to ask a different question. "Speaking of Zahied, have you heard from them since, or Raiden and Sheeria?"

Kaza shook his head. "Zahied, no. I can't get through to him. Raiden's communicator was working but hasn't answered yet. I guess that's the good thing about leaving Zoudiva and Mitis at True Hiro. At least this way we know where they will all be."

"Captain!" called a voice at the other end of the hall. Val turned to see a disgruntled Keppal marching over. "May I have a word, please?"

Kaza sniggered, "I guess that's my cue."

Val looked confused.

"I sort of told him Acarlie was dead and you wanted to kill him. I better go and confess. Chin up, kid," he said and slapped Val on his shoulder, knocking a spoonful of porridge away. "Don't let her tantrum get you down, you're doing fine as a guide."

He stood up and walked over to the white tigian.

Acarlie lay on the infirmary's bed looking up at the white ceiling. A small widow seeped sunlight into the shaded room above her. She stared at the beam of light and watched the tiny dust particles dance in the soft air around her. She had sat with a frozen pack on her head until she felt it had completely thawed into cold water and left her with a damp head. The swelling had gone down and the ship's medic, Roscopp, had cleaned and bandaged up the cuts. Only now she felt her head begin to ache from the frozen weight and finally took it off and let the air heal the rest.

She heard Roscopp's footsteps walking in and turned to see the tall, dark, bald doctor entering the room with a tray, bowl and water.

"How are we feeling, elementalist?" he asked while setting down the tray on a table beside her.

She groaned and sat up. "Terrible. How far are we from Eloma?"

The bald doctor pulled a small torch from the pocket of his white coat and checked her pupils. "Watch my finger, please," he said and moved his finger from side to side closely monitoring her pupils. Once he was happy he put the torch away.

"I'm afraid we're still a few days away from your home, elementalist. You must be patient though and use this time accordingly to heal, both mentally and physically."

That seemed almost impossible to her. "That's easier said than done, doc."

"Call me Roscopp, everybody else does," he smiled at her.

She returned the gesture with a weakened smile. "Okay. But how am I supposed to? My home could very well be destroyed, you don't know what that's like."

"Well, no, I don't. I never had a home to be destroyed,

you see." He kept the same smile on his face. Acarlie suddenly looked up at him realising she may have said too much. He continued, "Most of us on this ship never had a home to begin with. We could not be blessed with the pampered life of the elementalists, no offence."

She smiled and nodded but remained silent.

"Most of us here, what the rest of the world calls 'pirates', are merely men and women who were left behind. Every man you see on this ship has his own story of why he chose the life of a smuggler. Maybe it was because a young, pretty woman broke their heart, maybe it was because war and divide left them with no family; maybe it was their own country's lack of jobs, or maybe it was because all their lives they grew up without any causality." His last example he said more personally.

"Is that what happened to you?" she asked.

He looked up and reminisced. "Yes, my first life I was a cabin boy for a trading seaship in North Angland. No parents nor many friends my own age, you see, so I matured quite fast. I was moved from one ship to another, from captain to captain. I was spared many of the times if we were ever boarded simply because of my age. I used this and started training under the ship's medic, making myself useful, and soon the profession defined me. Eventually, however, on a drunken night I found a man half beaten and left to die in an alley. It seemed this man had made a stupid bet that he could sweet talk three sisters into sleeping with him all in one day. Suffice it to say he achieved his mission…"

Acarlie let out a small laugh at his story.

"…But apparently he didn't take into account that these sisters also had two older brothers who heard about his little escapade. Thought they would rid the world of this sweet talking philanderer. I took him in and fixed him up."

"The captain?" Acarlie asked now, with a smile on her face.

"Yes, young Mister Caines thanked me by offering me a job on his vessel once he found out I was a man of the sea like himself. The ship was only a seaship mind you, nothing like what we are in now, but the pay was good and he turned out to be not just a good captain but a good friend too. You see we are all free men on this ship. We answer to no world leader, nor do we take any account of divides. We accept men, women, children of all races and have no prejudice towards race, age nor sexuality. Captain Caines is our leader, our king, but he also has to be our friend. In a world where a single man controls a group of hard working men he has to be fair, even be one of us. Most of the time on this ship there is no leader."

"I don't understand," she confessed.

Roscopp stood up, poured her a glass of water and handed it to her. "You see, naval vessels who answer to their respective world leaders have a ranking system to keep the men in check by honour. But to a ship with no world leader honour means nothing for they have vowed allegiance to no man. A captain is still needed for otherwise there will be disorder between the men but the chosen captain must keep his men by a bond of trust and loyalty, if he doesn't he risks mutiny from his crew. I have been with several captains and have mutinied against three of them," he said, putting three fingers up. "It is easy for the power of leadership to go to a man's head and make him believe he is god among the rest of his crew, especially when out at sea where escape would usually mean death. Captain Kaza knows this and so must be a leader of the men but vigilant in fairness. We are a democracy, all equal, every voice is heard by the captain and taken into account in turn. He will rest with us, eat with us, drink and socialise; congratulate and counsel us when required for he must be more than a leader, he must be a friend."

Acarlie nodded, understanding. "Yes, I see your point."

The tall doctor smiled. "Then maybe there is something for you to learn too. For you are the elementalist. You are the leader of this whole venture for it is your pilgrimage, even the captain must eventually answer to your decisions as to your leo guide."

Acarlie again nodded at the lecture while sipping her water. "Yes, I understand. If I am to become the Elemental Lord I must understand what it is to be a leader. I must think of the people I am leading rather than my own selfish desires." Her words made her automatically think of Val and how she had been acting towards him lately. Guilt wrapped around her.

"Exactly," he smiled. "Oh, and in answer to your question, that's how."

"What?" she asked, confused now.

Roscopp pointed to her. "I can already see you feel better than you did before we started speaking. You asked how you can heal mentally when your home is in danger and I have just presented to you the answer: talking. By talking I have taken your mind from the issue and given you a moment's rest. Now go out and find your friend Val, or the captain or whoever, just go and talk with someone and take it easy."

Acarlie watched the doctor walk back around the bedside and towards the door. "Has anyone ever told you how good a doctor you are?" she asked.

Roscopp chuckled and turned as he left the room. "That's funny, that's exactly what the captain said on that night when I found him."

Acarlie stood silent, reaching out and taking Val's hand. The air around them blew gently and the heat from the sun settled down warmly. Distant birds still sang but everything else remained silent. So many eyes were drawn upon them Acarlie felt scared and gripped tightly onto Val's hand. After a moment she heard whispers from the crowd, "She has returned, Acarlie has come back," and the words "dishonour, liar, traitor, murderer and oath breaker" whispered from lips like a voiceless echo.

"How dare she return?" she heard one voice say, a sentence that nearly broke her heart all over again.

Eloma remained the way she had left it all apart from her elemental stadium. Her old home, nursery and school, the old small coliseum where she fought her very first Elemental Battle was now ashes and remains. Once word arrived that Elementalist Acarlie had returned home the whole town gathered to see her; however, she had not dreamed in her worst nightmares that they would react to seeing her again as they did. Her people, the faces she had known all her life now all stared over at her with such hatred and disappointment. There was in the crowd the local butcher; she used to play with his daughter along with the town doctor's son, and jump in the river on hot summer days. There was the old lady who greeted her every morning with a smile wide with broken teeth but full of joy. There was her old friend, the first boy she ever kissed, still with his golden dog by his side. An elderly tigian she used to call 'Old Mamma' who used to give her fresh apples and grapes that she grew in her garden. The list went on, she knew every face there, every one of them she had seen when she left and they had wished her luck, and now she returned, but everything was wrong. From a local hero and cherished member of their society Acarlie had returned a villain, a stranger to their cold, staring, and judgemental eyes of contempt. She could not bring herself to make eye-contact with anyone but instead held onto the hand of her only friend and made her way through a valley of disdain, passing the scorns and ignoring the contemptuous whispers that followed her, and down a long, lonely path to where she once had lived.

It was the sight of her ruined home that hurt the most. Once a grand arena in her eyes, it now looked an ancient ruin. A quarter of the oval shaped wall had fallen into a pile of rubble the town was slowly removing. Before it, the top half of her school and nursery was now an open top destroyed remains of how it once stood. Attached to the arena, the ancient school stood there with so much history, now all gone, and instead scattered tiles, bricks and concrete lay around. A tear formed in Acarlie's eye and her throat felt sore when she stood before it. Only now did she feel the pain that Mecroyles, Toshiro, Donolan and Chippenham felt. Her home with so many memories was now gone. She walked into the quiet remains of the old mansion. Everything had been removed now except the bricks and foundations that held it together; sunlight shone down on them and dust floated all around, sparkling in beams of light where a ceiling used to be. An old, red armchair was covered in the grey dust; she picked it up and stood it upright and ran her fingers down the arms. "I learned to read in this chair," she whispered to Val, reminiscing with a sigh of nostalgia. "My master, Elder Argo, used to sit me on his lap. I always chose to read a colourful comic book. He would wrap his arm around me and I would point at every word while I read. If I were stuck he would help me and teach me how to say the word." She squeezed a tear from her eye before turning to see the old kitchen, now just another desolate room. She almost laughed and pointed to it; Val remained silent the whole time and let her have her moment.

"Look," she said. "There is where Sheeria used to make her famous 'Elemental Pies', as she used to call them. She always told us they were made with magic but I always knew she only used the fruit from the trees in the garden…" She went to a broken window to point through at the garden but that too was gone, stone and rubble now littered the once green grass and wire and material scratched and pulled at the trees that still stood, the others burned into gangly black skeletons pointing many dead fingers at the sky. She sighed and leaned up to a wall, reached out just to touch it and feel all the memories and history come back, but even the wall felt dead.

"My home," she whispered and covered her eyes.

Val gently put a reassuring hand on her shoulder and pulled her towards him. "Come on, Acarlie. I think you've seen enough."

He took her away from the ruins and back up to the town's people hoping they would just point him in the direction of her old master, then get whatever item was needed and go. That was of course if Zane hadn't already got it.

He led her away from the ruins and back to the crowd, who still stared in a hateful silence, only now there was another standing before them, blocking their path. A tall, ginger, male human, his face covered in bandages covering a scar much worse than Val's.

"So she finally returns! I couldn't believe it when I first heard but here you are. You have some nerve to return here, Acarlie," the man shouted over to Acarlie.

When she realised who it was she ran forward wanting to embrace him, only Val held her back.

"What happened to you?" she asked fearfully.

The man pointed a hand bandaged to cover more burn scars at her. "*You* happened to me, Acarlie! *You* happened to this whole town!"

"But, Barry, I didn't do this!" she called back to her old training partner and fellow elementalist.

Barry, however, having survived what must have been a blazing inferno, stood with the town behind him. "Yes you did, Acarlie! You think we don't know about your pilgrimage? We watched every match, every fight and cheered you believing you would be the one to bring honour back to our town and instead you return like this! We heard of you killing Eliza from Toshiro, we watched you flee from Lord Zane; we watched *him* jump into your match in Lachine," he shouted, pointing at Val. "And we watched you embarrass yourself in the C.E.L. You do not even return with your guides, Acarlie. Where are Sheeria and Miles? How many oaths and rules have you broken? You dishonoured our town and hurt us more than any other, and when Lord Zane came to punish you for your crimes, it was *us* who paid the penalty! And now you return and expect us to forgive you?"

"Please stop!" Acarlie cried now. "Please, Barry, please stop!"

"Just tell us where Argo is!" Val called out and pulled Acarlie closer to him, shielding her from the judgement of her hateful family.

"And who are you?" Barry called back.

"I'm one of her guides. Sheeria cannot be with us right now but she can vouch for every action Acarlie has made on her pilgrimage."

"And what makes you think Sheeria is one to talk? We all knew Sheeria's story, she had run away from her family once before, and now she is one of Acarlie's group, the traitor of all elementalists. The one who doesn't even have the honour to terminate herself after breaking so many vowels."

"Just tell me where he is!" Val shouted back before Acarlie had a chance to.

"Elder Argo is dead!" Barry finally confirmed with a shout that brought an instant silence.

"What?" Acarlie asked, her eyes widened and clear tears now filling her lower eyelids. Barry stared at her and repeated, this time with cold, sharp words aimed straight at her. "Elder Argo is dead. He and all the other elders who trained us died protecting the school. Zane torched our home and when they ran around trying to save it he killed each and every one of them. It was the shock most of all, no one expected the E.L. to attack the school in retaliation for your actions. I'd say it was a broken heart that killed Master Argo."

"And where were you during this?" Val again tried protecting Acarlie by talking himself and not giving her a chance to.

Barry now stared at Val scathingly through his bandages. The answer was already standing before Val. "Where do you think I was!?" he spat back at him.

"The others." Acarlie began to weep. "The other elementalists, please tell me they're okay."

"The only children who survived were the ones who didn't stand in his way. He only needed to order most of them, they were forced to stand and watch. I am now the highest member of this school until we receive new elder masters sent to us from Chippenham. Well, at least I *was* until our honourable, High Elementalist Acarlie returned. So tell me, oh great leader, what is our next move?" he asked with a spiteful sarcasm Acarlie couldn't answer.

He continued, "Nothing? Well, let me tell you then. Do you remember our promise?"

"Barry," she pleaded. "Please don't."

"You remember, don't you? Well, you have returned and I'm going to hold you to your promise. Maybe it will be the only promise you can keep."

The crowd looked a little unsettled now; Val asked the question that was on everybody's lips.

"What's he talking about, Acarlie?"

"I promised him the night I left for my pilgrimage that one day I would return and give him a rematch," she explained.

This suddenly jolted the crowd with an excitement. Some nudged Barry. "You show her, Barry," someone said. The crowd took Barry's side instantly and glared at Acarlie.

Barry himself stood resolute with his arms held out. "Well, Acarlie? Will you fight me?"

"Please don't make me do this, Barry, you don't know what it's been like on my pilgrimage. I don't want to hurt you."

Barry now laughed wickedly; the crowd joined in. "Oh Acarlie, you think you're so high and mighty because you beat me on that day. You have no idea that I am now more trained in the Element of Unseen Forces than you ever were. Your pilgrimage has made you weak, you have learned all these other elements but now your strongest ally and home element is subordinate to mine. I have trained more than you have and am the more experienced wind elementalist."

"You don't look like you're in any state to fight, mate," Val called over. Barry responded by pushing his hand forward and suddenly Val was thrown back into the air to crash down with a thump with Acarlie screaming after him. Val groaned in pain as Acarlie came to him and reached down to help him up.

"You have two days, Acarlie! Two days for us to repair and clear out the stadium. In two days I will rid this town of its abomination and declare myself High Elementalist of Eloma!" He turned to his townspeople behind him. "Give them the room that journeying elementalists use. We will make this official. If he is her guide then she has everything she needs. We disown her so she will be treated like any other foreign elementalist on their journey, and she will also meet their fates."

29

Sphere's two moons sat in the sky and watched silently as the sun slept. They saw for miles across the planet whilst listening to passing clouds dance across the sky. They heard the stars burning millions of miles away, in galaxies so far they looked like stars themselves. They sensed the impending darkness somewhere in their solar system sitting hungry and waiting. They then looked down further into their master, Sphere, to find and watch the tool created to destroy this giant hole of black emptiness, this catastrophic mass of gravity. Past the few littered clouds of Racoves they searched. Down through the miles of sky and onto the outskirts of the small and destroyed town of Eloma they found the weapon Sphere had told them about, and he was looking right up at them.

Val blinked whilst looking up; he had never witnessed two full moons before. Zahied once told him it used to be a celebration in some countries because of how rare they were. When he thought about how much happiness and noise a large group of partying people would make he realised then how silent the night actually was. There was barely a breeze nor a single tweet of a bird, even the crickets had stopped singing and left him standing in a hollow silence. He looked back down to see the back of Acarlie as she stood outside her quarters also admiring the two moons tonight.

Val and Acarlie stood in a giant garden, trees outlined both of them and stretched down acres of land until a small hill was as far as they could see. The grass was perfectly mowed without a single weed growing and flowers outlined each section of the garden. Moon Flowers seemed to glow in the moonlight, sitting beside the yellow Evening Primroses, another nocturnal flower, that were expertly arranged around this tended garden, each one part of a pattern, sitting beside sleeping flowers that bloomed in the day. In the centre of this large garden was a pond rimmed with glowing blue stones in a path that roamed around the whole, secluded garden and gave an enchanted feel to it. The pond seemed so still it barely looked like water at all but instead a hole in the ground that mirrored the clear sky above and shone millions of stars up from a realm beneath it. Only the violet and deep crimson Night Blooming Water Lilies floating atop the relaxing water confirmed to them the pond's existence. Each flower seemed to give off a faint but pungent smell that wavered in the humidity of the air encircling them until Val himself thought he could even see the purple and violet mystifying energy known as Spirit surrounding them like a comforting aura of the night. Their quarters was a single large guest house a mile away from anything. Only a single, lonely road leading to the rest of the town connected them. The staff at this house had gone an hour previously and left the elementalist alone with her guide.

Val watched as Acarlie stood with her eyes to the sky; a falling tear caught the moonlight and glimmered as it fell onto her bare feet in the soft grass. She stood wearing a thin, silken, white gown that rested lightly upon her shoulders. As if she could sense him there behind her she then said over her shoulder, "The grass here is so…perfect."

He stepped forward and made his way through the warm mist of floating specks of dust, pollen and Spirit catching the silvery moonlight.

She closed her eyes and continued, "I always heard our Away-side's Quarters were the most beautiful and calming in the whole league."

"You've never been here before?" he asked.

She shook her head and replied with a heavy heart, "No, it's taboo for any home elementalist to creep into their Away-side's Quarters. The people who come here face an imminent death if they lose and so must be given one night of perfect calming solitude before fighting."

Val watched in silence as Acarlie then shivered. He remembered when she told him about these shivers on the elevator to True Hiro. Neither the temperature nor the breeze were the issue but it was Acarlie's heart that shivered when she looked out at a sight her eyes were not born to see.

"I am the only elementalist from Eloma to ever see this garden..." She blinked again and Val noticed another gleam of moisture building in her eye as she stared out onto this glowing vision of tranquillity. "...It's beautiful."

Val could see this garden hurt her eyes. He understood it wasn't the beauty of it that hurt but the fact that she was seeing it that tortured her. Her standing in this still and silent garden with only that glowing aura around her gently moving meant that her home had forgotten her. It was a message from the town that she was no longer welcome. Val stepped up again and this time reached up to gently rub her shoulder supportively.

After a moment Acarlie broke the silence again, voicing the weight she carried. "They hate me, Val. After all I've done, everything I've done for the honour of my town and..." Her hand covered her eyes and silenced her as she began to weep.

Val felt her begin to tremble and turned her around before she could fall and held her shoulders; he gave her no patronising words of comfort she didn't want to hear but instead only supported her.

She began to cry. "I don't have anything left, Val. No home, no parents, no friends. The world hates me and blames me for everything, Eliza, the C.E.L., Eloma. I don't even have Sheeria to guide me." She wiped her eye. "The only thing I have left in the world is…" her eyes caught his as he still stood silent before her, not daring to say a word that might upset her more. She didn't need to finish her sentence, the answer was before her. She flung herself into his arms and embraced him.

It was then that Val realised he was in a position not much different from hers. He too had nothing in this world, also without a real family, friends, even a name. He was a ghost without this mission. He was a nameless shell without any cause for existence. But the way she embraced him gave him everything. He noticed it wasn't the fact that she hugged him, it was the way she did it. She hugged him tightly like he was life itself, like he was the only thing in the world that mattered to her. All the while she did, all the while she had *him*, he had existence; he had the pilgrimage, the mission; he had causality; he had identity; he had Val.

Visions of her death flickered before his eyes again. He tried shutting them tight to push them away but her crying in his ear only reminded him more.

"*Kill me Val! Please kill me!*" the vision screamed behind his eyes. The knife buried in her chest spilt warm blood down his fingers.

"*No! Never!*" he wanted to shout at the vision. Still holding her in his arms he pulled her closer. "*I will never kill you!*"

She responded by also holding him tighter; the grip soon felt like a vice, like she had no intention of ever letting go. He reached up and thumbed her ear, their foreheads pressing together close enough that her eyes became one. Still he said nothing, words would be wasted in this moment, a history of spoken words created by their ancestors spanning back to a time neither of them could comprehend from a distance measured in time were all useless in this moment. Now he had her so close he felt he could understand her without words, the way she held him; the way she looked at him; even the way she breathed told him everything he needed to know, all else was wasted information.

There they stood, the two of them alone in a secluded space a mile from anywhere with only the two moons watching them, surrounded by the aura of the garden. The darkened sky glittering with stars decorated their view and the whole of their galaxy sat like a white disk stretching out into infinity. They stood together in synchronised harmony and so moved almost symmetrically when they kissed.

Acarlie lifted her hand and, to Val's surprise, she tilted the gown from her shoulder and let it slip down her body and stood naked before him.

Val's heart jumped and his legs twitched as he was suddenly looking down at the purest form of Acarlie. She reached up and embraced him again. With her slim, naked body now pressing against him Val's mind now raced with excitement. Ideas, dreams, visions; sensations and vibrations filled his mind as she kissed him again and guided his hands down her body. Of all these emotions, lusts and desires now filling his soul and exciting his body only one thought stopped him: *Responsibility*.

"Stop," he finally forced a whisper out before he lost himself.

She stopped but said nothing; they were still synchronised and so he knew her thoughts, *What's wrong?*

He answered her, "There is *nothing* I want more than this, Acarlie, and it pains me to do this but…your fight is tomorrow. If I cause you to lose concentration because of my own selfish desires I'll never forgive myself."

Still she said nothing. He knelt down and picked up her

gown. She watched his hands tremble as he clothed her again. He reached out to hold her cheeks in his hands and spoke into her eyes, "The only thing I want more than you, is you. Without you I am not Val."

She noticed Val now shiver; she knew that feeling all too well. Val's physical body screamed bloody murder at him, visions of her spread down on the floor and seductive small gasps of breath in his ear nearly drove him forward to go against his honour. It was what he wanted, it was what *she* wanted, but as much as it felt so natural and perfect, that didn't make it right. To take advantage of her in that state and either break their relationship, or even worse, her concentration during her battle would have been the end for her, for him.

Acarlie still stood in silence. Suddenly everything Val did was noticeable to her; he looked to have broken. He still stood trembling and kissed her one last time. "Now…," he said and took a step back. "If you need me I'll be having a cold shower…in liquid nitrogen."

She watched him turn and walk back leaving her there in the silvery glow of the night. A tear fell from her cheek again as her face twitched into a small smile.

30

Sheeria scrambled past some of the other tigians through the blazing corridor in her attempt to escape the mechanical monster now shredding its way through the ship. In a frenzied moment of terror and confusion she had lost her brother Audie and dared not to try to call his name in case she alerted Proto-Weapon. She found she had run in a circle when she reached a corner. Blood and entrails now soaked the floor and bones from torn apart carcasses now littered the floor like sharp pins she desperately tried to avoid stepping on. The ship was silent, but noisy at the same time. With a large window smashed open letting in sounds of the sky and whistling wind, extinguishing the small fires along with the sprinklers spraying down and diluting the litres of tigian blood into large puddles of stinking, sticky claret bogs. She leaned with her back against a wall and panted. Her head was scratched and now she finally had the time to realise it and rubbed her small wound. It thumped and was sore but was bearable enough to ignore for the while. Her heart, however, felt as if it were having a seizure, she had never felt so terrified in all her life. She felt she couldn't even breathe without making involuntary whimpering, weeping sounds. She rubbed her head again and noticed how much her furry orange hand was shaking. With the leos all but gone the tigians were next to the strongest creatures on Sphere apart from the ursas and here she was, as terrified as a mouse hiding from a starving cat, which seemed a giant monster in comparison. She tried to calm herself down, her short and insecure breaths were all she could feel as she leaned out slowly to see if her path was clear.

She was lost on this ship and completely on her own now but knew she didn't want to turn back. Down the hall she saw the crashed pod that Proto-Weapon had arrived in and the last of the fires burning out. The ship titled upwards briefly and sent a river of watered-down blood to dribble down the wooden floor and past her feet to congregate in a large puddle at the end of the hallway. She stepped out, the breeze from the smashed window suddenly hit her as a gale, her breath caught in her throat and she lifted her hand to block it from her eyes. A sudden and distant *clomp!* at the far end of the corridor stopped her and she witnessed the metal monster appear from a side door. She froze in her steps and felt her lungs suddenly seize again. Proto-Weapon stepped out with another terrifying *clomp!* as his metal feet stamped into the floor. He breathed slowly now but still every breath was as heavy as Death's own tombstone. The fires around his mane had now also subdued and mostly burned away but left large, burned slabs of black metal to appear from under his dark skin like a skull. The monster appeared covered from head to toe in blood and murder and holding a tigian ribcage in its hand, which it dropped in a bloody mess at its feet. Out of pure instinct Sheeria stepped back, her feet scraping against more bone and tissue of her brother tigians and tapping as she stepped onto the wet, red floor. Even with the sound of the wind, fires and sprinklers between them Proto-Weapon heard the tiny splash and jerked its morbid, burned, mechanical head to her. It swung around almost gracefully, except for the robot-like movements of its shoulders being slightly held back by their immense, metal weight. Its mechanical growl echoed down the hall like the laughter of Fate mocking her. Once its red eyes locked onto her, not waiting to see its obvious next action, she turned and fled, leaving the sound of its horrific, maniacal, digital roar to linger in the air. As she reached the corner she heard the monster give chase with a *doom! boom!* she felt vibrate under her feet. Her legs almost gave way as fear nearly overwhelmed her completely. She slipped in a small puddle of blood and crashed through a door with a scream. The door led to the ship's kitchen, with the open canteen on the other side. Knives, pans and other heavy and sharp apparatus were now at hand, which any other villain might have seen as being given a chance. All she could do though was jump over one of the metal work surfaces and hide behind it. She brought her knees up and trembled, hoping the beast would walk straight past. She heard the door slam open and suddenly the heavy, slow growls of breath permeated the air once more bringing terror and a tingling sensation that nearly made Sheeria squeak with fear. She covered her mouth and forced herself not to hold her breath but to breathe small breaths. Proto-Weapon stepped past, each step thumping the floor with the weight and force of a dropped oven. It stood over the work surface Sheeria cowered behind; she closed her eyes and sucked in a short breath through the gaps of her fingers. In a movement of a person who thought and wouldn't be classed as a mechanised being, Proto-Weapon reached out with its large, razor claws and scratched them along the metal surface as it took another slow step. With the screeching and unbearable sound of scraping metal now ringing in her ears and cutting right through her she wanted to bring her hand up to her ears but dared not. As either a tactic to lure out its prey or a movement of boredom Proto-Weapon continued to drag its claws along the metal surface Sheeria hid behind, his deep, malicious breaths joined in her mind with the terrifying screeching sound as a sabotage attempt on her nerves now screaming at her to make a sound and give away her position.

A fallen carving knife at her side caught her eye, shimmering in the light and giving her the slightest of ideas. She slowly picked it up, careful not to make a sound until she held it tightly against her chest. She would only have one chance at this and ever so slightly, ever so slowly leaned forward to see where it stood. As she looked upon the hideous burned carcass of Raiden's brother now turned into the greatest and most terrifying weapon ever created she felt slightly relieved it was half a step past her and scanning the silent kitchen. She sucked in another breath and this time held it, her hand trembled as she clutched tightly onto the knife and leaned more forward, waiting. Her moment needed to be precise and she waited for the metal neck of Proto-Weapon to face the opposite direction and afford her a good look at the wires on the back of its neck. Once she saw the yellows, blues and browns of the wires she finally took her chance, leaned up and threw the knife away from her. It clanged against the floor near to the door to the canteen. Proto-Weapon instantly turned around and charged toward the sound believing it to be a prey's mistake and through the door. Once she saw it leave she jumped back up and exited the kitchen through the same door she had entered it and almost collapsed again feeling her nerves now shattered and body limp.

A few minutes passed with Sheeria all alone on this mechanical demon infested ship in silence. All passengers now aboard this vessel had split apart from one another and all committed themselves to silence in fear of alerting their unstoppable, prowling predator. Sheeria counted the longest stretch of silence was ten minutes before it was broken by distant and echoing wails of despair followed by a crack, thud, crash or rip that commanded instant silence and started the timer again. She found herself on a familiar floor, the infirmary level. With all this confusion and fear she only had one thought, only one person she felt safe with; she had to wake him up, he would know what to do.

She crept along the hallway, hearing another distant voice cry its final vocal, knowing it was far away at the other end of the ship but still feeling too scared to run in case Proto-Weapon heard. She reached the door and slowly opened it.

"Raiden?" she whispered, the door creaked louder than her whisper as she entered.

The bed was empty.

"Raiden?" she said, louder this time. "Raiden? Are you here?"

When the answer came in the form of a deadening silence she stepped back.

Where could he be? He was far too injured to walk on his own. Thoughts and possibilities suddenly filled her mind with scenarios that frightened her. *The tigians here are desperate, they know Proto-Weapon is only here for Raiden, they have...no! please no!*

"Raiden!" she suddenly burst out and sprinted back through the door. *I have to find him! I have to find whoever took him before they give him to that monster!*

She hurried back up to the blood drenched tier of the ship and instantly the fear gripped her again, Proto-Weapon was somewhere on this floor but there was a chance Raiden was also. She approached carefully again, reaching out and touching the walls as she did so. She wanted to call but again knew to remain silent. With a silence so tense her ears became more valuable than her eyes. Every bump, snap and crack of tiny unseen things now made her jump. She made her way past more bodies, blood smears across the walls and holes trailed with long claw marks. She thought she heard another sound, a soft *clunk* that made her swivel and turn around, but again saw and heard nothing in the tense silence...until something grabbed her. She was yanked into a room with a hand over her mouth; she felt she nearly passed water but relaxed when she saw the familiar eyes of her brother staring back at her. He gently let go and began to whisper, "We have to escape this ship, sister."

"How though? I went for Raiden but couldn't find him."

"Don't worry about him, what's important is you. There is an escape vessel at the bow of the ship. My subjects wanted to leave without you but I couldn't. I sent tigians to their deaths looking for you, sister. Follow me."

She wanted to argue, to try to manipulate him into attempting to find Raiden but found herself following him. She was simply too scared and now with that thing wandering around wasn't the time to make a scene. He never let go of her hand all the while he led her through the ship in absolute silence. Within a few tense moments they managed to reach the escape vessel without incident. They walked along one of the top tiers of the ship, which was an outer-deck. Another hallway looked down on them from large glass panes to their left, as in the previous corridor where Proto-Weapon first arrived, and to their right was the long slanting roof of another corridor that dropped into the main deck below them.

"There you are, sir!" some of Audie's subjects declared as soon as they saw him and hurried over to claim them and lead them to the small, pod-like vessel awaiting their escape sitting at the end of the ship ready to safely leap into the sky. Sheeria still wanted to pull away; however, above them the familiar digital roar of their stalker, now looking down at them through the glass, presented their greatest fears.

"Quick! Get the President off the ship!" one called and forced them toward the vessel. Sheeria glanced up in horror as the metal beast pressed itself against the window; it was about to break through and drop down when something attacked it from behind. The window smashed and Proto-Weapon grunted as its head whipped back as it was now forced to fall straight over their tier and towards the slanting roof of the next. Before the door closed she only had a brief glimpse of Proto-Weapon now falling with something heavy, furry and equipped with shiny, metallic blue armour clutching onto it. The door sealed shut instantly and left her screaming his name as their vessel was ejected from the ship and away safely.

Having woken previously and seen the carnage his brother had caused, Raiden had since been following him from outside the ship. Once he saw Sheeria being hurried off the ship with her brother he took the moment to finally make a surprise attack on his brother and save the valiant tigians who were protecting Sheeria. With his weight and momentum the glass shattered easily and he timed it perfectly to grab hold of Proto-Weapon by its chest as they landed on the slanted roof and instantly began sliding down to the deck. Proto-Weapon needed a moment to compute the information it was suddenly receiving: one, its secondary target was escaping; two, its primary target had presented itself; three, it was falling; and four, it was being repeatedly struck by its primary target. Therefore, it did nothing, but allowed Raiden to continue with another two punches while they both slid down the slanted roof. Before they reached the edge of the roof Raiden tried turning around and grabbing hold of the edge but misjudged his handhold and fell straight off, along with his brother, but managed to process the information quicker than his deceased brother and rolled when he touched the floor, receiving only a few minor bumps and bruises. For Proto-

Weapon, however, this moment came too quickly for it to compute and instead slid off the roof, crashed into the decking like a piece of discarded machinery and straight through it. The whole ship felt the weight of its fall and rocked to one side. Raiden got to his feet when he heard the terrible sound of the failing of one of the thrusters.

"Are you okay?" he heard one of the tigians from above him call down. He groaned and slowly got to his feet and waved to them. The tigians pointed to the hole in the deck. "That thing fell straight into the engine room! It must have disrupted one of the engines!"

"Are there any more crew up there?" he finally called up.

"No! The ship is running on auto-pilot to the nearest land mass!"

"Then abandon ship!" he called up.

"What about you?"

Raiden noticed the ship rock again and begin to nose dive towards the sea below them.

"We don't have time! If I come up there my brother will chase me!"

"Who is your brother?"

Another crash below and a loud, painful and angry snarl screamed up from the hole and rang out on the deck.

"He is. Just go! Get off the ship and return once it is safe."

"But what about you?" they called back down but Raiden was too tired to answer; instead he staggered out towards the main deck of the ship. An endless horizon of ocean surrounded him and in the distance the Feydon skyships floated like tiny flies trying to reach them. The ship was definitely starting to fall to the ocean floor, a watery abyss looked back up at him as he reached the railings that narrowed at the bow of the ship. The other escape vessels had now ejected from their mothership and flew over Raiden's head while he panted and waited for the inevitable. Within a moment it appeared. Out from the hole it fell through climbed back his brother. Raiden looked over his shoulder and smiled as the beast was now in flames again but seemed not to care now and instead wore the flames like glowing robes, flapping in the wind.

He sighed and looked back at the horizon, he still ached and bled and was still weakened from previous wounds but now seemed not to care also. Instead he smiled; he felt strangely peaceful looking out to the horizon at the burning orange sun gleaming in the vast open blueness of the approaching ocean. *Maybe I'm dying?* he thought.

"You always were the stronger of the two of us, Val," he said to his brother and closed his eyes and remembered his brother, how he used to stand. Tall with dark cream fur, a red mane and ruby eyes, proud and smiling down with pride on his younger brother. With the look of their father also standing within him. When Raiden turned he opened his eyes to see his brother in the flesh. His posture was now crooked and bent like a feral beast with too much strength and power to know what to do with it. His fiery mane was now ablaze again and truly was a mane of fire. His ruby eyes were now a digital glowing red seeing through the metal plates covering that once proud smile. Raiden saw every detail, every scratch, every metal plate and stitching, every defile that Feydon had done to his brother but still only saw Valadad before him.

He sighed, grunted in pain and pushed himself away from the railing to face the burning malice before him. Raiden and his brother were facing each other at the nose of the ship that screamed through the air down towards the ocean. Raiden stood with three elements around him: fire before him, water behind him and air all around. Each one rolled their dice to see who would win. Valadad screamed once more, a tactic it assumed to frighten its target; only

Raiden stood smiling and with the last of his strength, standing tall and proud, lifted his arms, either wanting to welcome his charging beast of a brother back into his arms, to welcome him into a fight or to welcome fate to carry him away. He breathed his last breath on board that ship as Valadad leapt, claws out and ready to feast on his target, his digital eyes wide with feral rage and bloodthirsty ambition.

The distant Feydon ships witnessed the crashing skyship as it struck the ocean skin in a mighty, watery crash and sent a giant wave of white foaming water in every direction and crash down again as the bowel of the ship met the blue and white ocean. A giant tide appeared and rippled outwards into the ocean whilst the ship was instantly drowned and consumed within. A crash that they decided no one on board would have survived…

31

The rain fell in heavy droplets from a blackness above him. Mute missed thunder and lightning. Yes, they were dangerous and sometimes scary and violent but Mute loved that loose and wild energy of them. The anticipation in waiting for the next bolt to light up the sky and the roaring of thunder beckoning obedience of Sphere like a master would a dog. Mute wasn't very educated on his history but he knew enough to know that once, a very long time ago, humans believed in gods and deities watching over them, and it was storms that made him understand how they believed it. The storm he witnessed in Donolan almost made him believe in them himself, a heavy and angry presence was definitely there that night, but he understood like everybody else that the presence was Sphere. The elders taught that fact to humans many years ago now and they had soaked up the idea quickly. He never knew how or why though. In the rains of True Hiro, however, Sphere was absent. The rain had no direction but straight down, there was no energy to it. Outside rain fell in all different forms and pressures, some light enough to water the flowers and freshen the air and some with ferocity and malice slamming down in the form of hard hitting hailstones. Some even rained under a blue sky and revealed a rainbow, or so Mute heard, he had never seen one himself. He always wanted to though, he always wanted to make a wish on one. But down in True Hiro none of those happened, rain was just a gloomy time where water fell from the blackness above, always the same pressure, temperature and direction. He hated it. But as much as he hated it he also treasured it. Hiro and True Hiro were the home of the Element of Water and had been for thousands of years. He knew enough to know that water was the elixir of life. Without water, depressing as it was sometimes, life could not continue.

He sat out on top of one of the old buildings as he used to as a child. The city would be hunting him down soon and so he knew he had to stay above the city hopping from one roof to another or to crawl through the sewers below it. This option at least gave him the advantage of seeing what was going on below him. With his knees up to his chest and Fireshaver between his legs he hugged onto his metallic red katana as it was now his only possession in the world. To the right buyer it would have brought him a fortune; he could sell it, buy land somewhere in a country where no one knew him and live there peacefully. The thought did occur to him but something greater told him to keep it. Fireshaver meant so much to him that it was priceless, like it was part of him. He had never loved before, not properly anyway, he had lusted but never loved. He considered that maybe he loved Fireshaver for his red katana had never broken his heart, never let him down and always protected him. He knew it was only an inanimate object but he understood now that Sphere would never allow him to love a woman, so instead he would love this. He clutched onto Fireshaver tightly like he was embracing a woman, the way he imagined embracing Rezosa, until the edge of the blade dug into his shoulder and scratched his chest. The blood tickled as it ran down his belly. The underground riots of True Hiro had since died down with the rioters as the victors. The police force had pulled back their lines and more and more joined the freedom fighters' cause and increased their numbers. Led by their 'Slum King' the people of True Hiro were now beginning to become a force to be reckoned with but Mute knew better. He knew the people of True Hiro better than most because he was one of them. He knew their true colours – whereas some were true to their ambitions the rest were only joining because they were simply jumping at the chance to be part of a winning revolution as a means of becoming written into the history books, as well as finding the first opportunity to break away from the mundane and tedious normalities of life. These were the infestation he vowed to destroy, only now they were all onto him. The dark and drizzly draught of wind changed and Mute smelt fire once again and climbed to the edge of his platform and looked down at the streets with his eyes so perfectly made for seeing in dark places. There were fires all around, not the wild flames of battle any more but each fire was like a small candle flame from where he stood, and each small tip of fire had a human underneath it. The ground was glowing with hundreds of tiny, tame flames flapping against the drizzle and rain. He knew these fires all too well for they came every time True Hiro gathered, it was these fires that made the whole city gather like a town meeting, only in True Hiro a meeting was only known as a mob.

"We found this one here, sir!" called one of the rioters clutching tightly onto Mitis's arm as she was forced up through the mob, each holding a weapon, a solid club or a flaming torch. The crowd opened up for her as she was practically dragged up to Edwin, who stood with his people around him. She was finally thrown before him.

"She knows who the killer aeomon is!" the man shouted again.

Edwin was currently rallying his people to hunt down this crazed killer after his people all expressed their fear and worry about him. He needed to present to them all that he was now in power over the city and so took their side.

He looked to see the young blonde human he had spoken to one night previously now standing terrified before him. She began to tremble and look over her shoulder to his people now surrounding her. Some of his more violent and excitable subordinates had already started voicing their views and ideas of what to do with this scared woman. He sharply held up his hand before the crowd got over excited. "All right, that's enough everyone! Calm down!"

At first only a few heard him and remained silent while the rest still squabbled and shouted until Jacob beside him shouted louder and silenced them all.

The crowd was finally soothed enough for him to speak. "Thank you, Jacob. Now calm down everyone, you're scaring the poor girl." He stepped up to Mitis, who still stood like a mouse caught in a pounce of cats. He reassured her by holding onto her shoulders and speaking into her eyes. "Now no one is going to harm you. We are not animals here."

She shrugged off his hands in a defensive jerk and spat back at him spitefully. "Tell that to the group who tried to rape me!"

Edwin was unaware of this and took the accusation seriously. "What? Who did that to you?"

"I don't know but it was your men! Five of them chased me down, if my friend hadn't been there to help me they would have succeeded. I would have gone to the police too but again your men drew them away. Now there's no one left to look after the streets!"

"Jacob!" Edwin turned sternly as though he suddenly forgot all about his mob and this loose killer and addressed the situation seriously. "Assemble a loyal group and go and find who did this and anyone else you find has been taking advantage of our movement for their own benefit. I will not have rapists, murderers and thieves in our ranks sullying our cause."

The crowd clapped and cheered his decision and many volunteered for the capture. Edwin again had to address his people to reassure them all. "We are *not* the evil ones here! We do not fight for primal thrills of violence nor do we rape and pillage! We are fighting for our freedom here and will never succeeded if we have disloyal members of our army attacking and stealing from one another! Nor do we capture frightened women and drag them here like some prisoner of war!"

His last sentence finally caught their full attention. "Now, we need to all work together if we wish to fight our way out of this city, otherwise wherever we decide to go the city will follow us and we will never escape it, even if we are under the sky. We have to change ourselves if we wish to truly leave this place!"

He turned back to Mitis and continued, "I am truly sorry for your experience here. We all are." He gestured to the people around her who now all stood in a guilty silence.

Mitis stood still with uncertainty but managed to hold her composure and face him to ask, "Where is my kingnine companion? He was trying to protect me from the battle and was overcome with force."

"I know of the kingnine you speak of. At first they brought him to me just like they did you after it was confirmed he wasn't with the police force. I immediately recognised him as Elementalist Acarlie's guide and released him from my custody. He has remained a guest at my headquarters since and has asked me to look for his blonde human companion. I'm guessing that means you. So relax, he is fine, I will take you to him in a moment, but before I do, what is this about you knowing this killer on our streets? Is it true what my people say?"

"And what if it is?"

"Then maybe you're what we need to find him. He

knows you, you might be able to talk to him for us."

Finally! Someone who understands! she thought. "Yes, I think I may be the only one can get through to him. Please don't hate him, he's just lost at the moment. He is originally from True Hiro too, he's one of you. If I can get close enough to him I may be able to calm him down into giving up his weapon. Once he's subdued we'll leave the city and you'll never hear from us again."

Edwin thought for a moment, he silenced the crowd again, who had started shouting for retribution of their deceased, only thinking about what she said. "You say he's native to True Hiro? That would mean he would know the streets like we do. He would still have the advantage, but at least we know this now. Is there anything else you can tell us?"

"Only that he is not a threat. He just needs…someone…"

"Who does he need?" Edwin asked but Mitis remained silent before finally croaking under her breath.

"The person he needed the most is dead. I'm the only one left who could get through to him. Since Acarlie left I'm the only friend he has."

Edwin nodded and thought again. "In that case would you come with me? I promise your safety."

"Where are we going?"

"First to find your kingnine friend and then we are going to work on using you as bait to lure your friend into a confined place where he cannot escape."

"What!? No, I'm not going to let you hurt him!" she protested.

"I'm not going to, neither am I going to hurt you. But he will never show his face any other way." He signalled to two men behind her. "You two escort this lady. Only grab her, however, if she tries to resist."

"Am I under your custody?" she asked.

Edwin shot her a glance, like a parent to a frustrating child. "Only if you refuse to join me as a guest."

Mute hopped along from one rooftop to another. He even jumped down from one platform and landed on the butcher's shop he stole from at the beginning of his adventure but took no notice, only keeping his eyes on Mitis in the distance with the Slum King escorting her. Fireshaver, strapped tightly to his back, rocked while he ran and climbed. One window was left open and he climbed straight into someone's empty room and crept through the upper hallway. He heard the television on downstairs and the sounds of a chatting couple. He stopped at the top of the stairs and could not help but peek downstairs. There through the crack of a door he saw the two sitting peacefully. The man with his arms stretched over the back of the sofa and his girl sitting up against him, leaning her head against his shoulder. They were chatting some nonsense about the show they were watching; he didn't care for their conversation but instead listened to their voices, how they spoke. He noticed how relaxed their lives seemed even though they lived in True Hiro, how perfectly normal they were. The image burned a hole in his heart. How often had these two had a night like this? How many nights have they already forgotten because they have lived this night so many times that the memories had all scrambled together? Had either of them ever known the long, cold sting of loneliness like he had? Did either of them know how truly special they were? With his cold, jealous emotions beginning to build he felt Fireshaver begin to hum behind his back. A flash of a thought zipped through his mind. Maybe he would show them? Maybe he should take one of them away and leave the other to truly understand how important the other was and realise how late they were to truly express themselves?

This lesson would be hard earned but would teach them the value of love. He stood back up and felt the hilt of Fireshaver with his fingertips, hearing the sound of the two of them laughing at the television and feeling that burning sensation throughout his body and tingling behind his ears. He gripped onto Fireshaver and had taken the first step down when he hesitated. He realised what it was he was planning and instantly stopped. These thoughts were now his proof, he was truly evil. He shouldn't exist, there was enough evil in the world without him making it worse. He took one more glance at this mystery couple before leaving the hallway and climbing out of another window with only his mental scars, leaving them in peace.

"My Lady, I thought I would never find you," Zoudiva greeted Mitis as he saw her approach. He limped up with Hevana in his mouth and dropped it at her feet like a stick he wanted to fetch.

"Zoudiva! Are you hurt?" She knelt down and embraced him.

He smiled with his long, dog-like lips. "Only a few bumps and cuts. You forget I am a kingnine, My Lady. A species who was developed to kill a leo, a few humans and aeomon were no match. I just had to make sure I went easy on them."

"Zoudiva here has been my guest throughout the night. I made sure he had a comfortable night's sleep and a healthy breakfast," Edwin informed her. Zoudiva nodded. "This is true, My Lady, he also reassured me that he would send some of his men to look for you. At first I was sceptical about this man and his intentions but after a few hours I see no harm in him nor his goal. Did you find the Silent One?" he asked her.

"That's what we're doing here now, Zou'. I don't know

what this man has in mind but I think he wants to lure Dude out of hiding using me as bait."

Zoudiva suddenly growled and turned to Edwin. Edwin quickly spoke in his defence sensing the impending questions.

"We are not planning on harming you, Miss. We just want to catch this killer and you're the best means of doing so." He guided them with a few more of his men to a large, abandoned factory. Each black window had been smashed by some child's game and left uncleared, with shards of old glass scattered over the floor. The door opened like it hadn't in a century, opening with a noisy, wooden creak and nearly falling from its hinges. Rot had settled in on everything wooden there. Broken pallets and boards were thrown to the walls and only a large, rusting, blue boiler container decorated the room. All else was dirt, glass and stones around the floor. The room was very large but empty, only filled with a hollowed silence and almost perfect darkness. Mitis shivered as she walked in; a sudden fear crept down her neck and chilled her spine when Edwin walked ahead of her to a metal supporting girder. As he checked around she looked up to inspect the ceiling. What was once a second floor had now become only metal beams above her looking up to a black ceiling; some tiles from the roof had fallen through but still let in no sky, for there was no sky in this city.

"This will do," Edwin said and his voice echoed around them, "Do, Do, do."

He gestured for Mitis to come towards him. She hesitated out of sudden fear and nearly screamed when his men took her arms and gave her to him.

"Please don't be frightened," and the echo repeated, "nd, nd, nd."

He took her by her hand and gently tied her to the

beam. She wanted to struggle but even when she looked to Zoudiva he nodded reassuringly.

Edwin finally reached with a cloth to tie around her mouth. "Just relax…"

"Ax, ax, ax."

Once she was tied he went back to his men. He sent two of them outside to stand away from the door and encourage the killer to slip past them, then they went and hid in the shadows.

Mitis stood silent. After a moment it was like the room was suddenly empty again, only a soft draught drifted in as if lost and searching for refuge; after it saw the young woman tied and gagged to a dark bannister it became scared and flew away. Mitis sniffed and closed her eyes. She still didn't know if she trusted this Slum King but his method of catching Dude might work. He was the type to fall for a trap such as this and once she was unbound she would have the space to talk to him in person, but only if Dude had been watching. Edwin assured her that he would have knowledge of the city and since she was the only person he knew he would keep an eye on her. She just had to hope he was right.

Ten minutes in absolute silence passed slowly. For several moments Mitis believed they had all left and forgotten about her. She shifted her body around, her hands bound behind her back and against the beam, and tried to sit down. Another ten minutes passed, or so she believed – she couldn't see her watch, it might have been hours, days since anything had happened. Time disappeared from her like it needed a break itself and left her there alone. She wondered how long they would keep it up before Zoudiva insisted the plan had failed and came to release her, when she started to feel her eyes drop. She rested her eyes, closing them. Instantly the long forgotten face of her deceased lover popped into her head. Her Terry, how could she forget him? So much had seemed to go on that she had forgotten to grieve for him. His face morphed into Zane's and his into Val's and finally into Dude's. All this was her fault. If she could have just stayed out of Rezosa's business then she would still be alive and none of this would be happening. She had to make amends, she had to save Dude from what he was becoming.

A pebble rolled and dropped from a distant beam. Everything in the building heard it like an explosion and from the darkness above her dropped a shape. Seeing her there all alone and tied up he didn't hesitate to run to her. As soon as he did Edwin and his men sprang from their hiding places and quickly surrounded him.

Mitis tried to shout to Edwin through her gag to release her now but only a muffled, nonsensical sound escaped her.

Mute panicked and reached for his blade while they surrounded him. Suddenly that once silent abandoned factory seemed brimming with excitement, each voice bounced off every wall and echoed all around them.

"Stay there, don't move!"

"Get behind him!"

"Someone grab that weapon before he hurts someone!"

"Mrrfftted!"

"Edwin, release My Lady's gag and let her speak to him!"

Every weapon was now drawn and pointed to the silent aeomon, who stood defensively, waiting for an attack.

"Okay, okay, hold on. Everybody calm down!" Edwin shouted over the sudden confusion and walked over to Mitis. He reached up to take her gag off. "As promised, just please tell this aeomon to put his weapon down. We can settle this without any bloodshed."

Mitis gasped when she was released and called to

Dude, who stood warning anyone off coming any closer by pointing his blade at them.

"Dude, please, these men are not here to hurt you. They…"

A sudden *whoosh* silenced her mid-sentence. Everyone stopped as suddenly one of Edwin's men stood with an arrow piercing his chest. He only had time to look as confused as the rest of them before falling to the floor. Their prey had no bow and so this meant there was another.

"What was th–?" someone tried to say before he too was pounced upon by a heavy object that fell from the black ceiling silently. A tall, lean, hooded attacker pounced back up in a frenzy of attacks holding two, metallic blue, curved knives it expertly used to attack the group of humans. The moment happened so fast time had to catch up from its recent absence to witness it; however, it was a moment too late. Before Mitis could figure out what was happening all of Edwin's men were dead and Dude had tried to run away but stepped on a weakened floorboard and fallen straight through it. Edwin himself was standing over Mitis trying to protect her from this mysterious and violent being. Zoudiva, however, was still confused.

"What's happening?"

"What do you mean? You can't see that?" Mitis cried, cowering behind Edwin.

"See what? What's there?" he asked again but instead turned his nose and sniffed. He instantly recognised the scent.

The hooded killer spoke, a female, cat-like creature's face emerging from the shadow of her hood. "Kingnines only see in heat. An easy method to sneak past them if one could hide their heat signature."

"What? Who are you? Why are you here?" Edwin barked at her.

The hooded cat stood back and looked down at the human carcasses around her.

"I'm...hungry." She reached down and grabbed one of the humans by their feet and started dragging him away.

"You are the one following us!" Zoudiva called after her. "What is it you want?"

The hooded archer hissed back at him, "I don't need to answer to a kingnine! You, the ones created for the sole purpose of the extinction of an entire species. I will answer only to the leo!"

Edwin stood as terrified as Mitis was. He wanted to order this creature to drop his friend but found himself lost for words. He was no warrior, nor was he a king. He was only a man with a normal warehouse job. He could only stand and watch as his friend was dragged away and soon they were all alone again.

"Untie me!" Mitis screamed now and woke him up to his senses. He fumbled at first but released her, and she instantly shot towards the hole Dude had fallen through.

"Sir!" a voice shouted. Edwin looked up to see another small group of people running up, hearing the commotion.

Mitis climbed down into the darkness of where Dude had fallen. She instantly found him caught and tangled in loose rope with a wooden beam trapping his leg. He was conscious but in a very uncomfortable position. He tried struggling when he first saw her there, trying to escape, but found moving whilst still trapped under this beam brought him pain. He was caught.

Mitis looked around and saw his sword had fallen from his reach and left him there defenceless.

"Don't be afraid, Dude," she whispered. She knew she didn't have long. Soon Edwin would come to his senses and realise Dude was trapped down here. She needed to be quick.

Like a scared bird that had flown into someone's house Dude panicked a little but Mitis edged slowly toward him and reached out to finally touch his shoulder. His shoulder was bleeding from a previous wound and his scratched body was still covered in cuts and scars. She ran her finger around the back of his neck gently to soothe him. She hushed and whispered to him reassuringly.

"Please stop this, no more hurting people. These people are not going to hurt you. No one is. Do you understand?"

Their eyes met, his still wide with fear and uncomfortable panic and confusion while hers only shone with concern and patience. She needed to assure him she wasn't a threat, she didn't know what else to do and so acted on impulse. She kissed him. She didn't know why and thought this may be her only chance to get through to him that she cared for him, and to make him understand that she was there to help him.

In a moment of confusion Mute suddenly forgot his pain and became lost in his mind once more, this time not with feral and wild emotions of anger but something soothing, something he had never experienced before, something calming. He felt like he was falling back to reality and when he opened his eyes again he was looking into the eyes of the nurse. She stared back at him with a look he had never seen before, a look of pure concern. Like she actually wanted him safe enough to take it upon herself to find him, like she…cared.

Mitis glanced up when she heard the sounds of Edwin speaking to more of his men and explaining what just happened. She realised she didn't have much time and quickly lifted the beam from Mute's leg and released him. He tumbled to the floor and rolled, picking up his weapon, and jumped to his feet. With his sword back in his hand Mitis suddenly was the one defenceless and she stood back a little but needed to show him she wasn't afraid.

He looked down at Fireshaver, realised it was the point of her anxiety and sheaved it for her. He went to escape but found himself stopping; he wanted to turn and say "*Thank you*" but didn't want his stupid voice to spoil the moment. He turned back and in a movement of trust he stepped closer and held out his hand. She didn't move but allowed him to gently reach up and touch her chin, his fingers hesitantly reached up further until they were behind her ears and gently touching her hair. She still didn't move but kept her stare on him. He noticed this – she wasn't recoiling at his touch nor was she making any attempt to stop him. A voice from above broke the moment. He glanced up knowing he had to leave and took one more look at her. She wore an expression in silence like she was saying in his own body language, "*Don't go.*"

He blinked, "*I have to...I'm sorry,*" turned and escaped back out of the hole and ran away.

Mute ran as fast as he could. The others gave chase, the nurse and kingnine were amongst the group. The Slum King had now been withdrawn for his protection and instead a group of angry humans joined in the chase, trying to avenge the deaths he had had no part in. It must have been late because not many shops were open apart from the bars and strip clubs. Mute dashed past them all, he remembered running down this same street when the butcher's sons were after him for stealing that gammon joint; it now felt a lifetime ago. This gave him some assurance though, it meant he knew the back alleys better than anywhere else. This was his home after all. The rain still showered down cold and damp while he dashed through black puddles, past the neon lights of the clubs, smoke and the litter that clouded the ground. He heard the screams of Mitis calling him, how many times had she chased him now? How many times had she been there all along? He tried not to think but instead jumped up a familiar fence and climbed up on top of a large waste bin outside a food bar. A distant dog barked hearing the commotion and an alarm from a stolen M.V. screamed out through the city. Mute climbed.

He climbed until he heard no sounds of his pursuers but only the slam of the front door of the building he was climbing. As he reached the top he ran again to jump, when he found himself stuck on the edge. A gap far too wide to jump before him and a fall far too deep to recover from below him sniggered at his sudden predicament. The door from the roof began to bang and shunt until it fell through and his human pursuers now stood panting, trapping him once again. Mitis appeared again, pushing her way through them and trying to take command of the situation.

He saw that she was speaking but no sound was coming out of her mouth. He suddenly heard nothing but his own problematic inner-monologue presenting him with his final conundrum. Go with them and face the wrath of an army, colleagues of who he had previously slaughtered? Or go forward and hand himself over to gravity? To release himself from this prison of reality and give everybody what they wanted, what they were here for, but on his own terms? Rezosa was dead and now he would be soon too. He faced them all with his death to his back. Tears streamed down his cheeks while he contemplated. There was nothing before him worth staying for, they would imprison and kill him. Rezosa was gone and Val and Acarlie had left without him, there was nothing there left for him...except the nurse...

Her lips still moved and she also began to cry out for him but he still heard nothing; it wasn't her lips that made him hesitate him from taking another step back but her eyes. Her streaming, emerald green eyes were all he needed to see, the look of horror in her eyes when he took another step back, realising the truth. He remembered the couple on the sofa earlier that night. He remembered all those he had killed, he was a monster. Even if she did care for him, he would only end up hurting her. He didn't want that. He held his hands out and finally made his choice.

Mitis screamed at the pitch of someone who was witnessing a lover or family member dying as she could only watch the silent aeomon reach out and tip backwards and fall the long way down to the floor. Her legs gave way and she fell into the arms of a man close to her. Her body seemed to hollow out, her soul escaped and waited for the *thud*, which came with a loud smash of glass and a *crash*! A second later, silence again, a cold and unwelcoming silence, a silence that came with the scent of death...

32

:Tigian Keppal.

I hope this message reaches you well. I have heard about the injuries you received last time we spoke while leaving Chippenham. I want you to know I am deeply sorry for my part in all this. You, much like the rest of us here, have been swept away on this journey and I can understand how isolated you must feel sometimes being so far away from any of your friends and family. Tomorrow I will fight in my next Elemental Battle and so may not have another chance to apologise in person. I write this message in the hope that you will meet me on the outskirts of Eloma tomorrow at midday (13.30). If you ask one of the townspeople they can point you to a single road that leads you to Eloma's Away-side's Quarters. My battle will be at a quarter noon and so I will not have much time to wait if you are late. I will have sent Val to the stadium to prepare my entry for my upcoming battle by then and so I can only meet you alone. With the whole town now eagerly awaiting to witness me destroyed he had suggested I stay here at the quarters until the very moment I am to appear. I asked Val to send you this message at the break of dawn and to deliver it to the ship for you. Please Keppal, too much is on my mind and I must have an open mind if I am to survive my next battle. The quarters is a single large house with a decorative garden behind it with blooming summer flowers, walk to the hill to the left of the house. I shall meet you there at noon where I will be meditating for my battle.

I hope to see you there.

Your friend

Elementalist Acarlie:

Keppal stood in the spot where the letter asked him to be. The grass around him was open and the fields stretched infinitely beyond, behind him was the hill she wrote of and behind that was the quarters. He looked at a small pocket watch for the time. Sphere's days were twenty-seven hours long and so the clock hands seemed strange to people sometimes. With one large hand pointing slowly at the twenty-seven hours, a small dial and face was needed within each clock to represent minutes, otherwise it would seem too complicated to read. There were some clocks and watches around Sphere that used two thirteen and a half hour faces and would change from morning's face to noon's face at midday so that the hours didn't overlap on the clock, but in some places, like True Hiro, where the sun was absent, the idea was useless. With such long hours the people of Sphere needed a different way of noting time and so sections of the day were counted in quarters. From midnight to a quarter morn, half morn, three-quarter morn, midday; a quarter noon and so forth, unless they spoke in a digital or twenty-seven hour premise, where half morn would be 06.45, three quarter morn was 10.07(.5) and midday 13.30. This made it difficult in most cases. Keppal, however, was well educated in reading his little silver pocket watch and knew he was only a few moments early. A breeze swept past him from the open field and took a layer of cut grass and flower petals as gently as a baby's breath to dance and swirl behind him to the grassy hill. There was a row of apple trees sitting on top of the hill and hiding the view of the house she said she was in. He decided he would wait where he was but found himself restless after another five minutes and began to pace back and forth, then decided to walk over there himself.

After all this time, she has finally called for us to be alone. Not even Val will be here this time. Maybe this is the moment I have been waiting for. But then again, with her sending me this message it will make me a prime suspect again if she were to disappear... hmmm. He continued with his pacing around the soft grass while he contemplated. *But who's to say I have to stick around after she is dead? I am not on the ship any more, once she has left this planet I can easily walk into this horizon before me and never return...*

"Something on your mind?" called a voice from behind him. Keppal turned, expecting to see his target but instead almost groaned in disappointment, which would have given him away. Instead he forced a smile. "Good afternoon, Captain, what brings you here?"

Captain Kaza was now sitting on the top of the hill, sitting down against one of the apple trees with an apple in one hand and a knife in the other. He cut off a segment of the apple and bit into it.

"I was going to ask you the same thing, Fluffy," he said sarcastically, whilst looking up at the blue sky.

Keppal's eyes narrowed; he already knew the Captain was onto him but maybe he could use this time to persuade him otherwise now. "There's no need for name calling, Captain. I am here awaiting the elementalist. I received a message from her that she wishes to speak to me privately before her battle."

"And you just came down here all on your own to '*speak*' to her. No doubt you had a few words to say to her yourself," Kaza said and cut another apple segment.

"I have no idea what you're talking about, Captain. I have the letter right here..."

"Oh, use your brain, Fluffy!" Kaza now said and threw the knife down to stab into the dry mud at the foot of the tree and stood up. "Did you really think Acarlie would send you a message just to apologise? She's got more honour than that. If she wanted to apologise she wouldn't wait nor send any messages, she would come to you in person."

The realisation suddenly hit Keppal. He looked down at the words still in his hand. "She did not write this message?"

"Of course she didn't. I had Midia write that since she had the best handwriting. It only needed to fool you, which it did."

So it's a trap, she never meant to meet me at all. This was all Kaza's doing!

"Why would you do this, Captain? If you wanted to speak to me you could always have summoned me…or tied me to a bed and questioned me as before."

Kaza walked down from the hill and crossed his arms, the light from the sun reflected from his sunglasses and gleamed in Keppal's eyes sharply. "I wanted to know for sure what your intentions are on board my ship. If I asked you any other time you would only tell me what I want to hear."

"Which is the *truth!*" Keppal now spat; he didn't like being tricked.

Kaza, however, stood as cool as water and continued. "Maybe, maybe not. The only way I was going to make sure was to put you in a position where you could freely tell me what is going on."

Keppal now clenched his fists wondering what Kaza's plan was. It was only the two of them; an idea suddenly popped into his mind…

"All the while there are only two of us here you have no fear of being discovered. We are a mile from anywhere and anyone. You could kill me now, bury my body and go back to the ship and make up any story you like."

Keppal wondered for only a moment. Kaza was definitely smart, but so was he. "Your plan would not be solid then. I'm not saying I am confessing to anything, but how would I know you haven't spoken to your crew about your return? If I were to kill you how would I know that you haven't ordered my execution if you do not return? Also, how would I know you truly are alone?" He sniffed hoping he might be able to track any other humans around him, but smelt nothing. Kaza chose this spot well, all he could smell was the scents of the field behind him.

"I knew very well about that possibility, Fluffy. However, you don't insult me but my crew there. They are smarter than that and would not kill a person just on an assumption like that. It is hardly proof of your guilt if I were to disappear. For what I could have done is simply arrange this meeting then kill myself, or even better, simply hide somewhere for a day and wait for my crew to figure it all out and kill you. No, this isn't about killing you, it's about finding out whether you are a threat on board my ship and what you intend to do with the little Missy Elementalist."

Keppal stood still and stared out at Kaza, who stood before him stern and solid as though he had the unwavering resolve of a rock. The scene brought up a memory of Ursa Dusty in his mind. He had killed a larger and more powerful creature before – a human like Kaza would not be a problem.

"Now I am going to ask you one more time. You have no need to lie this time. Did you attack Acarlie?"

This time there was a silence, even the breeze seemed to stop, as if it had witnessed this scene as it passed by and stopped to watch what its outcome would be. Keppal looked up at the sky again and sighed. Kaza watched every movement, every gesture carefully. When Keppal's eyes looked back down at Kaza they seemed to change. Keppal seemed to have finally removed his mask and saw Kaza through his real eyes, only with a small, wicked smile bending the corner of his lips. Kaza had already known by then.

"*Why!?*" he suddenly roared, the breeze swept by again like it had seen all it had wanted to and ran away like a scared deer.

This time it was Keppal's turn to stand assertive and strong. He squared his shoulders. "Because I was ordered to by my lord Zane. He has told me everything about what you terrorists have been planning. It has been my secret objective to stop you."

"Did you kill Ursa Dusty back in Donolan?"

"The ursa was the first to discover my intentions. I had to silence him, as I now have to silence you. I don't know what your plan is, Kaza, maybe you have already trapped me into telling and maybe you have trapped me more so, but no matter. You're right you know, if I kill you, even if you did warn your crew, it's not proof of my guilt. I'm free to wipe you out now. Why though have you gone to all these lengths? This cannot all be about peace of mind for you; where is your security?" Keppal asked.

"That's the one fact you haven't got through your brain, you blind, arrogant bastard!" Kaza barked back at him smugly. "You think I need to go through all these tricks and mind games? You're looking in all these different directions and angles and being blind to the most obvious fact of all. You haven't even considered the possibility that I'm just going to beat you to a pulp!"

Keppal couldn't help but chuckle now. "You're right, Kaza. That would have been the last thought in my mind. I love your confidence–"

"And yours irritates me," Kaza countered.

"But if we are to battle, Kaza, let it be fair. Lose your weapons and let us fight hand to hand."

"But that wouldn't be fair, Keppal, but if you wish it…" Kaza took the long knives he had strapped to his legs and dropped them to the floor, then he also took the pistol from behind his back, removed the clip and threw them away. "…Now we are without weapons…Okay then, Fluffy, let's finish this!"

"Val, I want you to listen to me very carefully," Acarlie said. They were standing all alone amid the sound of an electric audience on the other side of two large metal doors. Val was stood with his hand on a bar ready to open the door for her entrance. He said nothing, but waited.

"Whatever happens out there today, I want you to promise me you won't interfere. I have beaten Barry once before. I can do it again but it won't mean anything if you decide to *help* me. Of all the elementalists I have to face on my pilgrimage Barry stands as the most important apart from Zane himself."

Val still said nothing. He didn't agree with this battle at all and didn't like the fact that she was being summoned to battle.

The walls around them were vibrating with excitement. Acarlie continued, "You see, if you help me it will prove to the audience that I was never the correct elementalist to win in our first battle. I am the High Elementalist of Eloma, this is my town and my people, whether they like it or not. But if I were to cheat in this battle, everything I have done on my pilgrimage will have been for nothing."

"But what if you lose?"

"I won't, Val. I have beaten him before and I am now stronger than him. I can do it again."

This answer still didn't satisfy Val. "And you mention cheating. Isn't there a rule about two elementalists facing each other twice?"

"Yes, but…"

"Then you shouldn't be battling in the first place. Acarlie, can't you see what this all is? Those people out there are not cheering for you. They don't want an Elemental Battle, they want a public execution."

His words were sharp but true, they cut right through Acarlie straight into her chest. She remembered standing on that very spot feeling nervous when she first fought Barry, her very first Elemental Battle. She remembered the sound of the audience then and realised Val was right, this sound vibrating through the walls was so much more angry and violent, they sounded more like a mob than a crowd of excited fans.

"It's not that I doubt your abilities, Acarlie, because I don't. I will promise not to interfere so long as they keep this battle fair. So long as it's just you and him with no surprise weapons nor contenders."

"No, Val, even then, I can take whatever they throw at me."

"That's a risk I am not willing to take."

"Promise me, Val!" she shouted now.

The sound of her introduction to the arena came with an instant booing, heckling and hissing from the audience. Val opened the door for her and shouted over the commotion, "I promise nothing!"

He expected a lecture, an order, a slap around the cheek and closed his eyes waiting for it but instead only felt her hand reach around and hold the back of his neck and pull herself toward him. Sometimes Val was a pain and hard to deal with but now so close to her battle Acarlie didn't have the time to argue nor become angry because of him. She forced herself to let go what he said and instead looked at it from his point of view, the way he had from the very beginning. He just wanted her safe, he was more of a guardian to her than Sheeria ever was. She felt lucky knowing that she had the only guide in the league who took the roll of protecting his elementalist so seriously that it sometimes meant going against everything in the league, and wasn't that what being a guardian was all about? She gave him one kiss on his cheek before walking out to the arena and into her next battle.

The instant heckling sound of boos and hisses greeted her while she walked over the dusty floor of her arena again. Barry was waiting for her on his spot again, his bandages had been removed to accommodate a special black mask that covered nearly all of his head but left his eyes, nose and mouth open, like a padded balaclava that pulled to one side, only his left cheek was unclothed. He had just finished speaking to the crowd and exciting them, filling them with anger and contempt, when he welcomed her into the arena. Acarlie ignored the disapproving hisses and walked with her head high against them all and straight up to Barry, where she knelt down and bowed to him.

Barry suddenly laughed, as did the crowd. "Grovelling isn't going to save you, traitor!" he shouted so the whole stadium heard.

Still Acarlie bowed. "I am bowing to my contender, Barry. May we have a just and fair battle."

Barry laughed again and saw what it was she was doing. He needed to win his crowd still and needed to show compassion, even for his traitor opponent. He knelt down and bowed. As soon as he did so the crowd silenced and even cheered him for his noble manners. Once they stood Acarlie had a moment to quickly look at the arena around them; still with an open top the arena now looked incomplete. A part of the arena had been demolished but had been cleaned up for their battle, wooden beams covered a very large part of the floor beyond them. Acarlie needed to ask, she knew the school was underneath this stadium, "Barry, is that where Lord Zane went?"

Barry turned and saw what she was pointing at. He answered honestly and without any spiteful comments, to her surprise. "Yes, it was a giant pit under the school. He exploded the whole thing, the blast broke away part of the school and since the stadium was on top, part of that fell too. Pit, I say pit, it's more of a cave or even a canyon that goes straight down until the light ends and blackness looks up. Most of the wreckage fell into the pit but the rest needed to be cleared up. No one knows how deep it is. All we can do is cover it for now. I promised the town we will start covering it up permanently after our battle."

Acarlie nodded. "Hopefully, if everything goes well in our fight, I would like to venture down there. I believe that was the whole reason why Zane came here in the first place."

"If you like, I can just throw you in there now? Just throw me a few punches and give the crowd their show and I'll give us what we both want."

Acarlie scowled, she was hurt by that statement. "There was no need for that, Barry. You're like a brother to me. I was not the reason for Zane's attack. Why can't you listen to me for once?"

"A number of possible reasons, Acarlie. Maybe it's because I am shamed by your pilgrimage and hurt by your decisions, maybe it's because I was left morbidly scarred for life after Zane came here when it was you he wanted…"

"But that was–"

"…or maybe it was exactly what you just said, '*brother*'. Maybe I am just sick of Acarlie, Master Argo's star pupil friend-zoning me to the point of seeing her as a brother."

Acarlie stood silenced, trying to comprehend what he just said and wondering if she had heard it wrong. Had she been that blind for all those years of training? She had trained with Barry all her life and they were roughly the same age and so it would make sense that Barry would grow feelings for her. And now she had returned home with this new guide by her side rather than the two she set off with. She saw the pain in Barry's eyes now burning with betrayal, contempt and resolve. She wondered how many years of pain she had caused him without even knowing.

"Barry, I–"

"Just get to your starting point!" he warned her.

She stepped back and turned.

"I want you to know, Acarlie!" he called out to her. She stopped and listened. "We're not even going to bury you here!"

She wanted to reply but rose above it and continued back to her spot.

When she was ready she closed her eyes and concentrated. She heard Barry call up to the audience again and since there were no elders present they had to start their battle with a countdown from the audience. Every number they called down seemed heavier than the last. She almost trembled with anxiety; as the numbers counted down they seemed also to slow. She took one final breath as the final number was followed by a scream that shook the air around them. Her eighth Elemental Battle had begun.

33

In a fight which should have been very one sided, the one word Keppal would have used to describe it when later telling his story would have been '*surprising*'. He admittedly underestimated Kaza at first and swung his first punch expecting it to end as quickly as that and was not prepared for when Kaza ducked under his arm and countered with a body hook straight into Keppal's solar plexus and a jab and cross hook into his chin, staggering him back and startling him.

Keppal had seen many fights while on duty and many fighting styles but never before had he seen anything like what Kaza was portraying. His stance was shorter than most and his guard was tight up against his cheeks. His hands were relaxed and even unclenched and were covering most of his face apart from his eyes, which peeked out of the top of them. He rocked from side to side in his dynamic stance waiting for Keppal's next attack.

He rubbed his chin. "An interesting style, Captain. Although your guard looks loose. Your fists should be tighter." He then took up his own position.

"A fist only needs to be tense...," Kaza said and stepped forward jabbing again into Keppal's chin, who now saw how slow he was compared with the human, "...on impact."

Keppal again rubbed his chin with the back of fist and held his guard up. "Interesting...I have never seen such a style before, Captain. If taught to a tigian it could a dangerous combination."

He jabbed to test Kaza's reactions; Kaza ducked back, keeping his high guard up, his feet moving fast back and forth. Keppal tried all he could to watch Kaza and the capabilities of this strange style. He waited for attack again from Kaza, who dived forward with more lightning fast jabs through Keppal's defence and jabbed his jaw. None of these jabs, however, had enough power to knock him out. With all these jabs to his chin, however, Keppal noticed his lower back begin to tire, and he worked out Kaza's tactic: to wear him out with small attacks. He also noticed something else about this strange, alien fighting style.

"You don't kick," he pointed out.

"Don't need to," Kaza countered and again side stepped and jabbed more and hooked another strong attack in Keppal's body and another under his chin. Keppal nearly bit his tongue.

He stood back and this time smirked; he had had enough playing around now and was beginning to hurt from this human's attempts. He decided it was high time to start fighting like a tigian. He snarled, baring his teeth and claws, and pounced at Kaza; one large bite into his neck would be all he needed to weaken him. He caught him as he fell and waited for his weight to press down on the pirate. The Captain, however, was waiting for this obvious tactic and rolled back clutching onto the tigian and with his back against the floor used his feet to throw Keppal back. Keppal tumbled and rolled back on his feet and pounced again. Kaza was already back up and swivelled around, catching Keppal's head and wrapping his arms around his neck and tried using his body weight to weigh him down. This tactic had never worked in a human and tigian fight before and this fight was no exception. Keppal forced himself back on his feet and reached up and grabbed the pirate on his back and threw him down with a *thud* against the floor. Quickly Keppal picked Kaza up, swung him around and threw him through the air to smack against one of the trees. The tree shuddered and threw apples down on them both, trying to force the fight to stop. Kaza rolled on his front with his elbows pressing into the ground with an agonising groan.

Keppal was panting himself now and stepped up to him. He reached down for Kaza, who, once feeling the clawed, white hands of Keppal, jumped up and thumped him in his groin. Keppal roared and moaned like any other male would and fell to his knees with his hands between his legs. Kaza was quickly enough back on his feet, grabbing the tigian's head under his arm again and ramming it into the tree. Again the tree shuddered, leaves fell around them and showered them with more apples.

Kaza then proceeded to stamp and kick Keppal like a thug would a helpless victim before finally standing back to catch his breath.

Keppal felt dizzy with pain but pushed himself up from the tree.

"You fight like an animal!" he shouted at him.

"I'm a pirate!" Kaza shouted back. "What makes you think I fight by rules?"

Keppal felt pain all over his head and bruising to his brow, but the gut wrenching pain between his legs was still the most painful.

"I thought you didn't use your feet."

"I lied."

Keppal growled and endured the pain and this time let out his wild anger, reached up for Kaza and dug his claws into his arm. Once Kaza yelled out in pain Keppal grabbed him with his other hand and threw him against the tree and pinned him up to it. He tilted his neck to one side and sank his teeth into Kaza's flesh. Kaza screamed, suddenly incapacitated with his arms still held down and pinned to the tree. Keppal knew all he had to do now was sink his teeth further and rip upwards and the fight would be over. He was already planning to run into the house behind the hill and clean up and deal with Kaza's body, but unfortunately Kaza still had one more trick up his sleeve. At first Kaza struggled but managed to position his knee up and used the tree on his back to support himself in striking Keppal in the solar plexus again. When Keppal recoiled in pain, he quickly wrenched his arm free and uppercut Keppal as hard as he could in his throat. It meant the teeth sank in further but meant Keppal gagged and gasped, releasing Kaza, who fell to the floor to grab his shoulder and neck as they bled and started choking on the floor.

After seeing his moment Kaza quickly jumped up and jabbed another strike into Keppal's throat and began assaulting him on the floor as Keppal suddenly panicked. With one final reverse hook punch across his cheek with enough force that Kaza thought he had broken his hand he won the fight. Keppal lay on the floor in a fit of gasps, hiding his head under his arms like a beaten child. With his victory, Kaza still felt he wasn't finished and started lifting Keppal's arms away from his head and punished him further until Midia and the other pirates came out of their hiding places.

"Stop, Captain, you're going to kill him!" Midia shouted. Everyone grabbed Kaza by his arms and pulled him off the cowering tigian.

After a confused moment Keppal caught his breath back and looked up through beaten and bruised eyes to see Kaza begin to calm down.

"I thought you said you were alone," he said.

"Guess what?" Kaza countered again.

Keppal felt defeated, and shamed because it was by a human, a lying, cheating human.

He sighed and with the help of the pirates sat up against the tree.

"So are you going to kill me now?"

Kaza was now picking up his weapons and waving away Roscopp, who wanted to inspect his bleeding wound. He stood over Keppal, assertive, and knelt down.

"No, I am not going to kill you. I knew you were the one behind the attacks. I also knew you were the one to inform Zane about Acarlie in Donolan. You killed Dusty and nearly killed Acarlie. I needed to sniff out this rat before more damage was done. Look around you, Keppal, and notice where you are. Look at what has happened to this town. Did Acarlie do this?"

Keppal sighed and groaned again.

"Answer me. Did Acarlie do this!?"

"No!"

"Who did? What's the name everyone in this bloody town seems to agree on when saying who destroyed their home!?"

"Zane!" he finally admitted.

"And who destroyed Donolan?"

"Zane!"

"And who destroyed Toshiro!?"

This time Keppal paused, he knew the answer but it pained him to finally admit it.

"Zane…"

Kaza stood back up and spoke down at him. "That's right. We have been totally honest with you, Keppal. You just chose to ignore the truth. Your stupid, fickle tigian brain couldn't see past the fact that your honourable and perfect Elemental Lord is the one trying to destroy the planet. He wants the black hole to swallow us all."

"That doesn't make sense! Why would he?" he asked.

"Why would *he*? What about *us*? Haven't you even asked yourself why *we* would want this? Zane wants it because he wants to die, Sphere's divide!" Kaza cursed.

Keppal spat blood down onto the ground. "But why? I

still don't understand why he would want to die!"

Kaza now looked back; he understood now what Keppal's problem was. "Because he's immortal."

"What? That's impossible!" Keppal stated and rolled on this front again to tend to a painful sting in his gut.

"Roscopp," Kaza ordered, "get him on the ship and out of my sight. Educate him on Zane. I can't even look at him right now."

"Yes, Capt'n!" his men confirmed and started picking up the injured tigian to take him away.

A moment later and only the dark haired quartermaster Midia was left beside him.

"Captain?"

"Yes, Midia?"

"Tell me again why you ordered us to wait. For a moment there I thought he was going to kill you."

He rubbed his neck again and looked at the fresh blood on his fingers then looked into the concerned face of his second in command.

"Because I knew the tigian underestimated me, as did most of the rest of my crew. At least this way I have taught him a lesson about humans as well as earned some good old fearful loyalty from my crew. All in all, a good outcome." He bent down and picked up an apple from the floor, feeling how tight and stiff his body was, and bit into it.

The crowd roared at every attack Barry threw at Acarlie, who parried, ducked and countered. It was a sound that became infinite, when one voice ended another was halfway through its sentence and so lingered in the air like static from a radio being far too loud. She concentrated all she could on her aggressive opponent, who looked to want her dead more than any other opponent she had ever faced before. But all the while she did, every now and again she heard small sentences from her once loving crowd, each one seeming to cut her deeper than the last.

"Kill her, Barry!"

"Rip her head off!"

"Fuck her up!"

She wanted to cry, but with Barry swinging attacks at her with such fire and enthusiasm she couldn't take her mind off him for a moment. He wasn't fighting to be seen as the better fighter, nor to take the title of High Elementalist, he truly and passionately wanted her dead. He tried using his mastery of their element and lifted her up to throw her back but she countered with her own and floated back down.

He looked surprised. "So you mastered the gravity of our element?"

"As well as the magnetism, yes," she confessed.

"Ah, but how about this?" he asked and suddenly threw his hand to the floor, a wave of energy seemed to explode outwards from him and took Acarlie back. She nimbly turned in her fall and gently set herself down.

"Actually, yes. You're using all of the elements combined to release a shockwave of electromagnetic energy."

"Then pray, show me, *sister*," he countered sarcastically, welcoming her with a gesture of his hand.

She looked all around at the stadium and remembered Donolan, the Bastard Camp and the C.E.L. "Actually, I don't think you'll want to see mine."

"Arrogant bitch!" he cursed.

They continued to fight once more to the roaring of the crowd. Acarlie kept her guard up all the time and mainly used her Element of Diamond in defence and attack, turning her arms to diamond and blocking his attacks.

"Come now, *sister*, you have more elements than that!" he warned and managed to catch her with a strike to her stomach but missed a chance to strike her chin as she pivoted away.

"Stop calling me that!" she shouted back, beginning to anger from his constant taunts.

"But that's what we are! You said it yourself, we're brother and sister!" he returned and finally caught her by surprise with a perfect kick straight against her skull, knocking her down.

She shook her head and jumped up. He tried again. This time she caught his leg and held it. "As you wish then, *brother*!" She sent a shock of electric energy through his body. He screamed and flew back. She managed to catch him and force him back further with the wind to tumble down onto the floor.

He only needed a few seconds to get back up while she ran to stay in range again. He jumped back up, jabbed her and struck her again. She tried parrying around him but only then noticed how much stronger and faster Barry now was as he grabbed her by the collar of her dark grey vest, pulled her into his range and cracked her with a strong punch that knocked her straight to the floor and nearly out of consciousness. He immediately knelt down and pressed his knees down on her shoulders and tightly wrapped his hands around her throat and squeezed tightly.

She choked and tried turning her neck to diamond but struggled with the concentration when her body only wanted to breathe. His hands were like a vice around her throat and squeezing tighter. She felt her blood rush and eyes bulge, the last thought she had was to quickly jolt him again with electricity. He jumped up and fell to the floor like his hands were burning while Acarlie gasped and choked loudly and involuntarily. He was the one quicker to his feet though and grabbed a fistful of her black hair and brought his knee to her nose in a horrifically brutal technique. She felt her nose pop and her head swim with pain again. He tried to punch her again but she again turned to the electric element and touched his leg and jolted him back again for a second to recover.

This now only infuriated him. "Stop that!" He took a step forward to the crouching Acarlie and swung a leg to punt her, when she turned and crossed her arms, turning them to diamond and letting his shin smack into them.

He yelled, screamed and fell to the floor like he had just kicked a rock and rolled around holding his shin. Acarlie was in a similar position but on all fours and wiping the blood from her face and taking deep breaths, trying to compose herself again. Out from the audience something hard hit her back. She sat up in pain and received another, hitting her in the back of the head. She screamed and looked down to see a gift thrown by a member of the audience in the form of a stone, stained in blood. She held the back of her head and looked up to see more stones being hurled from the audience. She cowered from them at first and in the distance heard the sound of her faithful guide screaming her name and jumping into the arena. She couldn't stand this any more. The hate and contempt from these people she loved she could handle but throwing stones was a different matter. How could they do this to her? This was her home, these were the only people she could say she knew like a family and shared all her memories with. These stones hurt her more on the inside than the bruises they were making. She screamed and swung her hand aside causing a large gale from around her to force all of the stones to fly away and stunned the audience.

Barry finally got back on his feet. Val still screamed from a distance as he tried to run to protect her.

Barry, however, saw him coming and with a gesture of his hand sent him flying back, where the audience began aiming their stones to.

"*Leave him alone!*" Acarlie screamed in her rage. Her body ached, her head swam with wild emotions and her eyes burned red with tears. Barry, however, turned back to her and using the gravity and wind, picked up all of the stones around her and threw them all at her in one movement. She felt like she was in the centre of a rock magically forming itself from many small stones, each stone pelted into her, the best she could do was kneel down and protect her temples, head and face. The stone cracking against her fingers hurt the most and flared bright red pain in her mind.

She screamed and wept in agony, her body felt broken, as did her heart. She had been near death a few times since her pilgrimage but never had she felt both the soul shattering pain of heartbreak and the annihilating torture of physical agony at the same time. She felt herself go limp, the same way she had felt when Electra defeated her in the C.E.L. She felt herself paralysed, more by the pain in her heart than that all around her body. She felt no alternative but to give in to her mind's desire to lie there and cry. She didn't deserve any of this. She would be killed by her home and family. And the worst part was Val would also die with her. She wished for the strength to get back up, when she heard Barry charging back to her. Fear and terror now came with acceptance of death; she was finally ready for it. It only broke her heart that it would come from the people she loved and also kill the man she cared for the most. The man she…

Her heart cringed, and with it came a flashing of blinding white light. Acarlie disappeared into the void of her mind.

Barry screamed and swung one final kick at Acarlie, who seemed to jerk up as though some new surge of power controlled her. She caught his foot and threw it up with such force that he left the floor and flipped over. Once he got back up Acarlie was before him, floating inches from the floor with her arms held to her side. Her chin was held high but her eyes were so…white. With no pupil nor iris her eyes were as white as the sclera, all white, absolute white…

He hesitated, not knowing what was happening. Her pained and bleeding face now seemed to change its expression. She now looked completely expressionless, blood still ran from her nose and down her mouth and chin and she didn't even seem to care about the pain. Nor for him, only a look of complete concentration. He shuddered when he looked into the white eyes. They seemed to not even notice him but look straight through him. She began to rise from the spot where she levitated. The wind, dust and air seemed to circle around her in a small cyclone, compacting tighter together. The audience stopped throwing stones at the interfering guide and stared at the strange phenomenon. Val, who had since protected himself with his electric shield, noticed Acarlie rise up again and knew exactly what would happen next.

"Not again!" he cursed and rolled to his feet and chased after her.

Barry, however, only thought this was some scare tactic she was using in her desperate attempt to defeat him and called forth his element but found it had failed him. Her strength with the wind around them was so strong it left none for him to counter with. Also he found her grasp onto the energy was so tight he couldn't even release the tensing energy of wind as she compacted it closer together until it felt so tight nothing could pass through it. In the end he could only cower down while she let out an echoing, wild scream of releasing energy and finally showed him the power he so desperately wanted to witness. Like a bomb exploding but without the heat or flames, a solid wall of energy suddenly struck Barry, thumped him and sent him back to the floor metres away. Val also felt this wave of energy, as did the whole stadium; it seemed to grow stronger as it stretched further until it was blasting the remaining, outer walls of the stadium away and spreading its energy to the town. The wooden boards covering the giant pit now scattered and fell down. From a bird's eye point of view a giant circle of energy looked to destroy the stadium; many parts of it fell apart until dust was seen blowing like an enlarging halo around the town.

Val got back up with a groan, noticing how many others were also getting back to their feet and wondering what it was they were witnessing. He had to stop this fight. If they threw anything more at Acarlie he didn't know what she would be capable of. He also knew she would not forgive herself if she woke to find out she had destroyed her home town. He pushed himself up, calling Staff and using it to help himself up before dashing over to her.

Barry also got back to his feet. Everything was a dusty aftermath around him. Only Acarlie stayed perfectly where she was, floating back down and staring at him. He wanted to charge her again when he heard her guide running to him.

"Acarlie!" he screamed. As he ran past he heard him say, "If you value your life you will not attack her," and then called again, "Acarlie!"

She seemed to hear him, her head flinched and she suddenly called out his name and fell limp to the floor. Val caught her and held her in his arms. Her control of this power was still becoming stronger, she was even beginning to wake up quicker. She found herself panting and out of breath in his arms. A silence was all around them and everything covered in dust.

"What's happening?" she asked.

"This fight is over!" he ordered her. "Let's just get this item and leave this wretched place."

He helped her to his feet. Many people had since fled the stadium and some more had climbed down to the arena feeling too uncomfortable to stay there any more and went to help Barry, who still knelt down in a confused defeat trying to work out what had just happened and how Acarlie's power had improved so much.

The two both limped over to the large, dark, rectangular pit, smouldering with dust and the mystifying darkness below.

"Is that it?" Val asked, still holding onto Acarlie.

"I think so. Barry told me that this is where Zane went." She paused. "I have to go down there."

"Well, not right now you're not. You're in no condition to do anything right now. I'll take you back to the quarters. You won the battle, Acarlie. I think everybody here will agree on that."

"What happened? What did I do?" she asked.

"You showed them all how you were the correct elementalist to go on this pilgrimage."

She sighed and wiped some dry blood from her face. "Did I hurt anyone?"

"I don't think so, only their precious pride."

"Acarlie!" cried a voice from behind them.

Val was the first to turn and found Barry had charged for them. He grabbed Val, reached for his knife and pushed him aside. Acarlie tried to scream but in his wild and uncontrollable rage Barry quickly ripped upwards, cutting through the air, slicing the wind and Acarlie's chest.

Val quickly grabbed his hand and twisted the knife from his fist and kicked him away, believing his attack to have missed. Only when he turned to see Acarlie, she stood at the end of the pit running her fingers up a large wound that ran across her chest. She lifted her hands to see the blood running down her hands and fell back.

He cried and reached out for her but her feet left the floor and she fell into the pit. He cried and fell on his knees watching her fall; her eyes never left his as she fell with a look of despair and horror in them. Small droplets of her blood chased after her like they were bravely facing gravity to bring her back and in a moment she was gone, swallowed into the darkness with only her wailing echo following her.

Val screamed and reached out for her, seeing his failed hand now trembling when it realised it was too short in catching her. The realisation hit him slowly: she was gone, she fell wounded into this pit. She was gone, she was... gone.

His breath was trapped in his chest, his heart stopped and his eyes instantly filled with water as the sentence continued on in his mind.

She is gone.

He heard the sound of Barry grunting behind him, slowly getting up from the floor where he fell.

This empty feeling of instant loss flared blue, red, yellow and every colour in his mind, finally settling on a red so bright it blocked out the sun. He turned with no other emotion but the purest form of anger burning in his eyes so bright it needed its tears to cool them down. Steam may well have evaporated from his eyes the way he turned to face Barry, Acarlie's killer, and stood in the stance of a creature Sphere had never seen before, a demon of pure wrath. For years after that day the children of Eloma told stories of Val's wrath, and exaggerated how many times he stabbed Barry over and over again...

FIN.

OUTRO

The dark and damp streets of True Hiro drizzled with a silent, brooding gloom. The sound of engines, buses and trucks filled the air as did the screams of playful children. The city rested after its excitement of all the riots, black holes, divides, new kings and serial killers. So much had seemed to go on and now the tides of change were turning, only they didn't know if they would be in their favour or not. They only knew darkness and knew not what the feeling of optimism was like. It was so new to them they didn't know how to take it and instead held it, but with unease and caution. They embraced their new king and a new army that was growing every everlasting night. There were now large parts of the city where the police had no jurisdiction and dared not enter. However, this did not mean crime formed in large places, instead groups of vigilantes appeared in the name of the Slum King and policed the city the way the city decided they would. These new pockets of revolution were democratic and so many people began to join them. Every everlasting night more and more appeared until soon the city was becoming something new altogether. The king above them was still too concentrated on his own power as tigians now ruled the country and so forgot all about their growing numbers.

Out on the outskirts of these pockets and in a space of no-man's land between the freedom fighters and the rest of the city stalked a hooded killer. She crept along the rooftops of her hunting ground. She was the predator the city now feared, from years' experience taught by her deceased husband she prowled the rooftops. They tried to catch her, they tried to hunt her but she was too clever for any of them. This whole city now belonged to her. Every time this Slum King thought up new ways to catch and trap her he only ended with more of his men dead, and more food on her plate. She was Umbra, she was Shadow, and in a city with no light shadow was all around her; she was in her element. She climbed up to the corner of an office block looked down at all of her potential new targets, all walking around like busy ants amongst themselves. Each one having not a care in the world not knowing that they had now a new god watching down on them, a hungry and wrathful god. Only, where she sat, perched another, dressed in tight black clothes to match hers. She turned to this new, younger killer and reached up to pull the hood over his head as if turning him into what she was.

"Now say the words," she commanded.

The new figure did as commanded and spoke from his hood into hers. "We are Paryii, we hurwuvive…"